THE BANK

THE BANK

a novel
by
Stephen Longstreet

Money, which represents the prose of life, and which is hardly spoken of in parlors without an apology, is, in its effects and laws, as beautiful as roses.
—RALPH WALDO EMERSON
Nominalist and Realist

G. P. Putnam's Sons
New York

SBN: 399-11658-3

Library of Congress Cataloging in Publication Data

Longstreet, Stephen, 1907–
    The bank.

        I. Title.
PZ3.L8662Ban   [PS3523.0486]   813'.5'4   75–40494

PRINTED IN THE UNITED STATES OF AMERICA

To my memory of
BERNARD M. BARUCH
and our conversations
about this kind of story

Certain major events in this novel are historically true. The characters and the institutions which involve their lives and are part of their personal story, however, are the invention of the author and are not intended as representing any family or persons living or dead. There never was an H. H. Starkweather & Company or a Starkweather-Unity Bank & Trust Company.

BOOK I

Money is the best bait to fish for man with.
—THOMAS FULLER

1

It was the day that the German kaiser abdicated and fled to Holland that Tyler Starkweather, in his spanking-new Brooks Brothers uniform of a second lieutenant, met Margo Crivelli at an afternoon benefit for the Red Cross, being held in the Steenshiners' villa in Cambridge on the Charles River.

Tyler was primed by the two drinks of well-aged bourbon Mr. Steenshiner had given him from his private stock. Margo was carrying a large red leather portfolio of watercolor drawings, from which dropped a sketch of Fifth Avenue in a rainstorm. Tyler picked it up from the marble floor and fell in love with Margo Crivelli at once. Margo waited a long time, being wary of any deceptive immediacy and spontaneity.

The Red Cross benefit that afternoon was hardly a failure, but the talk of a coming armistice discouraged some patriots from buying objects donated to the sale—a Tiffany lamp, a sealskin coat, a half dozen polo mallets, among other items—while a Metropolitan Opera star sang, "*Adieu mon amour, adieu douces fillettes.*"

Tyler, in the afternoon, offered to drive Margo back to New York City in his brother Andrew's old Stutz Black Hawk. Andrew, he explained, being in France, had been flying for the RAF. Tyler, too, had wanted to go Over There—had left Princeton to go to officers' training camp. But now he suggested they stop at the Red Lion Inn on the Boston Post Road for dinner. The wintry air was chilly; the car ride had numbed their limbs.

Tyler, who was eighteen years old, once inside by a warm fire, told Margo he was in love with her for sure. He insisted (over the lobster in drawn butter) it was true. Margo, cracking open a claw, looked at him with wonder. "Slow down. The war is nearly over. Hold your horses."

"I don't suppose I'm saying any of this just right."

"You're saying this fine. Only I'm a bit older than you and have heard it before."

"You're an artist—you should understand *better* something like this."

"I just draw fashions for the stores, mostly. I've got as many apprehensions about things as the next gal."

"You're not married?"

"Oh, God." She looked up at the raftered ceiling, the mortised and tenoned beams of the inn, and laughed. "*What* am I with?"

Tyler joined in her laughter—perhaps he was overcompulsively noisy. He figured no, she wasn't married. Or if she was, she wasn't living it. He still had the boyhood habit of believing if he hoped long enough about a thing, it would be so, some reciprocated favor from above. It wasn't that he really felt his system would work. Tyler had a good brain, was usually a clear thinker—logical, he felt—but in the matter of girls he was still unsure. He'd had some summer adventures in resort settings and was not a virgin. But he had remained a searcher.

Margo was watching him with an amused grin as she ate her hot apple pie with country cheddar. She was, he thought, all he had ever dreamed of.

"It was great you being able to know a Stutz Black Hawk is much more the rare car than the Bearcat."

"I'm full of all sorts of useless information. Pardon me, I have to tinkle."

He watched her move toward a door lettered POWDER ROOM. No female had ever mentioned her natural functions to him before. When she came back Tyler could see she was wary and puzzled by him.

"I hope you understand, Margo, I'm damn serious about us."

"I'll try, Tyler. And you try and see it from where I sit."

"We agree."

The host of the inn, a large man with too flushed a face, was over them, holding up a bottle, smiling down at Tyler in his fine uniform, Sam Browne belt in place, boots polished to a fine gloss, bronze insignia suggesting Roman legions.

"Lieutenant, I don't know if this bottle is the real Napoleon brandy or not. But it's old, and I want to offer you, a soldier of the United States, and your dear lady a couple of shots. On the house."

"I haven't been overseas."

12

Margo said, "But his brother Andrew flew with the RAF, lost a leg, married a French girl."

The inn host said, "*Nil desperandum*"—a Harvard man?—and filled three small glasses. "What the hell. It's been a great war." He joined them in a drink and, as the weather was turning foul outside, offered them the upstairs back bedroom for the night. "I like to see a young couple that really love each other and mean it."

It was a wide maple bed with carved wooden pineapple posts. Margo undressed quickly with natural, easy gestures, and Tyler undressed carefully; the boots were a problem, and he had never seen a naked woman under an electric light bulb hanging from a ceiling. He thought of the statue of Aphrodite Callipygos at his grandfather's. His few sexual experiences as an adolescent had been on summer vacations in the dark of public parks, and once the upstairs maid waylaid him in a linen closet in the Fifth Avenue home of his parents; a rather bizarre affair. The maid was, in college jargon, a joint gobbler. Now in the small inn room he felt, as he had read someplace, "a singing in his head," with a marvelous erection on hand. Margo had rather large breasts, wide hips, but a slender waist; her pubic hair was thick and black. He stood in a mixture of desire and apprehension.

They came together without talk, got on the bed, and Margo was ardent and noisy and he was delighted, amazed. When both had climaxed twice, they lay side by side, aware of their heartbeats—lay on the wide maple beds with the post topped by carved wooden pineapples, slowly smoking Murads Margo had produced from her tweed coat pocket. Outside the narrow windows were sounds of small animals in a nocturnal hunt for love or food and the call of a night bird. A kind of eerie hoot which Tyler recognized as that of an owl hunting, like the owls that came at night from near his grandfather's old carriage house at Shad Point below Norton-on-Hudson. The sound bridged his boyhood to his present manhood, to the just-done intimacies.

"Jesus, Margo, it was wonderful."

She exhaled a plume of smoke toward the ceiling. "It was good, but don't, Lieutenant, go building anything on it."

"I want you to be my girl."

There was a pause, a kind of sigh. "Here, put this out in the seashell there."

13

"I mean it." He wanted just then a reciprocated tenderness. "I want to marry you."

Margo turned to face him. "Look, Ty, never ask a girl to marry you after only knowing her five hours. You're a great big marvelous lover. You're honest and a gentleman and an officer. You're also a college Joe. They don't have wives at—what is it? Yale?"

"Princeton."

He reached for her and she slapped away his hand. The sweet kid was off his nut. "Don't touch. We have talking to do."

"No one has to know we're married, if you want it that way. I'll rent a cottage edge of town."

"And live off your allowance? Be practical. We've had a marvelous evening, a great night. You're charming, I admit it. Maybe we'll see each other weekends in New York."

"I don't have to live off an allowance. My grandmother left me a small trust of which I get the interest. And in a few years I can be a very junior partner in H. H. Starkweather and Company."

Margo sat up suddenly and as if a bee had stung her naked body. "What?"

Tyler blew out smoke slowly from both nostrils. "My grandfather founded the firm and my father is chairman of the board."

"*Mamma mia.*" Margo was out of the bed, her neck, shoulders, and breasts flushing much more than rose-colored. "I should have guessed," she said. "How many Starkweathers does a girl ever meet? You sure your name isn't Morgan or Rockefeller or Vanderbilt?"

Tyler tried to approach her but she backed away, arms held before her. He smiled. "My mother and father consider *them* rather pushy."

She gave a short involuntary laugh, more like a bark. He cornered her against a set of drawers topped by a spotted mirror and put his arms around her. "You're a snob in reverse, darling."

She ran her fingers through her thick blue-black hair. "Damned if I know *what* I am right now. One thing, I'm *not* in love with you. I mean you're nice, you're. . . ."

He kissed her and she kissed him back and she had a worried look on her face. She was sensual but not a promiscuous woman, not given very often to casual sexual adventures. She had had affairs, been desperately in love, been hurt. But this boy, so suddenly obsessed, so demanding and serious—she was at least four

14

years older than him. As they got back into bed to make love again in earnest, damp exuberance, she swore to herself, in the Italian of her grandmother, she would not see him again. *Io dirò cosa incredibile davvero.*

They celebrated, when it came, Armistice night at the Waldorf and then went to a party in the Village with some friends of John Reed, and spent two days in bed in Margo's studio on Riverside Drive before he went back to Princeton.

She came down to the college on the Pennsy day coach to weekend at Colter's Roadhouse and Inn in New Brunswick. In the fall Margo came for the Princeton-Harvard game. He gave her an engagement ring in the rooms he had taken in an old farmhouse smelling pleasantly of kerosene lamps. She put the ring away in her handbag, saying it was nonsense, and she cried for the first time in front of him. He asked her didn't she love him? Margo admitted she now loved him very much. But she insisted there was no engagement. Tyler, who had grown another inch in height and broadened a bit, said he would graduate from college, class of 1921, and he'd have her—this very fall—meet his family. They sat hand in hand watching a sunset, sipping hard cider and ginger ale. This was the first time Tyler had spoken of meeting any of the Starkweathers. Margo, for all her city wisdom and her awareness of Tyler's ardent love, still saw the Starkweathers as newspaper cartoon figures; the bankers, the trust makers, exploiters of Wall Street, as presented in the cartoons of Fred Opper and T. E. Powers in the Hearst press, as the bloated figures Art Young and William Gropper drew for the radical press in the *New Masses*. She knew, of course, she told herself all that was oversimplification. People could be very rich and still have the proper human instincts, a regard for humanity. Still, now sitting there after prolonged, detailed intimacies, the damn ring in her handbag, Margo knew in coherence and clarity it *had* to end, and end for good.

During the Christmas holidays Tyler told his family he was going to Lake Placid with some chaps for the bobsled runs and actually moved into Margo's studio. It was a marvelously happy, lightly boozy New Year's, just the two of them and the cat in residence. Margo lost her aloof evasiveness, and he had promised not to talk of marriage. Just live, live. Happy 1920!

This time Margo decided it was a parting for good, peremptory

15

and absolute. She didn't tell him she was going out to Hollywood to do the costumes for Clara Kimball Young, and she intended to stay there. She was back in New York City the week before Easter; the people who were to put up the money for the Lewis J. Selznick motion picture didn't. Margo had to pawn the engagement ring in Los Angeles to pay the train fare back to New York. They spent the Easter holiday together on Lake George in a lodge borrowed from a Princeton friend of Tyler's.

Before he went back to college, Margo agreed she would marry him when he graduated. Tyler told her she could have said that sooner. They were seated in the morning light in front of the lodge's stone fireplace, blazing with a burning pine log. They, not bothering to dress, were eating fried eggs and Canadian bacon Tyler had cooked. Outside a cold wind shook the lilac bushes. Margo asked why food tasted so good after making love, and Tyler said because they were both young and had demanding bodies and good appetites. He had, he added, two Kansas City porterhouses suitable for lunch in the icebox out back.

Margo, once back in the city, had some doubts about the Starkweathers of the *Social Register* taking any joy at welcoming "a wop daughter-in-law." The women in her family grew fat early and aged sooner than Anglo-Saxons. At least such was the tradition. Tyler would still look a boy at thirty. What was to come, she decided, would come. She secretly gave herself odds of four to one the Starkweathers would never permit the marriage to go through.

2

WALL STREET'S H. H. STARKWEATHER & COMPANY
REPORTS CORPORATE EARNINGS UP 25% IN
SECOND QUARTER OF 1920

NEW YORK—Second-quarter profits of the nation's corporations soared 25 percent on the average, but the typical company earned much less, an independent study by Starkweather & Company shows. The gain for most companies over the second quarter of last year was less than 3 percent, according to the Wall Street firm's quarterly profit survey of 1,429 companies by Starkweather & Company—the only Wall Street investment bankers rivaling J. P. Morgan & Company in size and earnings.

"One company in four had lower second-quarter earnings than a year ago, and if the spectacular gains of some basic-materials industries are excluded, the bulk of manufacturing firms showed a modest increase of 10 percent or 11 percent in the first half," the report said.

Biggest gains were reported by a few producers of basic materials which go into consumer products, increases of 50 percent to 96 percent in the second quarter over a year ago.

Profits of nonferrous metals companies such as aluminum and brass producers lead the economy, gaining 36 percent in the second quarter. Other industries which dramatically outpaced the nationwide average were steel industry profits up, oil profits up, chemicals and paper companies up.

On this September day the young man who emerged from the Wall Street subway station of the IRT was not thinking of the item reported in the financial section of the New York *Times,* a copy of that newspaper carried folded under one arm of his Harris tweed jacket. A jacket cut in the Brooks Brothers style so popular at Princeton and other Ivy League schools. He should have been attending the start of his senior year at Princeton.

. He was a tall young man rather on the lean side and, when he remembered, of a good posture. Regular features of what his Grandfather H.H. used to call "those goddamn Chesney fox-hunting faces from Virginia." Grandfather, getting on to eighty, still hated his wife's family, the Chesneys. He didn't come down to the Street more than three times a week, preferring his estate on Shad Point at Norton-on-Hudson. The young man made a grimace with his Chesney features. Well, the old bastard would be on the Street today ready to reprimand his grandson. Father would be present to agree as to the prestige, the social standing of the Starkweathers—and, of course, the reputation of H. H. Starkweather & Company, private bankers, underwriters of issues, international financiers.

The young man, Tyler Starkweather, came up from the cool, grease-smelling underground of the subway station, tilted his straw hat (called a boater by some) over to the right, and inhaled the warm air of the Street mixed with auto fumes and slightly of horse droppings. Pigeons whirled from old Trinity Church and its graveyard, which faced Wall Street.

Margo had told him in the Oyster Bar in Grand Central late one night, "It's a damn crazy street; a church and graveyard at one end and the East River to jump into at the other end."

17

Tyler sighed the way a young, alert, modern man was meant to sigh in 1920, one who had read *This Side of Paradise* and been commissioned second lieutenant at Camp Upton; if only the goddamn Huns hadn't given up the fight. The hundred-and-forty-dollar officer's uniform (with boots, Sam Browne belt, and spurs) had never been worn in combat.

He walked slowly down Wall Street, unaware he was not merely going to face his grandfather and father on a serious family matter, but moving into a historic event. Later he read, "A very attack on the citadels of money." He liked that phrase in the New York *Tribune,* describing what was about to happen as the clock in the Western Union window showed 11:57. Tyler was clearly half an hour and more late. He had spent the night with Margo, and he had made their breakfast on the gas ring—nearly fresh eggs and rashers of bacon, large slices of rye bread with marmalade, coffee in stoneware cups taken from Child's, Margo admitted—strong black coffee. How much more delightful than Princeton, H. H. Starkweather & Company, Gramp's Norton-on-Hudson estate, Father's damn Fifth Avenue Stanford White museum. Cold as Kelsey's balls. All of it didn't mean as much as a night with Margo in her Riverside Drive studio with forgotten cigarette butts, the pots of paint and brushes with which she created fashion drawings for Wanamakers, fancy catalogues of shoes, stockings, jewels. Margo thinking of herself as a creative artist with copies of Fuseli and someone called Matisse. Margo! And he nearly was run down by a Pierce-Arrow, then he went bumping into a dray hauling rolls of newsprint paper. He got a cursing from the driver with a three days' growth of beard and a threatening whip. "Fuckin' dude, wanna get yer ass broke?"

Tyler decided he sure didn't and made for the great slate slabs of sidewalk crowded now with people coming out from the buildings hoping to grab an early table or lunch stool before the noontime crush began. Tyler knew the Street was all about money and credits, bond issues, stock prices. Bookkeeping of profits and losses. German marks, British pounds, lire, and the world's gold supply. . . . And people going to a fifteen-cent lunch of a doughnut and a cup of Java—or ham on rye.

What happened at high noon on Wall Street that sixteenth of September has never been fully solved to Tyler's or anyone else's satisfaction. Wall Street was its usual hustle and bustle, bearer bonds delivered by messengers. Mr. Edison's stock ticker ticking. Two years after the end of the Great War the stock market was doing splendidly. On the corner of Wall and Broadway, H. H. Starkweather & Company and its rival, the House of Morgan, basked in their pride of having once floated war loans, established credits to the Allies. Only a few among the partners in both firms were suffering in their holdings of imperial Russian rubles. Catty-corner across the Street from Morgan & Company was the New York Stock Exchange—and Tyler noticed it was enlarging its space.

Unknown to him, some members of the British Cabinet had scattered over the English countryside to shoot grouse, read Horace, play golf, or place a bet at Epsom Downs, disturbed only by the thought that there might be a call from Downing Street. What if revolution was expected in Germany or some yammering about a corridor? Or ill-bred little Japs were stripping freeborn Englishmen down to their drawers and exposing their birthmarks to gaping coolies? So sorry. Misunderstanding. *Ah so.* The scandal of the rigging of the 1919 World Series by the White Sox was being exposed.

On the Street that morning—while Margo was still asleep in Tyler's arms—no big bond house had gone under in Paris or London. The Bourse had closed steady to dull. Time to resume the routine of commerce. Everything in its turn; even the League of Nations and all the oratorical pother about it could wait until one saw the market's opening prices, the banks' rates of exchange.

In New York the news was disturbed only by frequent wireless bulletins. Expert commentators vied with one another in redrawing the map of Europe in new colors. Armies were shifted from border to border with a fine disdain for transport, and confidential sources revealed wholesale changes in governments. Morning readers, however, preponderantly favored the comics over all the dire and contradictory prophecies of the foreign correspondents about a postwar world.

Just after dawn the last water truck had gone up Broadway from the Aquarium, wheeled east at Wall Street, slightly spraying the austere façades of the House of Morgan and H. H. Starkweather & Company as it turned and went on past the Stock Exchange Building. As the sun looked cautiously over the towers, the streets began to dry in spots. Then the trucks carrying the morning newspapers hurried by, catapulting tied bundles at the targets of the still-locked stands. Underground the subway trains thundered north and south to pick up the morning cargo of office girls, mail and bank clerks, runners, doormen, and bookkeepers. Flatbush and Queens and Harlem and the Bronx were stirring. The ferries and tubes were bringing Jersey's contribution, and commuter trains were rushing toward the terminals. Wall Street was waiting for them.

In front of the Starkweather & Company Bank Building blue-jacketed men were carrying moneybags from the armored trucks into the bank. Tellers behind their wire cages were sorting paper and silver currency, stacking the silver in the slots of the change-making machines. Last puffs at cigarettes were being taken before the massive brass-studded doors were swung open to admit the day's business.

In the lobby the elevators to the office floors were being directed by a man dressed like a field marshal, a clicker instead of a baton in his hand, the crowd deployed, some to one side and the rest to the other. On the left the elevators are locals to the sixteenth floor, and on the right side they take off nonstop to the seventeenth. On the first floor are the glass-paneled doors bearing the legend MEMBERS OF THE NEW YORK STOCK EXCHANGE.

Membership in the Curb Exchange, the Cotton Exchange and other commodity markets, the San Francisco, Chicago, and New Orleans exchanges, the branches in London, Paris, and Shanghai.

Below in the bank girls wheel ponderous posting machines into place and twirl wide sheets of ledger paper into the carriages. Files and safes are opened. Typewriters, adding machines, tickers are being uncovered. Row upon row of counter tops are being heaped with papers, and men with nimble fingers are beginning to marshal legions of figures.

The customers' room of the first-floor brokerage office had come alive at ten A.M., with its pine walls and massive red leather chairs. The list board inserted under the wall's molding static at the point of yesterday's closing prices.

In the bank Charlie Mott, doorman, was ordering the delivery and mail boys, swinging baskets full of deliveries. Following him, a trail of runners like a brood of chickens waiting to be fed from the baskets.

Old Maryatt, the head bank clerk, who had traveled all the way from Blue Point and his garden, was precisely on time, looked at his heavy snap-lid gold watch, and examined his loans list for the day. His red nose sniffed a comment on every account. The staff had long since learned to distinguish the range of meanings, from contempt to compassion, in those expressive sniffs.

Rose-Mae Cooley, Harry Starkweather's private secretary, entered as if she had been preceded by a fanfare. She stepped through the elevator door in the manner of an actress who, walking through the wings on cue, waits momentarily for a burst of applause to greet her entrance. A tall blonde with a flexible face, hard eyes, and a habit of looking away while talking with the greatest animation. Seven years she had held her job with the president of the bank and in that time had given the girls little to gossip about. Nothing deterred, the telephone switchboard operators have reconstructed her past, which included a stay at Vassar, marriage to a journalist that ended in a nasty, if unpublicized, divorce, and a more-than-generous allotment of affairs.

She walked to her office; the wire service began to babble. Berlin a listless market. I. G. Farben has been tapped for a new industrial loan, 100,000,000 marks at four and a half percent at 97, repayable in twenty years at 102. The office strategists whistle in admiration at the nerve of the Hun who pulled that one. In London the dollar is unchanged at 4.68¼. The franc is easier, 172 to the pound. In Amsterdam, Deli Batavia Rubber is 134, down a mere four points. There is a noteworthy recovery in the Shanghai yuan, up to 13.45 cents, a gain of sixty-five points to 28.92 cents. The Japanese yen is steady at 27.32. The Java florin yields five points and is at 53.25 cents, and the Straits Settlements dollar advances forty points to 55 cents. Among the South Americans the Peruvian sol is weak, giving way to 17.50, a new low for the year, but other Latins are quite firm.

Upstairs the head customers' men had arrived, exchanged pleasantries, and looked over their lists of the day's prospects; Farrington, the floor man, joined them. In a few minutes he went across the street to the floor of the Exchange to execute orders as usual until three o'clock.

Up in the brokers' offices the board boys adjusted their many-pocketed aprons, getting ready for the first sputterings of the ticker as early customers arrived. A normal day—until noon.

Tyler, as he walked, noticed building in progress. If anyone wanted to strike a blow against American capitalism, the radicals of the Village had told Tyler, Wall Street was the place.

21

Tyler wasn't looking forward to the lunch at the Bankers and Brokers Club as down Wall Street had come a small wagon, brown in color, with a canvas cover over it, passing the dawdling young man. It was pulled by a dark brown horse, and the driver drew it up to the curb at Wall and Nassau streets. The driver got down and walked away. No one later reported any suspicious action. No novelty were horses as a means of transportation. Tyler heard the Trinity Church clock at the top of the Street begin its respectful Protestant donging out of the hour—twelve noon. There was a tremendous explosion from the vicinity of the horse and wagon. Tyler spun around seeking to grab hold of something. A rising ball of white and bluish-white choking smoke rose. He saw yellow flames as the cloud rushed about shattering whatever was caught in the force of its concussion, whatever was blasted free to do damage. Brown and black plumes of smoke followed the first white cloud as fragments of iron and stone began to fly through the air.

Tyler stumbled into a doorway as glass started to spill down like sharp-knifed rain, and people began to fall, run, and scream with mashed limbs, cut faces, broken bones.

Skulls crushed like eggshells. Later it was reported that in more than half a mile, a vast circle of fury, glass fell from windows, becoming shards in shop windows, glass coming down from tall buildings. Five blocks from the explosion a man was killed by a heavy length of iron pipe catching up with him. Tyler looked toward H. H. Starkweather & Company. The granite front was scarred, windows blasted out.

The shock after the first explosion left only the smoke, the torn façades, and then he heard louder screaming as the wounded began to realize they had been hurt. The war he had missed, he thought as he choked and coughed in a cloud of dust and pigeon droppings and worse, must have been like this. But war was only between soldiers, men. Here young girls fell crumpled up as life went from them. Inside buildings fire was spreading—some office workers found their hair in flames and ran into the street. Bad burns were being suffered as high as the seventh floor in several of the office buildings.

A millionaire named Edward Street, a friend of Tyler's father, was killed; but he himself was never found, only a finger with his ring on it. J. P. Morgan's grandson, Junius Spencer, took a minor cut on a hand, otherwise, the *Times* was to report, "no other important Wall Street figure was hurt." Dead were thirty-five unimportant people and nearly 150 more or less damaged. Of the horse, little remained to be found but some scraps of hide and hair, and nothing much of the wagon.

Tyler, still in the doorway, found himself on his knees, his straw hat gone, dust on his jacket, and for some reason one of his two-toned shoes was off. For a gut-grabbing moment he feared he had lost a foot, but the shoe, empty, was by the curb along with crumpled copies of the New York *Journal* and a half-eaten roll. He heard the continual screaming and shouting, soon the clang of fire-engine bells. But his mind was too numbed to respond to noise. He hobbled over to the shoe, noticed his lisle gray clocked exposed sock had a hole in the toe.

Putting on the shoe, he stood and looked about him, then pushed his way through stalled cars, people that seemed to spin around in circles. Hysterical men, too. Oddly enough, he thought, the women, the flappers in their shingled bobs and knee-rolled stockings, seemed calmer, even if some were dabbing at a cut cheek or skinned knee. Shattered glass had been damaging. A Jewish girl with big black eyes held onto him. "Mister, it's crazy." He agreed, shook her off gently, and crossed to H. H. Starkweather & Company. The front was scarred here and there, as if shrapnel had gone off and gouged out chunks of stone in an irregular pattern. Tyler, looking across the street, saw J. P. Morgan & Company also had a pockmarked look. Both structures had lost most of their visible glass. Walking carefully through broken glass, Tyler saw a gray cat huddled in an empty packing case leaking straw.

The street-level banking floor of Starkweather & Company was done inside with black- and gold-colored marble, a great deal of shiny gold-brass grilles, walnut paneling, and heavy gold frames showing old oil paintings of New York harbor, downtown streets, the Battery, mostly of fifty years ago. All the interior was now chaos as Tyler pushed his way past old Charlie Mott, the doorman, his cap gone, his wings of white hair looking as if mangled by an egg-beater.

"It's a bleedin' shame what's happened here, Mr. Tyler, a bleedin' shame. H.H. so proud of the marble."

"Anyone badly hurt?"

"They're hollerin' too loud to be real hurt."

"It's certainly something, Charlie." The glass had done much damage to the furnishings, the deep leather chairs scarred, the marble, the paneling, picture frames. But except for some cuts and bruises, the clerks seemed merely to be making empty gestures or grabbing up ledgers, records, several girls holding bundles of stocks and bonds to their breasts like, Tyler thought, mothers grabbing their babies. One middle-aged woman was wandering about carrying an adding machine, shouting, "Clip together all vouchers!"

Tyler turned back to Charlie. "Is the elevator working? H.H.'s?"

"That it may be. Maybe, Mr. Tyler." Old Charlie was picking up shards of broken glass with his white-gloved hands. He had once told Tyler, when Tyler was ten and being taken to Sherry's for lunch, that he, Charlie, had been a drummer boy with Sherman in his march to the sea. . . . "Devastation, you never saw the like of it. Sherman's bummers they called us—devastation, Atlanta to the sea."

H.H.'s private elevator was off to one side down a narrow hall beyond the bank of public elevators, one of which was just emptying a packed mass of loud-talking people. The other elevator seemed stuck on the sixth floor. The gold vaults, Tyler knew, were in the subbasement. The sixth floor held certain special bonds and shares, safes of active issues that the house had floated, was floating, or about to float for various corporations, cartels, clients including some major and minor nations.

Ben, the black operator of the private elevator, was gone, run off, old Charlie said, most likely to see the excitement, stare at the wounded. From the street the noise was rising in pitch. There were more sirens, the honking of klaxon auto horns, and someplace a man was screaming in what could have been German.

"I'll take it up myself, Charlie."

Tyler had often been permitted by Ben to operate the elevator. He closed the doors, worked the lever for rise, and ascended slowly. Howard Harrison Starkweather had insisted his private "vertical railway" (as it had first been called when installed) move at a discreet rate of four miles an hour—in his early, hard-drinking days H.H. had a queasy stomach. Tyler, rather badly, stopped the ascent at the seventeenth floor, the top—three inches too high to meet the floor. He opened the fumed-oak door. There was a wide hallway of tapestries of goat-legged fauns at their approach to lust; two

24

bronze heads, Caesar and Homer; fresh flowers in celadon bowls. The gas fixtures overhead had been converted to electric bulbs ending in pinpoints.

A gray-haired woman with a long horseface and a very pleasant mouth was picking up spilled papers from the plum-colored rug. A bank of windows showed cracks, but no glass had fallen.

"What can it be, Tyler, what?"

"I'd guess a bomb of some sort, Munday. Maybe it's the Bolshevik revolution."

She looked at a Louis XIV clock on the wall. "You're expected. Go right in."

Tyler walked down the hall hung with Millet and Delacroix oils, a splendid rendering of women's flesh, a Rubens of Diana the huntress, and a tall Whistler girl in white. They were Harrison (Harry) Starkweather's, Tyler's father's, choice. H.H. himself, the grandfather, had about the public view of art expressed himself: "To show off your paintings at your place of business—it's like letting your pants down at a church supper."

At the end of the hall Casper Wilmot stood by the rubber plant in its Sung pot, and he made a *tut-tut* sucking sound as he looked at a gold watch, the lid snapped open in his hand.

"You're forty minutes late, Tyler."

"For Christ's sake, Wilmot, the city has been blown up and you're checking minutes."

Casper Wilmot was of medium height, medium plump, a plume of blond hair combed over a balding head, very blue eyes, medium-sized nose, "a woman's mouth," old Charlie said, and well-cared-for fingers. "Medium" expressed Casper Wilmot best. Banker's black suit, a wing collar, a dark purple cravat, gray spats. As H.H.'s personal shadow, confidant Casper was Boston Louisburg Square, Harvard, Phi Beta Kappa, lived with two aunts in East Orange, was a deadly skilled skeet shooter, collected Kipling firsts, and felt the Starkweather line was running down by the third generation. Tyler's brothers—Andrew in Paris, married to a Frenchwoman, Joseph a stockbroker *and* Village radical, red wine, sandals, beards.

Wilmot shut the watch case with a snap and returned it to its resting place, Tyler thought, just like William S. Hart in the films slipping his six-shooter back into its holster after drilling someone.

"Exactly, Tyler, you're forty minutes late."

"No excuse, Wilmot, none."

25

Wilmot opened one of the two ebony doors and motioned Tyler to precede him. The rugs were deeper and the pictures hid their true cost under very dark varnish. The room they came to was cheerful, furnishings not too massive, not too ornate.

His grandfather was standing at the window. He said, "It's like the damn Draft Riots of sixty-three down there, when the mob held the city for three days."

3

Tyler's grandfather turned from the window. At eighty, Tyler thought, the old blowhard looked fine, yes, fine his grandson thought. A nonquixotic grandeur about him. A bit stooped from his over six feet three inches of his prime, enough white hair left to give the shaggy look the Street remembered since the times when it was black and rising over his brow like a challenging plume. The stern features with the sensual mouth, the wise eyes, icy green-blue at times, and that domineering Starkweather jaw. A grim jaw still for all the loose old man's skin now hanging from it. An imposing figure that had frightened Tyler as a small boy, a presence in its broadcloth clothing, the square bowler hat. Also a smell of bourbon, good cigar ash, and the male smell of a healthy skin. Now, in old age, Tyler saw Grandfather was only a man who had lived well and hard and perhaps didn't admit his time was past. His deeds (or misdeeds) as founder of a great investment bank becoming part of the Street's history. Several historians *not* seeing Howard Harrison Starkweather with admiration, but admitting the glory.

"Hell, Ty, you should have seen the streets in sixty-three. Just after Gettysburg it was. Mobs of thousands, burning, hanging darkies from lampposts, cutting off their balls. Yes, and the police cracking skulls with big hickory clubs, like eggshells, and troops marching, maneuvering down Broadway, gunboats on the Hudson."

"It must have been fearful, sir." Tyler had heard the story of the Draft Riots a great many times and how Starkweather & Company had prepared to stand off the rioters if the mob ever got to Wall Street. H.H. armed with a 12-gauge shotgun. He'd have used it, too, and been stomped by the mob. No retreat, he had said.

H.H. opened a rosewood cigar box, thought of offering one to

26

Tyler, and shook his head. "I didn't blame the poor bastards. Lincoln had gotten Congress to pass a draft lottery for New York City. Needed four hundred thousand more men for that butcher Grant going into the Wilderness soon. But for three hundred dollars you could buy your way out of the army. Yep!" He cut the end of the cigar with the golden clipper attached to a massive watch chain. Lifted a lighter in the shape of a mermaid and when he had the cigar burning well, rotating it in his lips as he drew and exhaled. He smiled at Tyler. "The firm wasn't big yet then. A hole in the wall. It's been held against me that I paid the three hundred shinplasters, so did old J. D. Rockefeller, J. P. Morgan, oh, most of the well-off people in the city. No fastidious sensibilities on our part. We just didn't like soldiering."

"I rather enjoyed the army, sir."

"Yes, I'm sure you did. Country-club dances and food packages shipped to camp from the best shops. You didn't roll in the mud and horse turds and get a rusty bayonet pushed up in your gizzard. What saved the Union was what was *behind* the lines. People who kept the mills rolling, the steel being processed, the trains on our rails sent out to supply the feed to the armies. The South had enough food to feed Lee's forces there at the end when they ate horse corn and starved. And why did he and his men starve? Because their goddamn railroads were falling apart; they lacked rails and engines and steel mills. Chivalrous integrity wins no wars."

Down below in the Street the noise was growing in volume, but the smoke was clearing and police were roping off sidewalks and streets to keep out people and traffic. Ambulances came and went, wailing their shrill dirges.

H.H. looked at the end of his cigar. "I don't think today we'll lunch at the club. Kind of looked forward to a lemon sole." He spoke into one of three phones on his desk. "Munday, get us some trays of whatever they have down in our cafeteria . . . no, no damn custards or fried chicken. And have my son join us. Yes. No reporters. I have nothing to say on what has happened out in the Street. Just that we are open for business."

Tyler sat down facing the desk. The old gamecock was examining him with a stern eye over the cigar smoke, his yellowish teeth, but his own, showing. "I've always said anyone can go to hell or to the dogs in his own way to some inevitable consequence, and good riddance to him. It's been my way of life and Starkweather and

27

Company is something to outlast us all. It's one of the foundations of this country—damn it, Ty, *don't* you forget it. The muckrakers can't take away the fact of the railroads, the ships financed, the crops, the way we armed and fed and shipped out the AEF as a splendid fighting machine. It did save Europe's ass, didn't it? But beyond that. . . ."

Harry Starkweather came in, always the fashion plate, his son thought. A slimmer version of his father, much handsomer than his son Tyler. Silver gray, prone to biliousness, still played tennis. The hair thinning a bit at forty-eight, but wavy, and his clothes, cut in London, hung with a grace on the body he kept paunchless on the courts, by swimming in the pool of the Fifth Avenue house.

"Morning, Father." He nodded at Tyler.

"Hello, Dad."

"Morning, Ty. Father, there are dead people and millions in damage."

H.H. nodded. "Madmen get up pressures inside themselves. They want to hurt somebody. A bomb is the easiest way to call attention to the hot coals in their heads."

"It's the damn radicals. The Bolshies started it. I saw Mitchell Palmer, the Attorney General, last week. He's going to ship the swine out of the country."

Tyler looked at his father; a face deferential yet not patronizing. "Even if they're Americans?"

Harry Starkweather turned toward his son. "I wish I could ship you out. What's this nonsense of you wanting to marry some Polack?"

"She's Italian, named Margo Crivelli."

"Really?"

"Born on Mulberry Street. Graduate of Parson's. Draws fashions for Wanamakers."

H.H. nodded. "Commendable. And you love her, of course?"

"That's what this meeting is about, isn't it?"

Harry frowned. "Your grandfather and myself are broad-minded enough. We're no bluenoses or hypocrites. We understand a man has glands and, well, we're a lickerish family. And an honorable one—not just the Dutch-and-English-ancestry nonsense. I'm not a snob about that. You've heard me say any man if he has the stuff in him is as good as any other man or woman. But—"

Tyler found himself speaking. "It's unbelievable, *this* kind of

28

talk. I mean, pretentious reminders of old Dutch family, British ancestry. It's the way they used to talk at Newport, at Mrs. Astor's when we had a summer place there. Jesus, all that smug self-esteem. It's 1920—it's a new world."

"I agree, but old values still are valid."

H. H. stood up and went to the window again. "Ty, the Chinese have a great belief in family, in ancestors. Maybe it's all bushwa. Your father and me, we're thinking of the bank. It will be here when I'm gone and Harry is gone. It's one of the powers on the Street, and the Street, we like to think, runs the country. The whole shebang. You'll hear otherwise, but the Street *is* the country for all purposes, and it's a needed purpose. Credits, banking, the two-party system, all that the Street backs with money. I don't want to say Starkweathers don't marry Italians—immigrants' daughters, Catholics, or Jews yet, good as many of them are. Al Smith, Otto Kahn. Skip the aristocratic crap if you will—but we do stand for something."

"I'm aware of that, sir," Tyler said, swallowing hard; he wished he had H.H.'s self-assurance. "It all sounds, well, as if we've been guaranteed the earth."

H.H. turned from the window. He shouted, "Listen, boy! I wouldn't care if you married a bare-assed Hottentot or a Sioux squaw. But in twenty, thirty years you'll be H. H. Starkweather and Company. Your damn brother Andrew was to be the head and he flew kites with the RAF, lost a leg, and married that Frenchwoman, Sidonie. A hell of a lot Andy means to us now, running the Paris branch. And Joseph, a socialist stockbroker backing radical magazines, a boozehound. There is only you, Ty, only you. Harry and Kate are past breeding a new litter."

Jesus—Tyler felt the sweat run down his armpits—was all this naïveté or absurdity? All his life he had done things the Stark-weather way. Dressed like a Little Lord Fauntleroy, driven a wickerwork dogcart and pony in polite horse shows. Gone to Groton, seeing no fraudulence in the pretensions of a native ruling class. And Princeton, when he had wanted to enlist as a buck private and go to war. Taken dancing lessons at eight at Miss Bellaw's in his military drill uniform, moved across waxed oak floors with some smelling starchy little girl, learned table manners. All the years he hated; going from nanny to private school, to Culver. To prep school, a coach there who said you were best halfback on the team. Princeton, too gothic under its elm trees, and the posh eating club, the tradition of the sports-prone Poe brothers, Scotty and Bunny, and others talking of Pater and Art, the parlor snakes, the reading of Oscar Wilde and H. G. Wells. But it was always Princeton, rah, rah, and to hell with it.

He looked at his father. Class of '93, still of it. Margo, Tyler thought, she has broken me out of the mold, has cut an escape route, made a prison break for me. So, let them have it. Right between the eyes.

Harry said sternly, the way he talked to a client who doubted the comeback of royal Russian bonds, "Don't be a damn fool, Tyler."

"I might like being a fool."

"You're bright, you were always a good son and grandson. You were brought up properly."

H.H. coughed and put down his cigar. "So you've put your spoon in some girl's pudding. Young men get carried away—as if they invented the idea. But marrying, that, damn it, boy, is another dish. What's the matter with that Contrell girl you played tennis with all summer? All right, you want beauty? Old T. D. Otis' niece from Santa Barbara. You took her to the Rutgers-Princeton game when she came East. A damn fine body, amusing too—chitchat your head off—and the Otises, they're somebody. Kind goes to kind. Not just their paper mills, oil, shipping. I mean, Ty, the wrong marriage and you're up shit creek emotionally and no paddle. Look at that newspaper-publisher fellow with that chorus girl he's set up, and poor Stanford White, shot in the guts because he wanted a nice bit of naked girl on a velvet swing."

Harry said too quickly, "Yes, *yes*, Father."

Tyler smiled. Father was a bit of a stiff, a prude, and even as a club man of long standing who liked a blue story he most likely screwed in the dark when he went to Paris to visit the branch bank and André (Andrew) took him to that brothel, the House of All Nations, on the rue Edgar Quinet.

Harry seemed to sense what his son was thinking. "Ty, once you begin to think this thing through, you'll see it the family way. It's not just the family tradition and estates you'll inherit and the billions the bank will handle. It's what we owe each other—a duty. I'm no bigot, no defender of the Protestant Anglo-Saxon concept that made this nation. Oh, we move with the times. H.H. had lunch with Booker T. Washington and Teddy Roosevelt in the White House—helped establish Negro trade schools."

30

Tyler said, "I only want to get married."

H.H. waved off the idea of more talk. "Harry, let's drop it for to-day. The damn street bombing, and Ty is sensitive. That's the Chesney side of the family, a bit overbred like good racehorses. I'm not maligning your grandmother, boy. Just, a fact is a fact. Just tell us you'll do nothing rash like hitching up with this whatever her name is. And we'll talk again under damn better conditions. I'm taking the *Sea Witch* out of Sag Harbor next Tuesday. We'll all go up to Nantucket, eh?"

"Can I bring Margo?"

Harry flushed at this question. "Why, you young—"

H.H. held up a hand, smiled, put one still-strong hand on Tyler's shoulder. "Of course you can, Ty. Of course. A hell of a good idea. You're wrong, Harry, to be such a pernickety snob about the girl. I've nothing against her except taking her into the family. Yes, bring her, Ty. I want her to see your . . . your way of life and—"

There was a discreet knock on the door and Miss Munday came in, followed by two white-coated busboys from the bank's basement cafeteria carrying covered trays and by Charlie Mott with some newspaper extras headlined WALL STREET BOMBED; MANY DIE.

Miss Munday motioned the boys to set down the trays on a long Tudor side table. "I'm sorry we don't have much of a menu today, sir. There's some cold roast beef and the pea soup is rather good."

"That's fine, just fine, Munday, it will do," said H.H. "Just be sure of lots of black coffee. Charlie, what's doing below?"

"Carrying off the bodies, covering up the blown-out windows."

Harry took a newspaper, glanced over its first paragraph. "Nothing much beyond the headlines. Morgan building scarred, ours, pictures in later editions. Trading suspended for the day."

Miss Munday said, "The Stock Exchange has closed. The ticker is not reporting."

H.H. took a cut of roast beef on a plate Miss Munday handed him. "The English mustard, please. I wonder, Harry, if this will affect the market. People killed, injured, and we'll get blamed. The whole country has a cockeyed idea of the Street."

"They must catch whoever threw the bomb."

Charlie Mott said, "They figure it wasn't thrown. Nope, it was planted, some say in a wagon or dray. Come noon, she's set off. Boom!"

H.H. chewed a mouthful of beef. "Ty, go ahead, eat something. . . . Charlie, you were a city detective after they cleaned out the

31

Tweed gang from City Hall. What kind of miserable jackass would do anything like this?"

"Well, sir, these ain't Black Hand bombs—it's a radical or a nut with some personal idea of revenge against the House of Morgan *and* ourselves. It's one of those things. A gesture. Some stupe with his brains on fire. He's gotta hate something, somebody; he has maybe some direct word—God said for him to show 'em, the rich bastards—beggin' your pardon—using their terms. So he does. From time to time you get these bomber guys on the loose, and when you're a detective, you try to bag 'em before they do too much damage. Now, the Street bombing today was nothing too scientific. Most likely a nag, a wagon, maybe a couple of cases of real live dynamite mixed with, oh, say a quart or two of nitro, what the safecrackers call soup. Connected easy, say to a dollar tin alarm clock, then to some battery circuit to go off at dead noon. Zoom!"

Charlie nodded, pleased with his recital. Tyler looked at his grandfather spreading mustard on another cut of roast beef. The old man who should be thinking of death and punishment or rewards or punishment from his godhead. Yes, sitting there so calmly—as if he had a million years more—so sure of himself. Neither bomb nor rebel grandson seemed to have affected him. Sitting there under the old yellow oil painting of a blockade-runner on the high seas, the original *Sea Witch*. Not the present fifty-foot sleek yacht named after that paddle-wheeler English-built ship of 1862. In which H.H. as a young captain had run the Union blockades into Southern ports, taking out thousands of bales of contraband cotton. So, talk was, making enough to have founded the bank.

Tyler thought of the discrepancies between myth and reality. The past calmly chewing on a slice of roast beef. It was too bad there was no world of adventure left, no frontiers where a grandson could begin his own life the way he wanted it. Sitting Bull had been an attraction, Tyler remembered, with the Wild West show, the Klondike gold rush was over, all the buffalo were dead but for those in zoos. Admiral Peary had been to the North Pole, although some doubted it.

He chewed on a slice of dill pickle and thought of Stevenson's death in the South Seas a long time ago. And Jack London, a hero of Tyler's adolescence, had done himself in. Besides, *The Call of the Wild* was rather uncomfortable. He was remembering the summer on a ranch in Wyoming when he was fifteen. The dreadful skillet-singed food, the clapped-up cowboys sleeping in their stinking underwear, the cruelty to animals, the trapped wolf who chewed off his own leg when caught in a steel trap. And the fleas in the bunkhouse bedding, the castrating of the bull calves. No, Tyler had to admit, he liked comfort, the good life; why not servants, beautiful rooms, well-cooked food, clothes that were custom-fitted? It wasn't just that or being a Starkweather; so the maître d' always had a good table waiting. But it was fun to arrive at the Kentucky Derby in H.H.'s private railroad car, *Blue Sky*, even getting into the right eating club at college. It was all there and available, and if he had to give it up for Margo—yes, he would.

But no reason why he couldn't share all this with Margo. It might take a bit of doing. After all, Margo's talk of Marx and Emma Goldman, and evenings at Mable Dodge's, and hearing about John Reed, she doing a drawing for the *New Masses*, didn't mean everything to her. Not when it came to their love for each other. One could adjust.

Tyler saw no one was paying any attention to him, so he quietly left the room.

4

All the way uptown in the taxi to tell Margo of the visit, he brooded. Tyler was not yet fully aware, but he was beginning to suspect the reason for his father's opposition to his marrying Margo. The Starkweathers had not been among society's accepted four hundred in the late nineteenth century's "pernickety and perverse ideas of who belonged," as H.H. had said. Members of what felt itself exclusive society. There had been the problem of H.H. himself; too rough and too shady, some said, with his confusing explanations of how he got his start, his railroad stock raids. And the bank, too, had in its early days been involved with men who were too-clever operators of schemes and planners of how to corner some commodity. But it was H.H. himself who was too prickly for the best people. He had once chewed tobacco, and after an Astor charity dance he was observed to sit on his Newport villa porch in his stocking feet. Actually, it was not just faux pas behavior. There were remarks on "all the social bastards and climbers and the damn limp-wristed slobs dancing on their toes, and not any of them having a bloodline as good as their horses. . . . Their grandmothers drank from the spout of the teakettle."

Remarks like that had kept the Starkweathers out of what passed for the cream of society until the early years of the century. Then when pirates like old J.D., the part-Jewish Belmonts, the elder womanizer Morgan were accepted, the Starkweathers and their bank managed to become one with Astors and Vanderbilts. Harry and Kate Starkweather became gala hosts, givers of parties, fetes that made the social columns of "Cholly Knickerbocker" and the *Tribune*. Harry and Kate ("After all, she *is* a Van Rogen") relished, enjoyed, and fought for social success. Tyler saw his parents had to keep away various newcomers; miners with solid silver lodes, new dynasties of motorcars, cattle kings, brewers. Keep them in their place, maintain one's own hold in the proper social hierarchy. As a boy he watched his mother pontificate at teas and his father talk of his clubs. "Exclusive, but not bigoted, we have *one* Gimbel."

It was this defense of their social summit—the situation that brought so much pressure to bear on Tyler to "marry properly." Not only Harry and Kate's standing was in danger of mockery, but there was their daughter, Tyler's sister Pauline. She was coming out as a debutante that season. Hardly a time to bring a Mulberry Street Italian into the family when making the *Social Register* went back only a score of years.

H.H. had promised Harry he'd let them handle Tyler and his *bien-aimée* (as Kate put it). But now H.H. felt a little handling, with this own firm word added, would do the trick. It was not a thing H.H. felt was as important as Harry and Kate insisted. He himself didn't give a tinker's damn if the boy married a Digger Indian. But also he had an old man's desire to see his line go on and prosper. "Hell, I don't want to leave, as a dynasty, a retinue of show dogs." Harry was his only surviving son. Not the one he had placed his highest hopes in. Charles was his first choice; Charlie had been lost in a famous shipwreck, the *Titanic*, no less. And he feared some malevolent divinity might deplete the line. As H.H. grew older, grew old in a postwar world of inchoate chaos, he became more stubborn. He didn't like to be crossed ("even if I'm wrong").

Actually, the Starkweathers were unaware that already the whole pattern of what was called high society was by the early 1920's, even since the start of the World War, beginning to break up. And would soon become a kind of mocked group of a worn-out caste system to many. The time just ahead would see a Jewish writer of popular songs marry into the once-sacred ranks, Protestant society admit Catholics, even one or two Greeks ("*if* they're French"). In the speakeasies and nightclubs debutantes and their escorts were already mixing with prizefighters, film stars, gangsters—and a *Blue Book* member of one of the best first founding families of New Amsterdam marrying someone with, it was hinted, "a touch of the tar brush" of black blood.

Tyler was aware he was being forced (if he weakened) to uphold a pattern of society breaking down with a loss of consistency. A style and way of life his father and mother felt at ease in—and so dreaded to have it touched with any hint of gossip. A son seriously considering a wife outside the acceptable circle. . . . Years later, when a Rockefeller married his mother's Swedish servant girl, Kate Starkweather would admit, "Perhaps we were very foolish to be so stiff-necked. But it did seem such a naked and dangerous immediacy."

Tyler, for his part, saw his parents not as monsters or snobs, but rather as people living in an aspic of position and respect, congenially at ease with their equals. Tyler was too young as yet to understand the shelter most people erect around their lives, their hopes and aspirations. He merely saw that it was the family defending itself, and it was the damn bank. They were being unreasonable because they saw things only from their angle of observation. It was a good word, "unreasonable." He had been raised by the codes and taboos in which when one was unreasonable, one meant the unwashed making trouble; the strikers, the servants growing sassy, black sheep in drink and adultery. They were unreasonable. Now he applied the word against his father, mother, his grandfather. He hoped he had the strength to continue to be unreasonable.

The Crivellis of Little Italy, New York City, were not of peasant origin, not for four or five generations anyway, but formerly, in Molfetta, dealers in hides, horses, and mules. A group of brothers and cousins that had settled in Mulberry Street in the 1890's, some pushing carts of overripe fruit, some peddling plaster statues of saints, others trading olive oil and importing goat cheese. Became rich enough to be threatened by the Black Hand terrorists' organization; one cousin blown to bits by a bomb to show the others it was best to pay blackmail . . . *ora per sempre*. Margo, christened Majolini, was a granddaughter of a surviving Crivelli family who went into banking (rather, moneylending), became shipping-line passenger-ticket agents to the peddlers, pasta sellers, small shopkeepers, garment workers. Loans made at heavy interest, *very* heavy interest, on ships' cards, on credit for newcomers bringing over wives and bambinos from Livorno, Napoli, Palermo. With the National Prohibition Act creating a demand for alcohol, a few of the family were setting up portable stills to aid the evolution of the Black Hand Mustache Petes into bootlegging.

Most of the Crivellis were produce dealers, pork-shop owners, growers of Long Island potatoes. Few poor relatives, dealers in colored ices, at the povery levels. None owned a monkey or a hand organ. Margo's father, Joseph (Giuseppe) Crivelli, owned with two brothers, Jim (Giacomo) and Victor (Vittore), the Crivelli Bank on Mulberry Street; a storefront really, reached by ten steps, with one plate-glass window lettered ornately in gold: ITALIA AMICIZINA BANK. ITALIA STEAMSHIP TICKETS. G. CRIVELLI, DIRETTORE.

Margo had studied art at the Pratt Institute, then at Parson's, developed a talent for producing stylish long-legged fashion figures with great dolce dark madonna "wop eyes" that were catching on among store advertising departments. Her great hope was to get on the staff of *Vogue* and be featured with such names as Pages, Eric, or on *Harper's Bazaar* with Ertes.

Margo, at twenty-four, lived on the sixth floor of an apartment house on Riverside Drive near Seventy-ninth Street. A building a bit run down, but with high ceilings in the old-fashioned rooms and with dangerous wiring. There was a front-room studio with an expansion of window with stained-glass borders looking down on the Hudson, a bedroom with a terrace of vent pipes and tarred roof repairs, where she and her cat, Caesar Borgia, would take the sun, she under a bath towel and the tom making sniffing social calls at weedy shrubs set about in wooden containers. Sometimes, not often, she drew the drapes, sat in silent brooding for a day or two.

Margo was tall and, like her drawings, long-limbed, but rather wide in the hips and large in the breasts. Her olive skin and blue-black hair, cut in a shingled boyish bob, gave her an exotic look, a mysterious quality that was not at all her nature. She was frankly realistic, outspoken, given to the extremes of response. *Earthy*, Tyler thought, *and* practical. The sound of rain against her windows created a placid melancholy in her. Tyler was sure, by middle age, Margo would have a mustache, could run to fat. She had a comic and foul collection of Italian oaths and, unlike her mother, hated cooking, the mixing of sauces. Not for her the exploring *fidelini* vermicelli, pasta *fritto misto* dishes. She was a remarkable drafts-man. A gallery on Fifty-seventh Street featured her watercolors of the city and sometimes sold one. Twice a week she taught figure drawing at Parson's New York School of Fine and Applied Art at Seventy-ninth and Broadway. She was a favorite of the school's founder, Frank Alvah Parson; he wanted Margo to go to Paris and help run the branch of the art school there on the Place Vendôme.

She, at twenty-four, looked her age and had lost virginity six years before meeting Tyler. Lost it to a Hollywood actor with china teeth and an expensive wig. He desired to be mothered, he told her, and insisted on "incest." It had led in the end to an afternoon when she decided to leap from the Brooklyn Bridge, but a police-man dragged her off to the Central Street station house. Later she sat for six months in a dark corner of her grandmother's Bleecker Street flat, crying out, "*È troppo, è troppo*," and weeping. After which she took a portfolio of drawings around to the Fifth Avenue shops and decided to live forever alone even if, as the daughter of a Mul-berry Street banker, she had many suitors. . . .

Tyler took the old cage elevator of the Riverside apartment house up to the sixth floor and rapped on the deep blue painted sheet-metal door with its little card in a slot: CRIVELLI. He heard Margo's slipperless feet in the short hall; the door opened and he kissed her—all his girl and a mile wide, he thought. She was in a loose dressing gown, a lot of her exposed, and he kissed a naked very full breast. Then pressed one hand in the right place below, just where she liked it. Caesar Borgia, not relishing neglect, gave off a throaty growl. He was a tiger-striped cat of an amazing orange and yellow color. Margo often wiped her watercolor brushes on his fur to tease him. The large cat rubbed against their feet. Margo's short-cut hair was all every which way and she had the odor of a ready woman.

"*Bella, bella*," he said.

"What the hell was all the extra shouting in the streets?"

5

Holding her close, Tyler felt *if* he were wrong about Margo, it was a delight to be so wrong, a potent, exhilarating condition.

"Didn't you go down for a newspaper, Margo? Wall Street got blown up?"

"Good. All of it?"

"Just some street damage, busted glass windows. Mean. They think it was just one big bomb."

She smiled, put a hand on the back of his neck. "I thought only we dagos used the bomb."

He set his arms around her hips and led her over to her drawing table, looked down on the sheet of whatman board on which three young, willowy, impossibly tall girls, all with dark, romantic eyes, were modeling raincoats. Tyler kissed her again and she kept that ironic questioning look on her face.

"It's been a bad day all along the line, Margo. H.H. had me on the coals."

"I can guess why." She nuzzled her head with a brisk bump against his cheek. Her voice was firm, crisp. "I can guess for sure what the old crock said: 'Who the devil do you think, boy, a Stark-weather can marry? Who is this garlic-chewing bimbo? How dare you, a Starkweather, think of it ever? A little fucking, yeah, of the lower-class dame. A small intimate affair, yeah. But to bring her into our ritzy, high-nosed family, into our Fifth Avenue mansion, the acres at Shad Point. Horrors!' Oh, my aching society ass. Capish?" She sucked in air after this speech and waited.

Tyler shook his head, smiled. He sat down on the large sagging sofa salvaged from a bankrupt theater project. He pulled Margo down beside him. "I didn't agree to anything."

"You tell them to go climb a rope? You tell them it didn't matter what they thought—that this is love? Damn it, I want to know, did you fight for us?"

"Look, Margo, it was all haywire, confusion. There was the bombing and H.H. . . . Riding his high horse, the old bastard is something special to face when smoke is coming out of his ears. . . ."

Margo flared her nostrils, flexed her chest muscles. "So you said yes sir, no sir, Grandpappy." She turned her head away. Yes, Tyler noticed, just a faint dark line on her full upper lip. She went on, almost in a whisper. "You let them give you the family philosophy again. And tell you, 'Keep that scheming bitch away from our doorstep. Button up your fly and come home.'"

He seized one of her hands, which she pulled out of reach and looked at as if it had been scorched. He said, "Nothing like it. Listen, you've been invited to come out on the yacht this weekend. H.H. himself said so."

She looked at him closely, her head to one side, and kissed him twice on the mouth. "You poor dopey-benny. Ol' H.H. is treating me like any of the show girls he used to entertain on his boat—him and his butter-and-egg-men buddies—when he was in his prime. Just some sailing and screwing, so he can say, 'See, Tyler, my grandson, this Margo, she's *just* like any broad that comes out on this yacht.'"

Tyler tried to set himself into a controlled angry passivity. "Oh, damn it, Margo. You make everything sound like the plot of a cock-eyed Italian opera."

"Life *is* an Italian opera. Can't you see H.H.'s little scheme? If they want to meet me, the right way, let your father, mother give a dinner, and Grandpa, he can have us as weekend guests out on his place on the river. Where do they think I was raised? In a door-way?"

Tyler rubbed the cat's belly with the toe of a shoe. Margo, he felt, was not playing the game properly. There is a Starkweather way of doing things, his father used to say to him, "and the wrong way, rather unpleasant." Tyler didn't repeat this to Margo; it wasn't a text to reassure her. "We'll work things out. I'll be god damn firm; sure they understand I'm serious."

Margo reached for a cigarette from a cardboard pack of Murads and lit it from a folder of matches lettered TONY'S THE PLACE before Tyler could light it for her. Tony's was a Fifty-second Street speak-easy where newspaper men, show girls, taxi-fleet owners, depart-ment-store buyers, and college boys and their dates were coming to more often to drink very bad alcohol; the younger couples to think of it as an accessibility to life and real experience.

"If we don't get married, Tyler, in two months, we don't ever get married."

"We'll get married."

She repeated, "We'll get married. That is, *if* the Starkweathers don't break you down, put you in a nice warm pigeonhole just saved for sonny in the family history. No—I'm going to Paris to help run Parson's Paris school if we don't get married in two months. That's that."

"You're so damn angry at me. Well, I'm angry, too. Your atti-tude, well, it's goddamn lousy."

"You bet it is, darling. But I'm not going to hang around and have your family's idea of a proper guest list get into the way of *my* life."

"My brother Joseph didn't knuckle under to them."

"Joe isn't you. He's a marvelous born bum and rummy. He likes girls with soiled shoulder straps." She laughed and ended by making a grimace. "Joe isn't at all a proper Starkweather. You *are*, worse luck."

They sat and stared at each other as if testing the other's susceptible sensitivities. He felt she was wrong about him. She was seeing him from the height of being some years older than him. He still puzzled her. And an Italian family, you had to admit, was louder, more given to emotional display, public exhibition. No simplification of their sound and fury.

He had tried to explain himself one day when they were walking along the Jersey Palisades, picnicking high over the spinning coins of the river in the sun. Had tried to set out for Margo what family pride was like, social position and sense of duty and honor. She was in summer shantung of an amber color that day, coral around her neck, and she was eating an egg and cold salmon sandwich. She chewed slowly.

"They sound like those murder gangs and thieves down in Sicily."

In many ways, Tyler felt, she thought a lot like his brother Joseph. But then Joe was just a customer's man now in the brokerage office. Had been written off by H.H. and Father as someone not to head Starkweather & Company someday. His other brother, Andrew, called himself André now, had escaped, too, gone flying Sopwith Camels for the British, become a one-legged war hero, married, become a Catholic in Paris (worse, H.H. said, "than becoming a Democrat"). Andy was in Paris for good, with Starkweather et Fouchet on the avenue de l'Opéra, putting down, according to his last letter, a cellar of Château Latour and Rausan-Gassies and raising his kids as Frenchmen.

Tyler felt he was actually a stronger character than Margo, more stubborn, but she could outstrip him with talk.

"Don't you see, Margo, with Andy and Joe out of it, they'll have to settle for my way of thinking. So, hell, please come out on the yacht. It isn't what you think, not anymore anyway. H.H. hasn't been tomcatting for some years. I mean show girls, easy twat, on the yacht."

40

"Oh, god damn it all." Margo stood up, adjusted her dressing gown, walked stiff-legged over to the table, and looked down at the wash drawing of the girls in raincoats. She corrected a detail with a conté crayon pencil, drew quickly without hesitation, making instant judgments, having a firm, crisp line which gave her work so much more dash than the usual fashionable drawing of the period. "I don't know, sweetie, if we have anything left between us. Emotions wear out like silk stockings."

"You Italians dramatize too damn much." He was trying to hold onto her specific peculiar qualities that attracted him to her.

She turned to face him. "Yes, don't we, and with hand gestures, too! Like the Jews." She laughed. "Wouldn't it have been just nifty if I *were* Jewish? That would have bust a Starkweather gut wide open. Little kosher Starkweathers all over the place." She wanted to weep at the ragbag of contradictions that was coming between them.

"Listen, Margo, about Jews—both H.H. and my father are very good friends with the Kahns, Lehmans, Warburgs, Strauses, the—"

"I bet. But they don't invite them to Shad Point for dinner or for a day of bridge and prayers Sunday in the Whistler Peacock Room. I'm crowding you into a corner, Ty—and I'm doing it on purpose. You *or* Paris for me. Decide."

Tyler stood up and pushed the cat away with an angry side swipe of a shoe. "I'm not a naughty rag doll to be put in a corner, Miss Crivelli. If you calm down your wild Latin blood and get reasonable, I'll be at Tony's till five, and we'll have a few and be like it has been. My ritzy parents are giving a dinner tonight I have to attend, or I'd come back with you."

"Golly gee—what I'm missing."

Tyler again moved the cat away with a hard-pressed toe. "Oh, fuck off."

Margo said, "*Don't* kick my cat. Skip Tony's—come to bed."

"I thought we Starkweathers were a bunch of no-goods to you."

Margo folded her arms, said with a faint smile, "Just because I'm angry doesn't mean you're not habit-forming."

He followed her into the bedroom, where a plump Mexican Christ of wormy wood hung on one lemon-yellow wall and a few color reproductions of Juan Gris' Cubism shared space with a *New Masses* ball poster for a strikers' benefit—Kentucky coal miners.

They were, in the next hour, very compatible, tender, and aware

41

it had been a bad moment. Very earnest and ardent in their love-making, the old glow, almost innocence, was back. It was a time when the newspaper editorials in the *Sun* wrote of the postwar breakdown of morals and new, dangerously loose attitudes toward sexual freedom among the younger generations of the flapper she-bas and the parlor snakes, drugstore cowboys. Also of the rolled-stocking set and the first of the knickers, the plus fours for golf, and a certain freedom news writers had to express it all. Mr. Fitzgerald, Mr. Dos Passos. But actually it was—as with Tyler and Margo (no editorial readers—just young bodies)—as it had always been, only more people were writing about it and talking about it. ("The natural function of the sexes. Do I hear three cheers and tiger for it?" as Joseph Starkweather, down in the Village at Polly's Tearoom, expressed it.)

The Harrison Starkweathers' dinners in their Fifth Avenue house, just above and across from the Metropolitan Museum, were usually mentioned, often with an impressive guest list, in the New York *Times* and the *Tribune*, sometimes in the *World, Sun,* or *American* if among the guests were ambassadors. A listing of the dishes—even for a banker from Zurich or Threadneedle Street or a Scandinavian novelist who had won the Nobel Prize. The dinner Tyler attended was mostly a collection of Germans, bankers and financial experts with extra glands, it seemed to Tyler, on the backs of their thick shaved necks. Their wives appeared Wagnerian sopranos as to size, and the extra fat seemed to run to their wrists and legs. Wall Street was becoming involved in plans and loans to rebuild Germany, its steel, chemical-dye industries—the bank was interested in revitalizing the scientific instruments the Germans made so well.

Kate Starkweather had been a Van Rogen, one of the historic Hudson River Dutch families. They had lost their once-vast land holdings but retained some of the very old furniture. Harry and Kate Starkweather were well liked and people said it was a perfect marriage. Which it actually was; lived with simple straightforwardness and, to Tyler's knowledge, not at all dully. Perhaps a little too pridefully, some might say.

They enjoyed a summer month on their island in the St. Lawrence. Every other year, before the war, they went to Europe on a Cunarder, one of those big comfortable boats ("to avoid the raucous crowds on the French Line"). They were booked this year for Christmas in London with Sir Morris and Lady Manderson. The Harrison Starkweathers played whist and very skilled bridge and had started their married life with a mutual interest in brass polishing; they had, at the time, a mania for buying old brass. Ice-wagon scales, warming pans, hammered picture trays, and spending evenings with aprons on—using polishing agents, rubbing the brass items to a golden glow. In the early years they had played a vigorous tennis, and Harry from time to time worked on his stamp collection. Duties at the bank, however, as H.H. grew older, saw the brasses go back to brown dull surfaces, and Harry had never completed his hunt for the full Confederacy postage issue.

The dinner was good; a planked salmon, beef Wellington, after coffee "*mit Schlag*," as Kate put it. Tyler did manage to get his mother aside under the large Constable painting "The Hay Wagon."

"I don't want any discussions. I want a favor."

"Your father tells me you're being unreasonable."

"Just pleasantly unreasonable, Mother. I want you to invite Margo to the next big dinner."

"Ty, Ty, why are you so difficult? Your interest in girls is normal, I'm sure, is fine. When I was nineteen I didn't know I was foolish. I wanted to marry the horse groom in our Pittsfield place. What a preposterous idea. I came to see my infatuation."

"I bet he was something. Why didn't you?"

Kate adjusted two modest bracelets on her right wrist. "Have you met *her* parents?"

"Of course. And they don't think I'm good enough. After all, they're bankers, too."

"You know that remark is not amusing. Some Mulberry loan and ships' agency office."

"What was the horse groom like? You still look fine riding a long coupled bay."

His mother looked at him expressionless, but she could not prevent her neck flushing pink. Mother, he knew, could also get up a good head of steam when riled, as poor Dad knew from time to time.

Kate said, "I don't know why all my children turned out to be so goddamn nasty." She moved away, the tilt of her head showing her displeasure.

Tyler felt the scene mishandled; another brandy would do no harm. Father would be showing the guests his Daumier print collection; no, these were Germans; they'd see the Dürers. Tyler, carrying a refilled brandy glass, went out back by the stables, now garages, to the hothouse, where runty lemons grew in too-rich soil and humid air, also flowers without much scent—tended by Mother and brought to high color. A row of orchids in pots hung from a rack, produced blooms Tyler always thought of as cancerlike forms, abnormal organs. The whole evening seemed the highest idiocy; had he touched some secret corner of his mother's life? No, *not* Mother.

He sat on an iron chair painted white. To think things out. He had been told during his nursery life with Nanny Wilson, "Count ten, like a dear chappie, helps heaps to think things out." The football coach at the prep school said it his way, "Use the old noodle, Starkie." At Princeton the grind he had as roommate in his junior year—always waving his hands about, insisting, "Logic and reason could find the range on most everyday problems."

Tyler swallowed his brandy and spoke to the orchids. "Try it, you bastards, think it out. Ha, ha, ha."

6

The press, since the turn of the century, was always "making such a damn snotty fuss," H.H. insisted, about the Starkweather life-style: the beach house in Southampton, the villa at Newport, the 2,000-acre family estate, Shad Point, overlooking the Hudson River at Indian Hills—reporters claiming it has a fifty-room baronial mansion, a private golf course, stables, tennis courts, miles of trails, four swimming pools, a priceless art collection; add the twenty-room apartment overlooking Central Park in Manhattan of the Harry Starkweathers, the ranch in Copperwood, Wyoming, and the spacious home at Santa Barbara, California, and the impression was the Starkweathers lived well.

H.H. no longer attended the dinners his son Harry and daughter-in-law Kate gave. "Froufrou and damn silly exchange of gossip," he called such events. There had been, he recalled, great dinners at the turn of the century and before. All the fine eating places, Rector's, Delmonico's, and the amiable high-living people to eat them with. Chauncey Depew, Diamond Jim Brady, Representative Reed of Maine, Mark Twain. J. P. Morgan, that marvelously astute hulk of a man with a nose like a rotten tomato and the insides of a poet and lover of the flesh at times, yes, at times. His bank the only rival of H. H. Starkweather & Company. Hard armor-plated old J.P. when they were jockeying for control, for setting up a steel cartel or consolidating rail lines. And those Allied loans shared that sucked Woodrow Wilson into the war. . . . J.P. now dead.

H.H. sat on the big glass-enclosed porch of his Shad Point house—the press called it a fifty-room house, actually only forty-eight. He stared out into the night. Shad Point hadn't seen shad in the river for thirty years. Still, here on the river acres he had built this huge house of brick and stone with slate roofs and many chimneys, imported woods, stained glass. Built it in the nineties, when you could still get artists in, workmen, craftsmen, cabinetmakers, stonecutters. The world was going to hell in a basket since—any chucklehead could see that. Always was. He smiled to himself; you get old and you think things were better when you were young. Not true, not true. Neither were the street-corner prophets of doom with their flies open.

He'd been a widower for twenty years and liked it. He had been in love with Susan Chesney, then it became a travesty of marriage. . . . He drove off the cloud of memory. Still, there had been several women, not many, a few, and looking back in the serenity of detachment, he'd had it all; love, money, power, even a kind of dented fame. All now seemed worth nothing but a kick in the ass. What damn poet had said we all lived attached to a dying animal? Christ, yes. I feel as if I were seventeen again. But I know I'm just a bag of dry rot and brittle bones; the marrow is turning to stone and there are holes in my memory. The food has no taste, the whiskey little bite. Oh, I can sigh when I see a pretty girl and have hot whispering in my body—but let it pass, pass. "A dirty mind is a perpetual feast."

On the night river, barges with red and green running lights were moving slowly; a train someplace was blowing a banshee scream for a crossing and giving off a steamy panting. There used to be owls at Shad Point, but they were gone—the woods beyond the point gone. He was being besieged. New estates, new developments of fake Tudor and too-white colonial cottages were coming closer. He hadn't seen a fox on the place for years, and the river was usually stained with big oily patches, rainbow-colored and scum-fringed. He had seen floating horrors of dead cats and dogs washed up by the boathouse and dock no longer in use.

He thought of his grandsons and made a dour grimace. Harry had been a good son but had no breadth and spaciousness. And Harry and Kate's children had been a disappointment. All but Tyler, and now he, too, was acting up—the jackass in rut. Even as a child Tyler had been the rebel, the dreamer, the one who refused to let the pony have his way or let the nanny wash his ears. And once he had jumped into the river when a fish got away off his line. McKie, the gardener, had to jump in after him. Tyler was an outlaw till Harry and prep schools tamed him a bit. Now sniffing after a girl's skirt—a high sniff, the way they wore them *these* days. Of course Tyler was raised wrong. Overeducated, school protected, dude dressed, and *all* those manners. Hell, educated handshakers turned into dull people, wrote books without any real experience of life, and had the look of people who felt the rest of mankind smelled bad. Better a little frivolous coarseness than a year at Harvard.

The night wind rustled in the oldest oak. It was getting chilly too early in the season. Go in, get your shot of bourbon, get into the big lonely bed and sleep.

He never had trouble sleeping, never had trouble eating, drinking, never used to disappoint a woman, not in bed anyway; why did they all insist on the needless ramification of prolonged courtship?

The bomb explosion came back into his thoughts. Violence wasn't new to Americans. Just as soon lynch you as take your poke or horse or corporation. Helped by a pistol or a lawyer. So many try to steal you blind in business, trick you in a deal. . . . H.H. smiled. It was good, in a way, to test your mettle, to feel you had somebody facing you who had cunning and guile and yet you beat him—the game was worth it. Fisk, Gould, old Rockefeller, Jay Cooke, hundreds of names now carved on headstones or foundations. What of the bank? Tyler had in him the promise of something of mine; stamina, competence, strength. Tyler was good stuff, a little addled now by his glands. That damn Italian girl. First love, first fuckings of a young man are important to him. We should be sympathetically inclined. Harry didn't ever understand. Came a virgin to his wedding night with that Kate van Rogen. Tyler wasn't the waiting

46

kind—so you had to explain he had family duties. One didn't build the bank out of spit and flypaper. It took dedication.

Sticky items, women, hard to understand, hard to handle at times. Sometimes incredible naïveté on both sides. Jim Fisk had his direct way of putting it: "I tell you, Howie, cunt is the most important thing in the world; too bad we can only get it from a woman." Jim, he also got a bullet in his gut over a woman. Josie Mansfield—she got Jim shot, on a hotel staircase. A grand funeral, a lot of us from the Street attending. Jim dressed in his admiral's uniform, in a splendid open casket, uniform of his own navy, escorted by soldiers of his own army. A rascal, of course, but no man ever knew stocks, bonds, gold better.

Jim, who had gotten me, a callow rube, really started. Put me on a blockade-runner for the getting of contraband cotton to England. Farm boy to boatyard work, to codding off the Newfoundland banks. Then barge mate; hell, the subtle interrelations of seemingly disparate parts that make a life.

Polk, the butler, came out, a young husky with a square head, an English accent overpolished for use in the colonies.

"A bit too much of a chill in the air, sir. In you go."

"Don't tell me what to do, you cockney bastard."

"Bloody bastard, sir," said Polk, smiling, taking his arm. "Bit of a blazing blowup on the Street today."

"Just broken glass. Be a good lesson to the Street if it weren't for the people killed. Ever kill anyone, Polk?"

"Jolly well did, a whole blazing batch of Krauts on the retreat from Mons. Nearly got my dial smashed on the Somme. Did in one lot, me lads did, with the bayonet: Parry, lunge and right into the old gut or bash 'em in with a trench shovel, all the time a knee in the balls, and not think any the worse of it when the grog ration came up."

"I only killed one man. Not in war."

"Gave you the jollies, didn't it, sir?"

"Never had any feeling about it one way or the other."

They were moving up the grand staircase made of two colors of marble, past the row of family portraits, ruffles, whiskers, big noses, highlighted eyes, suits of armor, the tapestries, crystal chandeliers. H.H. no longer saw any of it; Harry's doings.

"Truth is it didn't bother me killing a man. I mean, no guilt feeling. But it gave me an idea how delicate and unique human life is.

47

Yes. One moment it is prancing and smiling, snapping its fingers, next moment it's dead meat, no more life in it than in a stone."

"Well, sir, don't go dreaming of any of it."

The bedroom overlooked the river. It was paneled in ancient chestnut and the bed was large. The dealer said it had been George IV's at Bath. H.H. had had the canopy removed when Susan died—curtains gave a feeling of alienation and withdrawal. By the bed was a Chippendale night table with a cut-glass container of water for night drinking if he got thirsty, also a sliced chicken breast on bread with the crust left on as he liked it, in case hunger came before dawn. It rarely did. Food had no taste anymore. Best was a shot glass of prime bourbon. The modern growing habit of drinking scotch he regretted—and speakeasy scotch at that—a damn snobbish poison. In bed, in his nightshirt, H.H. had never donned pajamas, "pimp clothes," he called them. He sipped the whiskey slowly, picked up a book. He'd read some of the Old Testament—a nightly habit—it brought sleep; "I have heard the reproach of Moab, and the reviling of the children of Ammon. . . ."

Polk switched off the lights all but one behind the partly opened bathroom door. The old sod, like all old men, had to flush his kidneys a few times a night or his prostate would give him hell. Polk took up the book, set it on the night table. "Good night, sir."

H.H. waved a liver-spotted hand and lay back, closed his eyes. Of late he had been dreaming a lot of the original H.H. Starkweather & Company of long ago, when it hadn't been much of a bank and the years of rivalry with Morgan, and of the Black Friday and the attempted corner of gold, all the floating of shares. . . . European holdings with Baring Brothers, the Rothschilds, Sassoons—and for kingdoms now gone. . . . The 1880's and 1890's of his prime, when it was free enterprise—hound eat hound—and they were all empire builders, not yet called robber barons. . . . Copper combines, steel cartels, the mergers of thousands of miles of cold-rolled, near-bankrupt steel rail. . . . The days of Silver Tabor, the Comstock lode mineral kings, and George Hearst, Collis Huntington, Stanford, Crocker. . . . That marvelous time he raced his private railroad car across the United States in three days and eight hours. . . . Just a big Baldwin, a diner, baggage car added; two chefs, six darkies, ten guests, women and champagne, tossing out the empty cases beyond the whistle stops, water tanks, junction points. . . .

48

Then back, back as he dozed off into a dark night off Charleston Harbor, ship's boilers with steam up, and seeking the mouth of the Savannah with the Union blockading gun frigates someplace nearby, searching for him, and then suddenly their nine-inch pivot guns blazing out on the dark sea plain and *Sea Witch* gray, slim, shallow enough to seek low water where the Union bottoms couldn't follow. In the dream it was all flames and smoke and he came away into another dream. The bank, the new building just finished that day, flawed by the news that San Francisco was burning, fallen into a great crack in the earth, disaster caused by an earthquake. The bank was solid enough on Manhattan's stone island. He had worn his square derby, a hammer-tailed coat, a choking collar, shaken hands with the Vice President and a Senator, a governor. The *World* and *Journal* had sent men with box cameras and flash powder . . . 1906.

A million years ago. Had been a chipper sixty-six that day and spent the night with that Polish opera singer, a prima donna, she had insisted on calling herself. Hairy to the navel. Near morning he dreamed again, river sirens of tug-pulled barges in his ears. The bank all flags, 1917, his grandson Andrew already for two years an RAF ace. Charlie Chaplin and Mary Pickford on a platform in front of the bank selling Liberty Bonds, the crowd singing "We'll Hang the Kaiser to a Sour Apple Tree." The year it added up to the bank collecting eighteen million dollars in commissions on loans it had negotiated for the Allied war effort. He was leading Tyler, dressed in an officer's uniform and Sam Browne belt and all out to be shown off. Then H.H. slept and didn't dream again. . . .

While the entire East Coast slept—but for night sports, watchmen—the day had begun in Europe, as a cable to Starkweather & Company indicated:

GOLD BULLION ON THE OPEN LONDON MARKET IN TERMS OF
BRITISH CURRENCY UNCHANGED AT 84s 93¾d PER OUNCE

Even with explosion in the Street, the grim bulk of the Assay Office lies immovable, like a watchdog, near the tip of Lower Manhattan. Gold is safe there. Still come great shiploads of bullion from every port in Europe. In the guarded storerooms of transatlantic liners it is stacked tier upon tier for its journey to the Harbor of

New York. Gold is running on the high seas toward its haven in this hemisphere. The earth is giving it up. From volcanic crevices, from timbered stopes and pockets it is being hacked out and blasted.

At the first light of morning on the docks the winches are lifting up the treasure from the ships' vaults. Neat stacks of oak boxes, hooped with iron, fill the armored cars. Police, guns drawn and ready, surround the bulletproof shapes. The trucks move forward, are loaded, and pick up speed as they pass taxis, pushcarts, and early, indifferent pedestrians. The gold convoy moves on toward the Assay Office.

There huge furnaces are melting the gold bricks, thousands of ounces at a time. The ingots are the chief ingredient of a bubbling yellow soup, some of it assigned to H. H. Starkweather & Company. To it is added the spice of gem-stripped rings, battered trinkets, gold eagles, moidores, sovereigns, louis d'or, medals, amulets, chalices, pen points, watch cases—all the mementos of hopes nourished, promises fulfilled, and symbols relinquished.

Sooty men in gray overalls dip their long-handled ladles into the soup and pour it, sizzling hot, into molds. Nothing is lost. Even the overalls ultimately go into the pot, and the gold flecks caught in their denim fabric are extracted. The gold dust in the air is imprisoned, too, in a chimney and turned back into the crucible.

While the ingots are cooling in their molds, they are stamped with their serial numbers. Sensitive scales weigh them, and recorders mark on their ruled sheets pounds, ounces, and grams at the moment of the new birth.

The batch going this morning to the banks on the Street is set out, waiting to be picked up.

Broken plate-glass windows of H. H. Starkweather & Company are being replaced.

7

A week after the bomb damage the Street was almost restored to its original state. The lost glass had been replaced but for some special sizes that had to come from an Ohio glass foundry. At Morgan & Company the scars and holes made by the explosion had been skillfully patched by craftsmen with a colored cement nearly matching the tones of the marble facade. But Starkweather & Company, at H.H.'s orders, had removed whole blocks of damaged stone sections and replaced them with fresh slabs. Several were already in place and had too clean a look that had to be toned down by several coats of dirty water.

In the bank the morning business was being done. While it does not seek off-the-street business, it does have a discreet corner of two cashiers and ornate grillwork for some ordinary banking procedures. Mostly the bank's business is municipal bonds, railroad issues, international credits, drafts, dealing in shares for clients and governments. It specializes in putting on the market huge blocks of shares, often with the aid of British connections. Much of its daily routine consists of meetings in various conference rooms and offices of company officials, department heads to discuss cables, coded letters, results of investigations, and plans with banks and exchanges from Cape Town to Tokyo. Those mysterious kinds of transactions (mysterious to the average man, anyway) of assets and currencies.

Harry Starkweather's office was the most guarded. Behind doors, a short hallway. It was heavily draped.

Harry was not so sure this morning that Tyler would not elope to Elkton, Maryland, with *that* girl. She was never referred to as Margo, just as "that girl," by him and Kate. Harry's office was always a delight to him. Classically Regency, "but with the proper amount of spread," the interior decorator had called it. The pictures were sedate, comforting; a small Claude landscape, a Homer watercolor of blue grouse rising to a hunter's shot. Harry, at his desk, inspected the day's prospects. Gold bullion, he noticed, on the open London market had gone to a hundred and twenty shillings and sixpence.

In Harry's office there is no intrusion of even the discreet noises of the outer rooms. It is spacious and orderly. The huge, crescent-shaped desk covered with plate glass. Besides the two telephones, nothing else is to be found on its glassy expanse. Behind the desk is a door that conceals a miniature bar and a bathroom. Six chairs stand at a respectful distance from the desk against the walls. Harry's swivel chair commands attention. It rises a bit above the sweep of desk and lords it over the six lower chairs.

He begins to study the opened page of the little notebook covered with minute initials followed by fractional figures. It is a map by which his course for the day's banking transactions is charted.

51

He will steer with care between the Scylla of the short loans and the Charybdis of the interest rates. His secretary, in her neat little office, is opening the morning mail. Advertisements go without a second glance into the wastebasket, business letters into a wire tray, and personal letters into a folder on the face of which she herself had penned an elaborate monogram of the initials *H.S.*

The morning market is opening with a flurry of selling orders and Harry studies the reports brought to him while a ticker works out its long paper tongue in a corner.

In London the Bank of England offered fifty-five million pounds at an average discount rate of one pound, three and eightpence against one pound, fourteen and threepence of the week before. The empire was going to fight a postwar depression if it had to, with cheap money. He knew the meaning of the reports from London that wages were down, prices higher for bacon and butter. Coal miners discontented. Amsterdam was weak and low. Banking schemes over there never easy to figure out. The rich burghers held onto their gold and rubber and spice holdings. And their money? How long could it stay at 7.5¼ guilders to the pound, 1.88½ to the dollar? Whenever the German inflation grew serious, other money would go into a tailspin. Still, Berlin looked stronger. Harry scanned the figures. The fixed-interest security market was dominated by the five thousand billion Reichsbank loan. An extra zero or two in the row of figures put there for some devious propaganda purpose?

One of the phones on the desk gave a polite tinkle.

"Hello, Harry?" H.H. sounded full of vigor this morning. "Where the hell are those overseas corporations' reports we've been setting up for clients?"

"On my desk, H.H. I just wanted to check them once more."

"You think this federal income tax that bastard Wilson put over is going to go creeping up and up?"

"Don't think so. Americans fought the British over unfair taxes, didn't we? It will peter out."

"Jesus, Harry, taxes are always unfair to our clients. I don't know, this *can* grow. Anytime a tax is put on, it isn't diminished with time, it grows like wind at a bean feast. How's the situation with Ty going?"

"I've had investigators at work. Hoping they'll turn something up. That girl, she's four years older than Ty, imagine!"

There was a chuckle, followed by a cough on the other end. "As

Nell Kimball used to say—Harry, she ran the best sporting house in New Orleans—'If they're big enough, they're old enough.'"

"I said, Father, that girl is *four* years older." The old boy was getting more than a bit deaf. And he had never been fastidious about what the telephone switchboard could hear.

"Did you say four? . . . You get a report the Germans are going to fall apart, with inflation going to run wild? I'd say to our clients stay out of their currency. Don't get the bank involved just yet. When inflation is really bad there, we'll see about acquiring steel and coal shares at the bottom prices."

"The Germans are hardworking people. I don't think their inflation is serious. If they had won the war, our royal Russian bonds would be in a healthy condition."

"Balls," said H.H., and hung up. Harry sat at his desk controlling his breathing. H.H. always seemed to think his son was still adolescent. Would there ever come a day when he, not his father, really ran the bank? When that whiskey and cigar-burned voice didn't contradict what Harry was sure were the most likely facts about events? The old boy was still thinking in terms of Civil War commodities, goose-feather quill pen and ink bookkeeping, and was too respectful of gold inventories. H.H. still read Adam Smith, the texts on John Law, and Ruskin. Even quoted Nell Kimball, a notorious madam. In Harry there was a persistent strain of ancestral puritanism.

He went to a large safe that blended artfully into the paneling and spun its dials, took out a series of thin blue cloth-covered ledgers. On his desk he piled them up, stroked them like a pet dog. He was rather proud of what they represented. He believed in it as some did in papal infallibility. H.H. had suggested the idea of it after the war ended, but he, Harry, had put it into operation.

These ledgers were as neat and trim as his sailing-boat models. Each one bore a small typewritten tag of identification pasted on its cover, which to Harry was like a proud name on the transom of a sailing ship.

BLUE WATER HOLDING CORPORATION	LUXEMBOURG
WARLOCK AND IRONSPINNER	LONDON
STANDARD TRADING SECURITIES	STATE OF DELAWARE
NEW WORLD INTERNATIONAL	BERN, SWITZERLAND
M. GUINEDOR ET CIE.	STOCKHOLM, SWEDEN
WU KONG, HOUSE OF	SHANGHAI

All these were the bank's creations for some of its special clients. Some were dormant; all were carefully set up and incorporated to dispose of assets, scatter responsibility, and avoid taxes. Certain of the bank's customers used them with the sure conviction that the legal proprieties were being observed. The bank only served as agent for these firms, received commissions and expense accountings, other high fees. Investing were federal and local judges, actresses, congressmen, millionaire Republicans, motion-picture stars, laxative heiresses, cigarette kings, DAR members, city contractors, and others who used these strategically scattered world firms to funnel assets abroad. To store gold hoards, to buy sovereigns, louis, gold bars, diamonds, and other hard values that one could actually hold in the hand or move from place to place when death taxes or estate levies were threatening.

Only Harry and H.H. knew fully the contents of the ledgers. In Shanghai and in Stockholm a few clerks and managers kept small suites of offices which had books filled with items in code and here and there an innocuously legal entry. Most of these companies hired vaults in the bigger native banks, but always through interlocking firms. It was all handled precisely, very legally, and was quite foolproof in 1920.

H. H. Starkweather was a respected and honorable bank and never stooped to anything like the deceit of certain other firms on the Street—like a notorious bucket-ship operation run by Boston Irish, just nearby, which horrified Harry.

Tyler was not very close to his older brother Joseph, not because Joe was a creature of diffident skepticism or the family disgrace. But Joe being five years older when they were growing up, the years apart had always seemed such a barrier. When Tyler was five, Joe was already playing grade-school basketball and didn't want a kid brother tagging along. When Joe was sixteen, in a stiff Arrow collar, smoking Fatimas, drinking beer secretly, putting his hands under the maid's uniform in the upstairs linen closet, Tyler was still reading *The White Company* and daydreaming of being a knight of Britain or the best swordsman at the court of Louis XIII.

It was only when Joe began to be featured in the newspapers as "the Starkweather radical" and the "Marxist stockbroker" that there developed a kind of understanding between the brothers. Joe in a porkpie hat with a hackle in the band, Tyler in Brooks Brothers Ivy League cloth.

54

The morning he found that Margo had acquired a new passport, had it in her possession, Tyler felt he had to turn to someone. Margo had been pretty bold about it, in that rich Italian contralto tone, when he found the passport in a handbag he had opened to search for a pack of cigarettes. After a night together.

"What the hell, Margo!"

"I wasn't kidding you," she said, standing by the big window watching the tugs and barges under the blue inanity of sky, going about their business as if nothing were changed in the whole world. "I'm going to be in Paris, Ty, by Thanksgiving, unless you show some spunk."

Someplace someone was producing the whine of a piano accordion.

"Damn it, I've been firm. I've laid it out plain to the family, I don't give an inch. They can toss me out of their damn dynasty, but I'm marrying you."

"Good. The next word *is*: When?"

Tyler broke a cigarette to bits in his fingers, let the shreds of tobacco fall to the green rug in need of cleaning. "When, when? Do you, too, have to go hammering at me, with my family giving me the elbow? I'll tell you when, Miss Crivelli—the day after my sister comes out as a debutante. October twentieth."

"My, my. And *my* family still fans their soup with their hats."

Tyler recognized Chopin's *Fantaisie Impromtu* on the accordion.

"I promised my mother I'd wait out that tacky society event." He smiled. "I made a deal, Margo. We wait, and in return you get invited to the deb party. Big doings at the Waldorf ballroom. Done over as old Venice, even a real small canal and a real gondola. Oscar himself to do the dinner. You'll be there to see us."

"The whole *megillah*?"

He had no idea what a *megillah* was, but she was hurting, he could sense that. He took her in his arms and kissed her and she said very low and husky. "Oh, Tyler, you're such a sweet dope in practical matters."

"There's a lunch at Sherry's at noon—I figured you didn't want to meet girls from Miss Beesley's School, the special chums, or the pimply girls down from Vassar. The big Waldorf spread is the one."

She studied his face closely, touching his cheeks. "Oh, sweetie, I'm not going. Not to any family affair until they invite me to the house."

"In time, in time."

"I'll try the boat. And a dinner with the Starkweathers."

"H.H. did want you taking the boat trip."

"Tyler, I really don't trust your honorable folks. Your dear old ma and pa. It's a cold, cold game they're playing."

"They're very decent people. Maybe not aware of the changes in the air but—"

"Ty, they've got detectives following me."

He didn't say anything, but he turned away and just looked at her. The cat, Caesar, was out on the terrace tapping on the French windows to get in. Tyler went to the windows, opened them, and the cat came in, stalked over to his scratching bar, ignoring them. Tyler said, "I told them they could investigate all they wanted and they'd find you as I saw you."

Margo stiffened, cocked her head to one side as if trying to get a new perspective of him. "You knew! You didn't resent it?"

"Of course I did. I yelled at dinner." He smiled. "No one has ever yelled at dinner. I told my father it wouldn't make any difference."

"Why not? There was that crazy summer with the movie actor I told you about. And I'm twenty-four, going to be twenty-five soon. I haven't lived like a nun. Nothing scandalous. But, well. . . ." She waved an arm in the air, leaving the sentence unfinished, suddenly reluctant to go on.

He went to her and put his arms around her. "I can't match you confession for confession, but it doesn't matter."

He had always instinctively avoided these kinds of scenes. Margo was weeping. She had been angry, thrown things at him, showed the hard edge of her temper. But somehow he hadn't expected Margo to cry again—it was out of character. Like the Venus de Milo in a slip doing a Castle dance step.

"All right, all right. I'll insist they stop the investigating."

She pushed her head—dropped it, actually—against his shoulder and wiped her tears on the cloth by rolling her head about, sniffing deeply.

The cat was at their feet staring up at them, making a mewing sound; he wanted to be fed and he didn't much care or show interest in these two bipeds engaged in their kind of yowling.

Tyler, leaving Margo's place, feeling something lost irretrievably, saw it was nearly nine thirty in the morning. Joe would be leaving from his Village flat for the brokerage office; the Stock Exchange opening at ten. Tyler was hungry, had left Margo's breakfastless. But first he phoned Joe from a United Cigar store, the phone smelling of bad breath, long-dead tobacco; the instrument grimy to the touch.

"Joe? Ty here."

"Hello, kid. Just leaving for the market."

"I need some advice."

"In a jam, eh? Gambling, broads?" Joseph Stanley Starkweather had a cheerful husky voice.

"Not anything like that."

"Look, I'm drag-tail hung over. Had a beaut of a row with Lily. Dames! What say to lunch at Lüchow's where the Pilsener flows? At one? Goodo."

The entire second story of the Starkweather Building held the well-planned floor space of its brokerage business.

MEMBERS NEW YORK STOCK EXCHANGE
CURB EXCHANGE, COTTON EXCHANGE
COMMODITIES EXCHANGE
Branches: Boston, New Orleans, Chicago, Los Angeles
Abroad: London, Paris, Rome, Shanghai, Rio de Janeiro

The Starkweather there had been Charles Chesney Starkweather, H.H.'s son, who went down in the *Titanic* in 1912. Joseph Starkweather mostly handled utility stocks.

The business dealings between the brokerage end and the bank were of value to both and to their clients, in the matters of family trusts, large holdings in industrial properties, the attending to heirs and "safeguarding the coupon clipping and dividends of widows and children," as Harry put it. "It calls for a great deal of knowledge of just how investment of trusts and changing market values can be held at peak condition."

Joseph Stanley Starkweather, his son, was a rather odd stockbroker, and only his family's name kept him in such a respectable, well-connected house. Joseph was the only member of the family aware that Tyler was bright, but still unformed.

Margo's visit as a guest on H.H.'s yacht, the *Sea Witch*, for a full two days' cruise around Long Island Sound began badly. She showed up at the club dock with Tyler at six in the morning, wearing comfortable but not properly styled clothes; a yellow sweater, gray pleated skirt (a bit crushed), and what looked like gray basketball shoes. A red scarf was wound around her head. She carried a brown paper bag which she said contained "girl secrets." Actually a bottle of gin (in case she needed a quick nip to face for two days these cold-ass bastards), a vanity case of various overage cosmetics, a change of panties, slip, and stockings for use when she sweated too much. She admitted to Tyler as they walked onto the yacht, "I sweat like a pig at a cookout picnic when I get panicky."

"Just keep calm, and don't yell."

"*Who's* yelling!"

H.H. in white flannels and old blue captain's cap cocked over to the left shook her hand when he greeted her on the bridge. "Well, young lady, you a good sailor? It's a bit choppy."

"You Tyler's father?"

"His grandfather."

She winked at Tyler, and a sailor led her below to show her her cabin. Tyler smiled. "She's a bit of a josher, H.H."

"God damn it, Ty, what's wrong with her remark? I *could* be your father. She's a bit big in the ass, like all Latin women."

"H.H., I love this girl."

"Damnedest fool words ever spoken by too many. Well, I don't intend to insult her or ask her to scrub down the deck. "

At ten the yacht cast off. It was an old yacht, still in steam to aid her vast spread of sail. There was a breakfast served on deck under an awning, and Margo met Tyler's father (his mother would join them at New Haven) and two ruddy-faced men who had already been at the grog (as they put it). Harry Starkweather, Margo put down right away as a stiff, a la-di-da gentleman, clubman, as warm as an ice wagon in December, and (poor gink) he was trying to be very nice to her.

"You know the Sound, Miss Crivelli?"

"Sure. My Uncle Giuseppe raises hogs near Oyster Bay."

"Poor Teddy," said H.H., attacking his ham and eggs.

"Didn't know there were any small farms thereabouts."

Margo put down her fork. "Small? Unk is the biggest pig man on the island. Take this ham on your plate—you ever see them slaughter a hog? The noise, the screams, and then scalding them, cutting them up in sections, like chopping up a pink baby."

"Really, *how* amusing," said a middle-aged actress married to one

58

of the ruddy men. She rose from her chair. "I'm going to upchuck. Don't mind me, dearie, it's the sea."

Tyler kicked Margo's foot. "You have no uncle who raises hogs."

"My cousin, really." She watched H.H.'s amused stare as he studied her. "Crude, huh?" she said to him.

"No, Miss Crivelli, you're shy, a bit scared, even resentful of us, and you're in a way sticking out your tongue at us."

One of the ruddy men said, "Crivelli? There was this chap in Rome had this huge palazzo—a count he was. I don't suppose he is related?"

"Of course not," said Tyler.

Margo stirred two spoons of sugar into her coffee cup. "Count Guido Crivelli? Yes, but a very distant relative. We're not so proud of him. A profiteer during the war. A money man, a—"

Harry said, "A banker?"

"Well, I didn't want to say it out loud, like a dirty word."

H.H. stood up. "We're opposite Bridgeport. There's a harbor buoy."

Standing at the rail with Margo later, Tyler said, "What the devil are you up to?"

"Getting them to like me. I'm not kissing society behinds. I'm not fawning at money and polished brass on a yacht. I'm being me."

"You're doing it all wrong."

"Go jump in the Sound." She turned away and she wished she had had another pull on the gin down below in the brown paper bag. She had expected to be angry, and here she was a bit scared of all of them. The old bastard was right. (Didn't he have a name? Why did everybody call him H.H.?) If she had any sense, she'd jump overboard and swim ashore, a good half mile. Maybe, if lucky, she'd drown.

Tyler's mother came on board and they sailed to the dock of the Saybrook Yacht Club. Here they all had dinner at the club in a room full of banners and tarnished award cups, ships' models, *and* Protestant food, Margo thought. All white bread, tasteless soups, no spices on the entrées that meant anything, and nearly everyone was hitting the booze.

Tyler's mother was charming, a bit frosty on the edges, fingering her pearls as if they were a hangman's noose. "You paint?"

"I paint, yes."

"You've known Tyler long?"

Margo found herself making that ethnic gesture, holding one hand flat, showing first the top, then the underside of it. "Fairly long."

Tyler's mother, poor bitch, you could see she was looking for something to talk about, not personal; you could catch the search in those society-page eyes. "This Picasso, what do you think?"

"What about, Mrs. Starkweather?"

"I mean it's all a jest, isn't it? A friend of ours brought back some jigsaw things of his—"

"No, it's the most goddamn revolutionary paint tossed in the face of the stuffed shirts of the world."

She had shouted it out, at least raised her voice a bit, for people were staring at her; lacquered shrimp impaled on forks, juicy oysters halfway to questioning mouths. Was it the "goddamn" or the word "revolutionary"? With Trotsky and Lenin in the evening's headlines. Margo wasn't sure.

Tyler's mother wiped with a damask napkin an imaginary dab of sauce from her chin and said, "I didn't know that."

The dinner at the Starkweathers' Fifth Avenue residence would go off much better, Margo promised Tyler. Present were two mustached college professors from Columbia—secret lovers, actually, but only Margo guessed it—a lady tennis champion, an Englishman in textile imports and his wife ("Visiting the colonies," Tyler whispered to Margo), and a fat journalist fresh from China ("Chaos, chaos"). Also some others Margo never really got into focus. H.H. was in Albany about some bill that was not to be passed, and somehow Margo missed the old bastard. He was on to her, but not unfriendly. As for Tyler's father and mother, they were all aspic-smooth surfaces, but you could sense that under the shiny cover they saw Margo as from the pushcart crowd downtown at Delancy and Hester streets, the wops and dagos out of Mulberry Street with their plaster saints and rosaries, wiping clean the ass of their bambino and stuffing in the pasta and olive oil.

Tyler's mother said over the braised rack of lamb *au jus* and the tomatoes Provençal, "You people, I gather, use a lot of veal."

Tyler gave Margo's foot a warning kick under the table. She kicked back violently and said, "Too much garlic in yours tonight— tell your cook."

"Too much?" said one of the professors. "Why, garlic, it's an Italian perfume, garlic."

"What?" asked the Englishman.

Harry Starkweather signaled the butler to serve the red wine.

"Been reading this book," said the journalist, "by a chap named Stoker, about vampires. Says garlic, great strings of it, whole cloves, you know, sure way to keep a vampire at bay."

"That's why," said Margo, "there are so many Italian survivors, because we stink of garlic all the time."

"Hear, hear," said the Englishman.

Kate Starkweather decided as she smiled and waved off the cauliflower *au gratin* offered her—decided even if it took the last breath left in her body—her boy Ty wasn't going to marry this dreadful person. She leaned over and took a silent sniff of the air. *Not* that the girl had any odor of damn garlic about her.

Later the young lovers were fighting in the taxi, fighting in the studio as Tyler tried to explain to Margo she was a goddamn stupid, stuck-up snotty bitch who was trying the patience of his family. "And fooling nobody! By acting boorish when all the family wants to do is to like you, get used to you, take you to their bosom."

Margo, near tears as she stripped off her gown, sank down on the bed. "Well, your old lady has the tits for bosom taking, even if I were twins."

They made love right then and were both surprised as to how fine and shaky it could be after an evening of taut nerves.

As for the Starkweathers, they didn't say no. And didn't say yes.

8

During business hours Joseph Starkweather dressed in a plain gray sack suit, pale blue shirt and collar, the collar usually open, a marine-blue tie pulled to one side. As a minor cog in Starkweather & Company he was, at twenty plus, ironic, amusing to those personal clients who saw him in his office. He was tall as his grandfather, had red hair always unruly at a time when young men buttered down their hair and parted it in the middle. When all men were hatted, he never wore head cover. He treated the stock market and Stock Exchange, where he had a seat (a gift of his father's on his twenty-first birthday), as a joke. Yet he was cunning, wise, and best of all, as H.H. put it, lucky. "I don't give a swift kick in the slats for anyone who isn't lucky. Joe's lucky, young, unstable, a son of a bitch, but a lucky one."

The conflict between grandson and grandfather was the result of the way Joseph lived. Married at nineteen, he had divorced a perfectly fine wife; Vassar, Junior League, a fine seat on a horse, one of the Van Reinhardts of Oyster Bay. He then moved into the Village with a Spanish dancer named Lily Overshaw, who was suspected of being a high yellow from Harlem. But worse than Joseph's crossing of the sexual color line, he also supported radical magazines, gave money to coal miners striking in Kentucky, signed manifestos of mill workers seeking a union shop in Paterson. He spoke of himself as a Marxist, arguing left-wing dogma with grimy men and short-haired women in basement cafés where they drank tea from a glass, the whole evening arguing about *Das Kapital*. Joseph calling Lenin "a good old Mr. Pickwick with wolf's teeth."

The East Side radicals and the members of the official Communist Party didn't like young Joe Starkweather's ironic comment on the coming world revolution and its leaders. They were more or less doctrinarians, fanatics. Joseph's sometimes cynical remarks about the one and only holy whole truth of Marxism upset them. But he supported so many of their projects, goals, crusades and could be shown off as "the millionaire Wall Street Marxist" that he was an asset to the party. Actually no millionaire, he might have hopes of some solid inheritance (if wills weren't changed). Truth was he lived mostly off his earned commissions.

Joseph in a gray worker's shirt, steel puddler's shoes, but wearing an old two-hundred-dollar Peel's tailored jacket from London, addressed strike groups and was photographed in the picketing of some capitalist nation's consul's office or on the piers protesting the deporting of aliens. He even getting run down by a police horse in Union Square during a Garment Workers' Union protest meeting against the sweatshop bosses.

Joseph Starkweather, "gilded youth radical," was always good for a newspaper story, and as the House of Morgan had a director's son who was also a left-winger, people did not hold it against either Starkweather or Morgan producing silver-spoon radicals. "They'll grow out of it," said one old player of the commodity market at Starkweather & Company, he preparing to take a flier in hog bellies futures and Red River winter wheat.

At twenty-two Joseph had been given up by his father and grandfather as a washout, one not fit to carry on the destiny of the family bank. H.H., after a few brandies, would indulge in hopes. "Someday some policeman is going to beat Joe's addled brains out with a billy club. I hope I'm here to enjoy it. Well, there's room for Joey in the family burial plot at Shad Point."

Actually, Joseph was not as intelligent as Tyler, but saw events with more clarity and as an irrational sequence. The brothers sat at lunch—Joe had preceded the meal with a pitcher of Pilsener beer, two very dry martinis, and touted Tyler off the *caneton à la presse*. He explained to Tyler over their sauerbraten and red cabbage that his kid brother suffered from that dangerous tribal mystique, duty to the family.

"Of course you wouldn't carry it as far as getting hitched against the clan's wishes."

Tyler said, "Didn't Lily want to get married?"

"They *all* do, Ty. All of those free lovers, women's rights Lucy Stoners. Free lovers? Ha! All alike, the advanced women, the tarts, lady poets, chorus girls. It's always in the back of their minds, the little gold wedding ring. No matter how they protest, even the girl comrade Bolshies, they want to live society's patterned life."

Tyler put down his knife and fork. He wiped his brow with the napkin, the overhead brass fans were buzzing, setting New York humidity into some sort of tacky current. Tyler remained uncomfortable and warm. In a corner two fat men were drinking brandy and singing low "*Zwei dunkle Augen*."

"You'd think, Joe, an artist, I mean Margo is really talented, wouldn't want the ties of marriage."

"Come off it. You're so respectable, Ty, you shine with it. You couldn't live, say at thirty, in what the family calls sin. You're a damn Pierce-Arrow, not a flivver."

"I'm not the studio-attic-and-sandal-and-red-wine type."

"*Touché*," said Joe, laughing and motioning to the waiter. " 'Owgust,' ein double martini, and bourbon for mein bruder."

"Ja, Herr Starkweather. Could I ask you somethink? Long Island Railroad is a gut stock to buy?"

"Anything is today, 'Owgust.' *Anything*." The waiter nodded and went off. "That's one of my smaller accounts. Everybody is beginning to buy stocks. That's democracy, isn't it? Aw, come on Ty, cheer up. I'm leveling with you. You asked me to give you advice. You're respectable. Not a stuffed shirt like brother André. Both you two have too much character, stubbornness. Brains even, I think, but Duty's Children, both of you. Can't ever be *déclassé.*"

"What's so wonderful about living in a cruddy flat among all those unwashed radicals? Not that I feel superior. Just, I suppose, finicky."

"Of course," said Joe, putting an arm across the tablecloth and pressing his brother's shoulder. "You're so frigging right. For you it wouldn't be the life at all. You're Byzantium, not Montparnasse, eh? And you'd fall out of grace with H.H. and our old man. You're one guy who can't find himself living in a cold-water flat raising up shitty-assed brats. Or live off your wife. She make any real money with those fashion drawings?"

Tyler laughed. Joe was always amusing and usually brutally direct and close to the facts as he saw them. Joe was young enough to have a good opinion of himself and clever even if frivolous.

"I love you, Joe, but I don't understand your way of life. Happy it's working for you. . . . Coming to Sis' debut?"

"Hell, no, not that *opéra bouffe* ritual. Truth is I wasn't invited. They're scared I'd bring Lily."

Tyler tried to focus on Joe's gesturing hands, the fingernails a bit in need of trimming. "You happy, Joe?"

Joe took the martini set before him and held it up at eye level. "Happy? I see happiness as a limited amount of contentment. You understand, Ty? Roaring, laughing, scratching, fall down, happy as a grig. Whatever the hell is a grig?"

"Anything animated and diminutive, like a grasshopper or a small eel."

Joe slapped the tabletop. "Three cheers for a Princeton education. But back to family tenacity. My advice is, Ty, give up your *ménage* and any plans for rice in your hair. Marry some nice *saftig* daughter of a corporation lawyer, even a girl who rides sidesaddle at Piping Rock horse shows. Best of breed. Good kennel papers full of the proper little orthodoxies. . . ."

Joe, it was clear, was looped or close to it.

"Joe. Thanks anyway. I just wanted your opinion. Really you're as much a bastard as H.H. and our old man about my situation. I mean your opinions are set in cement, just as theirs are."

"Well said. Yes, let him who is without bigotry cast the first judgment. . . . There's a coconut-custard pie here you mustn't miss. 'Owgust,' das pie mit whipped cream."

64

Tyler felt sad; he loved Joe, yet they were so far apart in everything.

Tyler shook hands with Joe outside Lüchow's and decided he didn't want to visit Starkweather & Company or even Margo. He took the subway uptown, breathing the cool captive air in constant reuse. He felt the subway fitted his mood. The underworld of Homer, and he was a poor version of the wily Ulysses. He spent the afternoon at Dan Moriarty's speakeasy at 216 East Fifty-eighth Street. A basement joint under a brownstone stoop; one went up to a steel door and an opening showing part of a head, mostly a wary eye. Inside, a plain redwood bar and taciturn drinkers, always some Irish doormen, a few strays from the New York Yacht Club, undergraduates from New Haven, Cambridge. A Haig & Haig box with a tiger-striped orange cat in it nursing her kittens. After two of the joint's version of whiskey Tyler fell into conversation with a geezer who claimed to be a Romanoff prince named Mike, a writer named Benchley, and a boy from New Haven who wore a bowler hat and raccoon coat; the boy from New Haven insisted Ann Pennington of the *Follies* was "the bee's knees."

Tyler stayed the night at the University Club and in the morning lay in the fissure between dream and waking, answering all the problems of the universe but his own.

Kate Starkweather and daughter Pauline, in the afternoon, were at Mme. Eloise's just off Fifth and Forty-ninth. The fitting was taking place of the gown Pauline would wear at her coming-out party. She was a long-legged girl, still free of disenchantment, decadence, pessimism. At eighteen, with hardly any breasts, and she had already cut her hair in a bob, Pauline Robin Starkweather was unaware she would become a type. Be the typical flapper, then move on to the look of the young married nightclubber—finally in two decades be the slim matron, mother of two children, seen in theater lobbies, the better speaks like Jack & Charlie's, feel the brevity of poignancy. Just now she was a rather excited teenager being fitted by Mme. Eloise (*née* Ethel Rosenblatt) while Kate, her mother, smoking through a jade-colored cigarette holder, walked around her daughter. "Rather skimpy, Ellie."

"Chic, madame, *très* chic."

Pauline was admiring herself in the big three-view mirror.

"Could you maybe pad it out, I *mean*. . . ." She placed her cupped hands over her chest. "Like kinda snazzy—huh?"

"Absolutely *not*," said Kate. "Just enough is enough."

Harry Starkweather in his Regency paneled office was reading a document the bank's legal department had sent down. Harry enjoyed the sight and sound of legal language, those tight-knit phrases they held down, closed the loopholes of those who did not hold an agreement, a contract, sacred: "Thirteenth: No contract or other transaction entered into by the Corporation shall be affected by the fact that any director of the Corporation in any way is interested in or connected with any party to such contract or transaction or himself is a party to such contract or trans. . . ."

Ah, it was like a good wine, a fine heady wine. Most legal texts on the Street, binding, solid enough, were just warm Coke.

H.H. had had a good lunch at the Bankers and Brokers Club. Mutton chops done just right. He had told Ollie Wilson of Morgan's you couldn't get a good mutton chop anywhere else in town. Well, maybe Keen's. When James Gordon Bennett was stirring up the city, there were a dozen good places for a mutton chop, thick, broiled properly. Ollie said yes, Jimmy Bennett—a self-made man who worshiped his Maker.

H.H., back in his office, was on his second afternoon cigar, was going over a prospectus of a new stock issue the bank would handle for the National Grange Harvester Company of Kansas City. A hundred thousand shares to be offered at 32, the bank, of course, to make its commission and also buy in for some special clients. Yes, farm machines by National Grange—NGH—was right up there with McCormick and International. Would be as good an investment as Carnegie Steel, Du Pont, even General Motors, now the self-starter was replacing the auto crank handle.

H.H. turned to the commodities report in the *Times*. NGH sales of its new issue, the demand by the brokerage houses would depend on the market of what it harvested:

Wheat, No. 2, red, per bushel	$0.88 £ ⅜
Corn, No. 2, yellow, per bushel	.63 £ ⅛
Rye, No. 2, Western, per bushel	.62 £ ¼
Oats, No. 3, white, per bushel	.45 £ ½
Four, Std., spring pats, bbl. 195 lbs.	5.45 @ 5.70

All this was food—bread—and far more. It was an old man's memory of the sun and earth, rain and snow and frost, and a mild sky. It was men, those he had known, who plowed and sowed, fertilized and harvested, who hoped and were disappointed and hoped again. Grain charts and estimates of wheat futures were prophecies of the outcome of an ever-recurring struggle with the soil and the elements. Reports of storm and blight and havoc by pests were the outlines of the drama, tragic or happy ending of the plot written in the storage records of the grain elevators, the cargoes of lake and ocean steamers and the carloadings of freight trains rolling over the plains.

Over the Middle West, the Deep South, and far into the great bulk of Texas the corn was a billowing sea of green, oceans of a wavelike moving tide . . . like a sea. . . . Yes. . . . He looked up at the painting of the paddle-wheel steamer breasting the crests of storm waves off Hampton Roads. He closed his eyes and sank back in the deep reclining chair . . . to run at night past Union steam frigates . . . no running lights . . . full steam up. . . .

BOOK II

Historically, the seller always comes before the buyer. It is the man who wants something to get rid of who comes hawking it round, and not the man who wants something who goes round trying to get it. . . . High-class finance consists of sitting round using your judgement. . . .

—EDWARD WELBOURNE,
twentieth-century historian
Cambridge

9

It was twilight of an April day, 1862, when the blockade-runner slipped out of Savanna-la-Mar on Jamaica's west coast, the steering point on her compass rose reading northwest. The ship, a long lean vessel built in Liverpool, was of shallow draft, a side-wheeler capable of very high speeds, faster than any unit of the Union blockading fleet patrolling off southern ports and thirty-eight hundred miles of rebel coast. The *Sea Witch* was painted a grayish-brown so that she merged now with the coming night and was hardly visible. Below in the fire boxes they were burning anthracite coal, which would not produce much smoke to escape from the two slanting funnels. She had loaded part of her cargo at Nassau in the Bahamas and in her last port of call had taken on a cargo consignment of lace, silk, cloth. But her main holds held three thousand barrels of gunpowder, seven thousand rifles, half a million each of cartridges and percussion caps. On the return trip she would carry back for the English market a huge load, bales of cotton desperately needed by Britain's mills.

For running the blockading fleets, both ways, the owners of *Sea Witch* would earn two hundred thousand dollars. One more successful round trip and the investment in ship and cargo would be paid for.

The sea began to kick up spume, flecking the tops of the waves, and *Sea Witch* rolled a bit but did not decrease her speed. At the teak wheel the whale-oil lamp burning by the binnacle cast up a bronze light on the chin-whiskered sailor with a jaw deformed by a chew of tobacco, he handling the spokes. The captain at his side wore a gray top hat, swallowtail coat, and red waistcoat. He was peering ahead into the now blue-black night sugared with stars. The captain was a young man, tall and wide-shouldered, with a too-

71

prominent nose, very large hands. He had come on board from a dance at the Planter's Club, a bit rum-dazed, but was now inhaling deeply and exhaling; just a hint of fruit and a scent of green rot from the island shoreline they were leaving coming to them on the breeze.

He was only twenty-two, but it was an age when youth matured quicker—he was to say much later—when few attended to years of higher education, and the seeking sons of New England were often itchy-footed, gristle-heeled—went to sea, went west, into trade, even some at rope's end to hang like overripe fruit on some wilderness plains tree as a failed outlaw.

The captain—still recalling the smell of lemon blossoms, jasmine, and *jusquiame*—felt *Sea Witch* tilt as the rolling current of some sea river caught them. Behind were pinpoints of shore lights fading out. From below came the thud and sweet sound of the Boulton & Watt engines turning and over the side the splashing of the paddle wheels. A normal yet special sound the captain relished, never grew bored with. He expected it, just as he knew his legs would steady him no matter what the weather.

"They'll never build anything finer than this ship, Dani'l."

"Aye, sir, aye." The helmsman spat carefully, skillfully an amber jet into a box of damp sawdust at his feet. The captain liked a neat ship. "But she's nothin' compared to a McKay tea clipper bound for Chiny past the Macao on the Canton run, a hundred and seventy-two days out of Boston to the Whampoa trading hongs, *and* back."

The captain was no romantic—not with such a formidable nose—and while he had been raised in a boatyard and had sailed his own skiff at seven, been a Gloucesterman at twelve in the hard work of codding off the Newfoundland banks, he thought sails outdated, impractical. He was a modern man, an up-to-date fellow, so he thought of himself. On his toes, the main chance, a man was what he made of himself, good luck was better than a handsome face. He was not ever to be naïve enough to live just by these New England Protestant ethics, yet he held them as doing no harm to one's thinking. As his father had put it, "No one was going to sell Howard any wooden nutmegs."

The night grew darker. "Be sure the watch is on deck, and wake me if you sight a ship's light."

"Aye, Captain Starkweather. You figure any Yankee gunboat this far south?"

72

"I don't figure, but don't want no thirty-two-pound pivot gun off a steam frigate shoved up my ass."

He wanted to get out of the party duds, soak his head in a bucket of sea water, and sleep. It had been a hard three days pleasing the English shipping agent who represented the owners and trying to gain reliable information of Confederate rebel ports being blockaded and in what strength. He had not meant to take the British governor's sister, so long of tooth, so peach-skinned and white-rumped, to bed. It was in the secret dealing in deliveries of rice, tobacco, cotton, indigo that he had met Jim Fisk, Jay Gould, other men. They talked big and sassy, speculators who carried gold coins by the jeansful, smoked Havana cheroots. Men who escorted the big, marvelous women with behinds like Morgan Red quarter horses. Howard Harrison Starkweather, callow, wary, unsure of himself, decided money was nothing to save, but a good thing to handle, to multiply by cunning and daring. So he hid his fears, his ignorance and had gone out as mate on the blockade-runner the *Iona*. Ten days out of Wilmington she had made Cork, where Howard saw to the taking on of coal, then making for Liverpool. A great deal had happened since then. As when Captain Barabee, who was to bring the new ship *Sea Witch* out on her first trip as a blockade-runner, fell and broke his thigh dockside, cursing a hackney-coach driver, and the owners had decided not to delay the sailing. For the Union had its spies on the docks for information on Confederate commerce raiders. The orders were for young Howard Starkweather to take her to sea and stop in Jamaica for added cargo. He was aware a letter from Jim Fisk had praised him—and also no other trustworthy captain was available.

If anyone would have asked the young captain if he had enjoyed his romantic adventurous life, he would honestly have answered he was not a goddamn romantic, and he didn't particularly call his life adventurous, just part of going to sea. However, no one asked him the question. He knew—under all his fears of funking it—his reason for being where he was. Partly a belief in his luck; he had been born with a caul. And also that he had a good opinion of himself. He was surprised to find he was brighter, keener than most seafarers, had a splendid sense of business, and now he knew it. He had no false conceit once he battered down his doubts—was neither offensive nor given to coarse actions, mean ways. His drinking and whoring he usually kept under tight control. He could never get

73

fully over the Bible-thumping sermons of the white clapboard churches of his boyhood. He had a residue of the New England sense of guilt that held him back from senseless hedonism, the full filth of Jack Tar ashore. He had long since decided religion was a good thing for some people but not as scientific as bookkeeping or the charts in Bowditch's *The Practical Navigator*. A text he had studied for years.

He was, he hoped, on a sea trail that could lead to riches. No more to be dreaming of the hard-scrabble farm of his grandfather, his wind-bowed father, his gaunt mother, the rocky acres cleared, the hard winters, the smell of the snowed-in cow barn when a blizzard raged and the animals stood smoking in the warmth of a barn and chewed their cuds while he milked a dozen of them before dawn each day—his hands red and cracked.

Howard, in his cabin, came away from his past to find Blacky, the eleven-year-old Indian—mostly Indian—mess boy shaking him awake. Blacky was wary for his years, the color of terra-cotta with clever, searching eyes, oversized, very even teeth. He was brighter than most of the crew and had so far escaped below-deck buggery by carrying a sharp Bowie knife and sleeping in the slop chest with his sea pants on.

"Captain, lookout says something comin' fast on the starboard."

Howard felt his guts contract—he choked back panic, a banging headache; in his mouth a coppery taste. Last night's shore-going finery, hat and tailcoat, white linen pantaloons with under-the-heel straps were scattered about. Naked, he sat up and reached for blue pants and a flannel shirt.

"Tell the mate to keep up speed. Be right up. God!" He held his head and walked to a wash stand, splashed several handfuls of water over his head, and tried to find the leg of his deck pants with a poorly steered foot. A hell of a time to meet a five-hundred-ton Union gunboat or a steam frigate. He just about kept his teeth from chattering.

On deck the dawn had come up like congealed bacon fat—silver gray—and some birds were silently skimming low over the waves—giant petrels and fulmars—where flying fish were foolishly leaping about. Howard saw the sighted ship was still far enough away not to be made out clearly. But from her black smoke he decided she was burning wood. He held on as the sea bumped itself like an unruly horse.

Matthew Winslow, the mate, a short man with ginger hair, a square-cut beard, and a plain walleyed face, was holding a brass spyglass on the sighted vessel. "I'd say, sir, she's about six knots slower than we are. Maybe more. Couldn't swear."

Matt was a mate who never took a chance, never had a solid opinion. Would never make captain.

Howard took the glass. A side-wheeler, ship rigged, larger than *Sea Witch,* carrying three masts with jibs flying. The cloud of black funnel smoke growing thicker. "Spanish, I think, Mr. Winslow. Old, burning wood. Keep your course."

"These contraband runs, Captain. If it weren't for the pay. . . ."

"You'd be digging potatoes and shoveling shit in Maine."

Howard felt better in the rising sun and accepted the tin mug of hot black coffee Blacky handed him. He took two strong pulls on the scalding brew and opened his mouth to cool the passage of the coffee.

"We'll make for the Savannah. I want to come on it just at twilight. The moon will be in its last quarter—a good dark night—when we make a run."

"Had the gun made ready, Captain. The lads will handle it shipshape."

Howard looked over at the six-pounder on its man-of-war carriage roped to rings in the deck. Matt was a jackass.

"That damn stovepipe couldn't stand up to anything with more firepower than a shotgun. Going to leave it behind in Charleston."

"Be unarmed, Captain?"

"Best weapon we got, Mr. Winslow, is our sea heels. Speed, speed *and* luck, and we'll outrun a whole row of Dahlgren cannon."

Blacky took the cup from him. "I been packin' up the rolls of the shiny stuff."

"Use the waterproof stuff for covers."

Howard had invested for his own profit in ten bolts of Hong Kong silk.

Back in his cabin he inspected the bundles Blacky had made of the bolts of silk. "Add some more cords."

"Ladies gonna make theirselves pretty for the sojers."

Howard smiled. Blacky had attached himself to the ship on her trial run, having been stranded—if his story was true—by a ship that sank at its English pier. Blacky seemed to be particularly alert, could even read some and write a fair hand. He would never talk of

75

from where came. "I'm a free man. I'm nobody's buck nigger boy." And his face would screw up and the agony almost jumped out of his thin body. Then he'd laugh like a blue jay.

"Blacky, silk is silk, but one thing I'll never understand is how people act the way they do. With their whole society coming down on their heads, still buying frou frous."

"They're itchy, Captain. Everybody is itchy all the time—so they scratch and they dance. *You* itchy in port."

"I'll kick you humpbacked."

Howard pulled on a cord tied around some of the bolts. "Don't suppose silk replaces too much gunpowder and stands of rifles."

"Confederacy has only got one foot on the ground," Jim Fisk had told him six months ago. "Is just feeling pain—not yet a sword in its vitals." They had been sitting in a Canal Street saloon, sipping Kentucky sour mash, and Jim was expansive, happy, amused, and cunning as ever. Sharpening the waxed spur ends of his mustache with fat, ringed fingers and keeping himself suppled with whiskey. Jim was plump, a solid square head on a big body. He was hearty and you had to like him just for the fun of being with him. And you could trust him—the wartime pirate that he was—whereas you couldn't trust his partner, Jay Gould, the puny little scut who coughed as if he were dying—coughed into his fist. Said he had the bad lung ailment, and you saw he never had an honest grin in him, just a kind of pious smirk.

Howard knew the two rascals had some small shares of *Sea Witch*. Lord knew what other Northern gentlemen were the major owners; very respectable, you could be lead-pipe sure—churchgoers, attending Henry Ward Beecher's church and thanking God for their big meals, smoking at the damask-covered table, and not thinking (among the family) of their plump soft women with whom they pleasured.

Jim Fisk had said over their cut of the rare beef and potatoes tucked under, "It's popular business, blockade-running. I'd say, Howie, there's about fifteen hundred vessels in the fleet right now, and half a million small arms have already been delivered to the rebs. Down in those plantations they used to produce over five million bales of cotton a year before the war. That was something to deal in, son. Even now they have a million and a half bales at least on their wharfs, just waiting for us to get it out. It pays even better than a shovel and wheelbarrow and an invitation to take what you want in any bank."

"Who's making the money, Mr. Fisk?"

"Everybody but the hoe hands. Whatever you bring into a rebel port is going to make more money than a royal flush."

10

Sea Witch felt the tidal suck as she rounded Tybee Island, and an edge of moon—irrelevant and frivolous, the captain thought—showed in a light mist. Howard looked at the compass and began to figure; if he went in on a slant, he'd still have recognized points, McQueen Island and Cockspur Island. That should give him direction for the mouth of the river. But what if the Union had already put troops on Tybee and sighted him in that trickle of moonlight? To the northeast those thin beads of light could only be the Union blockade boats, ready if they sighted him to come down and tear out his ass.

He motioned the sailor away from the tiller and took it himself, retracing in memory the maps he had studied in desperate urgency under the hanging oil lamp in his cabin for the last two nights. Somewhere off to the southwest was the Tattnall plantation, and as the paddle wheels of *Sea Witch* spun, he could somehow feel the tide pulling him off course. He had to find a harbor entrance point; he had moved barges here just a few years ago. Stay with what you know was a good rule.

Fort Pulaski in the outer harbor, that was it. He looked up to see sparks coming from his two funnels. "Damn it, Mr. Mate! We're showing flame from the stacks! Have them down below wet the coal before they toss it under the boilers."

The mate, after a quick look around as if hunting something he'd lost, went below. Aft, three sailors stood by watching the night, with buckets of sand at their feet. A hell of a lot of good that would do if the blockading fleet tossed red-hot cannonballs at them. Somehow that was unscrupulous, unfair warfare. He wondered if the cannonballs were kept cherry red at all times, or was that just sea gossip?

The boom of cannon came from the northwest, and he picked up the speaking tube to the engine room. "Moses, you forget trying to keep sparks out of the stacks. Pour it on. I want every bit of steam you can get. Full speed. Full, you *hear*, Moses?"

"I hear," said the British and black Gullah voice of Moses, the engine-gang boss. "She going to jolly well shake herself right to bits."

"Let her shake." He wondered from what direction he had heard cannon fire. The Union naval strategists fired randomly at times. He didn't have to wait long for direction. A string of lights on some ship's rigging in the mist was moving. He saw the flash, two flashes, as the cannon fired, and felt the protest of concussion in the air, still far off. Nine-pounders, he figured, and just out of range. Yes, two splashes two hundred yards to starboard showed that for the moment he was safe. Safe as a shoat with two dogs hanging on her ears.

He turned southwest, still wondering just where he was in relation to the river's mouth. Another shot, and he could hear it whistle. Like a shrill call and a death moan of a dappled gray horse he had known as a boy, a horse that died of the blind staggers. Union guns this heavy, he had heard, could at three hundred and fifty yards penetrate three feet of oak, six of pine.

He felt *Sea Witch* had been hit by the last shot, but high up; bits of funnel metal fell on deck. He turned the ship some to port and saw the edge of Pulaski, Fort Pulaski. He had his point of reference now to the harbor and river in the five-sided mass of masonry of the fort. He had visited it once with some bargemen and whores and a keg of hard cider. Howard had gone to the grave of the Count Pulaski who was killed hereabouts during the Revolution.

Howard wondered, for one moment, as he spun the wheel, if he was mistaking the lazaretto for the fort; lazaretto, the quarantine station and slave hospital. But no, he knew those gray walls with sphagnum moss on the trees, fetid fungi in puddles. Again he heard the whistle and the moan, and the lights were closer, three clusters showing now. Union frigates were closing in by the height of the mast lights. From the direction of the shore came the cry of a loon or a bittern.

The mate was back, sucking air through his mouth. "They're hound-dog close, Captain."

"See what damage has been done besides the stack."

He could feel *Sea Witch* responding to the increase of the steam pressure in the boilers, could feel the throb of her like some creature boiling in a pan, only a hundred times louder, as they churned up the sea.

78

Howard didn't pay any more attention to the moving clusters of lights behind him. He could outrun any Federal tub in the service—but *not* a lucky shot or two if they bushwhacked him by some surprise, like a frigate where it shouldn't be.

Blacky was at his elbow, pulling Howard's jacket sleeve.

"There's some more."

Howard looked to where the boy was pointing in a new direction, and it was more than just lights. It was the real shape of a Union ship and he could make out the spiderweb of rigging, the one huge funnel, the animated shapes of men under battle lanterns, bent over gun carriages. He could even hear voices giving command. A ship between him and the river mouth. And well within gun range. He felt his scrotum tighten. The bushwhacker had been there all the time, gotten close in during the moonless hours and the mist—unseen by the shore batteries. He tacked at once and so sharply *Sea Witch* heeled at an acute angle and the port paddle wheel beat only air for a moment. The frigate must have fired her guns and Howard had turned just in time. The sound of the shells roared in a mad pitch, *very* close.

The mate was back once more. He had torn open the collar of his tunic and, for some reason, had stuck a Colt Navy revolver into his belt. "Just holed one of the stacks, Captain. Cut two guy wires."

"How close you think the one trying to cut us off is?"

"Closing fast at three hundred yards, maybe."

"Maybe. Well. . . ."

"He's got us fer sure, Captain."

Howard was smiling, hands on the oak spokes of the wheel. If he couldn't smile, he'd have to show concern. But he was feeling nothing of the fears that had come so far with him on this trip. He'd hate to lose the ship now, the cargo, his few rolls of silk. To come so far in calculated impudence and be failing in his obligations now. No. He didn't give a tinker's fuck about the cargo now—it was *Sea Witch,* and him and them, the hunted and the hunters. Maybe that was too fancy a way to look at it. If only the bit of moon went away and he was sure of just where the shallows were. "Matt, go forward and start tossing the lead line. Going to low water where they can't follow with their big hulls. They draw what?"

"Thirty, forty feet of water."

"Get the lead line over side and give me readings."

The greedy swine of owners had put down just enough coal to get to an East Coast Southern harbor—to make more bunker space for cargo. He didn't dare take to the open sea now, with the scoop shovels scraping the bin floors.

"Thirty-two!"

He could sense the shallows of the harbor's fringe now. He didn't know how. Perhaps it was the sound echoing back from the bottom by the thrashing of the paddle blades. Perhaps he had this sense of *knowing*—being born with a caul had to give one some sixth sense. He looked up at a clearing sky and saw Sirius—the Dog Star—and the Perseid darting through the sky scattering stardust—or was it just an illusion? Anyway, his lucky stars.

"Twenty-eight!"

This time he'd test his luck. He did not move the wheel. He could feel the bottom now as the keel touched, just flecked on shell and sand. There was a scraping, a clearing, then a rasping under him. The sensation of refloating. He was over loose sea rock. Nothing for it but to go on. If he hit a reef, the rebels could come out in small boats—under fire—and take off cargo if he didn't sink. But he was sure his lucky stars were there for the hull to slide over sand. There was a thump hard enough on something down there, perhaps a wreck. He prayed not to show a dent or crack in her oak-planked gray sides. He was still calm enough to think that damage to *Sea Witch* would be like leaving an ugly scar on a beautiful woman's face. The ship had given him pride and forbearance—and the extremes of responsibility.

The lights of the frigates were dimming, scrubbing out. The moon had at last decided to bed down in the clouds. No Union hull around could follow him without a great risk, seeking a channel through shallows for which perhaps it had no charts.

Blacky was by his side, carrying his galley cleaver on a shoulder like a rifle.

"One of them got trouble."

Howard looked to starboard. Sure enough, one cluster of lights, very faint, seemed listing to one side. "They've run aground. Have a hell of a devil's own time trying to pull her off."

"Twenty-six!"

He was aware his shirt was wet; dampness, too, was in his hair and he could feel the sweat, like acid, rolling down into his collar. Well, he wasn't riddled like a colander by the Dahlgren thirty-two-pound pivot guns some of the five-hundred-ton gunboats mounted. His hands trembled, and he motioned a sailor to take the wheel.

"Keep her steady as she goes."

"Aye."

Howard felt suddenly very hungry. His stomach seemed to be howling for something to be put into it. He told Blacky to have cookie issue rations. "And get that rum jug in my cabin. We've all earned a swallow."

"The moon is back."

"Who cares?"

He looked up and saw stars, the whole heaven just sprinkled with them, winking down at him as if saluting his luck. He held onto the side of the skylight to stop the shakes. He'd land this cargo, and those Southern pricks better not give him any of their aristocratic disdain.

11

The Yamacraw district of Savannah was mostly given over to blacks; the workers of forges, timber shapers, loaders of ships (in peacetime), and haulers of the city's refuse. The blacks were still mainly slaves, and since Fort Sumter many had been moved into the back country. Captain Howard Harrison Starkweather, stepping in his freshly polished boots among the horse apples and the muddy ruts where the crushed shell had failed to make a solid street surface, wondered why he didn't have Donald McCann come to him rather than walk through this muck. The queasiness after his blockade run had left him. He saw they cut it high on the hog in this rebel city—there were still well-dressed folk.

He came to a stop, glancing up. The sign, painted some years back, had been weathered but he could still read over the big shed-like structure the words

D. D. MCCANN FORGE AND IRONWORKS
COMMISSION MERCHANT, FACTORING AGENT

There was the glow of charcoal burning red in the back of the shed and dark patterns of iron beams, rusting chains, and parts of machines the use for which he didn't recognize. He walked over a cinder surface to where broad pine boards made a corner of their own and knocked on the door lettered NO PEDDLERS. D. D. MCC.

Four blacks at the brick-held charcoal fire were lifting what he saw to be a ship's drive shaft out of the inferno of cherry-colored coals; lifting it on a chain hoist. As he watched, they lowered it onto a wide anvil and began to attack it with hammers, sparks flying, the blacks naked to the hips, pounding and grunting with effort, paying Howard no attention. He was about to knock again when the door was opened inward by a short stout man, red bandanna handkerchief knotted around his collar, his long near-orange hair greased and hanging limp on the side and the back of the neck, the face ending in a small tuft of maroon beard like a wise and wily fox's. The man held out a hand.

"Jasus, Starkweather, were it yourself they were firing at the other night?"

"They were, McCann. Hot breath down my neck."

"Come in, come in." He yelled at the work crew, "Damn ya, still tickling that shaft! Hammer, *hammer!*"

The room had no ceiling, just walls, one dusty window, and way overhead the grimy rafters of the building.

"Good laddies, these naggers. But ya have to stir 'em."

Howard saw a pine table, two chairs, a fumed-oak varnished file, a letterpress, and two brass spittoons. This seemed to be the furnishing. The only decor a colored print of a wheeled sulky, a horse named Big Prince straining to break the two-minute mile. And various ink stains on the back wall as if flung there by a brisk but careless shaking of a pen.

"If you've come for iron, my mon, its harder to find than gold."

"Don't need much, just to patch a shot through a funnel. A few square feet of very thin plate."

McCann tapped the table with short thin fingers. "Ah, well. I'm tearing down some iron railing from balconies someplace; maybe I'll steal you some thin stuff. But the war, it's taking all the iron and brass, and there never was much in the South. No, you Yankees, you know a war is iron and cloth and foodstuff. These damn planters—their infinite diversity of life is hound dogs, whiskey, cards, and callets."

"What's a callet?"

"A wench, a cunt."

McCann produced a bottle, blew dust from two blue glasses. "They do make a fine peach pressing. Not scotch like at hame, but it will do. So you're now captain, heh? I knew you'd never stay a bargeman. We did a neat trade in those days."

They sipped, and the hammering outside went on. Howard lifted his glass for a refill. "I've silk this time, fifty-two yards of it."

"Your own bit of profit? Well, if I can't find iron, I may have a use for the silk." McCann leaned nearer and whispered as if he suspected someone was listening behind the door. "You sail when?"

"Nine days. Loading bales now. Prime long-staple cotton. Liverpool. Hope to get out and away on the tide, the ninth, on a dark night."

"Jim Fisk trusts you, Starkweather, so I do, too, in these drumlie times. Jim is a fine high-handed bastard, but he'll play fair with you, me."

"He's been square to me." The peach brandy, or whatever it was, had a good taste and he knew he'd have to bargain with the little Scot over the price per yard for his silk.

"Now, laddie, I've been watching the contraband runners carry off the cotton and bring in the doodads and the few weapons. How long do you think this war will last before they get their beating?"

"You think, McCann, they'll lose?"

"Have to, mon, have to. A cause doomed by their absurdity. No banking system worth a domn, no gold reserve, no metals, no metals at all but old rusting nails and river hulks, and a transport system about as good as a leaking teakettle—not any large industry, no nest of factories, no trustworthy currency. No war ever was won by courage and gallantry alone. It's not soldiers at all that win—even the poor sods who take a field and hold it or fall back, and generals don't matter on fine horses waving swords. No, it's credits, rates of exchange, the sound of gold wins wars. Two years and the gentry and the red-necks, they've had it. Down to eating horses and wearing wallpaper for clothes. Still economics, lad. Ever read Adam Smith?"

"No, I will."

"Well, talking sense gives me rheumatic twinges." McCann reached under the table and brought up a japanned iron box. It was unlocked and he took out a bundle of papers. "These now are letters of credit from Baring Brothers, Lundon, and the Rothschilds. Paying for some cargoes, and I've been buying them up from the planters and agents, those getting cotton past the blockade."

"Barings and the Rothschilds are sound enough."

"Dinna I know that? But now, Starkweather, I want to get them to New York. There's movement and contact through the lines.

But risky. I'd hate to have these found in some woman's drawers by a groping Union officer. It's a risk I can't take. I've four hundred thousand in banking credits in this small bundle, aye."

The Scot leaned back in his chair, smiled, took a sip of his drink, and wiped his neck with the red bandanna. "I want you to take it to Jim Fisk's agent in Lundon, on Threadneedle Street, for me."

"That's a big risk, bigger than some Nellie's drawers."

"Hm, yes *and* no. I've been thinking yer a champion sailor, the way you come upriver. And. . . ." McCann rubbed the tips of his fingers together. "I've been supplying some of the Union frigate captains with what makes life more pleasant on sea patrol—fresh beef, mutton, some of this peach pressings. Not a bribe, mind you, *just* keeping up friendships. I'm sure they'll do an auld friend a favor and not patrol a *certain* sector out at sea some dark nicht."

Howard laughed. "You're a crafty son of a bitch, Mr. McCann. One who knows more than I'll ever know."

"Don't put yourself down. I'm just a bit older. Then it's settled? You carry the packet fer me. I'll give you the name of Jim's agent. I hope it gets to New York before England comes in on the side of the rebels. They're starving fer cotton, the bloody English—their mills shutting down, the ferment among the workers is bad, hunger and anger may bring the British lion in on the rebel side. That will kill the blockade-running trade and prolong the war, laddie. The place to be in is New York. It's the marketplace for the trading in shares, supplies. Give up the sea—join me there if things change."

"I'll have the capital for it, McCann, in three more round trips of *Sea Witch*."

"I don't envy you. It's here on land—millions to be made. Like the Erie steamcar shares by Drew and Gould. Oh, they play it like a fish on a line. It's a grand big land, Starkweather, and once this war is done for, there's the opening up of the resources of copper, silver, coal, and timber. The country, it's like a virgin lass waiting for Robbie Burns to put her on her back on the brae and spread her legs."

"Good farmlands and homesteading."

"Stay away from plowing and clearing forests. The town bankers and jackal lawyers will steal it all back. No, no, it's the speculators and the bankers who grow fat. Don't go being a farmer."

There was a knock on the door, and a barefoot yellow girl came in wearing a brown shift, her hair tied up in a crimson cloth. A perky girl, well made, gourd breasts, frisky legs. She wore silver earrings set with bits of what looked like rubies.

"Shake your tail out of here, Flossie," said McCann. "I'm entertaining a sea captain."

Flossie nodded, not at all put out. "We needs coffee at the house. And is the captain genilman staying for suppah?"

McCann made a mock frown. "You know there isn't a pound of coffee in all the county." He turned, leaned over to unlock a red painted cabinet, and took out a cloth sack of what, by the smell, was prime coffee bean.

"Take this." He casually patted the girl on the rump. "Will you stay for dinner, Starkweather? I have an idear to propose. Perhaps of mutal value to both of us. About the future."

"Be happy to dine with you."

"Yes, a poor widower's plain but hearty fare. Well . . . go along, Flossie."

The girl laughed, a rather pleasant bray, her earrings shaking, and she went out. Howard noticed her feet, even if unwashed, were very shapely. He decided he'd been too long at sea. He gave McCann that male glance of wonder that is half leer, half envy—a questioning stare. But the Scot was sliding the letters-of-credit papers into a heavy tan envelope and dipping a pen with an ivory shaft into an inkpot in which several blue flies had drowned.

"Yes, I have sixteen hundred pounds of the best Brazil bean for the gentry. But they should be buying gunpowder and French cannon. I offered them sixty bronze cannon now on the dock in Naples, cheap as whale shat—and they said they couldn't raise the money. But coffee is no trouble to sell them by the bag."

Howard watched the heating of a red wax stick over a candle, the dropping of it on the four corners of the tan envelope. McCann pressed a seal set on the end of a wooden grip into the soft wax. He held up the seal for Howard's inspection.

"It's me father's shilling he gave me when he threw me out of the hoose at twelve and said, 'Donnie, ya hungry bastard, go earn yer own bread.' Never spent it and use it as me seal." He handed Howard the envelope. "Samuel J. Wurdemann, King's House, Liverpool. Right off the docks. He'll have a letter from Jim, so you'll know it's Samuel."

"You sure you want to trust me with this?"

"Now, we'll go wash up fer supper and take a hot toddy."
McCann corked the bottle with the palm of a hand. "It's a good
cook I have. No haggis and sheep leavings. Flossie's mother, Nan, I
bought her twenty years ago in New Orleans. Sad sight to see hu-
mans sold and bought. Being a good Presbyterian, I never
trafficked in human flesh myself."

"I'll have to leave early. Promised some folk to sit in at poker.
You could join us."

McCann held up his hands, waved them about. "I don't hold with
cards. And there will be hurrs there, too, I'm sure. I don't hold with
loose paid women, and not just because they're costly."

"They deliver your money's worth, McCann."

Outside in the shed the hammering had stopped. McCann
rushed out and Howard could hear cursing. He hefted the envelope. Perhaps the smart little Scotch bastard was right. War was
made by money and credit, metals, steamboats and steamcars, and
moving the wheat and the corn, the hog bellies and hams. It went a
bit against his New England upbringing to see a righteous wrath as
bookkeeping. Not just to please some Old Testament Jew's God.
There was a residue of solid Christian fears in Howard—he never
fully enjoyed pictures of Greek gods clutching their *membra* in
drunken orgies.

Eleven days later *Sea Witch* slid out into the night, with a patched
funnel and some fresh paint on two new planks that had been replaced on the starboard side. The ship was heavy and sluggish,
loaded with bales of cotton, not only in her hold but lashed down
under waxed tarps on her deck. Howard stood by the wheel, its
spokes in the hands of two sailors, they still trying to clear their
heads of their recent debauches. The night was soot black—as the
phases of the moon had predicted. There was a breeze blowing
from the northwest. In two hours of slow careful movement they
were out of the harbor. The swells of the Atlantic rose and fell; the
ship dipped and danced.

Howard ordered two-thirds speed.

12

James Fisk, Jr., was born the son of a Vermont peddler of tinware, dry goods, and notions. For a while he followed the family

trade. Jim admitted to a free-living youth, never the proper New Englander, being neither frugal, pious, nor given to a sense of guilt. He drank, he tumbled the farm girls off their feet in barns, he enjoyed the pleasures of the body, money, of jewels, and a taste just a bit too garish in dress.

At the start of the Civil War he became an agent for the New York stock speculator Daniel Drew. Jim liked the economic activities better than life as a wagon peddler and, at one time, feeding and caring for a traveling animal show. He journeyed south into danger, moving contraband cotton and handling sales of army blankets for contractors. He managed to outwit his partners until they bought him out for 60,000 dollars, a sum he put into a share of the blockade-runner *Sea Witch*.

Jim was florid, a gross feeder, drinker; his gains or money losses did not diminish his love of women, the good life. A solid hunter of flesh, food, money, impressive, with extended mustache, dressed or rather overdressed, Jim was welcomed to the wilder ballrooms of society. He was a partner in the Wall Street brokerage Fisk & Belden, the ornate letters in leaf gold on its doors very large. It impressed Howard Starkweather the first time he saw it.

With a liberal handing out of cigars, whiskey, and introductions to pretty women, Jim was a master of the manipulation of stocks. To Howard he said, after a night of their drinking and bedding two actresses at the Astor House, "You can't get to money or women if you don't like money or women. You don't catch flies with vinegar."

This was in the spring of 1863, and Captain Howard Harrison Starkweather was residing in New York City, living in Mrs. Murtle's boardinghouse (room and supper, $6 a week) on Cortlandt Street in sight of the ferry slip. The boarder was a large young man with a heavily tanned face, a seafaring feller, said Mrs. Murtle. "A man what keeps to himself, comes home sometimes at a wee hour a bit tipsy—sometimes says he's been over to Brooklyn to hear the Reverend Beecher preach, says Beecher is the greatest man of Gaud with words as an orator since St. Paul."

Howard could have stayed at the Astor House; he had more than fifteen thousand dollars in gold, owned a large French watch in a heavy double gold case, two dueling pistols with etched inlaid silver barrels, kept in a rosewood case. In his wardrobe was a new clawhammer yellow coat and a spanking gray top hat, the brim of which the house servant ironed smooth to the proper curl after a rain.

Sea Witch had made three round trips under his command, Southern parts to England and back. Between his share of the runs and his profits in his personal transactions in silk cloth, tobacco, some Venetian glass, he was well off.

Howard read the *Herald* and the *Evening Post.* The country was not on the gold standard. Monetary values were in paper money. Gold was scarce and hard to get, so interest rates were high and manipulation of private bank notes, stocks, and shares was a splendid business.

MCCANN & STARKWEATHER was the sign on Broad Street just around the corner from Wall Street. A narrow shop front, diamond-shaped glass panes in a small window. Two steps up into a bare yellow room lit by gas. A room with an ink-stained table and behind it, the former cabin boy, Blacky, now called Chauncey Wilcox, clerk, with black arm-cuff protectors, his waistcoat red and shirt showing—no jacket. As the clerk he asked if you wanted Mr. McCann. Or Mr. Starkweather. There were two small offices with turkey-red carpeting behind two double doors beyond the clerk's domain. McCann to the left, Starkweather to the right. A plank storeroom existed out back, where lived the young clerk Chauncey Wilcox, with his dark wise young face, his look at fourteen hinting of knowing more than he'd ever say.

McCann & Starkweather dealt in railroad stocks, in commodities, shares in firms contracting with the Brooklyn Navy Yard for certain metals, loading stores on warships, connections with chandlers and suppliers to the army. They serviced clients buying futures in raw hides, horse fodder—clients like Jay Gould, James Fisk, Jr., Erie stock manipulator Daniel Drew. Often the partners went speculating themselves in casks of salt pork, Spanish cork, kegs of sherry, lengths of copper telegraph wire.

The war was still at its most brutal. Grant was bogged before Vicksburg and until that fell, if it ever would, the rebels had the Mississippi River as a highway. Abe Lincoln still lacked a general who would fight below the Potomac and take Richmond.

It was Jim Fisk who had produced the two actresses. Jim in his cape lined with red silk, his top hat three inches higher than most. He was mad about the theater, with a never-satisfied gargantuan appetite for fame, money and, as he admitted, "I fuck like a stoat."

In the suite at the Astor House Howard found the polite redhead was called Amy, and the big brassy blonde was Josie. Both were rather on the large side, but that was the fashion, Howard had been told. "In New York, Howie, it's size and firmness that counts." Jim lifted his glass high. "Ladies, my friend Howie has come from the war. Treat him kindly."

Amy said she didn't like whiskey—her father was Irish and he drank it—she preferred bubbly, she added.

As the girls began to shed ruffles, pins, belts, dresses and petticoats, lace-trimmed drawers and striped stockings, Josie insisted, "Never mind the fancy French drinks, Amy dear. There ain't nothing worth drinking between whiskey and champagne."

Josie Mansfield had a Middle West voice, a small talent onstage, and Jim was seeking to place her properly in some theater, as his discovery. Amy was convent-raised and amazed at the world. She admitted to Howard she played the viol in a three-girl band in a tearoom.

As the night progressed, it was clear Jim was in love with Josie, and Howard was attracted to Amy O'Hara, whose father, he regretted to find, was a captain of police (she pronounced it *poo-leese*).

The two men came out of the Astor House at noon, the actresses still sleeping, two twenty-dollar gold coins left on the mantel. Jim and Howard inhaled the horse-scented air of Broadway, and Jim waved his cane at a hackney coach for hire.

"Jim, Amy can read music, speaks French."

"I tell you, Howie, someday I'm going to fall into the trap—marry and raise me up a batch of children. Isn't that Josie a lalapalooza?"

Howard watched a soldier with his arm in a sling standing at the curb staring at the crowded street traffic. There were many shabby soldiers in the city, hundreds of hospital cases. Some were being formed into an invalid corps to police the city in case of riots. The war was not going well and Mr. Lincoln was asking for a new draft law.

"I can't see you, Jim, not you, in slippers and smoking a pipe by your fireplace."

"Loving makes me hungry. Let's go have something to eat at the Indian House. You like Amy?"

"I never knew a viol player before, in bed, I mean."

The eating place was on Fulton Street, run by a German family, was a sort of club for speculators, brokers, army contractors. Herr Ott welcomed Jim and Howard.

Top-hatted private bankers, promoters were eating the roast goose, the side of beef, river shad featured by the place. Cigar smoke and the scent of spices hung under the low ceiling. Jay Gould was carefully cutting up a veal chop while Barney, his clerk, a lean rake of a youth—with a prominent gold tooth, who hardly ever spoke in public—sopped up gravy with a slice of bread. Gould had a reputation of being morose—or so Howard had heard—also predatory and destructive.

Gould and Fisk were partners in several schemes ("Damn odd of Jim to pick that abomination Gould," a man told Howard).

Jim and Howard set to cutting up their meat. Jim, drinking whiskey, got to explaining the situation of the war with a flourish of his knife, as if it were a sword.

"Abe better find himself a general. It's not going good, the war."

"Good enough," said Jay Gould, sipping wine and water. He was a delicate little man and a dainty eater. Howard felt amused as Gould addressed him. "Don't you think so, Starkweather?"

"Why ask me? I'm no war expert. But the contraband trade is certainly petering out."

Jim nodded. "It is. The blockade is tight now as a bull's ass in fly time. Hasn't been a good cargo of cotton reaching England in two months."

The clerk, Barney, said, holding a napkin to his mouth and speaking as if from behind a wall, "The *Ocean Queen* was sunk off Pensacola, cargo, four hundred casks of gunpowder, five thousand stands of Crimean War muskets. Etc., etc."

"Would you, Starkweather," asked Gould, "take out another blockade-runner?"

Howard chewed thoughtfully. He was still feeling the effect of the night's drinking and the delights and demands of Amy. "Nope, Mr. Gould. My partner is in Philadelphia buying Studebaker wagons, gun carriages. I've left the sea."

It was a word Howard liked, "partner." Strange that he should have a partner and he Donald McCann, ironmonger, commission merchant, trader, and contraband dealer of Savannah. But after the sinking of *Sea Witch* it was clear the Union blockade was too

90

perfected to take a risk with cargoes—and lives—in or out of Southern ports.

McCann had put it to him after he saw *Sea Witch* wrecked.

"It's New York, Washington, or Philadelphia. We both know trade, so mon, it's no reason we can't be partnering. I'll match yer poke. I've a bit of cash on deposit, as you know from handling my letters of credit. What say?"

So it was done, a firm created, the little shop rented, set up to deal in shares, contracts and through Jim, Gould, and Daniel Drew, even old Vanderbilt now and then, the Commodore ("And a fine bastard he is, laddie, a skinflint but smells of money, comes from his pores like sweat. But we'll take his business tossed our way").

Howard looked at the fragment of meat on his fork. "Donald has some people in Philadelphia wanting to move in on the Jackson and Vicksburg Railroad when Grant takes the city there. To issue shares and extend the rail lines down to New Orleans in time and into Indiana, Ohio."

Gould just continued to eat. Jim sipped whiskey. "*If* Grant takes Vicksburg. He's been there, what is it, sixteen months?"

Howard said, "Thousands of bales of cotton within reach of that road."

Herr Ott came with the after-dinner bowl of hot punch for all but Gould. The talk ran to the rumors and gossip about the war. It was hard, Howard saw, to assess the true value of what passed for news.

Gould liked to expand on his knowledge of events to his table companions. "The South is desperate. Its supplies of cannon and powder, medical aids and drugs, nearly gone. Only Judah Benjamin, that smart Jew, has any sense of economics, of real war— among those romantic, gallant Southern fat cats and blowhards. Now, to bring England into the war on the side of the cotton planters is their real hope, eh? The South has to have one great victory for England, so it may send Lee to invade the North."

"Jay, you're dreaming," said Jim.

Howard wasn't so sure it wasn't true, an invasion.

"Lee, Jim, is massing seventy-five thousand troops," Gould said cheerfully. "Aiming for Philadelphia, Pennsylvania, moving to encircle Washington, seize Lincoln and the whole Congress, the gold

91

of the nation, then dictate a peace in the White House."

"Jesus H. Christ," Jim said, "it's opium-pipe smoking."

Howard sipped his toddy. "It's a possibility."

Jay Gould, small and neat, his foxy face pale, put a polite fist to his mouth as he coughed. Howard studied him. Clever, but mistrusted, wealthy, but not showy. A good family man who didn't abuse drink or hanker for fast women or fancy cuisine.

Howard asked, "You have private information, Mr. Gould?"

"I get the Richmond *Gazette* smuggled through the lines for me. I know J. E. B. Stuart is gathering horses. His scouts have been measuring the spring runoffs of the Potomac at Berkeley Springs, the north branch."

"When," asked Jim, "you think Lee will cross over?"

"June. Low water, good weather. Don't put any money in the bank at Chambersburg. He'll loot it."

This got a big laugh around the table. Howard said, "Bank robbers."

"As your partner, McCann, says, they're beginning to understand you don't win wars with just muskets."

"I don't know," Jim said to Gould, who was pulling on his starched cuffs until an inch showed out of the sleeve of his brown snuff-colored jacket. "You're all rumor, Jay. They've neglected the rail lines—most of them are streaks of rust. Sure, they've got food, the corn, the wheat to feed to their armies. If they had transport. Why, half their soldiers, poor bastards, haven't shoes. It's failure of moving supplies, not shortages. Lee can't supply his army for invasion"

"Eh, Starkweather?" asked Gould.

Howard put his thumbs under his watch chains, chains not as thick as Jim Fisk's, but impressive enough. "It's the only thing they have left to do. If Lee invades, he'll destroy railroad rolling stock, kill off herds . . . yes, loot the banks."

Jim was muttering to himself, a cigar in his mouth. Howard felt Jim was figuring out the rise in the cost of replacements—what rail stocks to sell short. Howard was learning; he was a student of banking now, investments. He had no plans to go to sea again—had never really liked the sea, not since his boyhood in a boatyard driving in wooden divits into oak hulls or working on fishing boats in freezing blizzards, battling drunken barge crews. That was for people like Mr. Melville; to write of the poetry and mystery of the ocean life. Howard Harrison Starkweather did not waste time on excessive introspection about sea life. *Sea Witch* he mourned. She had been battered to bits by two Union ironclads who had enough shallow draft to follow her through Saint Helena Sound up the Horsebow Bend branch of the Edisto River—more like a stream than a river. And stand off a mudbank and fire exploding shells into her hull among the cattail reeds of South Carolina. It had been just at dusk, with the fireflies not matching the gouts of orange flames that sent canister shells around the hull and into the muddy banks. Still, Howard had been able to save at least two-thirds of the cargo as night fell—drumming up two dozen blacks and their ox-drawn wagons, horse carts from three plantations behind the bend of the river. Chauncey Wilcox had saved the ship's bell.

13

Donald McCann had let his thin rust-colored beard grow out longer, wore a disgracefully tailored lumpy suit and square-toed country boots. But his linen was always clean and his cravats tied with skill. He sat in his office of McCann & Starkweather, looking up at Howard tapping a chair leg with his cane.

"You swallow rumors easy, as if eating oysters. This talk of invasion no one knows if true or fraudulent."

"He has crossed the Potomac! No rumor! It's Lee coming north!"

"Some of the rebels, scouts, and bummers maybe are stealing laundry off clotheslines and getting the trots eating green fruit. No one's sure it's Lee in force. I dinna know, you dinna know. But I've some shares to sell in coal mines at Mauch Chunk and Pottsville, and this will play bloody hell with them. Bring me facts. . . . Or are you off again to see some wench?"

"Don't be facetious, Donald. I've got something. There are fifty thousand stands of muskets being put together in the Union Steam Works in this city."

"Who would ya sell 'em to? The Sioux Indians?"

"They're on goverment order. They need hickory timber for cutting up into gunstocks. This girl I'm knowing, her father is a police captain along the waterfront. Captain Matthew J. O'Hara."

"They're not all dishonest, the police. You're not pondering the mutability of human conduct, are ye?"

93

"The police have been issued four-pound hardwood clubs, three feet in length. They have a surplus of two barges of solid hickory timber going at a cheap price. We can buy it and sell it for rifle stocks. Captain O'Hara says they have no great interest in holding the surplus wood in storage."

"Yes, the police are much maligned. You're a domn perceptive young man, Howard. A hedonist also, of simple straightforwardness. Union Works will buy the wood."

It was not fully a lie about the wood and Captain O'Hara, father of Amy O'Hara, Howard's love. Perhaps it *was* surplus and the captain would not ask too much "to sweeten the transaction."

He was aware Amy was a rather poor actress and a bland viol and cello player, had a temper, and he suspected she had been taken by Josie to dine with sporting gentry. Amy was young, lively, and daring, and skipping the convent and her French, sexually had a sense of ambivalence. He loved her, he admitted, loved her with a fervor that betrayed his New England upbringing, his dividing of all females into good women and whores. If Amy was a whore—she certainly was not a virgin—she was not greedy, and the trifling lengths of silk, a golden brooch with a cameo head of some Roman Caesar as gifts were not much. Add truffles and goose livers—a passion of hers at table, which he didn't mind.

Amy lived with her friend Josie Mansfield in a flat on the street behind the Astor Place Theatre. A flat paid for by Jim Fisk, as he paid for the baskets of food, hothouse fruit, the cases of wine, the tulle drapes, and Josie's rings and earrings. Josie was greedy. Amy was not. Josie was lazy, with fatuous guile, and told lies. Amy had an adolescent naïve quality, was quick on her feet, and she insisted she never lied. The nuns at the Convent of the Holy Spirit, north of the Colored Orphan Asylum uptown, had taught Amy to tell the truth, to go to confession, to sew samplers, and to cross herself when a funeral passed; there were a great many of those in the war years. She had been seduced at thirteen by the drawing teacher who visited the convent. "After that, well, Howie, as you might say, I wasn't above rubies."

If Josie was in bed with Jim Fisk, Howard liked to take a walk with Amy, she in her long sweeping dress and her little sunshade and neat feet in high kid shoes with a row of buttons. They liked to walk in Battery Park. He thought: She's special. It wasn't that he

94

and Jim hadn't had good times with other girls and, as Jim put it, "No holds barred." But Howard was aware he had grown most fond of Amy. He even felt a bit more ashamed of the recent past, the wild group idea of fun and frolic among jouncing breasts and high laughter of other women. Now, watching sedately—two ironclads passed the Battery steaming for Sandy Hook, the Kill Van Kull, to duty at sea—he stood with Amy as the clumsy ironclads sent up black stack smoke. . . . He pictured the wreck of *Sea Witch* in a world of dead leaves, in mud, pollen, frog spawn, rusting away.

"Why don't they sink, Howie?"

"It's a matter of mathematics—very scientific."

"They're ugly."

"They are. Wouldn't take one to sea for all the gold in the Grand Turk's harem." He studied Amy's porcelain fragility; for a large girl that was rare.

"You've been to Turkey?"

"Once, Amy, on a lime juicer. Streets full of starving dogs and the women all veiled and none under two hundred pounds. They smell like wild parsley."

"You've been to bed with a lot of women, haven't you?" It was not said in a tone of recrimination.

"Over half a million." He laughed and took her arm.

She looked at him and smiled. "You don't have to lie to me. I've sinned myself. But Father Mallory says if you've really meant to repent—I mean, you confess and return to a state of grace—it's like you've never done anything."

"It's a grand way of seeing things, Amy. Aren't we sinning when we go to bed, grace or no grace?"

"Yes, Howie, we are, mortal sinners. I tell myself the Virgin Mary herself will understand I can't marry a Protestant—so. . . ."

It was what he enjoyed about Amy, her eccentric zeal for mad logic. Her direct simple version of the world. There was no derision or denigration in her. She depending on her version of the saints and rules of her church which she managed to decode in her own way, favoring her version of things. Amy was actually brighter than Josie, Howard decided, and she could be trusted—he hoped. He felt like informing Jim that Josie was actually unfaithful to him, bamboozling him. But then Jim wasn't really faithful to Josie either. He did promise he would be when they were married. Jim

Fisk had at times this vision of the domestic life and the raising of a family. "But not today, not tomorrow, Howie—someday."

Howard had no intention of marrying Amy. McCann had said, "Keep yer *amour-propre*, don't marry a hurr." Howard didn't want to admit to himself that one didn't marry a fine loving girl who had slept around, been handled like merchandise by other men. Young Howard Starkweather, a person of his time, would have rejected any idea he was unfair not to believe in the double standard. There were two worlds for men, and only one for proper women. It was not too clear in Howard's mind, but he lived by that kind of male privilege, and so did most of the city. Bedroom indignities one reserved for hired rooms. Yet Howard felt the system was moral.

A big florid man on a glossy black horse, his shoulders very wide, his legs long, his face hairless but for the chin tuft, rode up to them. The big man, in his long-tailed blue coat, brass buttons, high wing collar, cap with a gold badge, dismounted and talked to the animal. "Easy there, me beauty." His voice and stance were those of a man sure of himself, physically able to engage in rough-and-tumble even if his badge of rank and the stripes did proclaim him a New York City police captain. Captain Matthew O'Hara was known, so Howard had heard, as a man with the back of his hand to the lowly criminal and as a user of the hard hickory baton he often carried, with which he had split open two skulls. Against a professional who was armed, the captain carried a Smith & Wesson that he used with rapid fire, if not too much true aim. A man with a self-sufficiency and given to pontification over his whiskey.

He looked at the ironclads. "Ah, the damn iron pots with teakettle tops are goin' to meet a bit of a storm."

"Morning, Captain O'Hara."

"Mornin', Captain Starkweather."

The policeman kissed his daughter's cheek and made a gesture at Howard that could have suggested a greeting, perhaps a warning. Or, Howard thought, a mere sign of a ubiquitous male understanding. Captain O'Hara in his youth had been sent to study for the priesthood in Ireland with the Jesuits at Enniscorthy. But he had burned a British army barracks at eighteen, and so while he knew Latin and wrote a fine hand, had read Cardinal Newman and St. Augustine (he told Howard he liked the saint's text "O Lord, make me chaste, but not just yet"), he had run for it, "scarpered out of Mountjoy Prison, come to New York, and decided between becoming a dock thief or joining the police, which in a lucky day I joined."

The captain liked his work, invested in real estate, took his share of "honest boodle," admired his wife, Mary Martha, his six children, of whom Amy was the only one who didn't knuckle down to his wishes and whom he admitted he perhaps liked the best. "She's got the Celtic feeling for the theatricals in her, like meself."

He told them of an invasion in Pennsylvania. "Lincoln has this new feller, General Jarge Meade. Lee is moving fast. But he's not got Stonewall Jackson this time—Jackson, he's dead as an Orangeman that a wall fell on."

"Where is it all?" Howard asked.

"Damn if they know. Past Chambersburg, near Cashtown. Telegraph is stingy with detail. But the hooligans are loose on the streets here."

"They'll be celebrating—if there's a real battle."

"And we win. . . . Oh, Captain Starkweather, I can't be getting you the load of timber. There's talk of street rioting here, over the draft drawings, the lotteries coming up. So we're carving out more clubs, enlisting more men. Would you like to be a deputy in the citizens' defense force?"

"No, Captain O'Hara. I'm sorry for these poor bastards, the folk being forced to enlist."

"Don't be using such language in front of my daughter. She's convent-bred, you know."

Amy showed an inch of tongue. "Oh, Daddo, you use worse yourself when you've had a drop and you're kicking the furniture."

"Never mind what *I* do. You might bring the young feller home for supper to meet Father Mullvany. That's my cousin from Cork. Green as goose turd, fresh from the seminary in Rome."

Howard was aware Captain O'Hara played the stage Irishman at times and used his brogue a bit too much. But he was a solid and clever officer. His men trusted him and feared him, which was what he wanted.

"I have to go now to plant some plainclothesmen I'm putting around to test the temper of the hoodlums."

"You couldn't see your way clear to sell me *one* barge of the wood, Captain?"

"It's the higher-ups that say no. . . ." He winked. "But I'll talk to thim about it."

97

That evening McCann paid the captain twice what had been asked for the wood in the first place and sold it for a five-hundred-dollar profit to the rifle contractor at the Union Steam Works the next day.

There were still no details of any great battle in Pennsylvania. Both armies, a huge collecton of men, cannon, flanked by horsemen, seemed to be wandering like blind men and any moment expected to stumble together.

The city waited in expectancy, as if holding its breath for some thunderbolt to burst in the sky.

Amy had moved her things to a small flat Howard had rented, furnished, from his boardinghouse landlady, Mrs. Murtle—two rooms on the top floor, four flights up—and he and Amy had moved in with her hatboxes, cello case, and canary. There was a view south to the harbor and the Narrows; by leaning way out one could see Brooklyn and on Sundays view Beecher's Boats, as they were called, taking the pious and the gentry to the Brooklyn church. "Beecher is a real rouser," said Amy, who had gone there often, "even if I'm a convent-bred girl."

Smelling of lemon and jasmine scent in the bed with Howard, she snuggling closer in his arms. "He's a grand man, this Henry Beecher, and they do say, it's rumored, he's not above lifting a skirt and unbuttoning his manhood while giving advice privately to some lady of his pious congregation. Would you believe that?" They were eating from a terrine of pâté de foie gras Jim Fisk had sent them. Howard watched Amy lick the spoon. "A man's a man, anyplace."

Outside there was a lot of traffic; iron wheels on the cobble, the drays dragging cargoes to the ships waiting for them—or the thousands of kegs and barrels branded u.s. All the poor sods in the army and navy, he thought, that would be eating the salt pork and already-wormy hardtack piling up on the docks. He touched one of the pendant amethyst earrings he had given Amy. "Amy, darling, I'm away for a few days. McCann wants me to go to Pennsylvania."

"What's there?"

"Something stirring. Several banks there want us to take over their green goods, some of their paper money."

She wiped her mouth on his naked shoulder, hugged him. "Oh, dear, damn it, just when I'm not dancing or playing music at Pas-

98

tor's, you have to leave me so alone." She began to brush cracker crumbs out of the bed.

"I know. Amy, we are thinking of expanding the business. Putting out shares in coffee, banana companies, rail lines in South America. I'd like to set you up properly. I mean permanently, as all mine. I love you, you know that."

"Do I know that?"

She looked at him, turning to him in the bed, her figure healthy pink, her face expressive of joy and a bit of teasing, too. "Make me know you love me. Tell me more."

"Why the hell do all girls want words? Haven't I showed it? We haven't been playing red rover or pulling taffy, have we?"

"Not on your tintype, we haven't. Maybe I love you, too. Awfully much. And, say, you're right about Josie Mansfield. Faithless, mean, and she doesn't wash as much as she might. Always pouring on scent and talking when I'm playing Schumann's *Arabesque.*"

Howard wanted to say more but he mistrusted words in emotional matters; truth was, he still feared any woman that was not for hire by the hour. There was something very remarkable, he knew, about a relationship with a woman—for all human incongruities— who was more than bought flesh. But he was not sure he could put it properly or that Amy would not laugh at him. Instead they made love, limbs locked together—rolled about a great deal on a bed that could have been softer. But they were young and limber, their bones not yet brittle.

Near morning, the windows open to the hot night, the voices began to cry: "*Wuxtra: Great battle in Pennsylvania. Wuxtra!*"

99

BOOK III

Make money, money by fair means if you
can,
if not, by any means money.
—HORACE, *Epistles,* Book I

14

McCann & Starkweather, for a small firm, had been doing very well when in April President Lincoln had used the Conscription Act passed by Congress, had demanded the drafting of 300,000 men, the conscription to begin on July 11 in New York City. It was an unfair, dishonest act, Howard felt, for it contained a built-in escape hatch for the rich and well-off; any man picked for the draft, if his number was called, could buy himself out of serving as a soldier by a payment of three hundred dollars. Sanctioned by money, an exclusive group would avoid the war. Both John D. Rockefeller and J. P. Morgan, hundreds of other businessmen were among those who were to pay the fee and avoid fighting for their country.

New York in the third year of the Civil War was a city with a population of about 815,000, and fifty percent of these Howard recognized as immigrants, born outside the borders of the United States and with no or only fragmented allegiance. The potato famine and crop failure had driven great numbers of Irish peasants to pack into the reeking holds of steerage passage across the ocean. More than 203,000 of them were living in the slums, the poverty areas of the city. Doing the meanest kind of rough work and barely existing; illiterate, looked down on with condescension and no pity.

Now, in the summer heat, Howard, like McCann, Fisk, Gould, and the rest of the city, waited for the final results of that Pennsylvania battle. It was the three-days Battle of Gettysburg. After the fourth day McCann said to Howard, "It was a close thing, laddie, *verra* close."

Neither the battle nor the failure of Robert E. Lee to force a victory cheered the New Yorkers. Meade had permitted Lee and his forces to escape.

Howard and Amy avoided the boiling July weather by spending

a few days at Asbury Park. On their return, the city seemed ready for some sullen event. July 11, a Saturday, came, the city gripped in sultry, damp summer weather. The drawing of numbers for those who would become conscipts was to begin. The various provost marshal's offices scattered around the city expected the usual grousing, but no trouble; the poor knew their place in Dickensian society. No police guard was requested, and the city's more than a thousand patrolmen had other duties.

Howard entered the open green door of McCann & Starkweather on one of those hot humid New York summer days that boiled tempers. Howard himself was in a scowling mood. His neck showed the angry red marks of heat rash. And he had somehow the night before, while he and Amy were sleeping on mattresses on the roof of Mrs. Murtle's boardinghouse, it being unbearable in his rooms, hinted at marriage. An honest impulse there in the night. It had seemed then a thought that would make his life something more meaningful. He did love her and time was inexorably ticking away. But at dawn, the air still heated and with a disk of orange sun proclaiming the day would be hotter, he wondered at his rush to become domesticated, settled in (or was it down?), tied to the rituals of a social pattern called marriage. McCann, a widower, had called marriage "female parasitism and of no guaranteed durability."

The drawing of draft numbers for Mr. Lincoln's army would begin today, and Howard had a thought; it would be an escape from his problem to go off to war, get shot at by shell and ball, even worse luck to be torn to bits or die in his prime. A young man who had so many hopes of making something of his life. He was only half facetious in his self-pity.

He found Donald McCann and Chaunce Wilcox in the lean-to behind the shop, where, having pulled up some floorboards, they were digging in the earth with short-handled shovels, McCann puffing, Chaunce digging like a badger.

"What the devil is this, Donald?"

McCann had his collar off and two handkerchiefs tucked under his chin. He, too, had an aggravating heat rash. "What are we doing? We're taking precautions, that's *what*. Lend a hand."

"Digging a cellar to hide in if there's trouble today?"

Chaunce flung a shovelful of earth out of the pit; he was grinning, enjoying the excitement in the city. "Mr. McCann thinks there will be shootin' and lootin'."

104

"Nonsense." Howard avoided getting his shined boots within range of the flung earth. "The poor bastards may not like it to be shipped off to slaughter, but they'll go like sheep. Don't they always go?"

McCann scratched at his neck. "Perhaps, perhaps. And will you be going if yer number is called? Eh?"

"Been thinking of it."

"While you're thinking, go get the ironboxes in my nook, and we'll be burying them here and putting back the boards."

It seemed to Howard foolish to be burying their records, their share holdings, and a pound or more of some gold and silver coins in buckskin bags. But McCann was senior partner. By noon the floor was back in place, several heavy timbers placed on it. Chaunce was set to pouring tepid water from a pitcher over their soiled hands. While their necks burned worse than ever from the heat rashes.

McCann put on his detachable shirt cuffs and collar. "Now, let us lock up and get to Ott's eating place to hear the gossip of what's going on. You better be sure yer sweetheart stays indoors. It may come to riot, rape, and worse."

Chauncey Wilcox was delighted. He gave an Indian yell. *"Wha-hoo-wah!"*

The Invalid Corps, Howard felt, would keep order. Commanded by a Major Ruggles he had treated to drinks, it was made up of soldiers recovering from wounds, various malingerers, walking cripples, and was mostly used to patrol and guard armories, arsenals, and places that produced munitions of war. Most of the corps scratched, groused, hoped for discharge or easy fatigue duty.

As Howard walked back to his flat, he saw the city was still in ferment and in mourning, stunned by the long, long casualty lists of Gettysburg. Now they would see their sons and husbands picked up by a draft-lottery wheel and sent out to more dreadful battles. His landlady greeted him, broom in hand. "While those who kin pay will be free to live in their fine mansions on Fifth Avenue along Central Park, be waited on by their house servants. Damn niggers brung the war."

"Now, Mrs. M., it's too hot to get riled."

The bald unfairness and the heat in the slums frayed tempers. Howard was aware it was against the well-off and the blacks that the rage grew. The provost marshal's offices opened and clerks began to spin the drums containing the numbers from which the new recruits would be picked. Amy had left a note: "Gone to the folks. Meet me there for supper. A." Some street speakers had hinted with disquieting prophecies of what the drawings could produce. The newspapers in New York had been printing violent stories about the inequity of the Conscription Act. There was an organization, political in nature, Howard had heard, called Knights of the Golden Circle, which hinted it might use force and violence in the city to oppose the draft. But it was mostly talk, he decided. Still, there were rumors that the Knights and their supporters were going to take over.

He thought, strange times. I'm stranger to myself. I'm always trying to get on top of things, of difficulties, keeping alive, I tell myself, and always kicking. Watching, waiting, hinting, taking. Mindful I have limits, aware I'm balanced on one foot as in the air on a tightrope. Certainly the city is too upset. I don't lack, call it a belief in myself. Wary not to drop into false games, the unimportant games of the world. (How like a thousand bodies with one head a mob is.) Don't make too many mistakes. The thing to know are the odds against you *or* for you. Now this mad city—how do I stand? Now? Today. To hear people, there's a great gout of what is called nostalgia and remorse about what the country has become. Hell, it's just growing up, Bible-drenched, wanting a good life. I suppose that's what McCann sneers at, "a conscious perfectibility of the world in order, and its face washed and talking to God in white clapboard little churches. Society, laddie, is a whore, but she's there to live with." McCann feels wise, but me, I'm an orphan among strangers in this city going crazy. All I can do is go on betting on my future. I'll die sooner or later and stink like everyone else. But what the devil. There is a growing disturbance in America. We're impatient, unsteady in our opinons. . . .

He walked among shouting people, shrugging his shoulders.

It's still good to be among the people, some of them. There is something angry but full of sensation about the country. We're all living in a magnetic field—that trick Jim Fisk does with steel filings and a magnet—being pushed together to live in havoc and fury, faced on all sides by the human condition. Like these angry people always in flux these days, that's what a man had to know and face.

("No draft!" shouted two men across the street.)

There is always a turbulent pressure and you have to ride out the times like a ship at sea with a flooded bilge and all hands at the pumps. Call it style, tone, that is what living is all about.

106

("No draft!")

People gathered more and more in the street—were shouting and calling out, massing in front of the U.S. Arsenal at Seventh Avenue and Thirty-fifth Street, and a police sergeant and fifteen men were there to stand guard. Talk was the crowd was not large, nor did it appear to be in a mood for rioting. The police were making themselves comfortable inside and had locked up the building.

Howard walked over to a district draft office set up at Third Avenue. The lottery-numbers drum was spinning and the crowd gathering outside muttered, shouted, cursed but did not interfere with the first drawing from a listing of 1,236 names.

"The number," a fat man told Howard, "demanded from the district calls for two hundred and sixty-four more names. Final numbers would be picked on Monday. Do 'em good to get out of the city. Wouldn't mind sojering myself—only I'm too old."

Supper at the O'Haras' was never a subdued meal. Son Neal was a professional tenor who sang "Kathleen Mavourneen" and "The Snowy-Breasted Pearl" at Tony Pastor's. Captain O'Hara sat stirring a dozen Bartlett pears in a basin of ice. He was cheerful as the two younger daughters set the table with a clatter of silverware. "It was as I said, Captain Starkweather, noise in the streets—nothing much. They'll howl and they'll curse, but they'll go off to war like good little puppies after a stick."

Mrs. O'Hara was a wide woman with big blue eyes and small teeth. She looked up at Howard from fanning herself. "You'll be paying the money not to go?"

"Hard to say. There's the business—and our contracts. . . ."

Captain O'Hara began to slice the pears, handing them around the table, where four or five of his children sat—Howard was never sure of how many there were. "If I were not on duty and needed, and were a young man, I'd maybe be liking to see Virginia and get my mitts on the rebels."

Neal, the tenor, adjusted his tiepin. "Would you, Daddo, go on your black horse?"

"I would, Neal boy."

A small boy of ten tapped on the table. "I could be a drummer boy."

Mrs. O'Hara wiped a young mouth next to her, the baby, Hughie, and fed his toothless gums a slice of iced pear. "Amy has been tellin' us, Captain, you're thinking of settlin' down."

"We've talked of it, yes."

Amy frowned, a bit of pear held halfway to her mouth. "Oh, Ma, I told you *that* in confidence. Nothing is settled."

Captain O'Hara chewed a pear, pursed his mouth, winked at Neal. "Well, if I meself had to do it over again, I'd be a soldier boy, a dragoon that could trot away."

Mrs. O'Hara said sternly, "Shouldn't you be at the stationhouse, Matt O'Hara?"

Neal said, "There was shooting down by Five Points."

"It's all the result of a lot of blathering by Horace Greeley and those newspaper fellers." O'Hara rose and put a chunk of ice into his mouth. "Well, Howard, you don't mind me calling you that? If you and Amy do want to make a go of it, you have my blessing, the O'Hara blessings of my grandmother: 'God bless you—and hold you in the palm of His hand.'"

"I'm goin' to be drummer boy," said the ten-year-old.

Amy reached across the table as if to slap his face. "You'll do no such thing, Michael."

Mrs. O'Hara added, "And don't be actin' up in front of Mr. Starkweather, or I'll really give you the back of my hand."

Michael got up and muttered a four-letter word he had heard but didn't know the meaning of.

Mrs. O'Hara turned to Howard. "What did he say?"

Howard shook his head. "I didn't catch it."

Later, the night still steamy hot, he and Amy walked back to the boardinghouse arm in arm. Both feeling a mood in the city that seemed to make a different sound. Even the barking of some dogs had a note of fear. Or, Howard wondered, was it only their own mood?

"You didn't mind me telling Ma? She's not so sure I'm really living with Josie Mansfield."

He said he didn't mind and he didn't know if he wanted his number to be called up or not in the next few days. They slept again on the roof and the feeble breeze that came at morning was not cooling. They descended early to their room, still in their underwear, to keep the amenities. Even the notes of the Sunday church bells sounded heated.

Bells that broke the morning atmosphere of a not-too-quiet New York City Sunday. Good Christians began to gather prayer books for the walk or take a carriage to church, often two or three generations of New Yorkers in each family group. But some church folk did not venture out that Sunday. Not all was exquisitely at ease in the city. Chauncey Wilcox, mingling with the street-corner groups of roughly dressed folk, found them debating and shouting at the news that a dozen or so well-known rich men whose names had been drawn for the draft had at once paid their three hundred dollars and freed themselves from the army duty. Detectives merged with the coagulation of the outraged groups. One could not yet call them mobs. The undercover men heard of weapons being collected: bricks, clubs, pistols, and whatever could strike or stab or bash a head.

The slum districts were active all day with tippling and cursing and a great sadness, too.

Chauncey said to one large man with ginger-colored chin whiskers and carrying a club, "Is there going to be fighting?"

"There will be, bub, you can bet on it."

"And shooting?"

"God forgive us, not on a Sunday." The large man crossed himself.

Chaunce and groups of street boys delighted in following the gathering groups who muttered, scowled, and cursed and spat very often. The mobs seemed to the boy confused and not at all sure of anything but their anger, their despair. Chaunce went across town and then uptown, as if testing the quality of the rage in various sections of the city. He wondered if he should report back to Captain Starkweather that the mood was mean. Instead he found some dirty-faced kids roasting mickies over a fire on a lot near Central Park, and so he joined them in eating charred potatoes nearly too hot to handle. The church bells continued to ring.

15

Early Monday morning at the boardinghouse table Howard and Amy heard the fire engines being hauled by horses through the streets. Mr. Mandel, a dry-goods bazaar clerk, buttered his bread carefully. "It's a sad day for the insurance companies."

Amy set down her cup of tea. "They'll not burn the theaters, will they?"

Miss Bedford, a schoolteacher, reset her uncomfortable teeth in place with her tongue. "It's the schools they'll burn. The Irish brutes. They hate education. The pope desires to keep them brutish and ignorant." She folded her napkin into a silver ring lettered *N.B.*

Howard said, "Miss O'Hara is Irish Catholic."

Miss Bedford said, "Is she, now?" and sailed out in her brown trailing skirt to carry a saucer of milk to her cat—who was not to be found for three days.

"Amy, don't go near the theater. I'm going out to assess the temper of the people in the street. Don't worry, I'm taking my pistols."

Amy made him promise he'd take good care; the way she looked at him he decided *if* he did marry, she would be his first choice.

With the two light French pistols, loaded, in the pockets of his jacket, he went out to the smell of charred wood and burned timbers. He had left off his top hat, his collar and cravat. It seemed best to wear an old sea cap. The gentry, now that the truth was out that most of them were paying the dollars to stay out of the draft, were in danger of stopping a dominick, as a half brick was called.

There were some fires set in the night still burning, and people gathered to watch the engine laddies do their work. No one made any effort to hinder them in their job. A hostile environment of physical violence did not yet show itself. Howard spoke to Superintendent of Police John A. Kennedy standing in a hotel lobby. "No reason for alarm, but we've got a guard on the Arsenal. Thousands of rifles and pistols stored there. Hot, isn't it? And humid."

"It's both," said Howard.

"Humid as New York can be in July. But clear, and people seem to be up early."

Howard nodded. Superintendent Kennedy wasn't too bright, but he knew how to handle crowds.

Moving on, Howard saw people on the West Side, groups that could be nothing else but a determined mob moving north along both Eighth and Ninth avenues. Scouts and wanderers were active in the side streets, shouting for workers in factories and shops to join them.

"Throw down the shovel! The hammer! Come along!"

Anyone who tried to stop this recruiting was given the choice of either shutting up or getting a fist or club on the head. There was trouble and bits of roughhouse, Howard saw. The mob massing together was gathering on a lot just east of Central Park. And it was armed. Mostly, Howard thought, as an old-fashioned mob out of a print of the French Revolution: clubs and staves, knives, pistols, hayforks, and old muskets.

An old man with a wagon spoke to Howard. "Ain't it grand?"

The householders in this fashionable district around the park looked out from their breakfast tables. They sensed a nervous instability in the shifting angry crowd on the weedy lot. For to them it was from this residential area the men came who had paid the price to have their names withdrawn from army service—this world, a mob speaker shouted, "of velvet drapes and bow windows and fat bellies."

The mob began to stir like some giant ungainly creature, forming and re-forming itself, shoving Howard with it, turning south, breaking into segments like an earthworm dividing, one section going down Fifth Avenue, the other with Howard down Sixth Avenue. He had no fears for himself and he could have pushed his way clear, but didn't. It was still a sort of game to him. Weapons were held high, voices were loud against Lincoln's war, curses were flung at the police and the provost marshal. The columns merged together at Forty-seventh Street, heading for the draft-lottery drum at Third Avenue and Forty-sixth Street. All frivolity and the mere watching of events were gone from the moving mass. Howard decided to drop back. A woman carrying an ax grabbed his arm. "Oh, we got 'em now, by the short hair!"

Howard saw thousands of milling, excited citizens.

Other draft officers were attracting their own angry crowds. The Broadway and Twenty-ninth Street office had a guard of seventy police standing tense and worried under a captain and three sergeants; sixty-nine men were rushing to the Third Avenue office. The cripples and battle-scarred men of the Invalid Corps took up their weapons and they, too, went to help hold back the mob at the Third Avenue office.

Superintendent Kennedy, in his office, set electric sparks flashing to tap out on police telegraph hookups:

TO ALL STATIONS IN NEW YORK AND BROOKLYN
CALL IN YOUR RESERVE PLATOONS AND HOLD THEM AT THE
STATIONHOUSE SUBJECT TO FURTHER ORDERS.

The police force had more than two thousand on its official lists, but Kennedy knew there were many slough-offs, easy jobs, desk cops, and just plain loafers. He figured only about fifteen hundred or sixteen hundred officers were actually patrolmen on active duty, ready with their heavy hickory hardwood clubs.

Captain O'Hara came in wiping out the hatband of his cap with a handkerchief. "It's getting out of hand. They need a taste of the club."

"Hold your water, O'Hara. I'll decide."

"They were throwing rocks at my house."

Kennedy smiled. "You sure not at you?"

The Third Avenue draft office was in serious trouble. For six blocks around in all directions the mob held control. Carriages were stopped, horses frightened. Howard saw a team unhitched. Passengers were pelted, made to run for it, top hats dented or knocked off.

The cry was *"No draft!"* Posters appeared crudely scrawled with the same message: NO DRAFT! The mob, feeling its strength, was pressing the police hard against the draft-office walls. The Black Joke gang went into action. The Black Joke was actually Volunteer Engine Company No. 33—Howard was a member—and like so many volunteer fire organizations, it was really a social club made up of men who gathered to gamble, tell tall stories, and they enjoyed brawling in the neighborhood saloons. Howard decided to avoid Engine Company No. 33 in its charge.

The Black Joke boys had heard their fire chief's number had been picked for the draft, and they were determined. "Raid the office, smash the wheel, burn the records!" Howard decided to go find McCann.

Donald McCann had bought a house, two stories of brownstone, with lace curtains, a Biedermeier set of parlor furniture, and stout oak doors, just east of Fifth, on Twelfth Street. Here he and Nan, his cook and housekeeper, and Flossie, her daughter, made a comfortable place of it with too many chairs and china closets bought as bargains and the fine wine in the cellar. For McCann was a man who claimed to know the taste and vintage of many wines. Perhaps he did—and knew Flossie's body, from the sassy easygoing way she acted, Howard thought as he pulled the bell tug of the McCann place. After some time a pair of eyes looked out at him from a few inches of glass set in the solid door.

"It's me, Flossie."

Bolts and chain were moved and Howard went into the red-carpeted hall with oil paintings on red blocked wallpaper—pictures of half-draped women in Roman times, gilt frames that caught the light from half-drawn velvet drapes.

Flossie had her hair up and wore shoes now—was a bit more forward than in her Savannah days. There was gossip McCann had married her, but Howard felt Donald McCann was not a man for such romantic actions. Howard felt, thinking of marriage, a perceptible fear for his own future.

"He's in the book room, Cap'in."

McCann, in a dressing gown, slippers, pipe in mouth, was standing among stacks of books piled up in disorder. Books on chemistry, biological texts, tomes on metal processes, all of which he read as some people read novels. He turned to close the heavy wooden shutters on the big double windows.

"That damn fool Police Chief Kennedy, I warned him to clear the streets early."

"He couldn't have, Donald. Too many of them."

McCann turned and tugged on his little beard. "If I had the time I'd head for Jersey. But there's too much here." He looked over the carved teak bookcases, the cabinets with mineral specimens. "Aye, here I am trapped by possessions. Have you, Howard, read Ecclesiastes on the vanity of vanities? No, you haven't."

"The hell I haven't."

"No offense, laddie, no offense." He patted Howard's arm. "Now, this thing is bigger than any of the city chowderheads think. There's the burning, going to be bigger burnings. Lord knows I hate to make a good thing out of people's misery. Still, one must listen to the auguries and test the way the wind blows, eh?"

Howard grinned and pushed some heavy books off a colored cherry-wood chair so he could sit down. "I know that, Donald. You're a true Christian."

McCann cocked his head to one side to stare at his partner. "Mock me, I've human weaknesses. But I'm not one to go out when it's raining soup, with a fork. Now, Howard, we're going to buy up whatever our purse can permit—the burned-out places, damaged houses, looted warehouses, spoiled stock."

"Are we?"

"The owners will sell in panic for whatever they can get. Once it's explained to them as the Aristotelian acceptance of logic."

"Who's going out to face them, find them in those streets? Have you been out there?"

"Don't intend to. We'll just wait out a few days of riot, King Mob

113

to do his work, then we'll go out and hold up our gold and do business. If we don't. . . .

Howard rubbed dust off one of the books, *An Essay on the Principle of Population,* T. R. Malthus.

"Someone else will."

"It's land values of New York I'm thinking of. Let them burn the houses, the waterfrontage. We'll pick up Fifth Avenue corners and nice bits around the park. There's the future in real estate. Ask the Vanderbilts, the Astors. . . . You'll stay for dinner? Nan has chicken pot pie and salmon cutlets."

"No, I'm helping out the police."

Superintendent John A. Kennedy still did not take the street violence as a civil uprising. "Oh, it's just my fellow micks given to a bit of temper and to the lark of breaking in when they could get hold of some whiskey. I can handle things." He dressed in a civilian suit, ordered his open carriage, picked up a light bamboo cane and, so armed, decided to see what was really going on along Lexington Avenue around Forty-sixth Street. Soon he saw the smoke and then the fire. He got out of his carriage and began to walk toward Third Avenue.

Chauncey Wilcox was with those who knew him, greeted him.

"It's the Kennedy!" someone shouted. Before Kennedy knew it, they had rushed him and a man in a worn army uniform, a discharged soldier, no doubt, knocked him down with a roundhouse punch. Kennedy at once sprang to his feet and struck his assailant with his light cane across the face. Chaunce seized hold of it and Kennedy was knocked down again—this time he was stomped; work shoes and boots began to kick hard at his prone body. Struggling to his feet, he was seized, lifted, and tossed over an embankment onto stones piled up for street repairs. He managed to get to his feet, was clubbed, but like a bull ring animal, was still able to get up again and make for Lexington Avenue. He was rescued by Chaunce and a man named John Wagan, for whom the mob still had some respect.

Chaunce shouted, "The superintendent is a dead man."

With cheers the mob turned back to the fire. Kennedy was covered with a sack by Chaunce and taken away. At the Bellevue they counted seventy-two bruises on him, two dozen wounds, many serious.

114

Soon the news of Kennedy's fate spread. The police commissioner, much against their wishes, would have to intervene. Two were stuffed-shirt politicians, but Thomas C. Acton took over and decided on repressive measures against the mobs. He had all of Manhattan Island to bring under control. Acton turned out to be a man who could go days without much sleep, never getting out of his clothes at the police headquarters at 300 Mulberry Street. He was the commanding head of both the police and the army forces available. These he merged in order to try to put down the city's rebellion.

Heavy fighting continued in the streets and there were now bodies underfoot. The police, though badly mauled, were themselves doing dreadful damage with their heavy hardwood clubs, skulls being crushed by their tremendous blows when they could get in a good club swing.

Captain O'Hara mounted—the horse nervous, its bit foam covered, he with a torn sleeve of his uniform—ran across Howard on Third Avenue.

"Don't you know there's mob rule runnin' mad?"

"I do, Captain. What's being done?"

"You go down to Mulberry Street and join Police Commissioner Acton's citizen deputies. You'll be saving your own hide. Tell me, is Amy safe?"

"She promised to stay off the streets."

"I've got to go the the house to see to the missus and others. Get them to relatives in Brooklyn."

Howard found the Mulberry Street station full of battered police, a smell of blood, sweat, and urine, the click of telegraph keys. Police Commissioner Acton was receiving messages and sending them out by the hundreds. He was a tall rather plump man with muttonchop side whiskers like a tiger's muff. Even worried, he had an ironic set of features, just now scowling but suggesting competent strength. He ordered some weapons to be moved from storage and looked at Howard standing by his desk. "You're Captain O'Hara's son-in-law?"

"No. Not yet, anyway."

"Said you were a sailor. Handle cannon?"

"I can."

"Good. Till the army sends us real help, I'll use what I can. You'll find four cannon out back of the station—see if they're in order."

115

"What about powder and shot?"

Acton looked at some telegraph messages handed him. "Let's see if you're a good hunter." He read, looked up, and shook his head.

"The mob is beating the police every place. The Invalid Corps is being brought into action. Fifty limping convalescing soldiers, armed with sabers and muskets. They marched up Third Avenue into a barrage of paving stones, bricks and, I'm sure, a dead cat or two."

"I'll go see about the cannon."

From all parts of the city there was gunfire like rolling octaves of thunder and the merged shouting of the crowds.

Acton was reading the latest telegraph message when Howard was back in his office, face smeared with muck, his hands dirty. "Commissioner, I've found six barrels of coarse gunpowder in the cellar of City Hall."

"Damn hazardous place for it."

"I'm placing the guns across the avenue. Let's hope the powder is not too damp. And I've robbed a monument of 1912 cannonballs."

Later, standing, waiting by old iron, Howard remembered McCann quoting an old Scottish minister. "He used to say all the world's a stage and the play is badly cast."

What was most puzzling to Howard in this confusion, danger was what passed for the real world. Why was it so different from God's world, the one he had been taught as a child? That was not a world of riot, of shares, of selling and issuing of bonds or deals in gold and wheat futures, hog bellies, ships' timbers. That Rockefeller hanky-panky on coal oil coming up from the Pennsylvania earth. God's world is always belonging to someone else. I am supposedly a parvenu (as Jay Gould puts it), a stranger, I work in a world of total ambition, on greedy projects, and with a kind of predictable lust. ("Mr. Starkweather, these powder kegs are damp.") I manipulate, I know losers and I know winners. I want to run with winners. What is puzzling, now that I may die today, is the scarcity of motives beyond gain. McCann and myself, it isn't just for money. Even if we like the cash, the gold butter-colored coins—not even power. We don't rush at people or kill them as the mobs are doing right now. No, not just for power. Maybe we're proving ourselves in a profit-and-loss setup. The value of position, that's it, sitting on top of the pile. Now, clearly life is short. I may never get there.

(Some snipers were firing from rooftops; someplace tormented horses were screaming.)

116

I'm me, extraordinarily myself, all absorbed in living, a concentration of effort that I ride; anxious, competitive. Wholeness of self is what I try for, a control over the disorder of others. I keep in myself a confidence of purpose. That is not just wealth and social grace. For that I don't give a shit about. Just *look* at today. The world is futility, meanness, and anarchy. I wish it were not so. Loading cannon, I mix dread, hope, and anxiety like layers in a sandwich. What I like is the color of life, the tense drama. I guess I'm hunting for an answer.

("They're coming.")

16

As Howard redeployed his cannon, he saw companies of National Guards and volunteer groups in the city, more or less organized or organizing. There were reports of seven hundred soldiers, also sailors on warships anchored in the Hudson. There were garrisons in the Brooklyn Navy Yard, on Governors Island, at Fort Hamilton, and elsewhere rimming the city. Artillery, field guns, howitzers could be brought against the mob, but for two days it had been only the police and the Invalids against the rioters. A thousand citizens were being sworn in, including many who had paid to get off the army lists. Commissioner Acton reported that from the bloody battle field around Gettysburg, fought just a few days before, cavalry and infantry, dozens of artillery batteries, about ten thousand soldiers, were coming to be used against the mob.

Chaunce, still roaming the streets, heard rumors of the arrival of the Michigan State Volunteers, the 13th Cavalry of Rochester, troops from Buffalo, National Guard regiments, all backed by grape and canister and disciplined army rifle fire.

Chaunce was knocked down—he was jarred but not injured—he got to his feet and ran. Ran blindly, turned several corners, and at last stood panting under the wooden awning of Moses Smith's Saddler Shop. The smell of smoke and something dreadful burning—a dog or a human body?—made him gag, and he felt suddenly how foolish he had been and how mean and dreadful was the excitement he had been enjoying for two days. Fear shook him like a green-fruit colic—and he vomited into the gutter. He felt his bile bitter in his mouth. Feet, heavy treading feet, were coming close

117

and the boy shrank back into the shadowed doorway of the saddler's. A group of large women ran past screaming with sweating joy at the fortuitous chaos, carrying bundles and several holding up bottles from which they drank in quick gulping gestures. Dirty children were dragged along by their arms and some dogs circled them, barking, then they were gone from Chaunce's sight like a bad dream. He turned onto a broad avenue littered with loose bricks and broken glass sparkling like stars in the sunlight, a dead horse, several bodies like heaps of rags.

Someone called his name and he saw Captain Starkweather, who pulled him behind a rampart of packing cases and overturned carts, behind which his cannon stood on dusty wheels.

"What the hell, Chaunce, are you doing?"

"Running, running like the devil."

Several men in civilian dress were unpacking powder in cloth bags.

"You stay here with me. Wipe your face. Eat this." He handed the boy a stale heel of a loaf of bread.

Howard looked uptown toward where a great black cloud of smoke was rising in sinister design into the heated air. At its base red flames twisted. Chaunce chewed on the hard bread. "That's the Armory, all them people in it burning up." He began to weep and continued to chew on the bread.

The rest of the city was active in its fury of fire and violence. The major victims were blacks. The rioters could hardly lay hands on the rich army evaders, the draft-board officials fleeing to safety.

Mobs moved to burn out police headquarters, and Howard tried to move his cannon. Two hundred police held the place, and all the badly wounded patrolmen who could be rushed in past the mob. Commissioner Acton, in command, set himself to hold this Mulberry Street command post. Informers and detectives had brought in tales that the mobs, once past this police stronghold, were going to take over the financial section, destroy Wall Street. Break into the banks for the heaped-up bags of gold and silver coins. Also they planned to burst into the vaults of the U.S. Subtreasury.

Howard said, "The powder is worthless."

"We are going to put down the mob and take no prisoners," said Inspector Daniel C. Carpenter, commander of the force positioned outside the headquarters to bear the brunt of the first attack of the growing mob.

118

Acton said, "So we're fighting to save Wall Street? Not to stay alive. Get a gun, Starkweather."

Inspector Carpenter moved one hundred and twenty-five men up to Mulberry and Bleecker streets as the mob filled Broadway, its street and walks, from housefront to housefront, waving weapons and howling "like banshees." Howard, with a shotgun, figured there were ten thousand men and women in the mob, led by a giant carrying an American flag.

"Go back!"

"God damn the war!"

"We'll fire!"

In front others carried a big board with the lettering NO DRAFT!

Like an advance guard of fear before the slowly moving mob, raced panicked blacks, some with carts loaded with merchandise and household ware owned by white masters, materialists who feared property losses, whipping up horses as they rushed along in some hope of safety. Howard thought, And I'm here defending my pile, and McCann's, Jim Fisk's, Jay Gould's. *Where* are they?

Inspector Carpenter moved his men forward in ranks of fours, banging into the mob's advance line at Amity Street by the La Farge house, where black servants were being savagely beaten. One of the mob, carrying a big stick, rushed at the inspector as he moved briskly at the head of his men, his nightstick at the ready. The two men came together in a crush of limbs and flailing clubs. Howard used the butt of the shotgun, smashed in the skull of the attacker, killing him on the spot with one blow. The inspector killed the big flag carrier with a club blow, then one of the bearers of the sign: NO DRAFT!

The inspector smiled through a soiling of blood and brains. "Thank you, Mr. Starkweather."

"Watch for bricks from the rooftops."

Howard felt sorry for the mob. They were desperate exploited people, and now their situation was becoming cruel; in turn *they* would be crueler.

Shots and bricks showered down on the police; several were badly hurt. Still they came on, taking their losses, killing and disabling as they went, muscled arms and murderous clubs doing dreadful damage wherever they struck. Howard dropped back to try to find Chauncey Wilcox.

It took only about fifteen minutes for the police to turn back the mob, set them on the run. Wall Street, the money, bank notes and coins and bookkeeping records of speculators and industry were safe. Dead and dying were discovered crumpled up or thrashing about wherever the police ran down some fleeing person. Chaunce was asleep under a table at the Mulberry police station—the heel of bread still in his soiled hands.

Even the worst day must end. The mob held the damaged city as dusk came down. Howard sat on a bench, the shotgun across his knee, police sleeping all around him. There was no doubt about it, he thought, a great city had been seized by its poor, its workers, the idle, and all those attracted by violence who had joined in "for the fun of it."

Soldiers were still not available. The police during the night were on the defense or on the run. Fires burned everyplace, great flames leaping over private homes and public buildings. Horses trapped in stables behind homes and in livery stables were neighing and breaking out, their huge eyeballs rolling in mindless frenzy.

Just before morning at the Mulberry station Howard woke Chaunce, made him wash up in a bucket of water. "Now, I'm taking you to Mrs. Murtle's boardinghouse, and I'm locking you in."

"Aw, it's still going on."

"Didn't you have enough? You want a shot in your britches?"

"Didn't cry, did I?"

"Damn well did. Come on. Stick close. Walk behind me."

The streets were like some wood engravings, Howard thought, he had once seen in a popular copy of Dante's *Inferno*. Ghastly shadows were articulated in old walls; flames were licking at wood here and there. Shapes of people dead or crawling, some with a sort of epileptic cry, and all around looting, no doubt. Howard held the shotgun at the ready, got to the boardinghouse, and found Amy in a dressing gown asleep in a chair. She came to his arms in a little tripping run. "Oh, oh, I dreamed you were dead."

"Not dead." He kissed her and he knew he was going to hear more about being married; now, how the hell did he come to be thinking of that with the city about to become a war zone again?

"It's my father, Howard. There's been talk they're going to kill him. He's been leading the clubbing squads, and they're going to kill him."

120

Howard said the captain was a grown man and could take care of himself.

Returning to his post, he thought of this business—of how frail was the grip one had on the path one's life took. There had been forming in his mind for some time, and now it was beginning to focus, forced by the action around him, a hope of a better understanding; there is a kind of reverberation inside a man's life that goes on, carried forward by what one has done and is doing. We begin, he felt, all of us who move with the times, we start like these mobs, with the deed. We act bravely or as cowards. A life becomes austere or runs wild. The doing and becoming *is* the human conflict. I've seen it in people—have for a long time. We are hot and passionate. I'm part of it—because insatiable—and we don't like to see clearly at such times. Wanting, driving. And if the nation suffers, if society suffers—look at these streets—we wonder where the devil is a moral order?

(There were flames in the sky, much smoke, heavy rifle fire.)

So we go on, he mused, stepping aside as a crowd of running, shouting people chased by. Things get done, get done and are irrevocable. In any life—take mine—it's not just heedlessness and pride. I've always tried for discipline, a personal order. McCann says I'm a man in conflict, hunting for expression, but I avoid, so he says, the hard interminables and "stay fierce under the breastbone." Hell, today I'm certainly beginning to think of the consequences of the tendency to raw action. It's a turbulence in the air today—a pressure like a steam boiler. . . .

Now in the embattled day, Howard knew he was no longer a boy grown up. What maturity he would have, it had been born here in these riots. He could only refine this maturity, sharpen it. He knew there would never be a better world; yes, *that* was the lesson of today.

("They're hanging a darky on Third Avenue!")

17

Tuesday, July 14, dawned, the city well washed by a rain that had not stopped. The smell from charred ruins filled the air; the smoke of smoldering timbers was evidence of the damage the city itself had suffered. The sodden mob, few aware of the massive harm done, was out early. Its fury was now desperate as it saw the growing masses of armed forces made up against it.

Howard had left early to join the Special Volunteer Police. Amy talked to Chaunce, worried over her father, as they sat in the boardinghouse parlor.

After the boy was gone, Amy stood at the window, her hands over her ears; the firing was heavy, and now there was added the thumping sound of cannon.

Chaunce, on his errand, saw by midmorning street barricades being erected at First Avenue; piling up rubble, wagons, dismantled lampposts, street poles, boxes, barrels, kegs, and even the furniture from looted houses. There was talk, by Donald McCann later, that some French refugees from the 1848 street riots in Paris had suggested barricades in New York could hold back police and army charges. Chaunce found that from Eleventh to Fourteenth streets on First Avenue the barricades solidly snaked their way.

Neither side had much use for prisoners. Troops with cannon manned by trained artillerymen began to move in to help the hardpressed police under Captain O'Hara.

One regiment ran into the mob head on. The men fired volleys and cannon poured their loads of grape and canister into the massed bodies. Men and women were torn to pieces.

The colonel of the regiment, well satisfied, told Captain O'Hara he had given the mob "a whiff of grape" and marched his soldiers back to the Arsenal.

Captain O'Hara went back to the scene of slaughter, on horseback and alone. He lived nearby and was still worried about his family and property. He was too proud—too heated up by events to think calmly—to take an armed escort with him. Riding to his house, he found his family, Mrs. O'Hara and the children, had gone off early to relatives in Brooklyn. Chaunce, on his way to deliver Amy's note, saw him pass just as on Second Avenue someone pointed him out. "The murdering captain himself." A half-dozen men leaped forward at the mounted police officer and tried to pull him from his horse. He also became the target of brick throwers. Sensing his danger, O'Hara got off his mount in a hurry—"God damn you riffraff"—and took refuge in a saloon at Second Avenue and Nineteenth Street. He still had no respect for the rioters nor feared them.

122

"Damn apes—they're all crazy." He left the saloon to face the men and women howling around him. Chaunce saw him, pistol out at the ready.

"Stand back, I'm the law." He intended to reach his horse across the street. Trying to shoulder past the mob, the captain was at once engulfed by cursing, battering, kicking men.

"Give 'im the boot!" Clubbed on the head, he was swept off his feet. Brutally punished by heavy shoes and boots and everything that could swing at a prone body, he appeared to Chaunce doomed to a horrible death. A rope was tied across O'Hara's ankles and the mob took turns dragging him around over the cobblestones, back and forth, hauled from curb to curb. "Oh, ain't he a sight? God-damn copper."

A slim elderly priest came forward. "I don't interfere with your actions, but the man's an Irish Catholic and so entitled to the last rites of his faith."

The priest performed his ritual services on the wrecked but still-living body of Captain O'Hara, then went his way. He uttered no word that Chaunce close by could hear, asking for mercy for the still-breathing man. He survived further torture of knives, swords, the blows of stones beaten against his head and body. And being dragged up and down the street like a trapped cat on a cord by cruel children. Thinking him at last dead, the mob left. Chaunce crept close to the battered hulk and the rags of a once-proud police uniform.

"Mother o' God . . . Mother o' mercy," the broken mouth said.

"Captain . . . Captain."

The battered lips moved, were wordless—sounds came faintly. The man lay in the street in the blazing heat of the day, no one but Chaunce coming to see if a spark of life remained or to offer him water. Some of the mob came back for more sport. Stones were thrown at his head and body. Chaunce said, "He's dead."

The fighting went on all over the city. But with most available military arms and ammunition kept from the mobs, the tide of battle was moving toward the growing forces of authority.

With so much military around, Donald McCann had at last ventured out to the gray-painted premises, the hanging oil lamps of McCann & Starkweather.

"Dreadful, dreadful, the unchaining and revenge of the carya-tids," he said to the walls. He was shaken by the destruction, the

123

burning buildings, the warehouses looted. It had seemed at first just land and property that could perhaps be turned to his advantage, bought cheaply. But the reality of fire, the smell of charred wood, the dead lying like horse droppings in the streets, heads split open by police clubs reached deeply into his Calvinist soul. A full sense of the evil men do to men came to him, and God's indifference, His turn to punish. For the first time in forty years he knelt and prayed while in the street booted feet hurried about in desperate errands. Women and children appeared to hunt among the dead for son, father, husband. Others to strip and hunt in pockets, pull off boots.

Five regiments of the Union Army in full war gear were being moved at all speed by steamcars and ferries to the city. Howard was able to get dry grain gunpowder.

Wednesday morning McCann, reading the newspapers, saw in print that the riot, the insurrection, had passed its peak, that its back was shattered, authority was again in control. "Why are they hooting for joy? It's Americans on both sides killing each other." Actually, the war in the city was to go on for three more days. Blacks continued to be molested, injured, and lynched. Field guns and howitzers commanded by Howard and others went into action against the rioting mobs. Saloons and groceries did a roaring business, were looted of their contents with no payment made. Chaunce, roaming through the streets again, found men, women, and children hurrying toward Yonkers, White Plains, carrying burdens, wheeling carts, frightened horses pulling loaded carriages. Lost dogs ran about barking. The smell of fear and fire and horse was strong all along the Westchester Road. Railroad stations and depots became battlegrounds for those seeking places on the steam trains. The ferry landings were packed, fights for position in line for places. "Crossing the bay," as a minister told Chaunce, "one wished for it to part like Moses' Red Sea."

By nightfall, under swinging oil lamps, Howard saw more trained battle-hardened Union troops moving into the city by the thousands. Sweat-stained in long worn blue, they came: the 74th National Guard, 26th Michigan, 152nd New York Volunteers.

The mayor issued a proclamation: all citizens of good intent to go about their business as usual, and all transportation to function once more. The rioters had been fully dispersed and the military forces now in the city would contain, control all illegal actions.

Archbishop Hughes, at his residence at Madison and Thirty-sixth Street, spoke from his balcony to about three thousand of the population. He was seated, as his arthritis kept him from standing. He wanted an end to the rioting. "Do you want my advice? Well, I have been hurt by the report that you were rioters. You cannot imagine that I could hear these things without being grievously pained.

Howard, bone-tired, unshaved, his clothes reeking, identified the battered body of Captain O'Hara in a blacksmith's shed on Lexington Avenue, where it had been dragged with several other corpses. Transporting the body home in a dray, Howard was handed a printed broadside issued by the city:

STOLEN PROPERTY

Police will search the districts of the poor to recover stolen items. Every person in whose possession these articles are found will be treated as a criminal—no excuses will be accepted that they were in the street and had been taken up to prevent them being burned. The entire city will be searched . . . so return all property removed from rightful owners.

But Howard thought life could *not* be returned to the hundreds dead. To find a coffin and a priest were the first tasks. The body lay that night in a black oak casket set on a stand in the shade-drawn O'Hara parlor—candles burning. Howard sat in the kitchen listening to the keening over the body of Captain O'Hara. The thin young priest's voice was weak but clear. *"Confiteor Deo omnipotenti. . . ."*

The last fighting was going on in the city beyond the walls of the widow O'Hara's parlor. The riots were a kind of message, Howard thought, one of shocking sadness, the futility and evanescence of what was society. It was McCann's "wolf world" all night, with the foxes snapping not at the grapes overhead, but at whatever they could get their teeth into. It was a half-baked culture, this America. (*"Benedicat vos omnipotens, Deus, Pater et Filius, et Spiritus Sanctus."*) Truth is, he now saw as he sipped from a glass of funeral gin, the country was still half formed, still a damn dream. We'll never really settle in and grow hedge roses. (That is Amy weeping—must go to her.) The people who are the mob exploding in rage are expressing their despair, in cruelty. They got cheated, were kicked in the ass on the way, and here in the Promised Land of milk and honey

125

found nothing much, so they've taken now to fire and whiskey, a stolen hat along the way, a pair of shoes. *("Te igitur, clementissime Pater.")*

It's me, too, who riled them up in their misery. McCann? Fisk? Gould? Vanderbilt? Morgan? Will they feel guilt as I do? Dreadful days, terrifying events. But how much can we understand, who to really blame? The truth is the average person can be destroyed when he gets in the way of what that wily bastard McCann calls "the hunt for the metals, the processing of resources, the control of the marketplace." Some of us have an oversized idea of existence. Captain O'Hara in his coffin, he had it, too.

Well, I have it, Howard admitted (and heard the priest read, *"Asperges me, Domine hyssopo"*).

BOOK IV

Buy land. They're not making it anymore.
—MARK TWAIN

18

Mr. and Mrs. Howard Harrison Starkweather were giving a dance and dinner party at their house on Fifth Avenue and Forty-first Street. A fine place, agreed the coachmen lining up their carriages; not as elegant and posh as William Marcy Tweed's house two blocks up at Fifth and Forty-third. But then Boss Tweed controlled Tammany and the spread of the boodle and the city contracts that made New York such a thriving bustling city. The Starkweather house, in the aquamarine dusk, showed itself to be three stories of yellow sandstone, marble window frames—a house with gas and lamplight glowing on white damask, candles burning in ornate chandeliers in the large parlor called the ballroom by the newspapers. A five-piece orchestra was already playing something Mitteleuropa, suggesting a promenade at Marienbad, the Bal des Anges at Nice.

There were those present who talked of their host—men in Prince Albert formal coats, there with their wives and daughters to add the sparkle of diamonds to the party. It was Mrs. Starkweather's birthday. Some men talked of just *how* secure was H. H. Starkweather & Company in its two-story building on Wall Street near Pearl? Starkweather fortunes had been swift in their climb. The firm had done well enough in handling the issuing of shares of certain Southern railroads and catering to those investors speculating in coal, iron and steel companies. Was it true the major bondholders of those rail lines, those on the board of directors, were running things badly? Certainly the roads still paid their dividends. Well, money was a problem to have or to invest; the banking business—yes—had its idiosyncrasies.

The servants moved about with trays of drinks—brandy juleps and Madeira—and while they were not in a livery as bold as those at Vanderbilt and Astor dinners, they were splendidly dressed for servants and a bit given over to a bold stare at the well-fed necks and bosoms of the women, the pink first flush of girlhood in adult gowns.

Mr. Starkweather's personal secretary came out of the library shooting out his starched cuffs, adjusting his wing collar. He was a handsome young man with an overlarge nose, face a bit dusty-skinned, wise very dark eyes to match a clever turn to the corners of his mouth. Chauncey Wilcox at nearly twenty had natural poise, and some who had to deal with him insisted *also* gall and arrogance. His blue-black hair, worn a bit long, was oiled, brushed up from a wide forehead. There were hints he was Spanish; ill-wishers insisted he was "sure as shooting part coon." Several sporting-house ladies about town insisted he was a direct descendant of the Shawnee Chief Tecumseh. While a gossip sheet, *Town Topics,* hinted Chauncey Wilcox was the illegitimate son of William Tecumseh Sherman. Chauncey himself admitted to nothing. He drove Mr. Starkweather's sporting rig at times, gambled at Canfield's, was inclined to seek his pleasures in what was to be called the Tenderloin district and its low-life dance halls.

He made his way discreetly and with grace through the gathering guests. Carriages were still unloading well-dressed guests on the avenue. He went up the wide mahogany and mother-of-pearl staircase and past its heavy framed pictures of Arab horsemen riding hard, Western landscapes of rather overdramatic skies. He hurried along a hall with much gilt furniture and tapped on a door, listened a moment, turned the gilt-and-crystal doorknob. He entered a room lit by gas mantels.

Mrs. Starkweather sat at her dressing table watching in the mirror her maid do up her hair, winding braids (not Mrs. Starkweather's own) over an ornate coiffure. She held a glass in her hand, sipping a medicinal-smelling drink. "What do you think, Nina?"

The maid stepped back and nodded. "It will do fine, madam."

"Let's try some bangs on one side."

Chauncey said, "H. H. is wondering if you'd mind coming down to greet your guests."

Mrs. Starkweather smiled, set down her glass. She was getting very la-di-da, the young man thought, but she retained in part also the manners of a little girl who projected her charm to get her own way. He was very fond of her.

"Of course not, Chaunce. Be right down."

"Happy birthday."

130

"Forget it, Chaunce—I have."

The gown Nina was hooking Mrs. Starkweather into was blue and gold and with large inserts, a train in the mode of the moment. Two rows of pearls comforted the now-flushed neck and chin. The fingers of both hands held rings from Tiffany's. Nina set a jeweled tiara on the titian-colored hair. From below in the ballroom came the sound of flageolet or a flute. Mrs. Starkweather wasn't sure which.

"My train, Nina." Followed by Chauncey and the maid, Mrs. Howard Harrison Starkweather went down—sailed, Chauncey thought—to greet her gathering guests. She wondering where they had, years ago, stored her cello.

Jerry Farnsworth, "social scrivener" (his own words) on Mr. Bennett's New York *Herald,* was already writing (in his head) the description of the gown as Mrs. Starkweather came down the staircase:

> Mrs. Starkweather is a lady who goes into society a great deal. She has a new dress for every occasion. And this was her birthday. Her gown was imported from Paris for the occasion and was made of blue satin, point gold-colored lace, and a profusion of flowers. The skirt had heavy flutings of satin around the bottom, and the lace flounces were looped up at the sides with bands of the most beautiful pinks, roses, lilies, forget-me-nots, and other flowers.
>
> We have it on the best information her extensive wardrobe contains evening robes in Swiss muslin, robes in linen for the garden and croquet playing, dresses for horse shows, *robes de nuit* and *robes de chambre,* dresses for breakfast and for dinner, dresses for receptions and for parties, dresses for watering places, and dresses for all possible occasions. . . .
>
> H. H. Starkweather, the Wall Street investment banker who has risen to prominence so quickly, indulges his wife in every way. But is not himself much interested in the society scene, being, it is reported, actively occupied in the scheme to launch elevated rail lines along many of the city's avenues. . . . President Grant's daughter and son-in-law, Mr. and Mrs. Abel R. Corbin, were among the most prominent guests of the evening. . . .

The library was a large room facing south, paneled in a polished golden oak, with leaded-glass doors on the bookcases holding many well-bound volumes. A few of which the host had read. The books

131

he really enjoyed he kept in his dressing room upstairs. Howard Harrison Starkweather as he approached thirty had not gone to fat, had not taken on a paunch. He had cultivated a large but well-trimmed mustache, not too sharply waxed at the ends. He filled out his good tailoring with just a hint of discomfort. He wore no rings, only three black-pearl shirt studs and gold-coin cuff links. Only his eyes betrayed a certain sense of worry, pressure.

He lit the cigar for the thin, rather peaked-looking, ruminative man facing him, lit it with a small swinging gas flame created just to light the host's good Havana cigars. The man had goitrous bulging eyes, but thought (it was clear) rather well of himself.

The host said, "Anyone not interested in transportation is going to regret it. That and land are the whole turkey shoot. This fellow Mark Twain said the other day, 'Buy land. They're not making it anymore.'"

The thin man, his sideburns like brackets to his face, inhaled cigar smoke and said, "That's pretty good."

"Yes."

"Jay feels the real profits to be made are in the Gold Room on the Exchange."

"Damn risky, Abel. The ordinary citizen doesn't trust or do much dealing in gold."

"But the nation is run on gold."

"Its credit is. But the average citizen, he rides the steamcars, the ferryboats, uses coal, things made of iron and steel. Feels there's always a demand for such things. Gold is to pack in a tooth or make a watch case out of."

"You sound like your cracked old partner. McCann." The thin man said it with a presumption of familiarity.

"I hope you have some shares of McCann Iron and Steel Company. He's producing pig iron and rolling steel equal to a Carnegie."

The library door opened and Zeeland, the portly Dutch butler, came in. It was rather daring and amusing, the host thought, to have a butler who was not English. Howard Starkweather enjoyed the shock of some of the guests at the thick accent of the dignified fat-cheeked servant.

"Mrs. Starkweather is cooming down, sir."

"Yes." He turned to Abel Corbin. "How's the President?"

"Bearing up. The damn pressures are not cured—like delegating a military situation."

132

The band was playing a lively Irish air. Howard motioned to the door. "We had hoped, that is, Amy, my wife, had hoped he and Mrs. Grant could be here tonight."

The son-in-law shook his head in a gloomy way. "National matters, you know, lay heavy on him. *Very* heavy. Christ, yes."

His host nodded and waved off a tray of anchovy-stuffed olives as Mrs. Starkweather reached the bottom of the staircase. After five years of marriage Howard had decided there was still a great deal of O'Hara in Amy. But her acute fears, sensibilities, grievances were well covered in her public appearances, and at times she yearned more and more for social success, meeting the right people, moving in the ostentation of those social circles that passed for the top layer of those descendants of smelly pelt traders, scow owners, land thieves, speculators in real estate; the towers of any aristocratic society. But let it pass; it pleased Amy at times; other times she mocked them: "They talk like they had a hot potato in their mouth and walk with a glass ball between their legs."

Amy looked well enough this festive night even if some qualified quack had insisted she had a delicate chest and a nerve condition with a Latin name. There was enough of the Amy Howard remembered from their days with theater people—the Jim Fisk and Josie Mansfield world—to prove useful to her, as now, in greeting people. Whispering in an ear here, kissing a cheek there, holding a hand just a second more, and laughing her silvery cheerful laugh; an amused sound at some remark perhaps. A bit too prolonged to have heard anything that amusing. A hostess has to cultivate a casually firm manner, ending with a tap of her fan.

Howard went to his wife's side and pressed her left hand. "Fine gathering. Happy birthday."

"Happy yourself, H.H." They exchanged cheek kisses while the guests applauded. The music struck up a bit of a polite English lancers dance tune, and he swung Amy out on the dance floor. Howard didn't care much for dancing, but Amy did and it was her birthday. Was she, he wondered, twenty-seven or twenty-eight? Whatever it was, it was also a kind of celebration to what a few years could do to turn a smuggler-sailor into one of the city's bright young bankers—manifesting an individuality and a taking of risks. He wasn't Howard Starkweather, ex-captain of a blockade-runner—its remains rusting and breaking up in some cursed malarial swamp inlet in the Carolinas. He was H.H. ("The Waldorfs are

133

here . . . but I don't see the Belmonts, H.H.") Odd how that had come about, to be called by his initials.

It had first been applied to him by Donald McCann the day it was decided the old partnership was to break up. A friendly, most friendly parting. McCann to go to Pittsburgh to attend to his iron and steel holdings, they being more to his interest than the firm of McCann & Starkweather. And Howard to go to opening a firm on his own. H. H. Starkweather & Company.

"H. H. it is," McCann had said as he emptied his desk, keeping just a few papers and tearing the rest to bits with his strong hands, hands with the red fuzz on the backs of them. "You're on your own nu, and since I've been such a good partner to you, don't take in any more. That's good advice. The partners aroun', they're not all as charming and honest a mon as I've been." He had laughed and slapped Howard on the back. "You're H. H. now, and stay that way. Hire men, give 'em titles, those you'll hire and keep—but not any equal partnership. Stay clear, too, of Jim and Jay, they're bone pickers. Don't go making a fat carcass for them to sharpen their beaks on. Ingrained skepticism is often better than having brains."

It had been a cheerful parting. He liked Donald McCann, owed him a great deal in making him flexible in society, politics, and the money market. But their ways were different. McCann was given to dealings involving iron and steel. He hadn't changed that much from his beginning and the McCann Forge. Howard had a wider vision of what a private bank and investment house should be; he enjoyed the nebulous dealing in hopes in shares, stocks and bonds, in which the true value was often a fantasy; in bills of exchange with firms like the Rothschilds, Baring Brothers overseas, the Gunzbergs in holy Russia, the Sassoons in Asia, mahogany-skinned men in Mexico City, Rio. He specialized at times and traded in the coins of Hong Kong, Austria. McCann was not daring enough, and worse, not interested. "You'll find out the chaos of power is greedy, out to grab the world like it were a chicken's neck."

The Street was impressed the way the new house of H. H. Starkweather had floated the shares of the McCann Iron and Steel Company, also its holdings in Red Mountain Iron Ores, Continental Railroad Supplies & Rails. A good public image—but low on capital. It was also nip and tuck that McCann would emerge stronger in the coming battle to supply the major railroads' demand for steel

134

rail, steel wheel carriages, pressed-steel car sides. To go up against the control of markets by steel men like Carnegie, Frick, and others. Buck them for the contracts with George Pullman, Huntington, Crocker's Central and Southern Pacific, Baldwin Locomotives Works, and convince men ready to span the rivers; to Brooklyn with spun-steel cables, cross the Mississippi, talk of even bridging the Hudson, the Golden Gate.

"No, Donald—I leave all that to you."

"It isn't just the product," McCann had said. "It's the trusts, the cartels. And young Morgan is moving towards control of railways, in copper, too. And old J.D. in coal oil. Others? Whiskey distilling, ice for summer, trolley cars, all being formed to drive the small firms to sell out or go to ruin. It is a grand and crazy time coming, H.H."

"If that's to be—let it come."

The dance music was still playing; he was aware he was dancing, Amy in his arms, smelling of some imported perfume and her own body odor (like apples in storage in a dry attic, he decided). Not very romantic but it was the way he liked her. It hadn't been an easy five years for them. He remembered Neal O'Hara singing, "Young love must go. For aught I care, to Jericho." The O'Haras were a feisty lot and had strong family ties. They were settled in San Francisco now, Neal running a theater there. Howard hadn't been as eager as Amy to move into the New York world of party giving, balls, and fêtes. . . . But it's not bad, not bad at all, he thought as the dance ended and everyone applauded loudly. While a servant dropped a tray someplace.

William Marcy Tweed had arrived with his wife. Tweed was a jolly man, crafty, with a large nose that Thomas Nast, the caricature fellow on *Harper's Weekly,* was drawing too big—a picture of fun to some; Boss Tweed, as many called him. Howard was there shaking hands with him, two of his Tammany captains, and their overstuffed wives. "Ah, H.H. You're doing yourself fine." Jay Cooke arrived, not to be mistaken, the butler warned a footman, for Jay Gould, who was resting his delicate stomach and nerves in the country. A rival investment firm, Jay Cooke & Company, but Howard liked the bulky heavy-bearded figure of the man and respected him. ("A blue-light Presbyterian nature," McCann had said of Cooke.) There was also a famous actor—Dion Something, Howard

135

remembered—who doffed his red silk-lined cape; how else to call it but "doffing," Howard thought as he shook hands with the still-arriving guests. Yes, doffing the cape as the hamola did on the stage of Burton's Theatre.

Howard told Chauncey it was certainly a splendid party and Amy enjoyed it. He standing at ease, being talked to in the library, smoking a good cigar, hands in his trouser pockets. Did they know it was all front? These men who were the powers in the city, on the Street. Successful in their work, their arts. The mocking turtle-headed lawyer Chauncey Depew came in to shake his hand.

"Ah, H.H., you must be making a lot *or* losing a lot to have such a spread."

"I can't know, Depew, until my bookkeeper does up the fiscal figures."

"You hear the story of the washerwoman and the randy preacher?"

The actor looked up at a picture of a landscape with a cow and a girl in it. "That would be a Corot."

"It would be," someone answered, "if it were not an Inness."

"She said, 'Too big for a man, too small for a horse.' Ha! Ha!"

The men were drinking old brandy in the library, and the laughter was loud through the good pungent cigar smoke. It was the only room in the house where smoking was permitted. Zeeland, the butler, again presented himself. "Dinner is being served, gentlemen."

Tweed rattled his watch chains with his thumbs, smiled. "Like any good cab horse, I can put on the nose bag. What is it tonight, H.H.?"

"Damn if I know, Bill. Mrs. Starkweather has been hiring the cooks."

Actually, Howard took a great deal of interest in food, good food. But it was one of those poses of disinterest men took during the period; of being controlled by their wives in the matter of decor, food, and domestic setting.

The Starkweather chef was an Italian, and the dinner of sixty people ate a celery-root remoulade, baked clams and country pâté, sweetbreads with *petits pois,* duck described by the journalist Farnsworth as *caneton aux airelles* with wild rice, *côte de veau* Normandy sautéed in Calvados, poached salmon in sauce Joinville. The desserts were listed by the reporter as cherry cake, *gâteau Bruxelles,* and

136

mousse crème Bavaroise. Wines were different with every course—he found the spelling difficult and had to follow the empties to the kitchen to copy the labels. It was a time when overeating and the fat girths to prove it were fashionable. Compared to an Astor or Vanderbilt dinner, the Starkweather spread was, as Chauncey Depew remarked to the actor, "hardly an entrée. A majestic simplicity."

Amy had changed gowns for the dinner and the journalist turned loose his best prose in describing her gown. "A rich blue satin skirt, *en train.* Over this there was looped up a magnificent brocade silk, white, with bouquets of flowers woven in all the natural colors. This overskirt was deeply flounced with costly white lace, caught up with bunches of feathers of bright colors. About her shoulders was thrown a fifteen-hundred-dollar shawl. She had a headdress of delicate gold beads."

It was two in the morning when Howard and Amy got into their nightclothes and into the big double bed. This was an age when husbands and wives spent a lifetime of sleep and breeding together in family beds. To separate each to a private bedroom was being talked about, but few went that far in domestic dislocation.

"Very fine evening," said Howard, buttoning his nightshirt.

"People thought so." Amy was taking her night's medicine prescribed by her doctor, Dr. Hawley. It had a strong smell of laudanum.

"Was a good birthday, wasn't it?"

Amy had already closed her eyes. Howard sank back on his pillow and felt tired, somewhat let down, as after every party. From below, in the backyard, came the tinkle of glass. Zeeland and the staff were taking out the empties. He fell asleep and dreamed he was at sea, a huge Union frigate firing its nine-inch guns at him, and no matter how he steered and dodged among the shallows, he could not elude the dark pursuing shape.

19

H. H. STARKWEATHER & CO.

Large gold letters against a solid black background over the door. A wide entrance of double doors with ornate bronze grille.

137

Inside varnished wall paneling, a brick floor, embossed metal ceiling, and globe gas lighting. The counters and cashier's cage were fenced by polished brass rods with an American motif on top (eagles).

The three clerks wore coats and wing collars, well-tied cravats, even if the cuffs might be trimmed by scissors to avoid showing they were frayed. Howard paid the clerks well, seven dollars a week. The head cashier, twelve. They were all males. An old charwoman came after closing hours, with bucket and mop and an old piece of shirt used for dusting.

Chauncey Wilcox, brash, decisive, but not insensitive, had a small office just outside Howard's bigger one, which was paneled, off to the left of the entrance that overlooked the street. It had a large plate-glass window with gold letters in one corner.

INVESTMENT BANKERS
DEALERS ON RAILROAD ISSUES
CURRENCY EXCHANGE
BANK-NOTE DISCOUNTING

Privacy Howard could have if he so wished—cut off from the street view and the street's view of him by light wooden shutters. The only connection with his past was an oil painting, made by a Charleston artist during the war, of *Sea Witch* running in a high sea, every detail showing sharply and a fine plume of smoke billowing out from her stacks.

Howard stood at the window reading the *Herald*'s reporter's version of Amy's party. . . . Well, at least he didn't say they had eaten their soup with their hats on. There was a sharp knock on the door to his office and Chauncey Wilcox came in. Dressed in a blue frock coat with gilt buttons, a gray topper set at an angle on his head, a cane under one arm.

"Very smart." Howard folded the newspaper. "You look like a wax window dummy in Stewart's shop."

"Thank you, H.H. Gold is moving this morning."

"I know. Anything illogical behind it?"

"You think it's Jim and . . . ?"

"Could be Baring Brothers in London. What is Western and Great Plains doing?"

138

"Not selling. We've had no offers this morning for any railroad shares."

"Morgan lying doggo?"

"Dull morning there, too. Gave their doorman two cigars for the information."

"Telegraph McCann I advise to withhold issuing any new shares until there's more excitement."

There was another knock on the door. A thin clerk, with the large red nose of a drinker, put his head in. Howard wondered how the head would look on a pole. (He'd been reading Carlyle.)

"What is it, Barbour?"

"Man outside with some hosses."

"Oh, yes. I'll be gone till afternoon, Chaunce. It's Amy's birthday gift, an extra one. Come look."

At the curb were two beautiful bay horses attached to a fine smart phaeton with a black leather hood, red wheels and shaft pole. A limping fat man in tight boots, a varnished coachman's hat, was flicking a whip, making a snapping sound, while manipulating a kitchen match between his teeth. The horses reacted as if on cue, arching their necks, scraping a hoof on the cobbled street surface.

"Well, Mr. Starkweather, ain't them two beauts? And the rig—there's only one other like it, and the Prince of Wales, he takes the reins to that one, Lillie Langtry at his side."

"They're not street-shy?" Howard patted the neck of one of the horses.

"You couldn't git them to bolt if you fired a cannon off in their ears."

Chauncey said, "Too frisky for Mrs. S., aren't they?"

"Tobias, I'll let you know tomorrow if I'll take them."

"Keep 'em a week, a year." He handed over the slender whip. "Just keep a tight hold on the reins and use the whip most for decoration. They don't need stirring up."

Howard took the whip and mounted the springy seat while the horse dealer unsnapped the check chain from the hitching post set in the sidewalk.

Howard wound the reins around his tan kid gloves. "What is gold this morning, Chaunce?"

"Ninety-four. Was ninety-one at closing yesterday."

"Hum." Howard flicked the whip in the air over the rumps of the

139

horses, held the reins firmly, and as the phaeton swayed on its springs, he moved off toward Broadway.

Howard Starkweather was often to wonder at the first five years of his marriage, appearance and essence. He had been undecided as to being married or not. But the murder of Captain O'Hara had sort of made him the presiding male. Neal, the oldest son, was not practical. He hoping for a career as a great singer. The children were in need of care and discipline. Mrs. O'Hara fell among priests who consoled her and set up masses for the soul of the departed police captain. To Howard marrying six months after the death of Captain O'Hara seemed the thing to do. Family life with the O'Haras was amusing, dramatic; given to laughter, tears, tempers, and Mrs. O'Hara taking to drink for some time in wailing anguish.

He and Amy had made a go of it. More than a go, he admitted as he held the reins and the marvelous horses trotted. There was for him and Amy still the attraction of their bodies for each other, and there was for him knowing someone was waiting and was close and trustworthy. He could talk out his problems, the day's market, banking, the partnership that was breaking up. And always of the future, as yet untapped potentialities.

He supposed it was true love. A subject on which he felt he was no true authority. They were happy in a feeling of camaraderie.

There was the problem of children. Amy wanted them, Howard was wary; too often a child is a vessel of ingratitude.

Dr. Welton Hawley, an imported Englishman with silver-rimmed glasses and a habit of chewing his lower lip, said Amy was too delicate to bear children. Her chest bothered the doctor. He was always listening to it—society women liked to be told they were delicate—and making *hmm* sounds and saying not to catch cold—he'd give her some medicine for warding off bronchitis, pneumonia.

Amy, on children, decided to let what could happen, happen. They couldn't give up sex, and they didn't care for the games where impregnation was foiled. But after a while it was clear Amy couldn't get pregnant. Dr. Hawley said she was lucky that way, *or* Howard *was* sterile. "Mind you, I mean sterile, but virile. That's what I mean."

"She did want them," Howard said.

"Some medical men think children help certain conditions . . . well . . . never mind. . . ."

"You hinting at bad lungs?"

140

"No, no. She hasn't been bringing up blood, has she? No, of course not. Just keep her feet dry and her body free from colds."

She had grown somewhat thinner and sometimes in the night she would wake, tell of some dream of an apocalyptic beast. The last two winters he had taken her to Warm Springs, West Virginia, to avoid the New York bad weather. She was brooding over not having children, and he would try to placate her with gifts. Jewels, a dressing table with three mirrors. She was neither passive nor compliant to her marriage. She knew her worth to him.

Her version of the world was often unreal, like the landscapes of dreams. She didn't seem to feel the loss of the O'Haras, who had all gone out to San Francisco in 1867 when Neal was made manager and director of a variety theater, the Star, on Sutter Street, and sent back a photograph of all the O'Haras looking perky into the camera lens, and a Mrs. Neal O'Hara added to the group. All of them dressed in their fancy best and looking healthy against a backdrop of Seal Rock and the Golden Gate.

When Howard drove up, the butler was sent to find Amy. She admired the rig and the two fine bays. She put on her smallest bon- ·net and her highest button shoes, and Howard drove through the park. Then north and across the Harlem River up to White Plains. Amy looked lovely—he held the reins, elbows high, and let her swish the whip. It was good country and the day was sunny without too much heat, all green and topaz and the smell of cut hay. Everything looked washed and clean. There had been rain in the night.

"It's a good place for buying land up through here."

"Oh, I'd miss the city."

"For the summer months, when it's hotter than hell's hinges. Along the river, past Tarrytown, there's a whole point of land I've my eye on."

"Please, Howie, I'm no country girl."

"We could keep a cow. Have cream and fresh milk. A French queen kept a cow. Milked her, too. But. . . ."

She adjusted her bonnet and flicked the whip at some elms by the roadside. Passed some garden statues with pubic moss.

"Stop treating me like I was made of glass, an invalid." She snapped the whip over the heads of the horses, which took it badly, broke into a run that gave Howard a bad two minutes.

"Damn it, Amy, you rattled them."

He held the reins tight and savaged them a bit and the bays ran on past a wagon hauling timbers and by a carryall with children in it from some public home, all in pale blue. It wasn't until they reached Rye Crossroads that Howard had the team under control. He was smiling as he relaxed hands and fingers.

"They're beauts, aren't they?"

"I want to drive them," Amy said.

"Maybe, someday."

"No, *now*."

"I'll have Nestor take you out for morning runs."

"No, now."

"All right, move over. Take the reins in front of my hands."

"Let go."

"Like hell. These nags would pull you right out off of the seat."

"Relax a bit, then. Let me feel the pull."

It was amusing. He and Amy hadn't really been together like this for some time. The setting up of the new firm, furnishing the fancy house, the condition of the market on the Street; it was either often a recession or a bull market in the wrong time. He'd have to see more of Amy. Perhaps in their homelife there was too much serenity and lucidity, usually—unless Amy got her dander up over something.

They had a good leisurely dinner near Yonkers at a river inn overlooking the Hudson. Planked shad and a Haut Brion that Jim Fisk had recommended. There was a delightful glow of moon by the river slipping endlessly by. Some banjo players were drifting in a sailboat, singing black songs. Across the river pinpoints of light showed how high the Palisades were on the Jersey side.

Coming back, the horses had lost their high-stepping vigor and were happy to pace slowly down to the Starkweather house, where Nestor, the old black groom who took care of the carriage, landau, and the horses, took them in hand.

"They're tuckered, Mr. Starkweather."

"They should be, we've had them almost to the North Pole. Think they'll do?"

"They'll do fine. They got class writ all over their pretty golden hides. I'll just cool 'em off and rub 'em down."

Howard and Amy both slept well that night and made prolonged and fastidious love in the morning. Howard dressed in his gray English suit, picked up his gold-headed cane out of the Chinese umbrella stand in the hall. He found Nestor in the coach house, smoking a short clay pipe and polishing the rump of one of the bays as if it were waxed furniture.

"You want to drive 'em downtown?"

"No, harness the chestnuts to the landau. Don't let Mrs. Starkweather drive the bays. You hear?"

"I hear. She got a good eye for horseflesh."

Amy was driving the bays within a week. Having bribed Nestor with one of Howard's suits, including a pair of needle-nosed yellow shoes, to take her and the bays through the park before noon. She had skill and good wrists. Two weeks later, as Howard emerged from his bank, there was Amy at the curb, holding the reins of the bays as they slobbered foam over their bits and trod on their own golden dung.

Nestor, at her side, in a varnished top hat, just showed the pink palms of his hands and shook his head. "Missus, she's strong-willed, she sure is, Mr. Starkweather."

"Damn if she isn't." He grinned and shook his head, too.

"Climb in," said Amy, "and I'll let *you* hold the reins if you promise to be careful."

He took it all cheerfully. "That's Amy."

She insisted, "No, that's being Irish."

Howard said, "No. The Irish believe that but they're no different from anyone else, unless it comes to whiskey and politics."

"For saying that, Howard, you can't drive my birthday gifts." From then on she often picked him up at the bank, the bays— named Pat and Mike (by Howard)—the envy of the Street.

Howard still retained a friendship with the speculators and sharpshooters he had known when he and McCann had first opened their bank in New York. But it was not a relationship he pressed—for he did not feel the future of his bank lay with the sharp methods and often the dishonesty that had prevailed during the war. The Street was still a jungle of shady operators, creators of wild schemes. But Howard Starkweather, like the Belmonts, Jay Cooke (not Gould), J. P. Morgan, felt there was more to be made by some sort of ethics. By having values that inspired trust from clients over a period of time. As he explained to Chauncey Wilcox while they inspected a new steel vault, "It isn't Old Testament morality here on the Street—that Jehovah is coming down to knock

143

me on the head—or any fear of sinning and being sent to Hell. It's just common sense to stay within the law, cut sharp corners sure, but protect the client all the time. . . . What do you think of this vault?"

"Looks solid. But a good box man could crack it, given time. Lots of time."

"Go soak your head. It's impressive. It looks trustworthy. You're to be assistant to the head cashier from now on."

Chauncey rubbed his upper lip, where he was trying for a sign of a mustache. "I'll be cashier within a year. I'm more cheerful a coot than old Bronson, and I can count and add a stack of bills faster."

"Ah, but Sam Bronson, he *looks* more solid. Chaunce, tone down your shirts, and less piping on your frock coat. Confidence is all a bank really has up front."

This young man, Howard thought, is all that is left of my early life. There were no more relatives left alive up in New England, all sleeping on rocky slopes among old slanting grave stones. I had in a way raised Chauncey from a cabin boy called Blacky—hungry, thin, and ready to bite the world—brought him along to a promising clever young man. Well mannered, even if aggressive. Honest; there had been many opportunities to tap the till, fatten himself personally on some deal.

Howard felt he knew the fiber of this part-Indian, Lord-knows-what-else that was now part of his life. Amy had once said mockingly, "He's the son we can't ever have. A son to you, isn't he, now? Confess."

He tried to remain phlegmatic on the subject, hadn't taken neatly to that idea. "I never thought of bouncing him on my knee or hearing his prayers. He does his work, is loyal and, I think, honest."

"Bulldust," said Amy. "And I'm sorry we can't have a kid, honest."

Yes, he supposed deep down inside, throwing off his reluctance to admit it, yes, he did look on Chauncey as a kind of son, part of the family. It didn't do to think too much in that direction; life is rigged with expectations that never occur. There was the dismal fact there would not be any Starkweather heirs to take over H. H. Starkweather & Company when he was old or gone. So perhaps it would be Chauncey Wilcox who, say in sixty, fifty years, would be running it all, the whole shebang. Howard didn't like to think of old age; the contemplation was depressing. Death he thought of as

144

being damn vulgar, a rotten system, badly planned, preposterous, nasty at the end. Just when you were getting the hang of things and had maybe built up enough sense to know what was up, the big bang in the back of the head and darkness, the nothingness of forever.

He began to notice the children that often accompanied women who begged on the Street or passed out broadsides against the saloons, against the smoking of tobacco. Dowdy women usually, stern of face. Dragging some raddled child by the arm, croaking out some song, holding out their hands for a coin for "the cause."

> Oh! Can you not help these sinned-against children?
> Oh! Should they be left to drift with the tide?
> Innocent, angel-faced rosebuds,
> 'Twere better they had in their babyhood died.
> Arouse ye, arouse ye, men of this nation!
> Vote down the vile saloons which ruin the young!

The antisaloon singer who worked the Street usually had two small pale children with her; the boy with a damp nose, a smeared face, the girl scuffing her worn square-toed shoes on the walk, head down as if ashamed of her mother's fanatic ways.

> The wide-open doors of saloons and low houses
> Waiting to greet them wherever I turned;
> At the bars and at wine tables sitting,
> The fallen of earth who purity spurned.
> Ah, sad! Yes, so sad is the dark recollection
> Of days of my youth in this Sodom of sin.

"How old are they?" he asked the woman one morning.

"Malvina is seven, Arnold is five. Their father lies in a drunkard's grave. Will you support our cause?"

He patted the boy on the head and gave each of the children a silver dollar and a five-dollar gold coin to the woman. "Get them some good hot food."

"You've children of your own? Do you want them to become the victims of the vile distilleries?"

"No. Not just yet."

That winter the three of them disappeared and he wondered as to their fate.

145

20

Howard was surprised to discover in himself such a large regret that he would father no children. And also how much in love he was with Amy. It had increased emotionally year by year. And all for *what?* If he, they, left no family? From his sea reading he recalled a line of John Donne's, "We are all prisoners going to the place of execution." Not a very cheerful thought. And to leave nothing of your own flesh behind. He could, of course, try to impregnate one of Josie Mansfield's friends. Raise himself up a bastard, but—it wasn't an infallible moral sense—he just didn't care anymore for the life of the Fisk circle, their mental coarseness; the cheap women; ribald, faithless, drinkers usually. Gesticulating, frivolous females *and* greedy. Blackmailers, the whole damn lot. He was happy he and Amy were done with them. Had somehow escaped.

Howard still felt an affection for Jim Fisk; a public figure, now more colorful in dress, louder, with a taller silk hat. Deeper voiced when ordering food and wine from restaurateur or hotelier. Still in love with Josie Mansfield.

"Well, devoting oneself to a long-drawn love affair is like coloring a meerschaum pipe. It passes the time . . ." as McCann put it.

It was a week after Amy's birthday dinner that a varnished brown-and-gold open carriage pulled up before Starkweather & Company, a carriage of gold trim, with horse gear of silver. A coat of arms of some sort was large on the carriage door. And Jim Fisk, Jr., himself, smiling and a bit larger than life, got out and entered the bank. He let Chauncey show him into Howard's office.

"Neat, neat, H.H.! Smells of money, and that's *better* than having it; just the odor attracts other money."

"I hope so, Jim, railroad shares aren't moving as well as I'd like."

"Dani'l Drew, he knew how to make railroads cough up. 'Never keep 'em solvent, print shares'—that was Dani'l's secret. Sorry I missed Amy's birthday. But had to be in Washington." Jim put a forefinger to one side of his nose and winked. "All kinds of ramifications. Going to be big things stirring soon."

"Costs too much to do business with fat-cat politicians."

"Only if you don't make a lot out of it for yourself. See? You have to prime the damn pump. The mudsills and barefooted turnip eaters, once they get to Congress and are shod, want to fill their carpetbags in a hurry. Still. . . ." Jim looked around and turned to Howard, held out a large cigar case. "Jay and me, we've an idea simmering. Not on the boil yet. Warming up."

The two men lit up the heavy dark cigars and sat facing each other.

Through the partly closed wooden shutters the business of Wall Street went on. Messengers trotted by; a dray of lager beer barrels seemed out of place. Across the way a rubber-tired hack stopped and let out several well-fed men, top hats acock over their laughing faces; most likely overfed, well liquored, too, from a lunch at the Bankers and Brokers Club.

Jim leaned forward, the cigar held steady by his strong front teeth, his voice kept down. "Now, H.H., this is all hush-hush—I trust you. We're thinking of a dance on the gold-market floor. We need some extra brokers to be buying for us on the q.t. Know what I mean? Take our orders, fill them, and keep mum. Might run the gold market up to a hundred and seventy-five. Even two hundred among the speculators. Yes."

"Gold at two hundred! Jim, you're daft."

Jim sat in a massive mock solemnity, then smiled, waved his cigar in the air, scattering ash on the maroon rug. "Don't say it so loud. Set you back on your heels, eh?"

"You have my confidence, Jim. But you're shooting at the moon."

"Don't but me no buts, H.H. Will you handle some of our buying orders?"

"When will you start?"

"Depends, depends, good friend. You can see we need a coherence, a mighty good cooperation in Washington, and—"

"Don't tell me, Jim. Just when you're ready—you and Jay—I'll start buying gold in lots you want. . . . How is Josie?"

"Flourishing. Say, she just said last night we don't see Amy and Howard much anymore. She's fine, a bit bigger and a lot sassier." The large man put his cigar into a silver ashtray on Howard's desk. "How much do you trust women? 'Fess up. Tell old Jim."

"Some, *yes*, some, *no*."

"I'd die for Josie. She is true blue. Everything just peachy."

"Then why are you worried?"

"Oh, not worried. Just so many fancy dudes around. Deep down she's really, believe me, a simple farm girl."

Howard puffed on his cigar. Josie was as complicated as a Swiss

147

watch, and she hadn't been near a farm—if she ever had been—
"since Christ was a cowboy," as they used to say during the war.
Still, every man has his weakness—some romantic imbecility hid-
den in him—and Howard smiled at Jim. "You've been very good to
Josie."

They talked of trade, shares, scurrilous gossip, promises of getting together with their ladies for an evening of "painting the town
red." As Jim Fisk left, a crowd of messenger boys, peanut peddlers,
loafers cheered him when he entered his open carriage. He stood
there, tossing out coins, before the coachman touched up the
horses.

Howard sat in his office and wondered how Jim's destiny would
work itself out. He was certainly the rootin,' tootin' rouser he
claimed to be; who had come from his Delilahs and Jezebels to a
final love—in Josie.

Jim was no shrinking violet. His monogram placed on everything
he owned or was connected with; he had lived in the full gaze of the
public. Scarcely had any private life. The whole town was talking of
his theater, his dashing four-in-hand, his holdings in railways and
steamboats. Even his private regiment, his toilettes, and his reckless
generosity. As for his influence on the community. Bad, Howard
decided. He had not only admirers, but imitators. These were out
to reproduce his bad qualities, not his virtues.

I like him, Howard thought. He isn't moralistic or parsimonious.
But he's wrong for me and what I want. Now, this gold scheme.
What have I let myself in for? Acting as one of his and Gould's
agents? Jim would never involve me too deeply in anything against
the law, knowingly. That's the catch; Jim, he's getting blind to reality. The Gold Room at the Exchange—could it be manipulated?
Have to seriously think this out. How can I refuse? And the business—H. H. Starkweather & Company needs it.

In the next few days it became clearer Jim and Jay's idea to lift
gold prices wasn't as secret as they felt. There were rumors and
gossip floating around the Street, deceit and credulity mixed; talk
about an undersea cable to Europe, a tunnel from Dover to France,
a canal to be dug across Panama. Scatterbrain schemes of this sort
were talked of and what could be gotten on the market out of them
for floating shares in these projects.

There were a group of young sparks, customer's men, junior
partners, middle-aged brokers and bankers (who like to feel

young), and these gathered Friday afternoons at Ott's Inn—after the market closed—to drink and sing. Howard often attended, even J. P. Morgan, if not off with a mistress on a yacht or in his private railroad car to attend some Presbyterian church meeting. Morgan was a solid man in his thirties, a few years older than Howard. A fastidious voluminous presence. His nose already enlarged and showing the first signs of its disease, like a ruddy sea anemone. Serious in gray and a square tan bowler, he motioned Howard over to his table while, by the fireplace, a group of young brokers were singing over steins of beer:

> Oh, Lil she was a famous beauty.
> She lived in a house of ill reputey.
> Menfolk came from miles around
> Just to see Lil in her low-cut gown. . . .
> Lil, boom-dee-ah-dah, dee-ah-dah-doo-day!

"You enjoy these things, Starkweather?"
"Once a week, why not?"
"The beer isn't bad. Ever had English ale?"
"In Liverpool, when I was a sailor."

> Now, clothes may make a girl go far
> But they have no place on a fille de jour.
> Oh, Lillian's troubles started when
> She concealed her abdomen.

> Lillian went to the house physician;
> He prescribed for her condition:
> "Madam, you have what the doctors say
> Is per-ni-shee-us a-nee-mee-ay."

"You must come out on a little boat I own. . . . There's talk those pirates, Fisk and Gould, have their eyes on the price of gold."
"I've heard rumors. The Street lives on and eats rumors, doesn't it?"
"They're testing the wind, Starkweather. They're fools, Gould, Fisk, if they think they can play with the Gold Room and not get burned."
"How much gold is there really in the United States?"
Morgan banged on the tabletop. "Free gold? Who the hell really

149

knows? What's under lock and key in the U.S. Treasury is off the market. Frankly, I know you have some sort of friendship with Fisk. I'm not being critical of you or your friends. But warn them they could be playing into a panic, a national panic."

> Lillian underwent baptism;
> She adopted mysticism;
> And every night she went to sleep
> She prayed the Lord her soul to keep.

Howard permitted himself a lopsided smile. "You have the welfare of the nation in mind, Morgan?"

Morgan laughed. For a young man he had a deep mature laugh. "Have any of us a loyalty beyond that to our own interests, to our firms, our country? Yes, that, too. I see it as being a bit of both. Firm and country. Those damn Jews, the Rothschilds. Oh, I'm not against Jews, they're often full of Old Testament morality; the Rothschilds do have this idea that they're Englishmen and Frenchmen first. Before being bankers. But somehow the shekels roll in. Ever notice the small irrelevances that spoil enormous meanings?"

"They have to prove themselves as citizens—the Rothschilds—we don't."

"Yes. . . . You like dogs?"

"If they're friendly."

"I've been breeding dachshunds. Let me send you one."

"Why, thanks, Morgan. Amy, Mrs. Starkweather, that is, would, I'm sure, enjoy a good house dog."

There was an invigorating calmness about the big wide man, a cool audacity even, if one got close, a joviality (and he was warning Howard off, out of a liking for him). Howard decided he'd make damn sure Fisk wasn't using him as a cat's paw.

> One night as she lay in her dishonor,
> She felt the Devil's hand upon her.
> She said, "My sins I now repents,
> But, Satan, it'll cost you fifty cents."

All the way driving home, he thought, I have to develop that inner stability J. P. Morgan has. That observant eye, the intuitive mind. An almost demoniacal possession that *thinks* like money.

150

He found Amy ordering the servants in the hall to setting out Chinese pots of growing oleanders, azaleas, and zamias.

"I want growing things in the house. Even if my mother always said they used up the air and killed people. I don't believe it."

Howard said neither did he.

21

"Oh, I don't mind his playing king rooster; it's the crowd he runs with it."

"I used to like it—you did, too. We had no qualms about a good old wild time."

"That was years ago, Amy."

His wife turned her back to him. "Button me up." It was a tight chiffon gown with much gold lace and puffed-out shoulders. Howard, in evening clothes—he always dressed too early—set his fingers to the task assigned to him. "We've changed somewhat."

"I don't feel I have, honey. Oh, I've added to my life a lot of furniture and more horses in the stable. But I like a bit of fun, a laugh, and the wine flowing. So do you, Mr. H. H. Starkweather, me lad. I don't cotton too much to the Belmont dinners or the Wall Street ladies' fancy garden parties. La-di-da and 'Milk or lemon, my dear-ah?' "

"All right, all right. We're going to Jim's theater tonight and out for lobsters and wine later. But not too often. Remember the nuns in the convent—the lessons in dignity and austerity."

"Oh, stop reminding me. . . . Josie's tailor is making me a driving outfit. The color matches the bays. It has a little top hat. . . ." She looked around at Howard and came to his arms. "Oh, Howard, I do make you happy, don't I?"

He said she certainly did, and yet he knew she did not feel fully satisfied with their life. Marriage was a precarious universe. And the bank was still a risky, shaky thing. Perhaps he should have gone to Pittsburgh with Donald McCann and made steel and iron.

It was a fine evening at the theater; loud music, a plot of sexual treacheries, and a funny drunk. Jim and Josie already a bit gay with

151

something stronger than wine; Josie, all in red, took to tickling Howard and Jim with her feathered fan.

At the lobster palace on Thirty-fourth Street they were greeted by music from Hungarians in red coats behind potted palms. Jim took bows and shook hands, and there was a maître d', also the owner himself, two waiters all ready to serve them.

Josie removed a half yard of glove. "Oh, Jimmy—for me order just a big porterhouse steak, lots of onions, and I'll start with a dozen bluepoints, very cold." She turned to Amy. "Listen to *this*." She smiled at the nearest waiter. "*Garçon, une bouteille de champagne.*"

"Been taking lessons," said Jim. "Make it *two* dozen bluepoints for me. And nothing under a six-pound lobster. Now, Howie, how about a good slice of roast beef to go with it?"

Josie adjusted her bottom, shoulders, and lace boa in the chair. "You stay so thin, Amy. I'm getting so if I eat an olive, it puts on a pound. Jim says he likes me this way—says it's his Turkish blood."

"You're looking just grand, Josie. Are those earrings new?"

"Jim is generous. How do you like keeping house?"

There was the popping of corks, the pouring of a taste for Jim to tongue and swish.

Amy wrinkled her nose as she sipped champagne. "Howard got these two marvelous bays for my birthday—didn't you, honey?—and. . . ."

The oysters came chilled on ice, done up with parsley, and surrounded by dishes of spiced colored sauces. Jim picked up an oyster on the half shell, poured some red mixture on it, lifted it high, and with a cheerful slurp swallowed. "You have to use the shell for carrying it. No fork, or you don't get the juice."

That night, undressing for bed, Howard stood winding his watch.

"I think Josie has settled down."

"Settled in, maybe. She's as bodacious like always. Why does Jim keep talking low to you and so serious, too? It's not like Jim. I mean, he's always joshing and teasing."

Howard pulled off his shoes, took out his collar stud.

"Oh, just some business he's involved in."

No use explaining too much. Amy was a wife who was not much interested in his business affairs, and she never did understand the intricate matters of stocks, bonds, shares, who were the bulls, the

152

bears, what was bucket shopping, selling short, and floating an issue. Howard didn't mind. "Truth is, Jim feels the folk from the city street, country, and Reubens from the farms all invest in what we offer. And they don't know much more about how it works than you do."

Amy was stepping out of her petticoats, one hand on the bedpost.

"Do you, dear?"

"There are times I wonder myself." He scratched his stomach and felt overfed and the alcohol flowing in his blood system.

"Imagine Josie—all that French."

"I've heard real French; her accent is blah."

At the end of the week Donald McCann came to New York. He had changed in five years since their partnership had ended, and Howard didn't know if for the better. He had widened; his beard covered more of his face and was frosted in places. His clothes were baggier, his collars higher, his cravats surprisingly gayer, as if heralding an opulent vibrancy.

Seated in Howard's library—Amy that morning had left, driving her bays to a church charity in Nyack—the two men were sipping a scotch that McCann was importing now by the case, and he had brought a dozen quarts along for the Starkweathers.

"This talk of a gold raid is nonsense. 'As the generation of leaves, so is that of men.' It can't be done. No, H.H., you stick to the railroads. It's you or that young Morgan galoot that are going to consolidate them one day soon into something worthy of the markets available."

"We have too many rail lines going bankrupt or not paying their dividends."

"Doesn't matter, laddie, not at all, opens up a chain of possibilities. It's a growing country; the red hostiles of the plains are being starved out or lynched in good Christian grace. Land opening up to wheat from horizon to horizon. Be not enough rails soon to carry the harvest to market, the steers to the packing plants. The future needs steel. I'm buying up ore land all along Lake Superior and going to have my ore boats, steamers carry it to the coke plant at Sandusky. Forget the gold idea. It's like cornering the market in snowflakes."

"It's an amazingly bold idea, Donald. I don't trust Gould, but Jim, well, he's kind of raised me from a pup."

153

"Let me tell you of James Fisk, Jr., a subaqueous roaring boy."

"Never made him out," Howard admitted.

"I've known James from the day he peddled tinware, needles, and—H.H., I think we could get a wee bit drunk."

"And that's a great deal for you to admit, Donald."

"Just the wee heel of the bottle. Hold yer glass up. Jim, now, makes a lot and needs a lot and so—"

There were voices outside on the avenue, and the clatter of horses in estrangement, as if rearing and someone trying to soothe them, and also cursing. Howard rose, looked out of the window, pulling aside the pale blue silk drapes.

"It's the bays."

At the curb were the phaeton with the two bays; one of the horses, Howard noticed, was bleeding at the shoulder. A big strange man, almost a giant, continued pulling on the check reins trying to hold the steeds steady while Nimrod and a helmeted policeman were lifting—like a valuable rug—Amy from the seat of the rig.

"It's Amy. She's had an accident with those goddamn horses."

Howard ran into the hall; there the maid was already opening the door and the large stranger, Nimrod, and the police officer, all three, were carrying Amy up the steps and into the house. Howard motioned. "In the parlor on the sofa. What the devil happened?"

He took one of her gloved hands, and as the men carried her, he saw one of her cheeks was badly bruised. A thin streak of very red blood was flowing from a corner of her mouth. It wasn't, he hoped, a hemorrhage.

Howard yelled for the maid to rush around the corner and get Dr. Millstein. "Drag him if you have to."

On the sofa Amy moaned but did not open her eyes. Donald McCann came in carrying a glass of scotch and he held it to her lips. But she did not swallow any. Carefully Howard wiped the blood away; the thin flow continued. He kept asking, glaring over his shoulder, "What happened?"

The big stranger said, "It was over round Thirty-fourth and the avenue; the lady was handlin' them critters well, but the horses were frisky and this tallyho coach four-in-hand comin' by the other way, going downtown."

Amy moaned, rolled her head about, the apple-yellow silk of the sofa staining, the heels of her small tan boots kicking about.

"And they were trottin' along. The horn and then the dogs turning on the lady's horses, nipping at their heels, upset the lady's team."

McCann got some of the whiskey down Amy's throat. She choked, coughed, and opened her eyes, focusing in turn on the faces around her. She seemed to make nothing much of the scene.

"The lady's horses ran away, hit a delivery van of Teller's Bazaar." The large man enjoying the interest in his story. "And the rig turned over and she was flung out. But she got up, cursin', floggin' the dogs with her whip. We got the rig set up again, and the lady, she said she lived up the avenue, and I figured I'd just come along to hold the horses' heads. They were skittish and rearing and—"

The doctor—a neighborhood stranger—came in buttoning his waistcoat, and he seemed to be chewing part of a meal at which he had been interrupted. He had a rheumy eye and a long chin. "Yes, yes, please step aside."

"She sorta passed out cold when we wuz a block away from the house. And begun bleedin' all over the traveling rug, so—"

"Thank you," said Howard, taking the large man by the arm. "Thank you."

"Sure—Mike."

The doctor, kneeling by the sofa, was adjusting a pair of gold-framed spectacles over his watery eyes. "Please leave us alone and send for her maid. . . ."

Howard was the last to leave the parlor and he looked down at Amy's face, very pale, her eyes now large and coming into focus. He heard her give a great gasp and cry out in some sound that didn't seem a word; he quickly closed the double doors. The hall seemed filled with the hush of desolation; McCann, two maids, Zeeland, the butler.

A half hour later Howard was standing by the library fireplace listening intensely to the doctor, who was holding a glass of the whiskey McCann had poured for him, but which he had not yet tasted.

"The blood, Mr. Starkweather, is from the lungs. I'm not yet sure which one."

"But it can't be consumption. I mean," Howard said, "her doctor, Welton Hawley, was sure that—"

"A very good man, Dr. Hawley," said Dr. Millstein, in ethical complacency, adding, "in *his* field."

"He felt she was delicate. There wasn't any coughing up of blood before."

"No, well. . . ." The doctor sipped his drink, held it out to McCann as if to agree it was certainly a splendid batch. "In some cases a kind of sack forms around the infected spot in the lung— keeps the consumptive matter encased, as it were. Then, regrettably, like today, some shock, blow, injury, and it bursts, and there you are, Mr. Starkweather."

"How serious is it?"

"Oh, very, I'd say, from what examination I've made. There are no conditions here for any prolonged taking of all symptoms. I would have some specialist in and various tests made. This German chap—Koch?—has done a lot of writing on lung infections, interesting papers and—"

"There's no danger to her life?"

"We don't know too much about what is called a dormant or arrest stage and what is termed galloping consumption. Why one case can last a lifetime, to a mature age anyway, and another. . . ." He shrugged, baffled. "I must be getting back; I have my patients' hours about now. I'll stop back later, and you call in your own medical man, Dr. Hawley, yes, a good man in his field. Best to have a consultation set up. Good day. . . . Thank you for the drink—no, really, no gift of a bottle. My wife, she is a teetotaler. Yes."

After the doctor had gone, Howard stared at McCann. *"Jesus!"*

"It's a shocker, H.H. And there's no real answer for it preying on people and the why of it."

There was a clatter of heels on waxed floors and Chauncey came in, hat in hand, eyes very wide, his face showing his worry. An expression very wrong for an Indian, Howard thought, or even a part Indian. Chauncey said, "I'm going down to the icehouse on Eighth Avenue. The doctor said to keep a lot of ice handy in case, well, it's hard to stop the bleeding."

Howard said, "Yes, ice."

22

Howard had no doubt that Amy's illness would be treated, the hemorrhaging stopped, and she would be cured. He believed in science, in progress, and if he were pushed far enough, he still, at that period, would admit maybe he believed in prayer. Amy herself, in a pink moiré dressing gown, did not look a consumptive—as the lung-illness victim was termed—she resting in the big bed. She insisted it was the cigars, cigarettes that caused her illness—for she and Josie Mansfield had once been heavy-smoking friends.

"The doctor is still not sure."

"Jim's cigars are very strong."

"Yes, maybe." Howard had a morning newspaper under his arm and had just come up from breakfast after studying the morning news and the shipping and market reports. "Well, whatever it is caused by, Dr. Hawley insists on you just resting. Not getting off your bottom in that bed for two months at least."

"And *then?*" There was fear in her eerie incomprehensible stare, as if asking for an explanation of this curse on her.

"Then he thinks you'll be able to do all the things you've always done."

"You'll not sell the horses? They're so—"

"No, no. Be like selling children." He leaned over and kissed her cheek. She smelled feverish, her damp brow warm, too warm, and the blue veins under her skin seemed bluer but for the two rosy spots on her cheeks, like signals of vulnerability, areas that seemed as if painted on by theater makeup.

If I hadn't had such faith in science and modern medicine, he thought, I would have to think she is in bad shape, thinner, weaker, and coughing with a more diabolical sound. He had moved into the small room next door, slept on a cot there, and in the night heard the hacking cough. He came to her several times before each dawn to have Amy drink some barley water. Dr. Hawley had warned him she might bring up blood, and if it was a prolonged discharge, to send for him at once. "And give her some laudanum drops."

McCann, on a visit, insisted that in Scotland people with the consumption were cured, "if not cured, their lives prolonged by going to a slaughterhouse, and when a good healthy steer had its throat cut, the sick person drinks a glass of warm animal blood."

But Howard couldn't see Amy driving up to an Eighth Avenue slaughterhouse and asking for "a pint of your best steer blood, warm."

"No, Donald, it's too ghastly an idea."

"Aye, we eat the animal cooked, but refuse him raw."

* * *

157

Howard tried to cut down on his hours at Starkweather & Company so as to be with Amy a great deal of the time. But there was suddenly an upturn on the Street, a place of small gratitudes and large hostilities. He was acting more and more as an agent for Gould and Fisk, and he had come around to a personal code of business conduct; if it broke no laws, he'd be an agent for them, handle their accounts. If not, he would make it plain to them the honor of his house meant a great deal to him. He didn't write it down that way—it sounded too fancy. Often our actions, he knew, are the sport of forces outside ourselves.

Gould and Fisk had their own brokerage house and other connections who handled parts of their effort. So perhaps they gave their shadier business elsewhere. Gould and Fisk were certainly becoming the talk of the Street, and Jim of the town, even more than before.

Howard told Amy, amusing her, watching her drink her warm-milk nightcap, "They have a real gift—corruptible conscience."

"So has Josie—she's seeing a man named Stokes, a Philadelphia dandy."

Fisk and Gould as partners had expanded into real estate. They owned the Opera House in New York Place on West Twelfth Street. Fisk was managing the place and was a solid theater buff, displaying himself to actors, actresses with large diamonds and a crimson silk cape. He lived behind the theater in a big overelaborate house and enjoyed the high life of the stage. Josie lived nearby and grew plumper and began to save her letters from Jim. Fisk ordered resplendent uniforms as a colonel of militia, and Howard and New York enjoyed the sight of Jim, with Josie and some actresses, seated in his open carriage behind a pair of spanking, smart trotting horses rolling through Central Park.

Howard saw Fisk as more than a flashy stage-door Johnny, cunning as ever. With Gould he was moving into the control of coal mines, harbor leases, ferryboats, and always railroads.

"Stick with Jim, my boy, you'll wear diamonds in your nose."

"A cravat pin, Jim, will do," Howard said.

"And I hope Amy, she's getting along. Damn it—it's really cruel how we can love one woman and suffer for it."

Jim Fisk, Howard saw, was very much in love. He had set up an iron gateway to Pike's Opera House with his and Josie's initials on it ("Nuzzling each other," Chauncey said). Fisk's office in the theater was of black walnut, Italian marble. The colors were mostly gold and scarlet and everything that could be fringed, tasseled, and ribboned was. Howard inspected the art; rather hefty erotic figures of bronze.

"Out of Greek legend, Howie, supposed to be fauns and wood nymphs having a time for themselves in the woods, and flower gardens. Let me give you a couple of statues."

"No thanks, Jim—make me too horny."

Jim owned over a dozen fine black-and-white horses, a phaeton, a barouche. "Four tallyho coaches, even my own sleigh, and a couple of glass-enclosed carriages." Jim Fisk took delight in driving through the park in one of his collection of wheels, often with Howard—sometimes with actresses—at his side. Jim Fisk usually in his uniform of a colonel ("A rank I bought") in the 9th Regiment of the New York National Guard.

"He's a sight," Howard told Amy, "like Barnum's whole show all by himself."

"I wish I could go on the rides."

As the heat of the summer percolated the city, indoors in Jim Fisk's office cakes of ice floated in basins in the *opéra bouffe* setting. A breeze from the river seemed to give the impression, Howard thought, of coolness without actually lowering the temperature. Jay Gould, small, serious, sat facing Jim and Howard. Fisk, with jacket and waistcoat undone, was fanning himself with a Japanese paper fan showing a mountain with a snow-topped peak.

Gould spoke in serene complacency. "You'll do well out of this, Starkweather. We're beginning to seriously make a move."

Howard said, "Gold is also on the mind of J. P. Morgan. Not just, he feels, its value as money, as credits in ledgers, there's the actual metal itself. Frankly, thinking of the gold bars in the U.S. Treasury, the whole national economy rested in that gold reserve."

Jim fanned himself, smiled. "We've been studying the Gold Room of the New York Stock Exchange. *That* institution controls the dealings in the floating supply of gold. Yes? Yes. Get it; you cornering the nation's currency."

Howard said, "The U.S. Treasury holdings in gold are about eighty million dollars of the yellow metal."

Jim nodded. "Yep. This *must* be kept out of the market if we are to capture all the free gold. We have to be sure the Treasury gold will not be thrown into the Gold Room of the Stock Exchange."

159

"You can't be sure."

Gould gave one of his rare smiles.

Jim dipped his hands into a basin of ice water. "Ah, when gold goes up, up and our fortunes with it—controlling the inflated price. The sky's the limit, Howie."

Howard felt a return of his old heat rash. "The major problem, gents, is to be sure President Grant will not move the nation's gold from its vaults to normalize the market."

Gould nodded. "You're friendly, Jim says, with the President's son-in-law, Corbin?"

Jim said, "Sure he is."

Howard picked up a bit of ice in a basin by his side, sucked it. "He's a cold fish, Abel Corbin."

Jay almost smiled again into his tangle of beard. "But a damn greedy one. Wishes he had four hands to grab things."

Jim went to the bay window and tried to open a section farther. But it was as open as it could be. The heat burned the defenseless streets. Jim leaned out into the hot night air. "Fill Howie in, Jay. He's got a good level head on him. He'll see if we have overlooked anything."

Jay Gould pressed the palms of his hands together. He had not removed his cravat or opened his high choker collar, taken off his frock coat. Yet he seemed cool and comfortable, even overfastidious.

"President Grant has demanding relatives. This son-in-law, Corbin, a wobbly speculator, actually is a front for some special people like us. We've given Corbin credit up to fifteen thousand dollars of gold for himself. Not telling him all just yet."

Howard didn't say anything for several moments. Then he looked up at Jay Gould. "As your agent, of course."

"Yes."

Howard wondered if it was a lie. Corbin was greedy and weak. But take a bribe? To pressure the President not to release the U.S. Treasury gold? Howard doubted that Grant was venal. Like so many people, Howard had admired General Grant and despaired of President Grant. But still the man was honest, had integrity, for all his ambiguity and that inscrutable face behind the cigar.

Jim was back from the window mopping his neck and face with a yellow silk handkerchief. Gould remained in his anchored serenity.

Jim smiled. "Our agents are active in Washington, explaining to the Senators and Congressmen that a rise in the value of gold on the open market will help the farmer, aid in his grain sales in Europe. Trade will jump forward. Gold prices must go up. Result: national prosperity. 'Go bullish on gold' is the message."

Howard frowned. "There's another Jay active on Wall Street, Jay Cooke and Company. This Jay is bearish on gold. He's out to lower the price of gold, he told me."

"Sure," said Fisk. "The bastard handles paper money, legal tender, government bonds. They been buying and selling goddamn millions of dollars' worth of paper, making fortunes from the goddamn inflated currency. Some big firms are allied to the Jay Cooke side. Oh, hell yes, enjoying the business in the rise of paper money. Well, we'll take *them* down a tack or two."

Howard left with some small buying orders in gold. "To test the air, Howie."

It was two in the morning when the hired rubber-tired hack that he had standing by drove Howard uptown. People were sleeping on fire escapes or sitting in a torpor on stoops in the night heat. All his long career as a banker Howard Starkweather was to believe in the gold standard, of the refined metal gold as the basic foundation ·of the nation's lifeblood. . . . That hot, humid night he decided that ·the rise in the price of gold would help the farmer, the merchant. What if it made money for some of the people on the Street? Like himself. That was to the good. He had never trusted the paper money or the dealings in other currencies, not too far. Starkweather & Company was very careful in its dealings in paper. Paper could be like a transient stranger who stole your watch.

Gold. He remembered, as the hack rolled north, a sermon from his boyhood in the clapboard church near the shipyard where he drove divits into hulls, his hands freezing in his mittens; the lanky preacher with a ring of brown chin whiskers shouting, *"Gold goes in at every gate except Heaven's."*

Some people never understood gold as lifeblood. Not even those bastards in the West, in their perverse behavior—wanting a currency of free silver. George Hearst, Horace Tabor, all those nabobs of Virginia City and their fortunes in silver. The hack crossed Fourteenth Street, deserted but for several drunken men and women who seemed in the heated night air to be howling at the moon. He'd go into gold himself for the firm, talk to McCann. It would be risky. But Gould and Fisk wouldn't have moved if they didn't have a plan they felt could keep the U.S. Treasury gold in its vaults. And he, Howard Starkweather, was helpful in their way to it. Through Abel Corbin.

The lamps were lit up all over his house as the hack came up to the hitching post and marble stepping block lettered STARKWEATHER. For a moment he had a vision of Amy stretched out pale and dead, and he flung some silver dollars at the hackie and ran up the steps into the house. Chauncey Wilcox met him.

"She began bleeding right after supper. But the doctor has stopped it."

"Why the hell didn't you send for me?"

"You didn't tell anyone where you'd be."

This was true. For some good practical reasons he had been secretive about his meeting, that late-night meeting with Gould and Fisk. He ran up the carpeted steps—and he had another vision of Amy coming down these very steps on her birthday. So fine-looking, so beautiful and happy. So alive, so gregarious, a felicitous hostess. *Happy?* It seemed the word had left this house.

Amy was propped up high on pillows; Nina, her maid, sitting by the bed, placed a damp cloth dipped in ice water on Amy's brow. The maid looked up at Howard and held a finger to her lips.

Amy was asleep, rather sunk in some drugged oblivion. She certainly looked drugged, and but for the flame spots on her cheekbones, she was paler than he had ever seen her.

The maid whispered, "The doctor gave her something to make her sleep. She isn't coughing up any more blood."

"Thank God, Nina."

He sat the rest of the night at his wife's bedside.

23

The June sun turned the surface of the Great South Bay in its gyrations to flickering silver coins. *Everything* is reminding us of money, thought Howard as the yacht moved away from the Long Island shore and the sky overhead was a blue so intense it seemed like a painting of a theater backdrop. He had not wanted to come on this cruise with all these men, official faces and the exuberance of camp followers. But Jim had hinted. "Very important person, our guest of honor, *very* important event."

Important, sure as shooting. President Grant himself, visiting his daughter and son-in-law, the Corbins, had accepted this day of cruising on the water. There, Howard thought, he is, U. S. Grant, six years after Vicksburg, the butcher of the Wilderness battles that finished off Lee. Now a bit wider, his hair touched with gray and cut much shorter than in the Brady photographs one could buy on Broadway. Yes, the President seated in a hickory deck chair in the shade of the striped awning. Glass in hand (amber whiskey, prime Kentucky bourbon), listening to Jim Fisk, who was being very cheerful in a coarse amusing way, while the other half-dozen guests tried, on the slightly tilting deck, to look as if born to the sea. Good thing the sea was calm, Howard thought, or it would toss these chowderheads off their feet onto their fat office-grown arses.

"You like sailing, Mr. President?" Fisk said.

A slow nod of the head upward. "Sometimes."

"How do you like the cigar?"

A nod. "Draws nicely."

Howard smiled. The President wasn't going to say much, and Jim could usually talk the devil out of his horns. All Grant really had to promise was that he wasn't going to release the government gold onto the market. Well, as McCann said, "No ducks fall from the sky fully roasted." That would take time. More whiskey, a few more cigars, a little confidential talk, perhaps below. With no pettifogging lawyers, speculators at the elbow.

Grant was reported as impressed by wealth, by show, and the easy way of the life of the rich. Jim had explained it was a world Grant had never entered before, and he was now a hero, too. The men with whom he was now surrounded in Washington and on this yacht lacked, Howard supposed, his hard values, his earnest efforts to keep to old tested standards. Look at the foxes and vultures on board. They were impressive, even at sea. A few in yachting caps, Gould in a silk top hat, some of well-fed proportions—clean-shaven, at least showing a well-curled mustache: Fisk had enlarged the ship's band and they began to toot away in the bow.

Yes, Howard thought, the President is feeling comfortable among all this well-being, smelling of money. And being entertained on Jim Fisk's yacht, the *Providence*—no actresses present of course, just good whiskey.

163

Jim Fisk, delighted to be entertaining the President, had put on his best uniform, set his ship's brass band to playing gay tunes (Grant had once said to Fisk, "I only know two tunes, one is 'Pop Goes the Weasel'; the other isn't").

So, yacht-borne, with bourbon glass in hand, cigar drawing well, Howard observed, Grant, the onetime business failure, army misfit, wood-kindling peddler, now pleased to be so intimate with the kings of the Street; stockbrokers, bankers, the nabobs that dealt in and made millions. Grant, it was clear, felt these people respected him for the wisdom, the skill (and butchery) with which he had managed to bring victory on so many battlefields.

Jay Gould now had his ear, hovering and whispering to the President as the yacht sailed on. Gould was explaining, Howard sensed, that the free ride of gold on an open market, to seek its own level, not hindered by the metal in the U.S. Treasury, was good for the country, the farmer, the merchant, the exporter.

Grant continued to sip whiskey and keep his cigar alight. The President said little. Fisk, his naval uniform unbuttoned, came up to Howard and winked.

"It's going just fine. Great little cruise."

"Jay didn't get any real promise from him?"

"Things don't work that way, H.H." Fisk made some finger gestures as if tracing a maze. "You go round, approach things from the blind side of the horse. Oh, it's clear he's seeing things our way. But he is the silent type. . . ."

Howard watched two boys in a yawl painted a pale blue tacking around them, both kids waving, and then the yawl heeling away as a breeze at a good slant for a tack caught them. "Too bad it's not to be in writing."

Fisk put an arm around Howard's shoulder. "Now, ain't you the josher? This isn't for the history-book Johnnies."

"Abel Corbin doesn't look too happy. And it's not seasickness."

"That son-in-law, he was born with that face and a wild hair up his ass. But we're filling his poke."

"What does Corbin say?"

"Grant had dinner at his house last night. He said it was a very jolly family scene."

"Yes, I'm sure, Jim. I mean about the gold."

Fisk made an O out of his mouth and exhaled cigar-smoke rings that the breeze broke apart at once. "Going as we expected."

164

There was an arabesque of movement in the water as a school of small fish passed. The ship's band was playing a Scottish tune, and two sailors were doing a hornpipe before Grant, who, expressionless, continued to sip and draw on his cigar. The sun was far to the west, a tarnished red ball sinking among the Long Island trees and shore ridges. Howard felt an inexhaustible calm in this dying day at sea.

Fisk adjusted his admiral's headgear and shouted up to the captain, "We can head back now."

"As you say, sir."

Fisk frowned, ludicrously solemn. "Tell me, H.H., aren't they supposed to say, 'Aye, aye'?"

"Not a rule of the sea. The British navy, however, rather expects it."

Gould was talking earnestly to Grant. The President had sunk lower in his deck chair and Howard noticed he had a nice color, the result of both sun *and* bourbon. His staff stood around or leaned on railings, rather apathetically.

Next morning Jim reported, "The President was very receptive to keeping the government out of the gold market." They were sipping coffee in the Hoffman House.

"You heard him say that?" Howard asked.

"The band was playing a bit loud, I admit, but Jay is cheerful this morning, and that fox, he doesn't smile much at anything. Why, he was actually laughing when he saw the Gold Room figures."

At five that afternoon Howard, driving home, saw the *Tribune* was calling Jay and Jim and his crowd of speculators the Goldbugs, hinting at something sinister in the making. But journalists were always writing things like this to sell their papers for a penny. Always printing suspected coups on the Street. Howard's mind was not entirely on the gold market. It seemed to him Amy was getting worse. Dr. Hawley had said everything in her chest was normal, heartbeat proper, pulse not bad. "Get her away to Saranac for the winter. Nice dry cold air. She'll be fine by spring. Women are delicate bits of machinery. Splendidly tuned, fine adjustments." Dr. Hawley was a bachelor, lived at the Yale Club. There was a sickroom smell in what had been their bedroom. It was now Amy's room, shared by Nina, her maid, who slept in the dressing room under a flickering night-light. There was also Clara, a large German nurse with many strong habits and a shelf of bosom. A deep voice that said *nein*

165

more than *ja*. She saw that Amy was fed, bathed, changed and assisted in her natural functions. Amy had developed a light sleep; like wild animals who awaken to a leaf dropping.

Howard had to leave hat and overcoat, cane and gloves outside the bedroom. "Der dust from outside *mit* the things in the air, they can hurt the lungs breathed in, *ja*."

Amy seemed all teeth and eyes, and her wrist, as he held it, was thin; he could feel the racing pulse like a watch's ticking.

"Wish I had been on the yacht with all you muckamucks. They have champagne and caviar?"

"Whiskey mostly, and a nice chowder."

"And girls?"

"The President doesn't stand for that sort of behavior. Jim has sense, at times."

"Have you seen the horses?"

"Every day. Chaunce is driving me these afternoons. Nimrod is getting a little creaky."

"I mean the bays."

"Yes, of course. He takes them out for a run round the park. Nimrod, he walks them in circles every morning to cool them off and gets them rubbed down."

"Don't let them get fat." Amy grabbed his hand; it was like being held by a fistful of fishbones. The dark rings under her eyes seemed to dominate her face. "Promise if anything happens to me, you'll never sell them to people who will mistreat them." She was no longer mischievous or given to tantrums.

"Crazy girl. Nothing is going to happen. We'll have a fine time this winter at Saranac. I've rented a lodge and we'll take the bays up and hitch them to a sleigh."

"Promise." She was tired, with completely desolate eyes.

"I promise we'll take them up by easy stages in a horse van."

"No, I mean you'll not sell them *if*. . . ."

"Don't be a damn fool, Amy."

She cried, and Frau Clara Klopfurtz said sternly, "You have been please upsetting the patient, *nein?*"

It was depressing. Howard had Chauncey move into the house and he learned to play whist and found he couldn't read for very long. Howard had a fairly good library. Some few books from his old sea chest and his youthful reading and a rather well-bound section of books he had bought at auction, liking the morocco bindings, the red and green leather, the gilt scrollwork on the spines. He reread Captain Ahab's chase of his fleeing goal. Such incredible persistence.

There was a volume by someone called Pascal, who had some sharp spiny things to say. "Man is neither angel nor brute, and his misery is that he who would act the angel, acts the brute." ✔

Such words were not very soothing. Howard would take a big nightcap of scotch and toss about a bit in a lonely bed and at last sleep, only to have dark dreams.

Chauncey Wilcox, as Starkweather & Company became more involved with the Gould-and-Fisk gold project, became the messenger between them and Howard. Chauncey was bright—had a look proclaiming privileged information. He kept his eyes and ears open and reported to Howard much more than the details Fisk sent over; Fisk hardly put anything in wrting. The talk about Goldbugs on the Street defeated any too-great interest in gold, at first.

Gold dropped to 125 in the Gold Room listing. Chaunce reported that Grant's son-in-law had a friend in the subtreasurer of the United States in New York, "who owes them favors. The gold lobbyists are active, feeding, badgering, and hinting at the rewards for favors to be done for all politicians who see things the Gould-Fisk way."

"Gold is still not going up."

"There's a big party—a real wingding—tomorrow night for Mr. Boutwell, Secretary of the Treasury. Mr. Gould is giving it."

"And he's coming, Boutwell?"

"He's accepted."

"Well, let's hear what he'll say in public." Howard was fully aware of the treacheries and misinformation of the Street.

"You're buying gold, H.H.?"

"Some, Chaunce. Just in case it goes as high as Gould claims."

"Going to the banquet? Barrels of lobsters coming down from Maine on ice. Also teal, mallard, prairie hens."

"No, I'm staying home with Amy. She's been coughing blood again."

"In the islands we cured everything with a sack of asafetida on a store string worn around the neck."

Chauncey reported in the morning on the Secretary of the Treasury, G. S. Boutwell. "He made it clear in his speech that the Treasury would keep hands off. He said, 'We would not heed the gold gamblers, and what is done on Wall Street is none of my business.'"

"I'm buying."

Gold rose to 133. Corbin, the President's son-in-law, as Chauncey reported, was handed by Gould a check for twenty-five thousand dollars as "profits."

In September Grant again was visiting the Corbins in their New York home. Things appeared to be going well. Corbin reported to Howard, "The President has ordered Secretary Boutwell to keep the U.S. Treasury gold off the market and keep it that way until the present struggle between bulls and bears is over."

"You've told Gould and Fisk?"

"Of course."

Gold went to 137. Howard bought and frowned. As a Gould-Fisk agent he bought for them in vast quantities.

The Street was like a battlefield, men jockeying for position. The Gold Room was always during business hours packed. Brokers and speculators releasing the strangest rumors. The dealings in gold dominated the market. One bought or wished one could. Many bought who couldn't afford to.

Donald McCann came to the city from Pittsburgh at Howard's urging, to get in on the gold market. Seated in Howard's office, legs crossed, showing elastic-sided shoes, woolen socks, he didn't seem impressed by Howard's inside information.

"It's all still blather. It's three months now since the talk started. It's now September and you really have no true evidence the President is involved in withholding gold. It's not Grant's style. He's a bit of a stick and humorless, not very sure of himself in polite society. But for him to make a privileged promise, with the humbuggery of these tricksters, ah, well, I have me doots."

"He may not be greedy himself. But his daughter, sons, they've got their hands out."

"It's still not the Grant that was at Appomattox."

Howard tapped his desk top with an ivory ruler. "*Nothing* is as it was at Appomattox Courthouse. You said so. It's other times. The full power of the age of steam, iron, steel, copper mining and river bridging, bigger ships to cross the seas. Markets for the natives—I quote you—'of the wild lands that need to be tamed and fed, to get a cloth to cover their arses.'"

168

"Whoa, Nellie," said McCann, slapping his thigh and laughing. "I sound that heady? And kilted in all those words? But to return to this gold raid. It isn't what I was talking about at all. It's still a world of caveat emptor."

"Gold is an item rising fast on the world's market."

"Just tell me for sure. Grant actually made such a promise? As Corbin reports to Gould and his goddamn Goldbug pool?"

"Yes, I believe some subtreasurer got a gift of a million five hundred in a gold account opened in his name. And others also had gifts dangled before their eyes."

"I'm sure."

"Gould told Jim Fisk that even Mrs. Grant was involved in gold speculation. The rumor of Mrs. Grant 'in gold' was sworn to by Fisk."

"Answer me, Howard. Did Grant?"

"I believe Grant made the promise. . . . Gold today is at one-forty-one. Buying?"

"Yes, and I'm jumping off feet first when I feel the whole scheme is going off the rails."

24

Howard was aware that the Tammany bank (the Tenth National) had loaned the Goldbugs nearly everything it had in resources, issuing certificate checks to buy gold "as if the checks were mere snowflakes." Fisk said the only collateral asked for was the gold they were buying.

Gould, Fisk, and the Goldbugs bought forty million dollars in gold for delivery, which Howard figured was actually about two times as much gold as was in existence on the free market.

Gold was at 144¼. Gould and his group had produced a major coup. So far.

Howard and McCann had made up a pool of their own. But McCann remained wary. He had developed a sarcastic conscience. . . . Taking the bays out for a run, Howard drove McCann up to Shad Point to show him the land he had bought. There was a threat of rain in the air, but it didn't fall. Howard cheerfully clucked to the horses. The animals needed the exercise since Amy could no longer take them out. The river was a spread of winking jade.

McCann wondered. "How far can Gould and Fisk take this thing with the imbecile gullible mob?"

"There isn't much more to take."

"All the gold floating free is under contract to deliver to them?"

"That's about it."

"Gold is gold. Free *or* in the national vaults; that's what worries me."

"The price rise is entirely justifiable—so far."

"It's a policy based on venal assumption."

"Well, it's a major coup. Gould has all the gold around, and he could demand payment in gold from those who had sold his gold, sold short and didn't really have it. Donald, it's a squeeze play of genius. *If* Grant stands, as he stood in the Battle of the Wilderness, solid, not moving back an inch in either direction."

"I think *we* should sell."

"Let's wait a bit."

The gold-shortage panic was building. The Goldbugs had all the gold, real and on call. For the nation to do business, produce, ship, import—gold was needed. On September 15, some newspapers began to suggest something was *very* wrong with the President and the people closest to him. Horace Greeley in the *Tribune* came out against "the huge conspiracy to corner gold" and demanded that the U.S. Treasury offer gold and gold bonds to ease the dangerous currency crisis. Howard heard that the other Jay, Jay Cooke, himself went to see Grant and Boutwell in Washington and laid out the whole Gould-Fisk scheme on the line.

Fisk just smiled. "We've put the screws on Grant's son-in-law to force him to earn his keep. We had him write a letter to the President, a real cry of anguish. Had him confess to Grant he was deeply involved and that the release of U.S. gold would not only ruin him, but the daughter and their friends, too."

"What will Grant do?"

"Save his family."

"Jim, we've been friends a long time. Do you trust Jay Gould?"

Jim twisted the ends of his mustache, laughed. "When I can keep my eye on him, and I can. What the hell, the Street is run on fallible human nature."

"Sure you can keep an eye on Gould?"

"He's too deep in to try to go stacking the deck on me. I'm a pretty wily cardplayer myself."

"I've gotten McCann into this. A bad turn in gold and he could lose his steel business."

Fisk tapped a diamond-wearing finger on the edge of Howard's desk and spoke very softly. "I don't have to keep an eye on you, do I, H.H.?"

"I'm placing orders for you and Gould. I will until you tell me to stop."

"Good, you and Amy, you'll be wearing jewels big as your nose."

They went to eat oysters at Ott's Inn. Howard always saw the world as a more cheerful place with Jim Fisk to talk to and share food with.

Thursday night Amy hemorrhaged badly and for a while was in a comatose state. It seemed, to Howard's horror, the flow of blood from that beloved mouth would never stop. There were three doctors and a nurse in attendance that night. Amy seemed to grow smaller, paler as she lay in the bed staring up at him, great fear in her eyes. Not permitted to speak, the trickle of blood being wiped from one corner of her mouth. He held her hand, feeling the race of her pulse, and then he was sent away.

He sat that night in the library, just one green-shaded lamp lit, hearing a church clock nearby strike two. The September air stirred a little the curtains, and he rose to close the windows, as if trying to keep out the world that was beyond the glass. He cut off the end of a cigar with a tiny gold clipper attached to his watch chain. A gift from Amy, that and several huge pipes and some English tobacco; but he didn't care for smoking pipes at that time, and he preferred Havana leaf to the Irish bogie mixed with Turkish from overseas.

Why was he thinking of tobacco with Amy near death? He didn't light the cigar, just rolled it between his fingers and was surprised to find he had crushed and fragmented it. As a sailor, a captain, the world was a chart perfectly Euclidean. But on land?

He started for the sickroom, but Dr. Hawley met him in the Venetian blue and gold of the hall. "No change, Starkweather, no change at all."

"Will she make it?"

The doctor suppressed a yawn. Hawley was a bit on the pompous side, but a kindly man if not dealing with fools—and he had been up since six that morning.

"She well may."

171

"What are her real chances?"

The doctor began to pull on a brown glove. "Starkweather, I want to be frank with you, I *must* be frank with you. Both lungs are affected. The right one, well. . . . " He made a gesture, gloved fingers wide apart. "That one is nearly gone. Yes."

"She going to die?" Associations of sensibilities were coming together in his chest, cutting off his breathing for a moment.

"We all are. Yes, your wife—sorry—she's going to die."

"Taking her away and—"

"It's beyond that. It's what some call galloping consumption. Regret that—"

"I'm sure you'll do your best."

"Of course. Must get some sleep. A full day ahead. I'll stop in around nine tonight. Oh, don't go to her, only accelerate her pulse . . . emotions are bad for her."

He saw the doctor to the door, his waiting carriage drive off, the horse hooves sounding like nails driven into his temples. He took another cigar and lighted this one. It tasted bitter and he let it burn in a silver ashtray, watching the ash grow longer, and the thoughts that came were of the good times and a blue vein on Amy's slim ankle.

It was at ten minutes past four that the nurse came down, expressionless, standing in front of him, her hands clasped together.

"*Ja, grüss Gott,* she is gone."

It didn't penetrate for a moment or two, and he picked up the cigar, carefully shook off the long ash, and replaced it in the tray.

"She's . . . Mrs. Starkweather is dead?"

The nurse nodded. And he was aware she was already the departed Mrs. Starkweather, not the living Amy anymore. There was a howl of anguish building up in his chest, expanding in his throat. But he didn't let the cry of agony emerge. He said simply, "I'll go see her."

"*Ja.*"

The windows in the sickroom were open; the illness-connected smell was almost gone. Some strange spicy odor filled the room. It was, he decided, the fresh linen on the bed, linen which Amy stored with dried lavender. That smell seemed to linger with him at some precarious emotional peak.

She lay so very small. Her eyes had been closed; she seemed to be

172

just dozing, her head on two pillows; a comb had been passed through her hair by someone else. She would not have approved, Howard felt; Amy never wore her hair like that—just combed back. He did not touch his dead wife. Just leaned over the bed, and he did not weep. But he was sick inside and he felt a crushing despair. Christ, the good things pass—like pickets on a fence. He would have to bear it, have to go on. But it seemed so futile and not at all like him, he thought. He had always been so aware of things— of his luck. Yes, one had to be lucky. But also one could master frailties, catastrophes. He was a man of his time. Believed—if luck held—he could control and direct his emotions in a great crisis. That he was master of his destiny. Even that he was a true stoic. Now all that seemed to crumble (how calm she looks) like those sand castles the children build on the Atlantic City beaches and the waves come in and dissolve them. He and Amy had watched that just the summer before after breakfasting at the Breakers (to put her away underground is abominable) and walking along the beach, the sand castles crumbling under the waves no matter how deep the moats the frantic children dug around them. He and Amy, she in fine well-cut white linen and the wide flower hat, and daring to take her shoes off to shake out the sand, and her stockings pulled off—laughing all the time—lifting up her skirts to run barefoot across the sand to the shock of the dowagers and ancient frumps in their deck chairs, under their sunshades (could she *just* be sleeping?). He and Amy, sand, sun, and antic bodies. . . . No more, no more.

He went back—firm steps, eyes straight ahead—to the library and had one drink of whiskey. No more. He seemed to have dozed off. Zeeland, the butler, was shaking him, a proper butler, fully dressed, but with no collar or tie.

"There's that *jung* person, sir."

"What?"

"That man, he's in the hall *und*—"

"No, no, I don't want to see anyone."

"I tole him—"

The doors shook, were forced open, and Chauncey Wilcox came in, hatless, jacket unbuttoned, his dark face scowling.

"The son of a bitch Dutchy said I couldn't see you."

"Amy. She's gone. She's dead."

"I know, H.H. He told me. Jesus, it's hard to think she. . . . But

173

listen, I had to see you, H.H. There is hell going to break loose on the Street in the morning."

"I don't give a goddamn."

"You have to. I know the telegraph man at the *Tribune*. I buy him a meal once in a while; he keeps me informed of things."

"Go away, Chauncey."

The young man looked at the butler, who turned and walked out of the room. "H.H. There was a wire late last night; a report of a rumor in Washington the President is going to release the national gold."

"There have been a lot of rumors." It was all just words—all words. Who really cares Amy's dead?

"I went over to Gould's house. Maybe I'd pick up a hint."

"You have been busy, Chaunce. Go eat breakfast. What time is it?"

"Sunrise in an hour. So I find Gould's house locked up. I got into the house, through a basement window. Got up to the hall, to Gould's private office. I found something."

"I'll go your bail. Good night, Chaunce."

The young man took a folded letter from his pocket and handed it to Howard. It was an ordinary stationery without a heading.

"It's a copy I made. Hadda light a lamp."

Howard read slowly. Some part of his brain took in the letter's contents. Most of him seemed indifferent to it. He couldn't fully come out of his torpor. But as he read on, he knew this was vital information.

Chaunce said, "It was unsigned—but it's to Mr. Corbin, I'm sure."

The contents made it clear that Grant had written the letter to his daughter.

"You see, H.H., it could only be Corbin who sent this or carried it over to Gould to show the game is up."

"It's clear the President, once he got wind of the full facts of the Gould-and-Fisk gold scheme, moved with his old push—like on the battlefield. Sent his daughter this personal letter to get her husband to sell *all* his gold stocks, *no* delay. The President makes it plain he rejects any idea that he is involved in any way with his son-in-law in connection with current events in the Gold Room.

"And so Corbin rushes to Gould with the letter, blurts out the news; the President wasn't on their side."

174

"I bet all of yesterday afternoon he's known. He didn't warn you?"

Howard was beginning to grasp the extremes of the situation.

"I'd make a good-sized bet, Chaunce, he hasn't warned Jim either."

"You'll have to act soon as the Gold Room opens." The young man was excited, waving his arms. "The President will wait a bit, to give Corbin time to sell out. So. . . ." He ran fingers through his heavy black hair. "So we begin to sell on the opening bell."

"Chaunce, I want to think. I'm all tangled up."

"You have to sell before the gold price breaks down like a shit-filled privy at the news."

"Yes."

"We can't dump everything. No time, no time. Dump what you can of your and Mr. McCann's account." Chauncey hunted in an inner pocket. "I've worked out a selling order at opening of the Exchange and at fifteen-minute intervals. Just sign them."

Howard took the papers and ruffled them. "I must tell Jim."

Chaunce said quietly, "He may know and *not* be telling you. Gould has gone into hiding."

Howard whipped his thigh with the selling orders. "Christ, suppose we, the Goldbugs, all dump at once. And suppose Grant decides *not* to release the gold he controls. Suppose, suppose. . . . Good night, Chaunce, I'll be at the bank at six in the morning."

"Yes, sure." The young man lowered his head. "You know I feel bad about Mrs. Starkweather. It just—it isn't anything I can say that would help how you must feel. But I do want to say it's like the time my mother died of yellow jack in Port-au-Prince—I was six years old—and. . . ." He turned and went out, closing the doors slowly.

BOOK V

Ah, take the Cash, and let the Credit go,
Nor heed the rumble of a distant Drum!
—OMAR KHAYYÁM, *Rubáiyát*

25

Little drops of whiskey,
Little mugs of beer
Bring the keenest sorrow
To the children dear.

Three middle-aged women, one holding onto a child, were chanting outside the Stock Exchange, lifting up petitions to be signed. No one was paying much attention to them. They were often on the Street holding up their papers, chanting their call to do away with Demon Rum, the saloon, and the drunkard.

Little drinks of brandy,
Little sips of gin
Swell the mighty torrent
Of disease and sin.

Howard, crossing the sidewalk, Chauncey at his side, was stopped by one of the women; she looking at him with the fanatic's eye, her clean but worn gray gown pinned together here and there to replace missing buttons. Her shoes had worn down. She pushed the sheet of paper at him, right into his face.

"You'll be signing for the good of those living in the hell of a drunkard's world. Better be dead than drunk."

He took the grubby black crayon offered and signed. He had some vague thought, it didn't matter; he hoped something would matter. The Stock Exchange was being mobbed, and the doorman, old Yancy, was having trouble keeping out most of the nonmembers, aided by two beefy police.

Little slips of paper
For the good cause cast.
If for prohibition,
Peace will come at last.

The Gold Room was in turmoil, buzzing like a demented bee-hive—even before it opened for business. Men in top hats spun about on their heels as rumors were passed from group to group. There were so many rumors that when someone hinted Grant would release gold, he was ignored. "Gold will go to two hundred before noon," insisted a large man with a red waistcoat and a battered nose, who kept shaking buy orders over people's heads. "Two hundred before noon, gents. I'm buying for the brokers, Belden and Speyer."

Howard, eyes red, his face drawn from his ordeal, moved toward the broker. It was like swimming in a sea of bobbing heads.

"Who you buying for, Murf?"

"You know, Belden and Speyer."

"In the firm's name?" Murf was a picknose mick, but no liar.

"Sure as shootin'."

Howard felt he was exposed in a public drama, still baffled by his role. He walked away, pushing past brokers gesturing their bids as the board opening the day's transactions showed gold moving up in the early-morning trading. It was hardly real to Howard. Was he participating in this vicarious bystanding? Was his wife dead? Was it true he was double-crossed by Gould? Perhaps even by Fisk? His energy was drained from him; the result of the long sleepless night, the shock to mind and body, of Amy gone. *Gone.* It was a bit more than he could logically face.

Chauncey shoved himself to Howard's side. He, too, had not slept but he seemed refreshed by the excitement around them; had changed his jacket even if his collar and shirt were wilted. The noise was rising in volume, canes and arms lifted up to reinforce voices.

"Fisk is buying through agents," Chauncey said.

Howard nodded. "Gould hasn't told him."

"What do we do?"

"Fill no more Gould or Fisk buying orders. Begin to sell our gold holding in small lots. Who are we using?"

"Connors and Feitelstein."

"Fine. Sell. Sell. Not too fast. Dribble orders out."

Chauncey looked about him. Gold prices were being marked up, still rising on the board. "The Exchange had a telegraphy key set up next door direct to Washington. If the President moves. . . ." He leaned over to whisper, "There's Mr. Fisk."

It would be hard to miss the man, Howard thought. The big man was the center of a human whirlpool, bidding and bidding loudly, a certain hoarseness in his voice as he began to buy all the gold offered.

Gold stood at 150, then at 160. The big man, his voice growing more strained, kept shouting, "It's gonna be two hundred today, boys."

"You tell 'em, Jim."

Howard hung back for half an hour listening to Fisk release a flood of platitudes. When he walked over to Fisk, the man was standing by the little fountain in the Gold Room that spouted and bubbled, indifferent to the noise, the bedlam going on around it. Fisk was splashing up handfuls of water from the fountain's base, splashing it over his head and neck, then sopping it up off his shoulders with a silk handkerchief. Howard was aware of the beast odor in the room, the sweat and windy results of excited bodies, the exhalation of frenzied men who were hardly digesting their breakfasts properly. The stench was growing more revolting, and Jim Fisk looked up, water dripping from the end of his mustache.

"Hello, Howie. Mad, mad, isn't it? Gold at two hundred before noon."

"You seem goddamn sure, Jim."

"Sure? Solid information. I've had reports by telegraph from Philadelphia, Chicago, Boston. Wild bidding, speculators out of their minds trying to get their voices heard. Look, it just reached one-sixty-six."

There was a shouting as the new price was chalked up on the big board. A man rushed by, his eyes wide, reminding Howard of an auger boring. He put a hand on Fisk's arm.

"Jim, you're being crossed. We're all being crossed."

"What? *What?*" Water dripped in beads down the wide face, down the broad neck, fell into a hopelessly soggy collar. Fisk pulled Howard to one side and spoke very low. "What the hell kind of a game is this?"

"Gould has a copy of a letter from the President to his daughter, saying he's going to release federal gold stock today."

"Jay? Jay do this. . . . Aw, damn it, Howie, we're old partners, we're. . . ."

Chauncey was pushing his way through to them. The noise in the Gold Room was still high, but it seemed to have a new tone, a kind of shrillness, aggressively outraged.

Jim Fisk said, "The son of a bitch, would he do it to me?"

Chauncey, straining to reach them, was showing a great deal of teeth, his lips and face muscles set in a kind of grim grin. "Secretary of the Treasury Boutwell has just tossed four million in government gold onto the market. It's the start."

Jim Fisk's face seemed to inflate with a damp conspicuousness—getting an extra supply of blood. He gave a bull roar and began to push his way through the now-agitated, milling mob. It *is* a mob now, Howard decided—reasonless, stunned but vocal.

"Jim will kill Gould," Howard said.

Chauncey half hooded his large dark eyes. "I get this feeling Mr. Fisk, he's been selling triple, over beyond his bellowing buy orders. Why would he have telegraph connections with Philadelphia, Boston, Chicago open?"

"You think he's selling out of town?"

Howard watched the sudden fall of gold prices on the board. He didn't feel anything; it was all still some ultimate pattern beyond reality. It was becoming clearer that Gould's scheme to corner gold was collapsing with a swiftness that was, Howard felt, like a sudden storm in the horse latitudes in the Atlantic.

Chauncey was pulling on his frock coat. "We're behind, not going to sell all your and Mr. McCann's holding for any price now."

"Dump everything for anything—Christ, this morning has burst the whole goddamn gold bubble."

He was right. In fifteen minutes in this evil-smelling room it was all over. The gold prices fell, fell. The condition of the room was sickening. Men were openmouthed in shock. Howard went into the hall. The building was packed with messengers, clerks. Brokers were running back and forth. He found a seat and sat leaning on his gold cane, chin resting on his gloved hands clasping the gold handle. He seemed to be the only indifferent ruined man in the building, on the Street, that Black Friday, the twenty-fourth. A Jewish investment broker he knew passed, muttering, "*Baruch atu Adonoi elehenu. . . .*" Out of his mind offering a prayer? Howard felt he was observing, recording the scene here and later in the street. He walked over to H. H. Starkweather & Company. He was most likely a very ruined man, or badly bent at the least. And he had a wife to bury.

Later that week, when he could reason logically, he wrote Donald McCann a long letter, of the scenes in the Gold Room and after. Of the rage, the horror on many faces as the gold market collapsed.

182

What madness, Donald, as the end came, the exhausted operators streaming out of the stifling hall into the fresh air of the street. In some offices customers by dozens were ruined whose margins were irrevocably lost, confronted their dealers with taunts and threats of violence for their treachery.

With night, Broad Street and its vicinity saw no letup. The silence and the darkness which ever rest over the lower city after seven of the evening were now broken by the blaze of gaslight from a hundred windows and the rushing of clerks from a hasty repast back to their overloaded desks. Until long after Trinity bells pealed out the dawn, I saw men bent over books, scrutinizing the clearinghouse statement for the morrow, taking whatever thought was possible for the future. I, myself, was numb. At the Gold Exchange Bank the weary accountants were making ineffective efforts to complete recorded business. That midnight of the bullion worshipers will be ever memorable for its anxieties and anguish.

Saturday brought no relief. I went through the motions of doing business. The Gold Board met only to adjourn. The clearinghouse being incapable of the task of settling its accounts, complicated as they were by each new fresh failure. Small brokers had gone under by scores. H. H. Starkweather & Company *may* survive, limping. The rumors of the impending suspension of some of the largest houses of the Street give fresh grounds for fear. The Stock Exchange is now the center of attraction. If that yields, all is lost. To sustain the market is vital. But from whence is the saving power to come? All yesterday shares had been falling headlong. Will the impulse downward continue? The frenzied men filled the corridors, overhung the stairway from which one looks down on the Exchange, saw mad tumult, heard the roar of the biddings. The end of the dream turned nightmare.

Howard walked among men ruined who stood staring at chalked figures that destroyed their lives. Bankruptcies were taking place.

Amy was buried on the land at Shad Point where Howard had planned to build a fine house for them. There was on the most northern section of the point, by the river, an old simple Colonial burying ground, free of sham and pretension. There were slanted and fallen gravestones still marking plot owners—stones, Howard felt, not ashamed of responsibility; weathered so it was hard to read names and dates. The graveyard had been almost forgotten, and it

183

was on his land. Here under two great elms on a slight rise of good thick wild grass, he stood by the freshly turned earth of a grave. There were present Chauncey and Josie Mansfield to stand by Howard, he in a dark hammer-clawed tailcoat, a black top hat and a silk mourning band tied around it. McCann was in Chicago fighting to save his steel mills.

Two gravediggers with whiskey-burned faces, their jaws disfigured by chaws of tobacco, watched, waited, indifferent to death and mourners. A long-faced young minister Chauncey had found and hired in White Plains would do fine, Howard decided. To say the few fragments of prayers on the fallible human existence. Do what little could be done to hurry away the dead woman inside the shiny golden oak casket with its silver handles, hurry her on her way. Amy had been born a Catholic, was convent-raised, but she had sloughed off the strict dogma and theology during their married life. Had let confession and states of grace slip away. Had been involved with Josie in the writing and assumptions of someone called Mary Baker Eddy. In her last weeks Amy had been found to be muttering, "There is no pain, there is no pain . . . there is no death. . . ." She knew better now, if she knew anything at all.

The minister was beginning:

> The new wine mourneth.
> The vine languisheth
> And the merry-hearted do sigh.
> The mirth of tabrets ceaseth.
> The noise of them that rejoice endeth. . . .

There was a warmish wind up from the river smelling of hay and clams. The last autumnal leaves of the ancient elms stirred. Howard turned his head and looked at the old gravestones, overturned broken. He would bring some order here, plant a hedge of boxwood around Amy's grave, and have something good lettered on stone placed over her.

> All joy is darkened.
> The mirth of the land is gone. . . .

He had two thousand acres here—if he could pay for them, if H. H. Starkweather & Company survived, if, *if*. . . . Chauncey Wilcox was watching him and Howard put a hand on the young

184

man's shoulder. . . . I am a widower, a sonless man, a childless man.

> In the city is left desolation
> And the gate is smitten with destruction. . . .

The old Jews certainly knew how to lay the agony on—entirely justifiable, I suppose—people being what they are. The young minister coot has a nice fine voice and recites as if he enjoyed every sorrow-filled sound of the text.

The minister finished, held the small Bible he had carried, but not read from, against his chest. Without lifting his head, he added, *"Requiescat in pace."*

Josie, wearing a veil, snuffed back a sob. "He reads beautifully. Amy, our Amy, would have liked it."

Howard took her by one elbow as the gravediggers began to thud clods of earth down on the casket. "It was good of you to come, Josie."

"Jim wanted to be here. But you know there have been threats."

"So I've heard." Howard made a gesture to Chauncey, who slipped a twenty-dollar gold coin into one of the minister's gloved hands. Howard nodded at the man. The minister nodded back, his gloved fingers ashamed of the gold token, and yet turning the coin over and over.

Just below them the night boat returning from Albany was coming downriver, all white with red trim, the paddle wheels thrusting at the river, people on its decks plainly seen. Howard stood watching the smoke of the tall stack scribble in the sky and he wondered if he should have stayed at sea and forgone domestic felicity. No, whatever star he was under, whatever blows or victories, he was now a landman and owned a filled grave to prove it.

26

No time for mourning. No time for anything but what Chauncey Wilcox called "the survival stakes." Howard found that the aftermath of the Gould gold disaster, at least a disaster for him and most of the Goldbugs—Jay Gould seemed to have sold out his holdings in time—was to try to assess the damage and never mind the scurri-

185

lous gossip. Starkweather & Company was hard hit. It had carried accounts for Gould and Fisk, bought, bought, and could not now get them accepted by Gould. As for the personal holdings of Howard and Donald McCann, they had only in part been sold in time, that wild insubstantial pageant of a Friday morning.

What hurt Howard most was he had had such grand plans for H. H. Starkweather & Company. Perhaps he could survive, perhaps he could manage to avoid the burden the Gould and Fisk account had put on him. The Street, after its first shock, was nearly catatonic, even piteously stupefied. But it slowly began to seek and do business again.

Painful to Howard was the attitude of Jim Fisk. Had Jim double-crossed him? Had he known early of the federal gold release? In time to unburden himself secretly, and not warn Howard?

From that creature of perfidy and ingratitude, Jay Gould, he expected nothing. That weasel-faced little man with his silent secret ways; one could expect only deceit and double-dealings. That *chinga tu madre*, as Spanish sailors used to shout. But Jim?

The Street's leading brokers still lunched at Ott's Inn. Howard was sitting over some baked duck he wasn't very hungry for—ever since Amy's death, somehow, neither food nor drink appealed—so sitting there, Jim came up to him, still as large as ever, a bit more of a network of wrinkles around the eyes, perhaps a slight increase in girth so that his blue frock coat with the gold buttons seemed a bit tight, and the collar pressing a wider neck. He did not act like a man who had demeaned a friendship.

"Ah, Howie, you been avoiding ol' Jim?"

"Been busy. Treading water."

Fisk sat down, pushed his gray topper back on his head. "You think I jobbed you, eh? Jobbed my friend Howie?"

Howard just shrugged, speared a bit of duck on his fork. Jim leaned forward. "I may be a shitassed son of a bitch, but I'm not as big a one as Jay. I didn't know for sure the President was moving."

"I heard you claim to have lost millions. But instead made millions."

Jim seemed to brush lint off his frieze frock coat. "Well, talk, talk. But believe me, I had no time to warn you, damn gyrations going on. I just plunged in. Making a big front of buying while I had some of my boys selling in Philadelphia, Boston—oh, you know—but I haven't counted up if I won or lost."

"You'll do fine, Jim." Howard stood up. "I have things to attend to. . . . I have counted up—I know I lost."

"You're not angry at Jim Fisk?" He held out a hand, big, pink, well cared for.

Howard ignored it. "Take care of yourself, Jim."

He had wanted to say more, wanted to shout. But it was best to control oneself when nothing can be gained by an outcry or a blow. Besides, Jim *might* be telling the truth. Time was short and confusion had been great.

It was common knowledge on the Street that Gould, at the first news of disaster, had taken it on the run, leaving his office by a back door. Fisk continued to brag boldly and claim he hadn't been warned. "I gave Grant's son-in-law, that shithead, a bawling out, called him a low-down scoundrel."

Actually, Howard was soon aware Fisk had made a fortune. Some sources insisted he made eleven million dollars on inside information the morning before Grant released federal gold.

Jay Gould moved quickly to protect himself and his holdings. He "owned" several judges and got out a dozen injunctions, court writs, stopping enforcement by the Gold Room Board and the Stock Exchange of any contracts he would have to settle. H. H. Starkweather insisted on the same treatment. The brokers acting for Gould and Fisk paid out not a penny for gold bought; their bids for gold stock were erased. Fisk had been too smart to sign any of the orders, so the brokers had taken all the risk on themselves. Not all brokers fared as well as did Gould and Fisk.

Howard wrote to Donald McCann:

> Failure to make good deliveries would have ensured the instant selling out of defaulters under the rule. As the majority of us bankers and brokers were inextricably involved, the only consequence would have been to throw us all into bankruptcy, thus bringing some $60,000,000 under the hammer. The market could not have borne up under such an avalanche. So it's been decided that the Gold Room should be kept open for borrowings and loans, but that all dealings should be suspended. One result of this complication is that gold now has no fixed value. It can be bought at one house for 133 and at other offices sold for 139. . . . I think I shall just stay afloat, that is all. The agony is so great in the city, it has made one feel as if Gettysburg had been lost and the rebels are marching down

Howard was learning the full essence of the sensation called "just afloat." The ledgers he inspected late at night under the gaslight showed he had been badly hit, between wind and water, as the Admiral Nelson saying was. He had holes in his hull, but he'd rig a jury mast and run before the wind. But thinking in sailor terms was silly. He needed cash badly.

McCann came to town—tired, but he, too, just, just solvent. They walked along the Battery, in a suggestion of spring, by the sycamores and elms, the grass showing green here and there; the hedges, tormented by dogs, horses, and children, showed buds and life. On the water—gray-blue water—steamers, ferries, schooners, and barges moved back and forth. The odor of mud flats and brine came to them as they walked.

McCann stopped to watch two steam tugs easing a Cunarder up the bay.

"Look up at the things that matter. It's still there, the need for ships' cargoes, the demands for notions, dry goods, and tools, for machines. Don't take it so ill. We were only badly bent. It's like one of those Damascus sword blades of fine steel. You can make a circle of it. It's steel that's limber and, released, it springs back good as new."

"Hard times for you, Donald?"

"That it's been, H.H. Bleak and a nasty go of it. I nearly lost the mill in Ohio. But I put it to the barstards on the board. I said, facing them around a table, 'Take the whole fuckin' plant, kit 'n' caboodle, from me. And who will run it for you? Puddle iron, run pig ingots, roll steel? Shape it and sell it?' Oh, I was good as Kean's Hamlet. 'You domn bankers on your fat arses—what can you do with a mill? And on payday for five hundred men?' "

"And they took it?"

"The plant?"

"The damn guff you handed out."

"Oh, of course they knew I had 'em by the short hair. You see, they're pious folk and love the dollar like they love their God. Maybe they could have found someone else to make good steel. But I was there, and I was willing. To serve their interests as well as mine is how I put it."

188

"What's your loss?"

"A good half me holdings; my shares as guarantee are in their vaults. But I'll be getting 'em back soon, someday. And you?"

The Staten Island ferry was coming across, its walking beam moving its paddle wheels at a steady rate. "I'm selling the house, Donald, most of the stable. I've a big mortgage on the land I bought at Shad Point. I'll move there. There's an old house on the property I was going to throw down. Now it's good enough till I can afford to build. The bays—the sight of them saddens me—I'll sell them; good horses—high in the withers, fine hock action."

"You'll be lonely, H.H."

"I don't mind. I can't be dancing in the streets. No mood for it."

"Marry agin."

Howard laughed. "You didn't. How's Flossie?"

"Don't mock me, mon. We are all only flesh at certain moments."

After watching the ferry move up to its slip, arm in arm they went to Ott's to drink hot toddies.

Slowly H. H. Starkweather & Company recovered. It handled shares in Midwestern steel-company issues; it represented Baring Brothers of London in some railroad promotions of the Western & Great Plains in California. There was a new clerk named St. Mars Chesney and a larger plate-glass window. Howard, at his most expansive moments, even took to walking the Street looking for a site that could be used someday to put up a really impressive Starkweather building. Of native stone, Vermont granite, three, four stories high, large windows on the ground floor trimmed with black marble, and heavy gold letters. H. H. STARKWEATHER & COMPANY, INVESTMENT BANKERS. As Jim Fisk used to say, "We swing through life as if there's a net underneath—just remember there isn't."

He was selling the house. It reminded him of Amy too much. Certain rooms never lost her odor of myrtle and somehow of stored apples. The money was needed to prop up the firm. He even had the mortgage increased on the acres of Shad Point. It still left him strapped for capital, and so he had decided to sell the bays. He could never enjoy them now. It was no good riding behind their polished rumps. It always brought back Amy's delight in holding the reins and making her little clucking horse mouth noise at them. He wondered if he were exaggerating his love for her, making larger the joys of their actual life together.

189

The Chesneys on Murray Hill—parents of his new young clerk, St. Mars Chesney—were from Richmond (they pronounced it Richmon'), Virginia. Living high on the hog. Captain Bixton Wade Chesney with a limp and a fine pointed beard and mustache in the style of Louis Napoleon; Mrs. Chesney, *née* Fairfax, of the Red Oak Fairfaxes, cheerful, wise as an owl, meek in public. Three daughters and a son, St. Mars Chesney, clerk at H. H. Starkweather, the hope of the family.

"Learnin' the bankin' trade, bright as a whip, but mannerly," is how Captain Chesney put it.

The captain (2nd Virginia Brigade, CSA) was a proud man burdened by debts, several war-neglected tobacco plantations, a burned-down gristmill. Anthrax raging among a once-fine horse herd in Georgia; those that hadn't been stolen by the freed slaves or the Union booters under Sherman. The proud blood of the Chesneys came from the founding father (out of Newgate Prison, shipped to the colonies in 1685 for sheep stealing, marrying an indentured servant girl). The last Chesneys suffered from the fact that the economic facts that were changing the nation were processes they could never understand. All but St. Mars. They still retained a feeling that trade and business were best left to overseers. They suffered in the city of New York, but they made do. They were excellent playactors, presenting to New York a façade of scatterbrained, aristocratic charm, living in style (on credits so far readily extended). There were the three daughters—solid sensible girls, handsome rather than beautiful—to marry off and the son to establish in a gainful career.

They needed a team and a carriage, and it was St. Mars who spoke of it to Howard, "Having heard, sir, you speak of wanting to sell the bays."

"Yes, the rig goes with them."

The captain invited Howard for breakfast one Sunday, and the rented house on Murray Hill was cheerful, the paint and wallpaper fresh. Added Mrs. Chesney, "Some of our heirlooms, suh, Mistah Starkweather, furnished it neatly."

Nimrod had polished and waxed the rig, brightened the bays' coats to a shine, and blackened their hooves. They looked splendid in the courtyard of the Chesney house.

Mrs. Chesney, wearing her cameo brooch with the head of Charles I on it, stood on the back steps and Captain Chesney introduced his daughters, Lavinia, Drucilla, and Susan. Not graceful Southern belles, but not forward or sassy or prone to flirt.

It was important the family had a proper "vee-he-kill and prime hossflesh"—as the captain put it—"to take the air in the park and visit the bazaars."

St. Mars inspected the bays and said they had good lines. He was an earnest young man of eighteen, with straw-yellow hair, a slight lisp, but a strong chin. Add a determination he could get what he wanted from life. He had none of the outworn ideals of his family. Howard felt St. Mars thought things out with a piercing clarity.

It was agreed the Chesneys could have the bays and the rig for nine hundred dollars. Payment to be made as soon as the family tobacco crop was marketed.

"Those damn Yan— dealers sure take advantage of a gentleman who doesn't have the gift of argufying on their level."

"I'd be glad to factor your crops, Captain. Get you the best prices available among the biggest buyers here."

"You are too kind. Lavinia, don't you go near that horse. You will, Mr. Starkweather, take as security some of the family keepsakes. Some pearls and—"

"No, I'll take an assignment on the crop, for the amount due."

"Very proper, very proper indeed."

Howard thought, Poor bastard, and those big girls to get rid of.

It took nearly a year to get payment for the bays and the rig. The Chesney crops had other claims against them. Back taxes, a burned-down drying shed for burley leaf tobacco to be rebuilt. Bills for hogsheads ordered and not paid for, going back fifteen years, while the Chesneys spent too little time pondering the mutability of business affairs. But Howard did get most of the horses and rig debt cleared up in time. St. Mars was turning out to be a bright young man, good-natured, with a specific quality in money matters. He and Chauncey were like two rival lovers, each trying to prove to Howard he was the favorite. Chauncey was the more practical in dealing with people. St. Mars was a remarkable salesman, presenting cool social grace, as if he were doing a client a favor releasing some new issue of shares of iron and steel McCann holdings or the Western & Great Plains Railroad building steadily eastward and south to the gulf, setting rail to bring beef on the hoof to Middle West packinghouses, planning routes for ore carriers from new developing Great Lakes mines.

Howard lived in the old house at Shad Point, penciling in plans

191

for the big house to rise "someday" on the riverfront. Zeeland, the butler—now also cook—and Nimrod, the handyman, were the only servants. Chauncey the lone boarder. Howard avoided anyone connected with the Gould-Fisk group. He was slowly building back his confidence, his resources; the firm, he saw, would survive after months of precarious equilibrium.

There was, of course, much talk of Jim and Josie. The situation between them was changing. Howard felt sorry for Fisk. Better to do as he, Howard, now did; visiting Madame Pearl's whorehouse on Twenty-third Street. Buy some bottles of wine on holidays and birthdays, give some small gold trinket to a favorite girl. But no commitments. No infatuation. It was not likely he would marry again.

He had—when desiring to be alone—taken to the reading of Balzac, volume after volume.

> In our society, the doctor and the lawyer are the people who stand to one side, and why? Because they have lost all respect for the world as it is. The lawyer's office is on a par with the gambling house, the courts, the brothels. Because they are places where the human drama is a scene utterly indifferent to our hopes. . . .

It was a world more real to Howard, at times, than the actual one.

> The city, you discover, is like a forest in the New World— here you have to deal with all kinds of savages who survive on the proceeds of their hunting. You, too, become a hunter for millions. To catch your millions you set your snares. Some hunt heiresses, others legacies, yet others sell out their clients hand and foot. And the man who brings in the most game, he will be praised, feted, and welcomed into the best society.

Christ, it's the Street, he thought.

When he tired of reading, late at night, he would sit and think of the pomposity and the pulsating world he knew and lived in. And his goal, was it just the piling up of gains, of position for himself? No, it was just rolling along with the momentum of doing what he had begun. No matter how many others crowded in, it was a world of manipulating money, and it created a strange and compelling individualism. Yes, it was the game of it that held him, even perhaps the perversities of human nature. The peculiar pleasure of dealing, trading in the end with mere numbers. Balances, losses, and gains recorded on paper. The winners swelled up with pride and greed like a poisoned toad, the losers moaning in exhaustion. When such moods of depression came over Howard, he would seek out the Chesney ménage—people essentially frivolous, at least on the surface.

27

It was two years later that Howard met Jim one night in the lobby of the Astor Theatre. Howard was taking the Chesneys to the play *Under the Gaslight,* celebrating Lavinia's engagement to Hugo Ellis Dixton, tanner and leather dealer of New Brunswick. Jim looked florid and unhealthy, with an outward jolliness yet a hint of inward self-inquiry.

During the intermission, Howard excused himself to smoke a cigar outside the theater; Mrs. Chesney had, she admitted, weak lungs and so none of the family smoked.

Jim came up to Howard just as he lit his cigar and was admiring how the lamps of the coaches made a kind of necklace of lights along the street.

"H.H., how are you?" Fisk's gloved hand was out. Howard shook it.

"Getting by, Jim. How are things with you?"

"Oh, always something. We haven't been seeing each other. Must be a year or more, eh?"

"Must be."

"Look, I've always felt you knew me—I mean that I'm not all hearty laughter. I've had troubles. It's Josie. I need advice."

Jim was an intriguer and wily—and a charmer. Careful, Howard told himself.

He listened. There was always about Jim this charm—for all his ideas of pleasure and sport, an earned reputation for rapacity, he was still a likable man. He talked now earnestly and was a deeply troubled man, he who had been so showy, and still was in a harrassed way. As he told it, Josie, his great love, had changed. "Gone wrong, H.H. Gone wrong as rain. You may have heard, huh?"

"Been busy—and not in a social mood."

She had liked to join him, Jim told Howard, to show herself on the Hudson River waterfront, Jim in an admiral's uniform, saluting the fleet of steamers he owned. For all his clown's exterior, Jim said he was a deadly serious and skilled man when making money and investing it.

But Josie was not a loyal mistress to Jim. She was greedy and sensual, Jim admitted, and she liked men—she liked them with a great deal of wealth.

"I do business with all kinds of people, H.H., and one person I associated with on a deal in a Brooklyn oil refinery was this suave society bastard, Edward S. Stokes. His background? The silver spoon. Folk out of Philadelphia's Main Line. A college athletic johnny. . . . Stokes is smart, but not a flashy member of the New York Stock Exchange, and likes blooded horses. Has this dull, Christer of a wooden wife and children at home. He was just ripe for Josie. God, *yes!*"

As Jim told it, Josie first met Stokes at Pike's Opera House, which Jim managed—there was a dinner date and a night of love. Stokes, it was clear, was like a being from another world for Josie, and she decided to break with Jim, move away from the world of the theater.

"The son of a bitch got an ornate nest for her. Now, Josie's a girl with a sense of bookkeeping and insisted I owed her twenty-five thousand dollars, as her shyster lawyer says, 'for past favors.' "

Fisk stopped to study the effect his story had on his listener. Howard wanted to laugh, but didn't. Poor Jim. Everyone knew of Josie and Stokes. . . . The bell was ringing for the second-act curtain. He patted Jim's arm. "I have to get back to my people. Why not lunch with me tomorrow at the Hudson Club? You can tell me all about it."

Fisk made a mock gesture of touching Howard's chin with a fist.

"You're true blue, Howie, true blue."

The Hudson Club, old in tradition (General Gates got drunk there in 1778 with Major André), was in sight of the river. Its food was good, wine cellar fair, and its members were businessmen, lawyers, dealers in grain, horses, land, and riverfrontage. There were better clubs and Howard was a member of two others. But Jim wasn't the type to be a guest in them.

Fisk came to the lunch with a white-piped vest, an astonishing cravat, frock-coat tails too long. He shook hands with Howard and

194

over the well-done sirloin and the hashed browns, the whole roast chicken, steins of beer, the hot biscuits, he talked, chewed his food, sipped, and told his story.

"Of course, I didn't pony up any twenty-five thousand she and Stokes wanted. Josie and me had a lot of mean and nasty words to toss at each other long ago. An exchange of, well, certain letters, dynamite politically, took place. But Josie did not get her twenty-five thousand for body rent. No, siree. Now Stokes is suing me, claiming he has two hundred thousand dollars coming to him from our joint venture in oil refining. A very sore loser, H.H. *Very* sore."

Howard grinned. "You didn't kind of tilt things in the deal? As punishment?"

"Look, Stokes, for a Philadelphia gent, doesn't act like one. He's got my letters to Josie—some of them—and these he claimed would prove that I had been criminally involved in dishonest dealings, like in matters of railroad swindles. And that with Gould, we two pretty much own a majority of New York's judges, courts, and politicians."

"It's well-known gossip, Jim."

"Yes, but here it's all written out in bragging letters to my once-true love. Why did I write to her? Trust her?"

"What now?"

"Oh, I announced Stokes was a blackmailer with letters. So Stokes and Josie sue me for libel. Libel! You ever hear of such a thing! Lawyers move in as usual to mulch both sides. Stokes, he's asking for two hundred thousand dollars and Josie now is wanting fifty thousand dollars instead of the original twenty-five thousand dollars for going to bed with me. I tell you, I oughtta been gelded like a steer."

"When's the trial?"

"In two days. I don't trust my lawyers, *any* lawyers. They'd hump a wooden Indian. Come to court with me. Just so I have a friend, *my* friend Howie, with me? You're still my friend; aren't you?"

Howard motioned the waiter to clear the table. "Jim, I suppose I am. Always will be."

"Good to hear it. . . . Oh, waiter, are there frittered clams, if not, soft-shelled crabs? You know, Howie, trouble only gives me a whale of an appetite."

The city enjoyed the talk of the trial, enjoyed Josie coming before the judge the first day in black silk, violet gloves, and just *one* well-placed crimson feather. She smiled at Howard. "Hello, H.H. Holding Jim's hand?"

Fisk, after that day's court business was done—mostly legal mumbo jumbo—went back to his office in Pike's Opera House. Always helpful to politicians, he told Howard he had a deal on to advance the New York Police Department its delayed payroll of two hundred and fifty thousand dollars. "Reformers with a legal move have for the time being locked up the city's money."

"To keep it from the Tweed gang?"

"Now, Howie, you know it's no use calling names. . . . What you think of the trial? There's a surprise coming for them; Josie and Stokes. I can just see them lunching at Delmonico's while right now I bet they're being served with papers. Being indicted for attempting blackmail by the grand jury!"

"One of your pranks, Jim?"

"No, no, this is on the level. It *is* blackmail. Look, gotta run. Right now I have something to do at the Grand Central Hotel on Broadway."

"I know where it is."

"Meet me there at four thirty P.M.; we'll have drinks and talk, eh? You can tell about your crazy plans for Shad Point. Going to put a wife in it?"

"Not that I know of. I'll see you at the Grand. Have to get a letter off to London."

"Jesus—it's good we've made it up. Couldn't go it alone."

They parted, Howard wondering how Stokes would take the indictment for blackmail. That could be serious for him and Josie if proved. Jim had great power and muscle in the New York courts.

Howard spent the rest of the afternoon dictating to Chauncey a report to Baring Brothers on the plans for a practical refrigerated freight car ("Goods train, Chauncey, they call it in England"). A car that could carry slaughtered steers, trimmed beef and mutton direct to market. It would be a good idea to investigate the plans and buy a controlling interest in the patents.

It was after four when Howard walked over to the Grand Central Hotel. There was the usual street traffic of the horse-drawn stages, the curses of draymen, the swearing of hack drivers. Around the hotel a larger crowding of people than usual. Howard pushed his way to where a beefy policeman with side-whiskers stood at the hotel entrance.

"What's up, Clancy?"

"Ah, Mr. Starkweather. There's been a shootin'."

"Anyone hurt?"

"You kin call it a murder. He ain't goin' to live, I hear."

Howard somehow had a crystal-ball vision. "Jim Fisk?"

"That's right. The bull's eye."

The hotel manager, wringing his hands and watching the stomping on his lobby rugs, told Howard how it had happened. It was at four fifteen that afternoon that Edward Stokes and Jim Fisk faced each other for the last time on what was called the Ladies' Staircase of the hotel. Both men were armed with pistols. Stokes, insane over the blackmail writ, without hesitation shot first. Down went Jim, and the wound was mortal.

The dying Fisk had at his bedside, in his once-gay living quarters, Jay Gould and Howard. Howard looked down on the once-brash, so lively figure, now prone on the bed. Fisk, he figured, was thirty-seven years old.

Just before breath left him, Fisk managed to say, "I was just paying a visit to a business associate's wife. Nothing more, when there was that prick Stokes on the staircase. . . . Shooting. God!"

Boss Tweed came in just before the last breath left Fisk's body, followed by Meyer Drood, the undertaker.

Gould looked down on his partner's dead face, and he coughed. "We'll give him a send-off to remember."

Tweed fingered his watch chains. Howard saw Tweed was already a Nast cartoon of the political dictator of the city and Tammany. The vast gut, the huge nose, the whiskers as lampooned in *Harper's Weekly*.

"Something fine, Jay. *Real* fine."

Howard picked his hat off a chair. "He had style."

Gould, never given much to talk, nodded and left. He seemed to scurry away, and Tweed frowned. "If it had to be one of them, why not Gould?"

There was still Meyer Drood with gray gloves on, standing in the background. He came forward, and Howard wondered at the travesty a corpse made of existence.

"If we may now, gentlemen, have the remains? To prepare."

The funeral rites, as Chauncey put it, were sure done up brown.

Howard rode with Jay Gould in the first carriage. The mayor rode in the second, and Tweed with two of his gang in the third.

Jim Fisk's passage through the city, in death, was fitting for a monarch, certainly a colonel or an admiral, as Jim had claimed to be. He had lain impressively large for four days in a coffin of rare wood with gold trim, the casket set up in his theater. The curious had passed the catafalque and stared. Then Fisk's remains were escorted to the railroad station by his regiment's band (muffled drums). Officers, ships' captains (full dress) following Jim's riderless horse led by a liveried groom. Burial was to be among his native stones in Bennington, Vermont.

Josie bought mourning black, but did not attend the rites for her late lover. She fled instead to Europe.

Howard hurried from the departure of the black-draped funeral train to change his clothes into something more cheerful. The Chesneys were giving a reception for their daughter Drucilla, who was to marry a member of the Van Bibber family (ships' chandlers) of Rye, New York. The Chesneys were more in debt than ever, but moving in better circles, with two daughters off their hands. Captain Chesney looked wrung out. He was turning gray and had a bit of palsy in his hands. Sipping champagne, he said to Howard, "Lord, I'd rather face Meade at Gettysburg again than go through these last two years once more."

Edward Stokes was three times tried for the murder of Jim Fisk "by pistol shot." The third trial ended with a guilty verdict of third-degree murder, a rarely used grade of guilt among the various definitions of homicide. His sentence was four years in prison.

Howard Harrison Starkweather, investment banker, testified at the last trial as to what he knew of the bad atmosphere between the two men on the day of the killing. He asked, and was permitted, to testify on the first day of the trial because, he explained to the judge, he was to be married the next day at St. Thomas Church at high noon to Susan Chesney, the third daughter of Captain and Mrs. Bixton Wade Chesney.

BOOK VI

Money alone sets all the world in motion.
—PUBILIUS SYRUS, Maxim 656

28

When Harry (Harrison Chesney) Starkweather was seven years old, he had trouble sleeping and would wake to see at the window a large black bear climbing the wind-shaken pine tree outside his bedroom. The creature would open its big red mouth and show huge yellow teeth. Harry would scream, and Mother would come rushing in, in her blue robe. She holding him close to her and rocking him in her arms with her assurances it was a dream.

"Now, now, Harry, it's all right, my darling boy."

"It was a bear."

"Yes, dear, but it was an imaginary bear."

"No, no."

He would fall asleep to her inexhaustible patience—Mother holding him in her warm arms, then put him to bed, and the smell of her and the yielding touch were with him even in sleep, infinitely subtle—but there. Sometimes he could hear Father shouting down the hall in a kind of bronchial barking, "Damn it, Susan, don't pamper the boy."

It was good to know Mother was there and that Charlie, his brother, a year older, wasn't. Charlie, who slept in the north tower of the Shad Point house (had twice climbed down the drainpipe, once set fire to his room). Charlie didn't know about the night frights, the insecurity of a small boy's ambiguous fears.

Charlie was Father's favorite. And the girls, Sunny, Phyllis, Christine, Father liked the girls, too. Mother would say to Harry, "Of course he likes you, Harry. He wants you to be a manly little fellow." And Harry would try and grit his teeth.

"It's just an imaginary bear, isn't it?"

"Of course it is, my dear."

Mother was strong-willed and she stood up to Father in their embroilments. She was always telling the children about the Chesney plantations and how splendid life had been when she was small: her own darky to fetch and carry and her own mammy. The fox hunters yoicking through the hedges on fine horses and stopping for a stirrup cup with her father, now called "Colonel" Chesney, lifting the silver cup to toast the red-coated gentry and ladies—and the baying hounds. Then off across the fields—harvest already in— and the foxes on the run—"Why, we had the fanciest red foxes in Oaktree County." A grandiose epicurean life, Harry was to think of it many years later.

Father would look up from his newspaper at one lament of Mother for the past; it was the first year he was wearing spectacles for reading. "Damn county jakes playing games, afflicting blight on their worn-out acres. Their asses sticking through their riding pants."

"Really, Howard, you might save your vulgarities for your low friends in the city." Mother spoke in refined cadenced tones that irritated Father.

They were all living at Shad Point the first year the house was finished, at least one wing of it, smelling of wet plaster and wood shavings and wallpaper paste. Solid stone, tapestry brick, stretches of slate roof, twenty-foot-high doors, leaded glass windows.

Harry was twelve—fastidious, but most of the shyness gone— when he was sent off to Groton. "The very smart school for making little gentlemen," Mother called it. The house was bigger by then. Father loved swearing at workingmen; the slate roofs—featuring lightning rods—covered a vast expanse. Charlie used to take Harry up to the roof to shoot at what he called hawks, but would aim his .22 rifle at anything on wings and sometimes made a hit. Charlie was the handsomest of the litter, Chauncey Wilcox felt. Even the girls, Sonia (Sunny), Phyllis (Phyl), and Christine (Chris), were merely pretty, but Charlie, Harry admitted, was striking-looking; his corn-colored hair, big blue eyes, and very long lashes all added to a fine physical appearance. His teeth were straight and not a bit bucky, as were Harry's and the girls'.

Harry liked his sisters and their governess, Miss Elm, who was very British, "Don't-cha-know," as Charlie mocked her.

Charlie didn't care as yet for girls. "They smell like cat pee, Hal, and they're weak. No muscles." Harry, not yet arriving at the unrealized dreams of adolescence, agreed.

It was sad to leave Shad Point and Charlie was at Exeter, playing football, writing essays that were sent home marked in blue pencil "Very neat and original point of view" or "Certainly a remarkable new idea on the subject."

It was the year after Harry was very afraid of moths, and when in the night they would be bumping against the screen, sometimes one fluttering horror got in. Harry no longer dared call for Mother; he'd thump on the ceiling with his bamboo fishing pole that Father had given him the year they summered on one of the Thousand Islands in the St. Lawrence. On the signal, Charlie would come down in his nightshirt and catch the moth, laughing all the time, reciting, "Their fangs have the poison of cobras!" Then, "All right, Hal, I've got the little bastard."

Several times Charlie lied about the capture. And the moth, all powdery and awful to touch, would flap against you, would still be there. After that happened a few times, Harry made Charlie show him the corpse held up in his strong brown fingers.

"Here's the body. That proof enough?"

"Thanks, Charlie. When they touch you, *og!*"

Charlie had no fears of nature's forms. He was lifting barbells and swinging dumbbells and Indian clubs and changing his mind about girls, grabbing Mother's maid, Sylvia, in the halls and she crying out, "Oh, you're a bad boy," and he getting under her skirts, rewarded with a hard slap. "Master Charlie's a *very* bad boy."

Once, after a moth capture, Charlie pulled up his nightshirt and in exalted nudity, doing an Indian war dance, showed Harry his hard-on.

"You ever get one of these?"

Harry had—several times—once woke in a tacky bed. But it wasn't something to talk about. Charlie was a wonderful brother. He never mocked Harry about the fear of moths; he taught him to box John L. Sullivan style in the stables and coach house. Charlie talked back to Father on their morning canter when Harry couldn't keep up with them as they rode along the river trail in the early summer. If Harry rode badly, truth was he was thinking of the story he had been reading the night before, one he had reread several times. He had traded for it with one of the grooms; a pearl-handled penknife—a gift from Uncle St. Mars—for the book. A lurid-covered book, *Riders of the Plain.*

He mouthed silently a section of the text he liked best as they rode:

Far in the background rolled the waving grass of a bound-less prairie; amid the silent wilderness of which towered the noble figure of the hunter-horseman, half Indian, half white man in appearance, with rifle, horse, and dog for his sole com-panions in all that dreary waste; though to the right a yelling pack of wolves were seen upon his track. . . .

("Damn it, Harry! Don't give the horse so much rein. Give her a flip of the whip, boy!")

To his left the thick, black smoke, in curling wreaths, pro-claimed the prairie fire, while in the clear gray eyes that looked from the thrilling picture forth, there seemed to glance a look of proud indifference to all and the conscious confidence of ennobling self-reliance!

("She almost threw you. God damn it, stop woolgathering, ride with your eyes open.")

Harry broke off his musing, jerked the horse's head around, feeling foolish, feeling exposed, naked as a worm. "I'm all right."

"Dad, you gave Harry a rotten old mare. She's too broad for him to grip her right."

"He picked her." Father that day waving his riding crop with the deerhorn handle, looking like King Arthur out of the *Tales of the Knights of the Round Table,* his mustache long and shiny, riding jack-et form-fitting with long tails, the proper riding breeches from London, boots with shiny mirrored surfaces. His black horse, Salty, strenuously maneuvering sideways, Father keeping a tight rein.

Charlie was as reckless as Father, taking jumps over bayberry and thorn hedge, riding into a stream with great splashing. He was stealing father's Romeo y Julieta maduro-strength cigars and one dreadful morning getting Harry to smoke one, at least begin, and he had to cat up in the tack room. While from their stalls the grays that pulled the carriage munched oats, their big crystal eyes staring in sorrow to see a boy in such a desperate sick state.

It was clear that Father put his hopes and faith in Charlie to take over someday at the bank. Everything in the family began and end-ed with the bank; H. H. Starkweather & Company. Always in capi-tal letters, it seemed to Harry, as there was talk of markets, silver in the British raj, floating shares and bear raids, a bull market and the price of gold on the Rand. What to others might seem megalo-mania was to the Starkweathers normal existence.

Charlie would have it all one day, and Harry would be on the board of directors, of course, and with some dignified position. But Charlie was hell on wheels, as Gramps ("Colonel" Chesney) put it to Father. "Chuck, his mind is as bright as a little red wagon." Years later, when Harry was the little red wagon that ran the bank, the heir and the head of the family, it seemed ironic (of whom? he wondered. Of God, of society, of the stars in their path?) that Charlie should drown on the *Titanic*, standing at the rail of the new ocean liner going down, smoking his last cigar, listening to the band trying to play as the icy waters crept higher on the tilted deck. Harry always insisted, when someone brought up the subject, they were *not* playing "Nearer, My God, to Thee."

The bank was one of the most imposing four-story buildings on the Street. But Father wasn't satisfied with it. When he took Charlie and Harry—they home for the Easter holiday from prep schools—to lunch at the Bankers and Brokers Club, they would first tour the bank with him, be greeted by Mr. Wilcox and Uncle St. Mars, both those dignitaries in winged gate-ajar collars and marvelous Prince Albert frock coats. Mr. Wilcox, manager and head cashier, and Uncle St. Mars, vice-president in charge of something important to do with trusts and floating issues of stocks and bonds. Harry imagined him, Uncle St. Mars, in a dream once, floating in the Shad Point lily pond holding engraved papers above his head.

Father would look about him in the bank, standing by the gold eagle set in the entrance lobby, and peer down the marble columns all in a row before the bronze enclosures where busy people did the day's business. "I'm going to build a really big bank building soon as I can get hold of the frontage in the parcel next door and all the way behind to the next street. It will be a humdinger."

Father's eyes would light up and he'd hum a tune and smile and slap Charlie and Harry on their backs. "Let's go put on the feed bag." It was impressive the way people called Father, in a respectful tone, H.H., and spoke with admiration of him on their faces as they talked. Sometimes they whispered in his ear, and Father would purse his lips, maybe twist the end of his mustache and clear his throat, saying, "Well, now, that takes a little thinking about, doesn't it? Yep."

Sometimes he'd whisper back, openly jubilant or doubtful. Father always seemed to present a sense of the appropriate.

Harry liked meeting the men Father knew. They would shake his hand and Charlie's. "Nice boys you have there, H.H." Or "Look like chips off the old block." Mr. Morgan and Mr. Belmont, Mr. Drexel, Mr. Villard—and Westerners, Mr. Harriman and Mr. Hill. Some who wore cowboy boots and a black Laredo ranch hat.

Mother and Father went to the opera and the horse shows. Gave fetes and balls at Shad Point, had people with French accents and titles, and sometimes even what Father called the White Jews. Father would not take any nonsense about the Jews. No cruel remarks or snide comments.

"I like 'em. You *can* trust 'em, people like Joseph Pedlock. They know the market and they have a damn fine family life."

Mother just held her facial expressions rigid. "Of course, Howard, your guests are always welcome. You know that."

Father caught the overtranquil intonation in her voice. "I want them *more* than welcome. I want my guests at ease here—no matter when or who. Not some damn decaying gentlewomen and clapped-up old floorwalkers."

"What language. *Really.*"

Mother could use the word "really" to show the contempt she had for the vulgar, the crude side of Father and the pushy clever people with whom he lived on the Street or entertained in town. Father once said, "You'd never have gotten my crowd out to that Chesney plantation for the mint juleps—the mint leaves bruised, not crushed, right? And all the darkies at twilight very respectful, carrying lanterns, standing on the lawn singing to the massa and missy and the drunken guests. Hell, you all were busted planters, drifting on bits of a past that never was."

"Really."

Father and Mother didn't get on too well during the years Harry was at prep school. You didn't have to be clever or very observant to see their irrationality toward each other. Most of the time polite, rather formal, chatting of the house, the garden, the water system (never perfectly in order until pumps were installed to fill the tanks in the great attic).

If Mother didn't care much for the Jews, she made an exception for Joseph Pedlock. He had fought as a major with the Confederate states, had shattered a leg in battle; had a most romantic limp to prove it. ("He isn't just one of *those.*") Both Charlie and Harry were aware of a wound that showed as a red raised welt on his neck, the result, they knew, of a gun duel in the streets he had fought in

Butte, Montana, when he was perfecting the Pedlock smelter process for refining copper and building up the Pedlock copper empire.

Gramps, when he was still alive, would sit on the great front porch overlooking the river, with Major Pedlock and Captain Starkweather, and while the ends of their cigars glowed like fireflies in the twilight, the three men talked of old battles and dead comrades. He, Harry, and Charlie, sitting below them on the steps, listened, making no sound, hoping they'd not be noticed and be sent inside to bed.

Harry got images of dead soldiers rotting like spoiled hay in the fields of Shiloh, which Major Pedlock called Pittsburg Landing, and Gramps' remarks of J. E. B. Stuart ("Not Jeb, like you damn Yankees call him") raiding behind the Union lines. Also a hard realism not in books; the shits from green fruit and the stink of wounds while some friend died on a plank floor, inch by inch, of gangrene.

When Gramps died, Grandma moved in with them, and when Mother would weep sometimes, Grandma would say, "That's the way it is, Sue. It's a man's world and it's our God-given burden to put up with. Harry, what are you doing there gawking? Go wash your hands and go out and play with your dogs." It wasn't that Harry made a habit of standing behind open doors or sitting late on the porch in the big swing, watching the fireflies down by the boathouse go off and on, hearing the loud voices of Mother and Father in their bedroom just overhead, the amenities of their public appearances lost. . . . Harry, he just had been sitting in the dusk, sulking; Charlie had gone off with some friends from Tarrytown for a beer bust, and Harry had been told he was too young and to wait until he had hair around his pecker. There was a threatening fragility in the night, Harry sensed, as Mother's voice grew in volume. Damn, he wished he were not here but with Charlie. Charlie was only a year older; at sixteen he acted as if he were already adult.

It was a warm early June night, and the windows were open. Mother's voice was cutting, not in that slow cultured way she usually spoke.

"Oh, yes, the proper family man, the adoring father. Rather the damn philanderer, that's what you are. Don't I know it now? You

207

only married me for a breeding mare. To give you children. You were still mooning over that theater trash you married, and very much your kind, I'm sure. A whore from the—"

It could have been a slap Harry heard. He felt his stomach muscles tighten, and he sat on the swing, not moving, fearing its creaking chains would show that someone had heard. Mother was usually not one to weep, and too well bred to strike back. "Really, Howard, it's only what I could expect from your kind."

29

For weeks Harry waited for some dread consequences—but only Mother's discolored eye grew better. The sole person Susan would confide in was her sister Drucilla, who was now twice widowed and called herself Mrs. Brooks. Aunt Dru, as Harry knew her, was thin and bony with some inner turmoil set in bile that had turned her very serious and *very* skillful in handling the estates of two husbands. She had a ten-year-old son, Nicholas, a rather pale and knobby bowlegged little boy with large staring unblinking eyes and a mouth usually slightly open. He always looked hungry and most likely was.

Aunt Dru was so involved with land sales and dealing in stocks and bonds she had no time for domestic duties. Drucilla had, Howard admitted, a natural gift for business. "Good as any man's, maybe better." However, she lived like a person always in doubt of having enough left for tomorrow. She and Nick existed in two unheated rooms, but for a gas ring, on East Fourteenth Street. They both lived on her cooked-up messes of gruel; she bought the gruel—a mixture of oatmeal and other cereals—by the bag at wholesale markets.

Aunt Dru came dressed in her greeny-black dress, either her only one or one of several of that style. She, on one visit, let Susan feed her and Nick, seated in a rocker on the big porch at Shad Point—nodding her head, from which she hardly ever removed a little cup-shaped hat topped with soiled feathers.

"Well, Susan, I never had much use for men. Oh, it's in the scheme of things—'male and female made He them. . . .' Nick, finish off that sandwich and have the cakes. Yes, Susan, you have a cross to bear—it's a Gadarene descent, living with a man."

"You should know Howard when he's in his lion's den mood. Isn't Nick eating too much?"

"Oh, a boy's stomach is like a mule's mouth. Stretch a mile before it'll tear an inch. Howard? I know him well. He handles some of my little trifling accounts. . . . The late Mr. Brooks. . . ." Aunt Dru would lean over and talk directly into Mother's ear, but very low. Nick was sweating a bit, having eaten the tray clean at his mother's urging. Harry took him around to see the dogs and Nick made throat sounds and vomited. He made Harry promise not to tell Aunt Dru.

"Ma, she says two visits a week out anyplace for tea and you don't have to keep an icebox."

"What do you eat at home?"

"Gruel hot, gruel cold. And two-day-old bread and lard."

Aunt Dru didn't feel one should waste time on cooking or worrying about clothes. "You gussy yourself up, Susan, and go cakewalking along at Newport or Atlantic City to please this man—so the man, he walks all over you. I had the late Mr. Brooks toe the mark, walk the line, believe you me! Nick, don't play too hard with Cousin Harry and knock out the knees of your stockings again. *His* father can afford them."

They all made fun of Aunt Dru, but Father said, "She's one damn shrewd speculator. Did a bit of a killing in cotton futures last month. You ever ask her how much she's worth now?"

Mother said, "We Chesneys never thought much of money matters."

"Which is why your father would have died a bankrupt if I hadn't taken things in hand."

That led, as Harry remembered, to a fresh fearful row.

From the journal of St. Mars. Chesney:

> Donald McCann tells me H.H. always insists a new ruling group in business has to be firmly aggressive, and if some call it lawless, the end result is what we should study. The ordinary people, who don't know the Street—says McCann, Scot Calvinist—have moral values they follow more or less, so does the Street.
>
> H.H. doesn't, McCann insists, like the words "common people." "Hell, he's just as common as anybody, he'll tell you. It's just the average man lacks the energy and drive that takes

chances, has the courage—maybe the gall—that keeps the country eating, moving."

It's true. I have observed H.H. and other big men of the Street; they do feel useful and creative. They're in some other world, McCann claims. "In another time they'd be rulers, generals, and not what the sensation-seeking newspapers call boodlers, label moneybags."

McCann insists they are not solidly united, as some think. They bite and scratch, fight, intrigue among themselves. McCann admits everything said against them—their bad habits, methods—is true but points to the changes in the nation's look, income, exports. Yes, there is the collecting of property into a few hands to replace the scattered unhealthy industries not efficient or technical enough to survive. Critics do say H.H. and men like him work for private gain and are not polite or silk-gloved. This goes for ditchdiggers, too.

They use people who control the Street, the nation's resources as a private pantry. But the clerk, the farmer, the small homeowner could benefit. H.H. warns against uncontrolled appetites for profits. He has no use for J. D. Rockefeller, who says, "God gave me my money."

H.H. is scornful of J.D. "S——. John D. Rockefeller is worth a billion. He makes his money by simply selling five hundred million dollars' worth of oil securities, then the market goes down and he takes them back at his leisure. Of course the market cannot stand the weight of his selling. He is the one man who knows what everybody else is doing, and nobody knows what he is doing."

As H.H. sees it, it's the investment banker keeps the capitalist world afloat. The public's, the banks' money is what he guards. Gold, credits, reserves. He has said to me, "We're a big tit, St. Mars, feeding out of short- or long-term loans, producing money for investment growth. The millowners, railmen, industrial boys come running to us with their industrial paper, shares to issue, their collateral. And we accept their promises to pay us back. We sell confidence. We hold secrets; we save investors from losses in bad companies that need propping up. Yes, sure, we take a fat commission and do have other people's money on deposit. And use it for our own ends for profit. But it's safe. We demand seats—true—on boards; *try* running a country without us. Anyway, we all die, we stink, we get buried; but the railroads, ships, factories remain. No irony like God's irony. Yep."

Harry was in his second year at Harvard, class of '93, when it was clear to him that the marriage of his mother and father was a disaster, locked in calamity. He had gone through the summer at Shad Point when he was on vacation from prep school, enjoying swimming and boating, hard games of tennis, loafing in the Pocantico hills. Yes, aware of friction on the domestic scene at Shad Point. But assuming (from what he had seen of the homelife of his friends and school mates as a weekend guest) this was the pattern of marriage near the end of the nineteenth century. It left him a bit flummoxed, as Miss Elm, the English governess of his sisters, would say.

Charlie was at Princeton (Howard felt the boys should be educated separately. "So they don't back each other up in any school, but stand on their own feet"). Charlie in a heavy turtle-necked sweater, a broken nose (it gave him character) and a chipped front tooth as reward for being halfback on the best football team that ever beat Rutgers.

One morning, Thanksgiving holiday, when they both were out in the skiff trolling for river bass, Charlie said, "You know, Hal, the old man is keeping this lady doctor."

"What lady doctor?"

"Oh, one of those new women, all for female votes and wearing bloomers and no riding sidesaddle."

"That's why Mother spends so much time in Newport?"

"You're slow, but solid. Once you catch on to a thing, it's glued in your memory."

Charlie was mocking him cruelly these days—but Harry knew his brother liked him. Charlie was a big man at Princeton; football captain, baseball pitcher, and the pride of Professor Weskitt, head of the higher mathematics. Charlie was a wizard at figures and Professor Weskitt called him "my young Euclid."

"Hey, Chuck! I've got a strike." Harry was feeling a choking sensation in his throat—strange, a father with a mistress, like in a French novel. But the fish on the line gave him an excuse for shouting in bringing the thrashing fish close and Charlie lifted it up by grabbing it under the gills.

"Three pounds, Chuck!"

"Maybe two, *if* you fill it with pebbles."

Harry didn't care for the rest of the afternoon talk as Charlie detailed Father's way of life. Harry had had several fumbling experiences with an older woman, wife of a dentist, in a Boston hotel room. Not fully satisfactory in her maniacal manipulation of his first time. Certain experiences needed further study. Harry had a slight fear of hell and damnation as an adulterer and yet a certain urge to seek the limits of what was called in church his "animal nature." Charlie was freer and rather foul-mouthed about his sexual adventures; he seemed to exult in the conquest of waitresses and salesgirls in the better shops. And once, he told Harry, as they rowed back to the boathouse—in Atlantic City with the touring Princeton Glee Club—he sang in a strong but controlled baritone, "I had me some beautiful black skin . . . a change of luck, they say, you know, to dip your wick in a Negress."

There were people who did not blame Susan for leaving Shad Point and her husband and going to live in Newport. She had been, she thought, a good wife, had borne beautiful children—ungrateful children. She had admired Howard's mind (she did not like to call him, as most did, H.H.). Had found him fair, protective, and in the end indifferent to her. Disassociated. "That bad moment," her mother said, "when casualness becomes cruelty."

Susan had to admit she had no sparkling mind, not any kind of wit. Her God and her church were vital to her, serious indeed. Not to be mocked by Howard's remarks that it was a church of the rich and fashionable and "handing out a basket with a sick turkey, some apples and nuts once or twice a year doesn't make life any better for the poor devils in those tenements."

It had been no use, Mother said to Aunt Dru, asking, reminding Howard what *he* did; handing out money to actors, actresses, rummies, and plain misfits. Worthless people who flattered his vanity and tipped their hats to him or fluttered their eyelids. And the gossip reached her—some of the actresses took off their petticoats and spread their legs for him up in his suite on the third floor of his new bank. She herself had found sex a doleful game, not distasteful, but a duty not to be prolonged.

Howard had stopped listening to her tirades. He would just smile, read his newspaper, or carefully trim a cigar and light it. Knowing she found tobacco a great evil and nasty-smelling. More and more, he'd just leave her, she in mid-sentence, and go off to the stables or the boathouse or have a groom drive him to the depot at Norton-on-Hudson and spend the night in town. He claimed at one of his clubs.

212

When Harry entered Harvard, Susan had finally reached the point when she could no longer live in the same house with Howard Harrison Starkweather. She had left his bed, rather, he had moved into the blue guest room, after Christine was born. She had begged off (when he was one night a mere animal full of physical desires) and he had called her "a frozen bitch and cold c---." (She never dared think of the entire four-letter word.)

That summer of 1891 Harry went to Newport, not to Shad Point, for the summer vacation. Charlie had gone out to a dude ranch in Wyoming to shoot elk and eat greasy camp cooking, as he wrote back, with some people who had his own reaction to the West; he sent Harry a picture with Teddy Roosevelt. He rarely wrote to his mother. Susan just said, "Charles, he's like his father, Harry. He's dispensed with manners, decency."

Howard Starkweather, age fifty-one, was like no one, he felt, but himself. He was honest enough to admit he had married Susan Chesney because she had a large desirable body, because it seemed a kind of thing to do; he liked the Chesney family. And deep down there was the hope he could produce from her splendid healthy body children, a dynasty, at least the start of one.

It was not that he had an insensitivity or felt Susan was not aware of what a marriage of pleasure had to be. He tried never to be dishonest with himself as to his motives, his actions. Physically drawn as he had once been to Susan Chesney, he had not been deeply in love. The relentless image of Amy remained, and he soon knew he saw in Susan virtues, wisdoms that she had never possessed. Yet she had been in their first years amusing, entertaining, alive, alert to the same surface of living that excited and delighted him. With Susan he found, he thought, a willing bed partner ("dutiful" would be a better word, he thought later). Soon it was clear she found sex rather boring and degrading. He once nearly brained her with a Biedermeier clock when he told her he missed her in bed when he had to be out of town and she answered, "Really?"

Susan was a splendid mother, but as he swore at her, "Damn it, I can hire nannies and governesses to wipe their dirty little asses and blow their noses."

"You want a courtesan, not a wife."

" 'Whore' is the word you're looking for, Mrs. S. Well, a whore gives value, earns her keep. Sleeping with you these nights is like—"

She had fled from his cataloguing of her faults in the marriage bed and spent two days having nausea spasms, taking violet drops, and weeping.

Howard had never had any guilty feelings when after the birth of their last child he began to have an affair with Naomi Richards, who made large clay sculptures in Greenwich Village of Diana the huntress, Leda and the swan. Naomi had a deep voice, dark gold-flecked eyes. Her family were rich people in San Francisco and owned silver mines and smelters in Cripple Creek, Virginia City. She was rather demanding sexually, which at first pleased Howard. ("We are, Howard, like the secret gods in Greek groves.") It all ended one day when Naomi suggested they invite Lily Cohn, who painted lampshades in the next studio, to join them on the big dusty studio couch. ("We will be at Mytilene on the island of Lesbos, where Sappho sang.")

As Howard was floating Naomi Richards' father's silver-mine shares, he merely excused himself and left. It was a mistake he did not make again; mix his sexual drives with business.

In the 1890's there was a great deal of business H. H. Starkweather & Company was doing. Chauncey Wilcox had proved to be hard and brilliant, able to handle the setting up of companies, corporations, trusts. While St. Mars Chesney, Howard's wife's brother, had turned into a polished and convincing salesman, saw to the disposing of various shares and bonds that H. H. Starkweather & Company handled for clients in America and Europe. From his pale topaz tiepin to cloisonné jardinieres on his desk holding chrysanthemums, he was in good taste.

Howard made the final major decisions, created situations more daring than St. Mars would have approved of. Chauncey, however, did not shrink from sales to firms and organizations that other investment bankers on the Street might not have taken. Howard tried to keep a tight rein on the young man, as on his horse, Salty.

Chauncey had grown heavier, his face had broadened, his nose becoming a prominent feature, "an Indian hawk's," Chauncey admitted. He dressed in the clubman's high mode, drank a bit too much at times, ate well with a gourmet's delight and a gourmand's appetite at the best places. He was known at Bar Harbor during the yacht regattas, at Saratoga in the racing season, an escort of Lillian

Russell. (Memoirs mention him in the sporting house of Nell Kimball when in New Orleans to see to a line of a railroad out of Southern California into the Delta.) He was often at the Hoffman House with John Drew, Nat Goodwin, was called by the New York *World* a *bon vivant* and *bon viveur*. He had never married after a whispering among the social set that "he's a British West Indies nigger." Chauncey was trigger-tempered and had been badly beaten one New Year's night at a dance hall on Fourteenth Street. He was a skilled investor and had made some large sums of money. But his gambling at Canfield's and other card and dice clubs, his bets on prizefights, horse races were costly.

Howard made no attempt to change Chauncey's life-style. And he often shared Chauncey's habit of relaxing on the massage slabs in the Sea of Marmara Turkish Baths, being slapped and hand-rubbed by two large Greeks. Smoking a cigar with Chauncey one night, H.H. blew smoke rings at the tiled ceiling when the Greeks left.

"You having yourself a time in life, Chaunce?"

"I'm trying, H.H. Jesus, I'm trying."

Howard chuckled. He felt lazy and relaxed. As if drained of the Street's poison by the steam room, and now his nerve ends were at rest after being teased with skill and little hard slaps. "Don't you get too much involved in joy. I'm going to pull together a copper trust with Joseph Pedlock to head it."

"Isn't that Morgan's child? He's been having his man Rodgers sniffing out the controls of some copper mines and smelters. Little fellows, but if he combines them and goes for the big round-up. . . ."

"I know. I know. But Pedlock controls the Pedlock process."

"What's that?"

"To purify the smelting of copper ore into pure metal by blowing compressed air through it."

"What does that do, H.H.?"

"Carries off most of the impurities. Trouble is the patent can't hold with all the infringing going on. Just make shyster lawyers rich. So instead of fighting in the courts, Starkweather and Company is going to put together one *big* copper trust. The way Morgan, I hear, is working one out for railroads and the steel mills.

"McCann joining him?"

"Donald is getting on, Chauncey. He may give in rather than fight. Take his share in stocks and sponsor opera stars, his latest idea of life. I hope my kids don't take to that. Opera!"

Chauncey closed his eyes, puffed on his cigar. "That's some boy you have in Charlie."

"Both good boys. Harry is all right. Too much mother."

"It's all finished there, H.H.?"

"Over a long time. Just kind of became a habit while the children were growing up. . . . Yes, well, get St. Mars to feel out the copper miners."

30

Among those who thought well of Howard Starkweather was Myron Carpenter-Garnier, president of the National Broadway-Manhattan Bank near Trinity Church. He was a plump man with faded muttonchop whiskers a bit on the long side, a man who earnestly supported evangelical Christianity in overseas missions, knelt in prayer on retiring, lived simply but well on Staten Island, and was dedicated to stopping the betting on horseflesh.

Howard had been sleeping with Myron Carpenter-Garnier's wife late afternoons at the apartment he kept in town. Fanny Carpenter-Garnier, twenty years younger than her husband, had found life an unmitigated bore. Howard met her ice skating in Central Park—at first he seemed a safe middle-aged gentleman with whom to have coffee and tarts, go shopping for ribbons. But it turned out he was not like Myron at all. He proved, twice a week, a delightful virile lover, making of sex an ostensible detailed drama before he got her into her clothes, mockingly singing, "Pale hands I loved beside the Shalimar." Then, all buttons, bows done up, drove her to the Staten Island ferry slip.

The National Broadway-Manhattan Bank had two generations of solid Anglo-Saxon-French-Early American family behind it, also a connection with the Vanderbilt shipping lines, and held the notes of some of the biggest whiskey distillers of the middle Atlantic states. There was a time when the bank had backed certain ship's captains who went blackbirding off the African West Coast, bringing back cargoes of slaves to be smuggled ashore in the Carolinas at six to eight hundred dollars a head.

Myron was happy to see Howard this afternoon. His liver was acting up, he was getting too plump. A flight of stairs would cause Myron to catch his breath. Thank God he had been a decent Christian, honest, hardworking, and Fanny would (God don't hurry the day) be left well off if he should die suddenly like Grandfather and Father, among all the marble and bronze, under the oak-raftered ceiling of the bank. So like a tomb, so like a gol-darn tomb (he did not use foul language or take the name of the Lord in vain).

"Well, H.H., sit down. Have a cheroot. A tot of rye?"

"Myron, you're a hard man, a fair one, a driver of good bargains who has gumption and daring."

"I serve." (Myron sipped the drink.) "I try. *How* daring?"

"Copper," said H.H. "Pedlock, Butte."

"Ha. Danged good, all three, like a gold twenty-dollar coin. You have something in mind?"

"I have. But it's big. What, Myron, are your assets?"

"Annual report just in. One hundred and fifty million satisfy you?" The banker laughed and shook like calf's-foot jelly. "Want it *all* in gold and silver, tied up in canvas bags?"

"Only to look at some of it."

When half an hour later they shook hands, Howard walked back to his office. . . . He'd have to give up Fanny. Myron was too fine a man to do business with *and* bed his wife at the same time. I've become too self-indulgent, Howard thought. I'd better stop before I find myself reprehensible. He was in a good mood and did a little jig in his office.

St. Mars sipped sherry in his study and wrote in his journal:

H.H.'s pattern of combining industries, of floating shares has now become a flood. Copper will be a really big one. Just this morning, looking over a week's newspaper clippings on my desk, I compiled a whole series of names and corporations that have grown on the ideas H.H. was among the first to create. Starkweather & Company of course sees others use his methods—take over the investment banking, to build up such

217

names and firms as Elbert Gary and John W. Gates, who creat-
ed the wire-nail trust. The Moore brothers ran wild, formed
National Biscuit Trust, a tin-plate trust, and the steel-hoop
combine. Gary to form the Federal Steel Company. Morgan,
National Tube, American Bridge, American Sheet Steel. With
Morgan's brain, there is General Electric, and in public utilities
William Whitney, Thomas Fortune Ryan, Charles T. Yerkes,
Peter Widener, H. H. Rogers, William Rockefeller to combine
gas and electric companies, trolley lines. Theodore Vail set up
telephones. Did business in shares based on the work of Edi-
son, Westinghouse, Thomson, Houston. A grab and seizure,
H.H. sees, of his methods, electric tools, machinery needed for
public utilities, public welfare.

I don't suppose the big businessmen of the nation will ever
erect a statue to H.H. He has no vanities in that direction.
"Christ, St. Mars, I'm just a natural-born individual, a native
doing things that help the country and also do well by me and
mine. I don't need the mob to kiss my ass, and much as I like a
lot of them, I don't think they have the horse sense to run the
country. Let them go into Congress and take their boodle." As
Chauncey Wilcox puts it, "He may sound hard and nobody
ever got rich picking up a half-dollar he has dropped without
meaning to. Still, I've never known H.H. *not* to keep his word."

St. Mars Chesney was given the task of making contact with the
copper producers, owners of mines and smelters, shapers of copper into wire to be strung over the cities on a forest of poles, tubing
for ships being built, distillery pipes, other alloys. H. H. Starkweather had set up the share selling of an issue for a Greenpoint
organization that cast bronze propellers for the Brooklyn Navy
Yard. And the telephone would someday go into *every* home and
office.

St. Mars had remained slim, his corn-colored hair still holding a
wave, his features more refined, mature; the nose perhaps a bit too
small. But, all in all, "a gentleman of standing and good ancestry
just by the look of him," as one sponsor said on St. Mars' admit-
tance to the Union League.

He had married a distant niece of Senator Boies Penrose of
Pennsylvania, a Senator very close to the political bureau and lobby
of Standard Oil. She was also related to Mark Hanna, boss of the
Republican Party. So St. Mars was a valuable member of H. H.

Starkweather & Company. Mrs. Chesney (*née* Penrose) had money of her own. They lived in a Tudor house on three acres between Great Neck and Oyster Bay, kept a forty-foot ketch-rigged sailboat on the Sound. They had three daughters, who in time rode ponies at the horse shows. They owned a Hoppner, Greuze, and several others of the Barbizon school. No Bouguereau.

The St. Mars Chesneys were not snobs and when they put down one of the first clay tennis courts, their neighbors were invited to play on it. St. Mars was chairman of the North Shore Republican District Club. There was good talk over cocktails by some members while seated on the Long Island Sound Yacht Club piazza. Waiting for the wind to turn, for the junior sailing classic event to be run off on Decoration Day—talk of St. Mars Chesney having a political future.

"You can trust young St. Mars. Need 'im in the right public office. All this bushwa about union organizing and this Bryan coming up for free silver and labor. Party needs new blood."

"Bryan, he'll never amount to much. But St. Mars would look fine up in Albany to begin with."

"The wind's turning. Finish your drinks, gentlemen, and put on your judges' badges."

However, at the club dance that night St. Mars shook his head at questions on running for public office. "I'm just an investment banker, you boys know that."

"We'll not give up. But it's good to have you on the Street. Too many Yids there now."

St. Mars just smiled. He had no prejudices against Jews. They had their own clubs. . . . Standing there in a blue well-cut jacket with the gold-plated buttons, his white flannels and rubber-soled white shoes, a slant to a yachting cap with the club emblem, he looked what he was. A pleasant bright young man who could be trusted not to betray polite society; solid, respectable—needed to help balance the muckers pressing out from New York onto the Island, north to Westchester, to Tuxedo Park and Spring Valley. St. Mars did not say anything about his meeting set with Joseph Pedlock in the morning.

St. Mars Chesney added to his journal, not mere personal events, but rather often notes of what he had observed and studied on the Street:

219

What no one can ever take away from H.H. is the basic idea of a combination of small industries into giants as the railroads spread out and the crops, the meat on the hoof, the coal and the petroleum began to attract powerful forces of banking and money. H.H. saw the pattern of the whole industrial system—long before others did—and made it a near science—saw its way of operating had to change and the solitary speculator or family trust could be taken over by joint-stock companies, by banks and operators with large amounts of money or credits. That by the selling of shares and bonds, fortunes could be made even before any crop was grown, steers raised, metal dug from the earth and refined. And, yes, before one rail was laid. Early men like Gould and Fisk had been raiders to seize and destroy. H.H. was a creator.

H.H., true, was for the idea of making combinations big enough so they could not be hindered or stopped. Bigger productions, trusts, combines, rings, pools, cartels, syndicates. For H.H. they could do away with small or underendowed and underfinanced companies. What will survive, he feels, will in time become fully efficient—and the multimillion-dollar producers will dominate the market.

H.H. saw this could be bad. "Still, there's science to it—leaping like a frog with a hot poker up its ass; new processes, better machines, creating more demands, and sales of shares. I've seen in ten years manufactured goods jump from five billion to ten billion.

"It ruined some, this progress—but it gave zest to seeking new markets."

What was not at first apparent was that men like H.H. and others controlled everything for sale in the nation. Controlled it almost from the Street and from their investment banks. There will be fewer industries, but you can bet, H.H. insists, the survivors will be bigger than anything yet seen. In the way Starkweather & Company made McCann Steel and Iron, one of the leaders in steel, just as much as their use of Bessemer converters. Rows and rows of Bessemer furnaces pouring decarbonized steel faster and cheaper. The issues of stocks went faster as McCann opened new plants, developed better processes. But it was Starkweather & Company, H.H., that actually created those steel plants by getting the millions to erect them. Others on the Street did the same for Frick, for Elihu Thomson, for Carnegie, the Homestead Steel Works.

Donald McCann came often to the Street—with a body bent

220

over a bit more, gray and paunchy, somewhat deaf now. But the icy eyes were alert and he grumbling—to report to H.H. that Mc. S. & I. plants were rolling twenty thousand tons of steel a month with a three-million-dollar profit for the quarter. "Iron is depressed. Steel is king!"

Now Howard Harrison Starkweather clients faced Sherman Antitrust Act enforcement. He wasn't fazed by it. He said, "I tell you forces greater than any man or group of men can't stop the making of combinations. And I'll be goddamned if I'll admit that the word 'trust' is a dirty word."

31

Riverside Drive was producing its best series of apartment houses. The Naples was tall and ornate and Joseph Pedlock lived on the top story in an apartment dominated by heavy rugs, dark-red velvet drapes, and overcarved *art décoratif* Vienna furniture; his sister Tante Longstrasse's choice.

Howard and Chauncey, arriving near ten o'clock, were let in by a maid who was obviously not able to speak much English ("You spaken Polski?"). They were shown into the large room facing the river and the park. Over a Spanish fireplace hung the John Singer Sargent painting of Joseph Pedlock, his wife, and their three sons, Sam, Ralph, and Egon (in the picture small boys with naked knees, Eton collars, big blue bows, and velour pants). Joseph Pedlock was painted, with a neat dark beard, holding a live cigar and the glowing end done in two tones of pink. (The picture is now in the Metropolitan Museum of Art.)

"Damn fine painting," said Howard.

Chauncey was looking over the rest of the room's art, not identifying the Copley and the Gilbert Stuart, studying some dark oils of Talmudic faces in female wigs or ritual beards, patterned by genuine gold watch chains, wing collars. A strong family, he decided—with roots in the American Revolution and wherever else the Jews came from in Europe.

Howard was looking at a small photograph of a Confederate captain of horse.

"That's me at twenty-three. All piss and vigor."

Both men turned at the sound of the voice to find Joseph Ped-

221

lock standing in the doorway leading to another room. "Hell, yes, Captain Pedlock, CSA. Full of romantic drivel. I had the rebel faith. Yes, indeed, in Judah P. Benjamin and Robert E. Lee. Now, Jeff Davis I wasn't *too* sure about."

Howard nodded. "A fine view up the river. You're comfortable, Joseph. Snug."

"H.H., it's lonely. The boys away, the rest of the family in Baden-Baden, Paris. . . . Let's get started. Anyone care for a drink?"

"Too early, Joseph. And Chesney isn't here yet." Howard looked at his watch after snapping open the double lids. "Gentlemen of breeding always arrive late."

Joseph Pedlock went to an old teak chest on legs; it looked rather worm-eaten, but the wide iron bands that held it together gave it a solid look. He took out some papers. "God's wisdom is often man's foolishness."

"Not if you had a smart lawyer."

"Got these yesterday from the vaults of my bankers, Wollfain and Ellenbogen, at the moment handling my copper shares."

"Good firm" said Chauncey. "I have here a list of copper firms we've found, been in contact with—they're mostly in favor of merging into a copper combine."

Chauncey took a paper from an inner pocket. "It's not complete. Chesney is handling the final details. But so far we seem sure of St. Paul Copper Corporation, Standard Refineries, and Ball and Kingston Smelters. Also we've twenty small outfits. All listed here."

Howard tapped the list with his fingers. "Now, Joseph, we can buy or control all of these mines, holdings, at a cost of about twenty-nine million dollars."

"Just like that? I've got good credit, but *that* sum!"

Howard smiled in amiability. "I've wanted to put together something like this for a long time. Morgan is doing it with railroads, with steel. He'll get around to copper unless we move first, aggressively. Combine, control, sell shares, and *if*—"

The maid showed St. Mars in, he in a morning coat, striped trousers, a white waistcoat with the thinnest of gold watch chains, a bit of jade hanging on the end of one. As usual he projected a sense of serene complacency, the quality of luminosity of a good salesman.

"The carriage traffic around Herald Square is nearly impassable. Sorry, Mr. Pedlock, H.H., Chaunce."

"Yes, something will have to be done or the city will become immovable."

Howard was impatient, gave St. Mars a deprecatory look. "I was just starting to explain to the major how we're going to handle the controlling of the copper companies. Merge them with the Pedlock holdings."

St. Mars took the small carrying case from under his arm and laid it down on a nearby table, opened it, removed from it a thick pencil, a batch of papers. "Now, to outline Mr. Starkweather's idea."

"Sit down, St. Mars, damn it. *Sit*," said Howard.

"I will." He sat, inspected the first sheet in his hands, flipped three over. "Ah, yes, the gist. We take title to the mines and smelters; that is, we will buy through two dummy corporations set up in my name and Mr. Wilcox's. Buy by turning over a check for twenty-nine million dollars, drawn on the National Broadway-Manhattan Bank."

Joseph Pedlock gave a faint grin. "Who's *meshugge* here?"

Chauncey said, "It's being drawn. The understanding—our secret—is that the check will be left deposited in the bank and remain there for a certain fixed period of time."

"Meanwhile, "Howard said, taking the papers from St. Mars and putting on his eyeglasses, "we are organizing the Trans-American Copper Combine. With clerks of some of the companies we take over as directors. Directors controlled by us. To this Trans-American Copper Combine we transfer all the mines and smelters, issue new shares, and for fifty-five million dollars."

Joseph Pedlock looked serious. "Not for cash?"

"No, for capital stock."

"It's beautiful, damn it, H.H., like a Hassidic rabbi's chant, even if it's a pipe dream."

Joseph Pedlock stood up and patted Howard on the back. "You should have been a Greek or a Yankee peddler. I'm beginning to see the light. You take this fifty-five million in capital stock to the National Broadway-Manhattan Bank and borrow the twenty-nine million. That covers the check lent to your first setup of companies bought out. I don't believe it—it's *too* simple."

"We still owe the bank twenty-nine million of course," said Howard, "but we then put the shares up for the bank—selling, we think, on the market at about one hundred or one hundred and one dol-

223

lars a share. That's a fair estimate, and with copper prices, need for copper, our solid hold on the ore and its smelting, we should get perhaps a rise, a price of one-twenty-five, one-twenty-six a share in time."

St. Mars said, tapping the table with the pencil, "We can work up a great interest in copper shares in the press. And it's good solid stock. Well worth investing in by trusts and estates. We should sell most of the fifty-five million dollars' worth. From that we repay the bank plus their rate of interest—and take the difference between the twenty-four million and the final fifty-five million—less costs—as profit."

Howard handed the papers back to St. Mars. "And neither we nor you, Joseph, have used a dollar of our own."

"H.H.! Morgan couldn't have done it better."

Chauncey added, "Just costs and expenses."

"We haven't done it yet. Just started," added Howard.

"Who," asked Joseph Pedlock, "will run the combine? After all, there is real copper to mine and refine. It's harder than printing shares."

"You, Joseph, as president and with a board of directors we shall carefully pick. St. Mars will fill you in. You know how to run mines and smelters. Also you'll retain enough stock for you to control through it and proxies."

Chauncey said, "No problem with the shares—good-sounding shares are usually bought by doctors, ministers, shopkeepers, lawyers, well-off farmers."

St. Mars carefully replaced his papers in his case and handed it to Joseph Pedlock. "These are your set, sir."

Howard added, "By control of dividends and passed dividends, too, the price of shares can be controlled and you will want to buy back a bigger control."

St. Mars said, "We'll watch J. P. Morgan. If he begins to smell a combine, he'll perhaps try to gain control. So until the last detail is final. . . ."

There was a shaking of hands all around, a sipping of cognac, and a tasting of honey *lekach* and cookies called *rugelach* sent in by Tante Longstrasse.

Joseph Pedlock lifed his glass. "There's an old Jewish toast and a hosanna—*L'chayim*; to life. And in this case, to copper. It's a hell of a different time from when I first went out to Butte. It was dirty work sinking shafts; hired gunmen to protect your diggings and ore cars. Now it's all done on paper by the Street, instead of burning freight cars, and your rivals getting rebates from the railroads on your shippings. They're *all* so smart. Rodgers for Rockefeller, Flagler, Harrison, Payne. They have no fear God can find them out—even behind a thousand walls."

"That's the way things are done," said Howard, sipping cognac. "Take Standard Oil. Their directors, fifteen of them. St. Mars, where do these hold other directorships?"

"Standard Oil Company of New Jersey directors have their asses in chairs as directors in innumerable banks, insurance companies, traction companies, electric light, gas and industrial concerns of every sort, including Mesabi iron range in Minnesota."

"Enough, enough, gentlemen. . . ."

Joseph Pedlock, after they had left, stood at the bank of windows, looking down on the apple-green park and the river. He was the same age, he supposed, as Howard Starkweather, who had also taken hard knocks; how he must have fought to emerge into the upper air—a luftmensch of business and banking. Yet we seem to come from different worlds. So much of his world is an impenetrable mirror to me.

To produce the copper at the best prices, to enlarge the nation's resources and be rewarded for it, that has been my whole purpose. But men like Howard Starkweather are to me as if from a different species. I'm as persistent, as impervious to past disasters. But. . . .

What a remarkable plan of H.H.'s for forming the Trans-American Copper Combine. And as had been said in this very room just a little time ago, without putting up a dollar of our own. . . . The nation was certainly speaking a new rhetoric in business, with a higher angle of vision.

He turned and walked past the wall of rabbinical faces and the members of his wife's family; the Manderscheids of Philadelphia in their George Washington wigs and ruffles. He stopped to gaze at himself at twenty-three, Captain Pedlock, CSA. All answers seemed to come easy then. All the future was there to be taken by a strong man who could handle circumstances and consequences.

A long time since the bloody shitty shirttails and the loose bowels in Virginia fields . . . the leg shattered by a Sharps rifle . . . the stink of defeat . . . the feeling of being vulnerable and alone as Lee rode his gray horse off into history.

Joseph Pedlock poured himself another three fingers of cognac and held it up to the picture. "You romantic son of a bitch, did you

225

ever imagine we'd be here and with such doings? Well, all good deeds must be punished."

Sharing a hack downtown to Wall Street, St. Mars said, "I still wonder if in the end Morgan will not take it away from Pedlock?"

Howard watched the parade of Broadway. It always was drama to him, the shabby people and the well-dressed, the hungry in worn clothing examining eating places. Crystal windows where were displayed huge red lobsters, staring fish resting on ice, great pink hams and game birds still in their feathers. Cases of caviar and cheese. How they must affect those poor and dispossessed, who just pressed close to look; do they wonder if the city could again turn to riot and civil war, as it did in '63? A balls breaker. No. Today the old displayers of rage do not seize guns, they seek the power of the purse. Get rich themselves.

"Even if Morgan in the end gets control, Pedlock and us, we'll have ten, fifteen years, I'd say, to get the best out of it in the handling of the shares. . . . You know, just here in sixty-three I commanded cannon during the riots after Gettysburg. The poor buggers were being sent off to war while the well-off bought themselves out of the service for three hundred dollars."

"Did you, H.H.?" St. Mars asked.

"There were dead lying all around these streets, even women and children, heads mashed in by police clubs. And the soldiers killing everything in sight. Oh, being killed, too. My father-in-law, Captain O'Hara, my first father-in-law, that is, he was beaten to death by the mob, horribly tortured. . . . Did I buy a substitute to go to war for me? My number wasn't picked. I never had to make the choice."

Chauncey thumbed his waistcoat's piping. "Me and Captain Starkweather were at sea the first two years of the war. Running the sea blockade for you Southerners. Remember *Sea Witch*, H.H.?"

Howard chuckled. "That's no ferryboat I have a picture of hanging in my office."

St. Mars produced a gold pencil and a small leather-bound notebook. "This copper combine is, sir, the greatest coup Starkweather and Company has yet produced."

"Christ, St. Mars, only if all goes well."

"It will. I'll prepare something for the journalists when the time is ripe. How soon will we alert our agents in Boston as to the shares available? Boston somehow seems the proper city, having the kind of people who would invest in the copper combine."

"Philadelphia, too," said Chauncey, closing his eyes. He had had only two hours' sleep and was still feeling the effects of the saloon and sporting-house visits of the night before. He was somewhat amazed he had become so accustomed to speaking of millions of dollars. It was good, he thought, being a champion of laissez-faire—nothing to it, he thought, half asleep. But an elbow soon was shoved into his ribs.

"Get up, Chaunce, we're at the bank." The hack had come to a stop and Chauncey shook his head, trying to clear it of any ideas of rest and sleep. There was a lot to do. The project wasn't going to be as easy as they had explained it in such self-aggrandized detail at Pedlock's apartment.

It wasn't easy, it wasn't smooth the next two months. But in the end the Trans-American Copper Combine existed and people on the Street spoke of H. H. Starkweather ("Smart, oh, really smart; H.H. runs a trim ship"). The firm became not the largest, but one of the most successful; certainly it had shouldered its way in among the important houses, ones that suggested millions, offering shares that rose in value. Usually.

It was the entry of H. H. Starkweather & Company into top-level dealings—with a weight of values and enterprises properly handled. A move into what (after the turn of the century) vaudeville actors would call "the big time."

Howard Starkweather was accepted as one of the important men on the Street; the bank was among the half dozen mentioned when one thought of the Street.

There were those who saw Howard Harrison Starkweather as a very able man to rise with—it would do to attach oneself to his coat-tails. There were some few "petulant bastards" (Chauncey) who said he wasn't simon-pure and recalled when he had been caught up in the Gould-Fisk gold scandal. The realists saw his worth, the romantics envied his skill; the public, those with money, bought his shares.

32

The year Harry Starkweather graduated from Harvard ("Hound-Dog Hal" in the year book) he was a tall, too-thin young

227

man who looked ill fed. Actually he had a fine appetite, but somehow didn't seem to fill out. He had a certain searching look, as if hunting with a timeless fatalism; wondering what the rest of the world was made of, its existence and conditions on earth. He had read a great many novels, done poorly in French and Latin, but made passing marks. Been excited by Emerson, repelled by some of Mark Twain's humor, and felt a bit ashamed of his sensuality. He came down from Harvard with some of the school's dislike of immediacy and spontaneity, a sober-minded young man.

He dressed well, but hardly with the dash and color of his brother, Charlie, who was working at the bank's overseas section. Charlie's collars were high, he often carried a cane, not one as heavy as his father's. Harry was a churchgoer but had no spiritual torments. At school he had been called a Christer and feared death, also rowdy men in saloons and venereal disease. He disliked vulgarity, bad taste, and the smell of people who often did not bathe—many didn't at the time. He was kind, tolerant, but a bit uneasy with people who were not in his segment of society. Not that Harry was a snob or a prig. He was shy. He preferred the prose of Dickens to Defoe (English Lit. 3), sang well, and enjoyed blacking up for the college "nigger minstrel shows." He never made any team on land but did row in the crew of a shell that beat Yale in his third year. Uncle St. Mars gave him a party at the yacht club after the race and hung his oar in the club's Clipper Ship Bar. He left behind at Harvard a comparatively too-casual sex life.

Harry had progressed from weekends in bed with a doctor's wife to the heavy embraces of the niece of a German professor. He had fallen deeply in love in Boston with an actress appearing in flesh-colored tights, Nellie Thomson, who sang "Little Yellow Bird" while walking around showing her sturdy legs, oscillating breasts, and a large cheerful expression. Harry never met her, but saw her perform at least a dozen times from a front seat at the old Howard and sent her one Christmas three pounds of Swiss chocolates with a Gibson Girl in color on the box. Inside a note: "Just say an admirer."

The first day at the bank, Father smiled and asked Harry to sit down in his office.

"Christ, Hal, here you are grown up and in the bank. Now, there will be no nonsense of you starting at the bottom. Charlie will one day run H. H. Starkweather and Company. And you'll help him. Our purpose is to serve and work at the acquisition and retention of wealth. You'll be well paid and one day you'll be a very rich man. You'll work your ass off, Chaunce will see to that. And if you get into trouble, Bonely and Rashe are our laywers. Don't become a drunk. A little advice. Pay for your fucking and do it with whores: don't dishonor any respectable girls. Gambling is a worse curse than drink or women. I mean at cards, dice, or horses. The Street, of course, is a form of gambling. This is the longest speech I'm going to make to you. I wish my father had made one to me as direct—and no pious hosannas. Life is nothing like the books or the ministers' versions."

Harry just nodded, seated across from his father, seeing him at his desk; the light striking and modeling H.H.'s features. Harry was suddenly aware his father was no longer young. He was mortal and would die before him. And all Harry could think of was, He prefers Charlie to me. He thinks Charlie is brighter, more substantial, skillful and faster, instinctively responsive to thinking things out.

Out loud he said, "Thank you, Father. You'll find I have assets and ideas." He wanted to add: You think I'm too much a Chesney like Mother's side of the family.

"And I hope lucky, Hal. I've always felt if a man is unlucky, his brain and abilities can go down the drain. Stay lucky. . . . Like your office?"

"Haven't seen it yet."

"Chaunce will show it to you."

"Just what will I do?"

"Listen, watch, store up facts like a squirrel for a hard winter. You'll be active in checking through our West Coast railroad shares. We represent Baring Brothers, the London bankers who put up or got the money and credits to build the Western and Great Plains Railroad in Southern California."

"Yes, I've read some reports Uncle Chauncey gave me."

"Good solid expanding rail line going into New Orleans, and Enoch Kingston, who runs it, is going to see it will carry most of the steers to the packinghouses."

"Seems to be spending a great deal of their income on expansion and not paying the dividends they could."

H.H. cocked his head to one side and smiled. "You'll do. Don't

229

jump to conclusions. But write me a report why you think the W. and G.P. is spending too much."

Chauncey Wilcox was pleased to have Harry in an office next to his own suite. He pointed out features. "It's small, Harry, but real walnut paneling, good Arabian rug (used to be mine), and the washroom has a tub and large mirror. There's a lock on the cabinet, but keep no more than a bottle of Old Crow bourbon. H.H. doesn't mind a ceremonial snort, but *not* any lushing."

"So I gather." It was all like the first day at prep school—still rather frightening, insubstantial.

"Two hours for lunch is fine. I'll escort you around to the steak and lobster houses. Get to know the bank, we have plenty of hired hands, I'm trying out this new typewriter thing—the girl typist is a flirty bit. But my advice is, *don't* play lift-the-skirt with the help. Anything else I can tell you?"

"Uncle Chauncey, I'm pretty serious, maybe too much so. I mean, I'm not witty or amusing like Charlie. I'm trying to say I'm going to take my work *very* seriously."

Chauncey lifted his hands toward the ceiling, palms up, and laughed. "All H.H. asks is we make a lot of money and please our clients."

"That's what he told me."

At first Harry shared a flat with Charlie in the Gramercy Park section ("a little Parisian pied-à-terre," Charlie called it) but Charlie had too many sporting friends with whom he had played football, gone hunting in the Catskills or in Wyoming, met in Saratoga saloons, even picked up at prizefights, on Atlantic crossings in Cunarders. Charlie had been to England three times and was to become a seasoned ocean traveler. "Known to all the stewards, Harry, and barmen on the big ships." Twice winning the ship's pool betting on the last twenty-four-hour run. "I like it, the sea—all horizon in all directions. I've got H.H.'s seaman's blood."

"I gather Father didn't really care for it."

Charlie would often appear at a late hour in their flat with some painted girl or a dignified lady who by her dress was of good society; she usually was carefully veiled and apprehensive. They would disappear into Charlie's bedroom for what later Charlie identified as "some slap and tickle."

Harry was a bit of a prude, and he liked order. Charlie threw things about and was not discreet about the undergarments of some of his women, who would, at times, forget some silken item or other. It was an era of many petticoats, corsets, and other things.

So Harry left Charlie and took two rooms down the street in a house with a green door. He was not celibate in New York. He had made a friend, a girl named Marsha from New Haven, who ran the Golly Wog Bookshop near Sheridan Square in the Village. She was a serious type with her brown hair worn in a tight bun and her nearsighted blue eyes behind rather thickish glasses clipped to her nose and worn with a chain attached to her rather prominent bosom. When at day's end, twice a week, Harry arrived at the shop around seven in the evening, she would turn down the gas, lock the front door, and they would go back to the living space behind the store. Here Marsha would let down her hair in a great coil—like a curious snake, Harry would think—take off her clothes, revealing a marvelously developed brown body. She would begin to kiss Harry ardently, muttering, "Mate man." They would finish a bottle of champagne kept cold in the tan oak icebox and then get into the brass bed. She was an advanced young woman who considered sexual satisfaction the "higher healing art."

It was a very satisfactory arrangement for both of them. They were not in love. Marsha was mourning a lover who had died in an Apache Indian attack on a horse-soldier patrol a decade before in Arizona. As for Harry, he felt he could fall in love only with a girl who was younger than himself. Marsha was ten years older. Besides, he did not consider premarital fornication training for a proper wife.

Harry was never sad after sex. Staying overnight usually, and as he washed up in the basin, not sure the water in the pitcher was fresh, he always felt there could be no doubt about his manhood. Such satisfaction often resulted in his getting back into bed with Marsha. But he was never late at the bank. Nine o'clock each morning saw him at his desk reading the telegraph reports from the West Coast, checking the railroad stocks, shipping tonnage, passenger income. He made reports of the loadings of cattle, wheat, machinery, also looked over dispatches from Europe from various agents of the bank.

He met the Van Rogens at the Long Island North Shore Yacht Club. Uncle St. Mars had gotten him a membership, and while

231

Harry didn't own a boat himself, he acted as a skilled crew member in the racing sloops' runs—usually on a triangular course to Norwalk across on the Connecticut side, to Riverhead on eastern Long Island, then if the wind was right, tacking back to the yacht-club basin.

The Van Rogens owned a sixty-foot sloop, the *Amsterdam*. They were very proud of the family's having been early Dutch settlers when New York was called New Amsterdam. Once, as rich mynheers, they had lived the life Washington Irving described, on their vast estates up the Hudson around Albany. But that was all in the past. They were a family going downhill, with many acres lost by bad crops and poor management and a flurry in potato futures Peter van Rogen had tried to make in commodities. They still had much land and the big old house in Patchogue, for musicales and teas, a house filled with rare furniture, old damask. They lived in hope Peter would yet make a real killing in wheat futures.

St. Mars made the introductions in the club dining room. "This is my nephew Harry. . . . You've heard of him, rowed for Harvard."

Peter van Rogen shook hands. "Of course. Really put your back to it. Your oar is over our bar."

"How kind of the club."

"Yes, this is Minnie and this is Katie."

"Minerva," said Mrs. Van Rogen, a fading blonde and a bit too much chin; Katie said, "Katherine." She was, Harry thought, pleasing to the eye, taffy-colored hair, most of it up in the fashionable pompadour. A girl just past adolescence, he judged, in a white sailing skirt, little blue jacket with stars on the collar. A silver boat whistle around her neck on a gold chain. As they would say at Harvard, "Unrealized and willful."

Harry decided—if events proved right—it would be hard to act on H.H.'s advice about being respectable with respectable girls. That day he handled the tiller on the *Amsterdam*; they came in second. Next week he was in the crew on a sail to Westerly, a two-day cruise, and they lay to at the Old Anchor Yacht Club hung with gonfalons, ate supper on deck as the lights of the clubhouse windows shone in yellow bars around the dimpling water. The orchestra for the weekend club dance was playing Victor Herbert.

Harry kissed Katie behind the dinghy and held her close, *but* respectably, as called for by one's finer sensibilities.

232

They became engaged that spring, but Minnie van Rogen made it clear it was to be a long engagement. "Katie is only sixteen—she's too young to run a household. We want her to finish her education first and see Europe."

"I understand," said Harry.

"You know, dear boy, my grandfather Matthew Vassar founded the college. He was a brewer in Poughkeepsie, and naturally Katie must graduate; it's family tradition."

"Of course, Mrs. van Rogen."

"Call me Minnie."

The Van Rogen family history was being fed to Harry with tiring persistence.

There was an engagement ring and the Van Rogens were entertained at Sherry's by H.H., and Susan came down from Newport. Aunt Drucilla, too—her clothes a bit out of date. Charlie was hilariously drunk, but not offensive, got his foot caught in an umbrella stand. They all went to a horse show the next week.

Harry was a disciplined lover and they never went beyond kisses and he lightly fondling a thigh and breast through several layers of cloth. Whenever Katie was down from Vassar, they went to the theater. After which, having escorted Kate to the family town house on Sutton Place, he would rush down to the Village, knock on the Golly Wog Bookshop door, and drag Marsha toward the brass bed. But that never more than twice a week, for he believed in controlled healthy living; ten minutes at an open window each morning on arising, swinging Indian clubs, a cold shower, and a run in the park weekends or at the Battery. All good for mustering one's self-esteem. He was discovering he was very intelligent.

Howard was pleased with Harry's interest in the bank, and while he thought the boy was raw and taken in by the Van Rogens with their too-fancy living beyond their means, he also sensed Harry would be happy with the girl. She had grace, a fairly decent mind. "Nothing to astonish the world," he told Charlie, "but solid Dutch sense of what is worthwhile and what isn't." Not his kind of woman, he admitted, but then he hadn't been very lucky with Susan, and his emotional attentions were at the moment scattered among casual affairs; one the lady doctor, Miss Rice, having married an Englishman and gone to live in Manchester. And Fanny Carpenter-Garnier had taken to Christian Science.

233

Howard, at the Hudson Club, sat at lunch with Harry and Charles that fall. H.H. favored mutton chops done just right. "Only myself and James Gordon Bennett really know how a mutton chop should be properly done. Not that I'm a food fiend, but a mutton chop is easily overcooked. . . . You're going to England next month, Charlie. When you are in London, drop into Simpson's on the Strand, mention my name to Walter, the headwaiter there. They do a chop better than anyone."

"What's the purpose of the trip, H.H., besides eating mutton?"

"Hal thinks Baring Brothers are in trouble. We have a million in clients' money invested in their projects. I want a discreet but *deep* checking of just what is going on, if anything."

Harry hated mutton, despised game birds, duck and goose, liked best a good rare cut of cold roast beef. "Charlie should go to South America, the Argentine. Barings are deep in investments in crops and cattle down there, and it's the third year of the drought. Their backing of rail lines and the beef business there could be a major mistake. No ultimate fulfillment of their hopes."

"Why?" asked Howard.

"If there is a drought for another year, there will be no cattle to ship, no grain to transport, and *so*—" He placed a section of cold beef, with just a touch of mustard and horseradish sauce, into his mouth and chewed.

Howard patted Harry on the back. "Hal's our disaster crier."

Harry tried to assume a look of worldly and discreet sagacity. He loved his father and someday H.H. would see his worth.

Charlie picked at his perfect teeth with a toothpick. "Harry, you're a fiend for digesting reports. I feel Barings are too big to be hurt. It has to rain sometime down there, doesn't it?"

"It could," said Harry. "But anyway there's going to be a wheat shortage."

Howard set down knife and fork, wiped mutton fat off his lips. "Pete van Rogen tells me he's in this commodities pool being made in Chicago. A corner in wheat they're talking of. Christ, it could turn out, I figure, like Fisk and Gould's corner in gold."

"I hope not," said Harry. "Pete has mortgaged his farmlands and house and is deep in the pool with some Chicago Jews; merchants, I think."

That winter Harry and Katie went skating on the ice near Peekskill with a group of friends; later the two sat in a farmer's hotel by a large fire of hickory chunks, drank spiced hot wine, and later, clothed, tumbled about on a bed upstairs, but decently, both agreed. Very decently, and Harry went to his own room in a fearful state and had to take the prep-school sin against God's commandment as a way out. They saw each other as often as they could, went to plays, to fetes, and planned a wedding in 1898, when Katie would graduate. They were undecided between living in a cottage H.H. would build for them at Shad Point or leasing a floor in a brownstone on the north side of Washington Square.

It was about this time they decided that using the tongue in kissing was permitted to engaged couples.

33

The place that Harry lived in, after he moved out on Charlie, was a third-floor flat facing a back garden of struggling trees and amorous cats; a house that prided itself on its respectability, its "tidy hours for gentlemen." Each tenant had a front-door latchkey, but strangers after nine at night had to ring the pull bell on the door to attract attention.

It was after twelve at night when Mrs. Griben, who managed the place, in her wrapper and hair done in twists of paper under a dust cap, knocked on Harry's door, woke him from sleep. He came to the door with a dressing gown slipped over his long nightshirt, still woozy from the superimposed remains of an interrupted dream.

"What the devil, Mrs. Griben. The place on fire?"

"There's some mad fella downstairs. I've put the door on the chain. Claimin' he's some sort of relative of yours. Now, Mr. Starkweather, if he's under the influence, I mean drunk, this isn't the kind of house to—"

"Did he give a name?"

"One of those odd ones."

It turned out to be Peter van Rogen, without a collar and tie, his waistcoat buttoned improperly, a man in a bad state, red-faced, sweating.

"Harry, Harry." He clutched Harry's arm once he was in the flat, had trouble talking through grimacing twitching lips.

"Lord, Lord, Harry, my dear boy—"

"What is it, Pete? Something happen to Katie, Minnie?"

"Worse, worse. For God's sake give me a drink."

"You smell as if. . . ." He not only smelled of drink, but the burst capillaries in the man's nose hinted at prolonged drinking.

He took the tot of rye whiskey Harry poured for him and sat down, mopped his face and neck with a big silk handkerchief. "Now, listen, Harry, you're already like one of the family. Close kin, I mean. I'm ashamed, and I'm ruined."

"What's happened?"

The man's speech came out in the wrong cadence, between sobbing.

"You know I've been in with these Chicago people—a syndicate—to make a corner in wheat. Well, we had it, god damn it—we *had* it in the palms of our hands." He beat a fist into the flat of the other hand. "Deep winter, the Great Lakes frozen over. We got the price of wheat up like it's hardly ever been up. We had contracts for most of it. A real corner, I tell you, Harry, the kind you dream of. , . . I'll have another snort."

"No. If it's a corner, Pete, in wheat, what's wrong?"

"Don't you see? We depended on the freezing of the lakes solid until spring and we having the wheat in our hands or contracted. Now the Canadian wheat ships, to destroy the shortage, are on their way across the lakes. They'll dump wheat, break the market price, ruin us. And we're committed to millions of dollars to be paid in wheat at high prices."

Harry took a sip of whiskey himself. "What the hell are you talking of, Pete? The lakes will be frozen over for a couple of months yet."

The large distressed man looked up, his eyes bloodshot and he sucking air through his mouth as if existing in some hallucinatory state. "Ever hear of dynamite?"

"Dynamite?"

"They're breaking up the ice to clear an open water path into Chicago and other lake ports. Canadian wheat will ruin me."

The resonance of the man's despair was, Harry thought, almost indecent.

"Let me get dressed. We'll go see H.H., my father."

"Yes, yes, of course. He certainly can stop those Canuck bastards . . . ruining a man . . . his family."

Harry picked up the whiskey bottle and went into the bedroom to dress. Maybe H.H. could get some coherence and clarity of the situation from the sobbing man.

Howard Starkweather always gave his address as Shad Point, New York, but he had a three-room suite at the Clairmont Hotel near Madison Square Garden, which he kept all year round. Kept for those times he didn't go back to Shad Point, kept, too, to entertain important clients or in which to give discreet little parties with Stanford White, James Huneker, H. O. Havemeyer, Otto Kahn, and others. At some of these evenings show girls were present.

Howard slept well and deeply at all times, and it took Harry and Peter van Rogen ten minutes to wake him fully. They had come out in foul weather—a night of wind and snow flurries—come from Harry's place, walking, as no free hack for hire was sighted in their search for one.

Howard had looked huge and angry as he opened the door, his long nightshirt nearly touching his toes, the hair on his head, on his chest showing gray. He was barefoot.

"Damn silly calling hour."

"Pete's in trouble."

"He's pretty well got a bun on. He's drunk, by the look of him. Hello, Pete."

"H.H., you have to save me."

"Not in a drafty hall. Come in. Look out for the vase."

It took half an hour for Peter van Rogen to give Howard all the details asked for. The end result, Howard saw, was a plain indication the man would lose about four million dollars as his part of the wheat combine's plan to corner wheat. Nearly a million was from mortgages and loans on his remaining Van Rogen land holdings, acres of farms, waterfront property, and his house. Some was part of his wife's trust and her two spinster sisters' trusts he was administering. Illegally (he hiccoughed), he had used them as assets. The rest of the money was from relatives, uncles and cousins on both sides of the family he had talked into putting up funds to join the wheat pool. "A sure thing, I told them, a lead-pipe cinch. God almighty, H.H., I've ruined half a dozen families *if* that Canadian wheat gets through the ice and is dumped on the market. What a foul trick."

"Oh, bullshit," said H.H. "Let's face facts."

H.H. had put on a smoking jacket with red velvet frogs, buttoned over his nightshirt, and had lighted a cigar. He stood by the fireplace rumpling his hair into greater disorder. "No dirtier a trick than trying to corner wheat. It's give-and-take, and I fear, Pete, the devil takes the hindmost. You're that, maybe."

"Can't anything be done?" Harry asked. He had never seen a grown man weep, come apart, shake so.

H.H. said, "First of all, that ice is thick on Lake Michigan off Chicago. They may not be able to blow a way across it."

Harry nodded. "I'll telegraph the Chicago newspapers for reports."

"Do that. Yep, and I'll try and get some information on the Commodities Pit, where the speculators operate. Pete, it could all be a rumor. The bears may be playing games with your crowd. Making a killing on just rumors."

"God's grace it is. God's mercy on an old fool. I have no right to do these things. I'm not a well man. I'm—"

"There's a cot in my dressing room. Go get some sleep, Pete. You haven't had much sleep, have you?"

Peter van Rogen confessed he hadn't shut his eyes for three days, hardly at all. When he was gone, had staggered off, shedding frock coat and waistcoat, tugging at his shirt buttons, Howard and Harry faced each other by the fireplace. "There's a saying on the Street, Hal, sometimes the bulls make money on the market, sometimes the bears. But the hogs *never*."

"Pete's just a pathetic fool, H.H. He's all family history and pride and easy living with no real assets but too much land he's not paid all his taxes on. Will he lose those?"

"The hell with those. It's the trusts he's looted, the people he's made promises to. I'll bet his books are crooked. He could in his abysmal ignorance and greed go to jail for ten years if those lake steamers with whea. get through."

"Will they?"

"I wonder, as I said, if it all isn't a raid by the bears in Chicago. Starting a rumor, even using a bit of explosives to start a drop in wheat prices, and Pete and his gang loaded with the high grain."

"What do you think?"

"I think, my boy, it's really an attempt by the Canadians to get their wheat through in cahoots with some bear group to bust the pool." Howard laughed. "It's damn clever, you know."

H.H. rubbed his chest. "Let's hope that ice is as thick as the head of that Dutchman snoring in the next room."

Two days later, the sky lighting up in the east, Peter van Rogen walked out from his big and fine house toward the yellow-brick stables. It was a slow thoughtful walk; dawn was just breaking. He had come back late the night before, loaded with horrible apprehensions, from a last talk with Howard Starkweather.

"It's no use hiding it, Pete," H.H. had said as they sat late in the Wall Street office, the gaslight making a hissing sound in the overhead fixture. "Six Canadian grain ships have made Chicago. An east wind softened the ice and the dynamite did the rest in certain hard places."

"I'm ruined, utterly ruined."

"You bought heavy in wheat with your pool at high prices to get control. Prices have been falling all afternoon as more ships are expected. Wheat is going to tumble ass over the teakettle. Face it—and let's think."

"What can I do? It's all *so* hopeless."

Howard tapped his desk with his fingertips. "No use trying to deliver the high-priced wheat. You've been jobbed, of course."

"Jobbed. What?"

"A group of speculators—I think, if my information is correct, the McCormick, Armour people—could have been setting up this Canadian wheat thing for some time. They've sold short millions and will cover their contracts with the depleted prices at which wheat is going to open tomorrow."

"Tomorrow?" Peter van Rogen seemed too dazed to realize fully the meaning of H.H.'s information. "My wife's sisters' trusts. I'm a criminal. What I did is illegal. And *all* the families—how can I ever face them?"

Howard looked at his watch, snapped the lid shut. "Get yourself a crafty, not-too-honest lawyer; get yourself declared insolvent and bankrupt. As you bought on margin, refuse to honor your commitments. Sue the wheat pool. Tie everything up in legal tangles. Stall, delay."

"That will not get back all I've already squandered."

"You're goddamn right it will not, Pete. Now go home and prepare your family. Get some kind of predated papers permitting

239

you to tamper with those trusts. That's what families are for, aren't they? To stand by?"

Peter van Rogen just stared as Howard began to turn down the overhead lights, leaving just one small flame with a blue center and an orange edging.

"H.H., the family honor, my social standing, my—"

Howard had just rattled the key ring in his hand. . . .

Now Peter van Rogen entered his stables, went into the strong odor of horses and their litter, a smell that he had always delighted in. Howard Starkweather did not understand family or honor at all. Peter van Rogen felt how could things come to this pass when the horses were still there and his spotted coach dog, Leo, all affection, was coming forward to meet him? Yes, an affectionate animal; at times he had felt only Leo understood him. He patted the dog's head and went back to the room lined in bird's-eye maple where he kept his fishing gear and guns. The stableman and his family lived just beyond the place, behind the stand of elms.

Peter van Rogen, from a cabinet he unlocked, took out a Henry carbine with the bright yellow brass band around its firing section. He inserted a full round of sharp-pointed shells. It was samurai time.

He calmly shot the spotted coach dog swiftly and skillfully between the eyes. He went out to the stalls and placed the muzzle of the Yellow Boy Henry against the temple of his favorite hunter, a riding horse named Prince Velvet, and sent a slug through the long elegant head chewing oats.

To do the thing properly, he told himself, he should go indoors and shoot Minnie. He was a bit confused on that point and too tired to think it out. There was the clatter of boots from the direction of the stableman's house; the shots had been heard. He put the carbine's blue steel snout just under his chin, pointing upward, and indifferently—*I have done what a gentleman has to do*—pulled the trigger.

Harry Starkweather and Katherine van Rogen were married just six months after the ritual mourning period demanded in respect for the dead. The wedding party, after the ceremony by a pastor of the Dutch Reform Church from Tarrytown, was held in the ballroom at Shad Point, a rather serious affair, a somber elegance. It didn't seem to be a time of too much joy, but rather of uncertainty.

Not only was the bride's father a recent suicide who had ruined all connected with him, but the lawyers and the courts, it was clear, would leave Minerva van Rogen and her two spinster sisters with very little of their once-ample trusts.

Katie looked healthy and very golden in the old lace wedding dress, and Harry felt now he had pattern to his life, all properly in order, and with Katie it would be a good traditional marriage of tranquillity in society and of some passion in privacy.

Minnie had not wept. She was solid stuff, Howard thought as he lifted a glass of champagne and toasted her with a smiling nod. It was not a large wedding party; it had been held down deliberately. St. Mars and Chauncey in gray frock coats and striped pants as best man and usher. With, in whispering silks, Harry's sisters, Sunny, Phyllis, and Christine, as bridesmaids with three of Katie's Long Island friends. Harry saw his sisters were growing up to look like Mother. (She, Susan, was in a Worth gown from Paris, severe but well cut.) Yes, good solid girls, no beauties, but handsome. He wished he knew them better—but they lived with Mother and had some of her cold naïveté.

Susan was polite to Howard, and he didn't say much to her. He felt he had in the perversities of Christian marriage been kind, but neither in love with her after the children were born nor faithful.

As the butler's helpers brought in the huge wedding cake, rumored to be a reproduction of a Venice palace, the orchestra discreetly played an old English maypole tune. Harry—*great God, I'm married*—with Katie on his arm felt a moment of panic; *my life is over, I've leaped into the future—is it all an inconceivable misconception? I'm tied to someone forever. My thoughts, my actions are no longer to be freely indulged in. From now on, meticulous exactness of conduct.* . . . He looked up to see Charlie hand Katie a naked sword with a gold tassle on its hilt and point to the wedding cake.

"It's Harry's grandfather's. He wore it in battle. You cut the cake with it."

The widow Chesney, with a slouch that was becoming a stoop, nodded, standing by Aunt Dru with her angular jaw, her defiant stare, as if all this costly affair were rather reprehensible.

The wedding party went rather quickly after that. Harry and Katie slipped out and were driven to the depot at Norton-on-Hudson to catch the upstate flier to Lake George and what Charlie whispered to a laughing bridesmaid was "the deflowering ceremony."

Minnie van Rogen and Susan made the gesture of kissing, shook hands, and hoped the best for their children.

Drucilla Brooks, with direct serenity, took away two bags of food, some cakes, and several cigars; the latter she would give to the janitor in the house where she lived, instead of any cash, as a Christmas gift.

When all the guests were gone and the servants and hired help from the best places in New York were cleaning up, disposing of the empty bottles, broken bits of food, collecting napkins, stripping tables, Howard and Chauncey walked down to the boathouse.

"Now I feel like the late Captain Chesney. I, too, have daughters to get married off. Weddings depress me, Chaunce; such a cock-eyed mixture of apprehension and hope."

"Mrs. Starkweather will see to the girls' meeting the right sort in Newport. They'll do well."

"Yes, no shenanigans there. Charlie's thinking of getting married?"

"Well, H.H., I wouldn't buy any fresh fish for a wedding breakfast for him."

"I'm depending on Charlie. Very much so. Hal's a fine son, but, well. . . ."

He didn't go on. Chauncey remained silent. He and Chauncey, they had been together so many years that often there was no need for conversation; they could communicate at times without words. By a glance, a gesture. Truth was, Howard had to admit, he was closer to, and understood, Chauncey better than his own sons.

34

Andrew Starkweather was born the year Baring Brothers, the English banking house, went under. The baby had been named Andrew Jackson Starkweather, on the basis of some vague claim of Harry's mother that the Chesneys were related to Old Hickory, as Aunt Dru referred to him.

The Harrison Chesney Starkweathers (Harry was for everyday use, and his father called him Hal) and their son lived in a new addition to Shad Point, a white Italianized villa designed by H.H.'s friend Stanford White, well known as a fashionable mansion designer and whispered about as a hedonist. It stood a quarter mile from the main house among maples and elms on a gentle bluff, below which the river moved at its usual pace while the white paddle-wheel boats churned past.

Andrew was a good baby who fed heavily at Katie's breasts. They lived simply; besides a maid, a groom, and gardener, there were a black couple, Wallace and Lacey-Mae, to serve as butler and cook, in what the Norton-on-Hudson *Daily Herald* termed "a household of good living without ostentation, set like some lambent jewel in a green world."

Harry was driven by the groom to the depot every day to catch the 8:25 A.M. into the city.

When the clouds closed in on the Baring Brothers' enterprises, there was a meeting in H.H.'s office at the bank. Charlie, back from Europe for four days, St. Mars and Chauncey, Harry and his notes, H.H. at the head of the long table used for meetings. Ashtrays at each place facing a red leather chair. There had been strong apprehension on the Street about the English firm.

Charlie, in a hairy tweed jacket, freshly shaven and scented, opened a folder he had set out. He had, Harry decided, a Jesuitical side, Charlie did.

"I must say," Charlie began, "we acted in time. We sold out much of our Baring holdings, those in trusts, too, and advised our clients to withdraw from Baring Brothers' offerings, enterprises."

H.H., lighting a cigar, sucked air and blew smoke. "Another sign of credulities and imbecilities. Those of our clients who did not take our advice will face losses, Charlie."

"Yes. Well, it was clear as I checked up on data we had that the whole affair was hopeless, South American investments ruined by drought and cattle disease. At the last minute the Rothschilds stepped in with some millions of pounds for Baring. Then the Bank of England also tried to aid them. No dice."

"Huh?" asked H.H.

Chauncey said, "'No dice' in crapshooting is a new gambler's term."

Harry sat doodling, making first a series of circles, then turning them into faces. He thought, Should I point out it was I, not Charlie, who had first drawn up the memos as to the true state of Baring Brothers? Yes, Charlie had done the hunting of facts and information in Europe, but. . . . Harry's train of thought was interrupted by St. Mars holding up a well-manicured finger and speaking.

243

"This means the Western and Great Plains Railroad—Barings' major holdings in North America, that is—can perhaps be facing a condition for reorganization?"

H.H. shook off his cigar ash onto the rug; he hardly ever used an ashtray. "Enoch Kingston is a smart operator. He and his lawyer, fellow named White, they'll try to take over, reorganizing W. and G.P. as their own company. What do you think, Chauncey?"

"If we can offer them a plan of needed money or work with them to reorganize, project a whole new issue of railroad shares in a new company, yes, it's something that could be very big for the bank."

St. Mars nodded. "Might. But now that J. P. Morgan is reorganizing a lot of small Northwest roads into a big railroad system, I'd say he is going to impress Kingston as the man to handle the W. and G.P. reorganization. Of course we don't know yet how bad the Baring disaster is. They may salvage something. They are known on Threadneedle Street as necromancers of the pound sterling."

"Hell, no, it's hopeless. Up shit creek and no paddle," said Charlie. "It's all kaput. It's everyone out to save what they can. I'll handle, feel Kingston out, H.H."

St. Mars smiled. "Charles, that's *my* side of the street. I'm meeting with Kingston in a week or so to show him some statistics."

H.H. frowned. "That's too late. Chaunce, find out where he is right now. We'll give him a bang-up dinner at Shad Point." He put a wry expression on his face and looked over at St. Mars. "Sort of keeping my hand in. You don't mind? Those who live by statistics will lose by statistics sometimes. So—"

"Not at all, H.H. Enoch Kingston is not actually in the city. He's someplace on the rails in his private railroad car, *Golden Eagle.* I'll try to locate him."

Charlie gave a whistle. "You should see the damn thing. A palace on wheels. Has a marble bathtub, a private kitchen, a regular saloon bar. And a big silver-plated bed, acres of it, in the sleeping compartment."

H.H. looked up from some notes he had been reading. "I gather Kingston doesn't travel with his wife. Sounds like a Kansas City whorehouse on wheels."

"I think he's a widower," Harry said. "A feisty one, I gather."

"Best kind," said H.H., absorbed in some private thought. He looked up. "If we can cut into Morgan's stranglehold on railroad reorganizing, we'll be the bank that is just as important as J. P. Morgan and Company in that hootenanny field. Christ, it's just waiting

244

for us. Nearly fifty percent of the American railroads are bankrupt, or running at a loss or being mismanaged. Just kissing our toes to help in reorganization. The bank wants a big share of that."

St. Mars looked down at his fingernails. "That means meeting J.P. head-on."

"That's right, St. Mars. Better than nose to nose—he's bigger there. Christ, I've known J.P. since the days before Fisk and Gould were interested in gold. He's a cockeyed marvel with selling shares. Cold as Kelsey's balls, too, but you can trust him. His word is solid. If he could only laugh, he'd be a good model of what a top-notch investment banker should be."

St. Mars said, "I don't know if humor or being friendly with mankind is any asset to the Street."

Charlie slapped St. Mars on the back as he rose and stretched. "No, Uncle St. Mars, but it helps you from feeling cornering the almighty dollar is all there is in the world."

Chaunce winked. "There's better things, eh? Like lounging, scratching, and farting."

Later Howard was standing at the windows in his office looking down into the Street, a rush of people hurrying home from the day's activities. Howard was a great window starer, taking some melancholy interest in the hurrying people, the Street emptying itself like a great gut after the day's trading. So much sold, so much bought, such and such; the U.S. Treasury figures, so much exported, certain quantities imported. All, as far as the Street was concerned, not physically real—no, just figures in books, listings on boards, posted bulletins, confidential reports. Never an actual bale of cotton, a hogshead of sugar, a farm wagon, or a bloodred side of beef hanging in any of the exchanges or offices. Howard turned toward a cabinet of mineral specimens, a gift from Joseph Pedlock. Copper ore, quartz with tiny veins of true gold, a ten-pound silver ingot, some rare and wonderfully colored rock formations all labeled in Latin and in translation. He delighted in their names: selenite, calcite, corundum, lavender jasper, malachite. He liked handling the large bluish-green sample of copper ore. They all proved in part the true inherent fact of physical existence.

For all his well-dressed appearance, St. Mars was a deep student not only of the money market and stocks but also of the position of the investment banks and the men who manipulated them. He hunted beyond the mechanisms of the Street's business. In his private journal he wrote:

> The investment bank, the private banker, holds the reins of power in national business by his position, not just that of a moneylender. He projects and organizes, if he's H.H., the issuing of stocks and bonds, aware that these add to controls—to the use of long-term credit capital as the power weapon. In growing nations there is an ever-expanding population needing more and more products, and industry smoking up more and more of the landscape, digging out of the earth, the ores to process. H.H. grew by seeing credits must be extended more and more to certain firms. And so in time the private investment banker *is* the ruling hand. H.H. buys, sells, permits, or denies growth. He and others are the begetters of capital and credit. The money comes in from the solid pushing and selling of shares, the floating of issues to investors, speculators, and the public itself. For this work there are the commissions, and a great deal of the total passage of money goes back to him, the banker, on deposit. Here, as H.H. puts it, "it mellows and collects not any patina, but goes out as investments in new deals, new issues." The boom is on and the banker who is only a promoter of securities is lazy; he can make national history.

St. Mars kept the journal under lock and key at home. He was aware of reaction against the private banker in some places, all the acrimonious controversy.

He sent on to H.H. an item in the *Times*, some remarks of a lawyer named Brandeis, with the comment in a neat hand: "Not all Jews are Joseph Pedlock." He underlined some of the text:

> Adding the duties of undertaker to those of midwife, the investment bankers became in times of corporate disaster members of security holders' "Protective Committees"; then they participated as "Reorganization Managers" in the reincarnation of the unsuccessful corporations, and ultimately became directors. The need for money gets the banker a seat in the management, on the board of directors. Even the stockholders' proxies deposited with the bank. When a banker entered the Board, his group proved tenacious, his influence usually supreme; for he controls the supply of money.

To which Howard added and sent back to St. Mars, "Well, what the hell is wrong in this statement? It's the whole secret of the success of this bank."

Howard watched Morgan & Company, for he knew only it stood so solid, firm, unblinking between him and the top position on the Street as a great national investment bank. He repeated the Street's jest that "when the angels of God took unto themselves wives among the daughters of men, the end result was the Morgan partners. . . ." But Howard never went as far as calling the firm "Jesus Christ and his twelve apostles," as the Bankers Club wits did.

The two men met from time to time in the club, sat together, H.H. and J.P., their big bodies set well back in the comfortable leather chairs, cigars smoldering, good balloons of brandy at their sides. No loquacity between them, but certainly a sensibility, if only for each other's reputation.

When Baring Brothers fell, they, a few days later, had their cigars and brandy together, their privacy respected by the rest of the men in the clubroom. With fools and bores they were given to a spurry spikiness.

"Your boy Charlie I wish I had with us, H.H."

"Trade you for Coster or Wright."

J.P. Morgan permitted himself a chuckle at the mention of his two top partners. "Yes, I bet you would. Your boy, he's been very active, showing admirable interest in the Western and Great Plains."

"We've done a lot of Baring Brothers' business with them in the past."

"Get burned much? Barings are down the chute."

"Hmmm. Not too much, we had warnings."

"Yes, H.H. I'm impressed with what you've done in the Trans-American Copper Combine. At least I looked the other way."

"And you think I should turn my gaze away from Western and Great Plains?"

J.P. sipped his brandy, his huge diseased nose magnified in the snifter. "I never give advice unless well paid for it. How do you like living on the river on your patriarchal acres?"

"Marvelous. Lots of trees—pines, cedars. I hope to have a dozen grandchildren living on the place someday—each in his or her own house.

"I like Long Island myself. Thank God the damn minuets and

247

quadrilles are done for. But I don't think my family are the breeders you hope for."

They finished their drinks and cigars in a pleasant mood—to all appearances. . . .

Howard was thinking of the Morgan warning (threat?) the next day when Charles and Harry came into his office. "I'm giving a little dinner tonight at Shad Point. Thought we'd all go up together on the six ten."

Charlie made a mock sad face. "Well, I suppose there's going to be a disappointed girl at the Winter Garden. How you think our meetings are going, H.H.?"

"As usual. We'll judge from results. Hal, follow the actions of the Western and Great Plains Railroad. I suspect they'll increase spending for new work, cut dividends, run down their own shares. They'll try to force a reorganization and seize the road for themselves. Kingston been chafing at Baring controls for a long time."

Harry agreed: "I think you're right. They were overbuilding, ordering new rolling stock—all at the cost of lowering dividends. Yes, it might point to that. 'Bout their connection with Morgan. Well . . . it's just . . . just. . . ."

"Come on." H.H. smiled. "Why the buttoned-down mouth? Spit it out, Hal. You're on to something?"

"No, no, just a vague . . . well. . . ."

"You suspect St. Mars is touching knees with Morgan on the quiet?"

Charlie, who was pouring himself a drink from H.H.'s private stock, stood still, openmouthed, glass in one hand, bottle in the other. "What! Ol' Uncle St. Mars? Him!"

H.H. rubbed the side of his nose with the knuckles of his right hand. "It's been sort of seeping into my own mind. He's kind of moved Kingston into his private files. He's been wishy-washy on certain things I've asked him to follow up. But I may be bad-mouthing him."

Charlie added, "He runs with that fancy crowd of Astors, Vanderbilts, those Four Hundred ginks. Living high and fancy."

"That's no crime," H.H. said, "nor any sign he's not wholeheartedly for the bank. Living high? Well, aren't we all?"

Harry said, "His wife's people are big stockholders in Northwestern rail lines, all Morgan-controlled. Appalachian coal—timber rights along the Rappahannock."

"Yes, maybe. Well, never shoot a soldier until you know he's taking enemy pay. We'll just see what comes of the Kingston matter."

It was not just H. H. Starkweather & Company that was involved in the upheavals, the crisis of the national railroad systems. Many other firms on the Street were wondering just what was going on. It was clear that Morgan was the giant manipulator in this matter. But that Starkweather was challenging him. If not a direct frontal attack, then biting into his flank. Morgan, with contacts at Standard Oil, the trusts in coal and steel he had organized behind him, had the power to strike back at any challenger.

But H.H. had slowly been building up his own powerful forces. Men and organizations that resented, feared the power of Morgan, his demands of full control, forcing the men and systems he worked with to put their personal holdings in shares in his vaults, turn over their stocks so they could not be manipulated behind his back while change was going on. He had no interest in stale, defunct controversies.

H.H. laid out his backers like a field marshal his reserve regiments. The copper people, some of the silver crowd, the cotton brokers, textile spinners, certain makers of farm machines—almost all who used Donald McCann steel. How solidly behind Howard? Not too solidly, but with promises and a dislike of Morgan, Standard Oil methods, the other steel barons. Howard felt he had solid deck planking under his feet, but would the ship sail?

Harry was good at getting facts and figures. Charlie was able to pound a decision out of most situations, and St. Mars and Chauncey were watchers of the market, the daily action on the Exchange; charting, planning, trying to predict in the dangerous numbers game of the Street what reactions were rumored and what was being talked about.

Howard had for some time felt that St. Mars, so clear, yet impenetrable as a mirror, might turn; if not disloyal, wonder what his chances were at Starkweather & Company with Charlie, Harry, and Chauncey closer to H.H. than he was. H.H., as always, had been tearing down the social importance, the proud poverty of the Chesneys. One could understand that, seeing H.H.'s bad relationship with St. Mars' sister Susan. Now hardly a wife. Separated from his bed, with her girls playing the social turns at Newport, Bar Harbor. Even going out to Santa Barbara and Pasadena. Riling, ruffling, H.H. . . . So, does St. Mars feel no loyalty to me?

249

35

Enoch Bancroft Kingston in his fifties was impressive to look at and impressing when one knew his reputation and record as a railroad builder. He suggested a man whose emotions were regulated by intelligence. He had a large, rather stern face, but with a sense of humor lurking around his eyes and mouth. He was one of those Westerners who were not born there, but migrated. As a youth during the Civil War he had been at the throttle of army trains at the siege of Vicksburg. Going west then to plan and create pioneer rail lines in Southern California. At first working for others, now it clearly appeared he had plans to take over the full control of the Western & Great Plains, having been for some time a large holder of its shares and major owner of the construction and supply companies that serviced the expanding rail lines. He had a reputation as a man with a temper—yet could also be as tactiturn as a stone.

H.H.'s dinner for him was well arranged to seem casual, but with some women bejeweled enough to show the glitter the city could produce. Harry and his wife, Katie, she looking well after the birth of their son. ("She's a nursing mother," Harry had whispered to Mrs. St. Mars Chesney. "The baby's upstairs with his nurse.") Mrs. Chesney, as was only to be expected as the wife of St. Mars, was herself a splendid dresser in puce and gold, highlighted with a neat but not gaudy collection of jewels. Charlie was absent, being in Canada talking to the board of the Bank of Montreal. Donald McCann had brought Madame Nalda Nassenda, the New Zealand-born opera singer—a favorite of the Prince of Wales; she had also had a rich dessert named after her. McCann had become a bit mad about opera and its prima donnas—Italian, Scottish, French, German—whom he escorted and some said now and then he made his mistresses. McCann had grown more than a little bent over since Howard remembered from their last meeting, the nose more pointed, decisive, his face wrinkled like a nut meat. But the voice still was strong and as crisply quizzical. In the study before the guests came, he spoke out. "Damn me, H.H." He shook the glass of scotch in his hand. "Haven't you got enough without trying to swallow railroad systems?"

Howard adjusted his ruby cuff links, saw to the ends of his bow tie. He was enjoying the fripperies of evening dress.

"Now, Donald, you know the law of averages. You aim at all tar-

gets and settle for what you bull's-eye. Now, you and Madame Nassenda?"

"You'll have problems with Enoch Kingston. He's none of your
suburban gentility."

Howard winked. "Having problems with your pretty opera
lady?"

McCann sighed. "It's no different, the state of one's emotions,
whether you're a mon running a cheap-john iron forge or piling
up steel millions. I'm a firm fool in that female direction—all
alarms and excursions—and that's no lie."

The sound of carriage wheels on the blue stone drive alerted
Howard. He pulled a bell cord by a silvery Corot painting, and
when the butler came in, he said, "If it's Mr. Kingston, have him
come into the study."

Enoch Kingston, when he strode in, was impressive, well over six
feet tall; now in middle age, he had turned bulky, gone to girth, his
weathered face audacious, but not arrogant. Howard was disappointed the man wasn't wearing his Western boots, just was neatly
tailored in black broadcloth, a choke-me-johnny high collar,
starched shirt with two black pearl studs.

"Glad to see you, Kingston. You know Donald McCann."

"Yes, yes." He shook hands firmly, not with any cruel crush of
fingers some men practiced. "Used a hell of a lot of Donald's low-
carbon steel rail extending our lines from the Panhandle toward
New Orleans."

H.H. pointed to some crystal decanters of drinks behind which a
servant stood waiting to pour. "You're not in New Orleans yet?"

"Inching our way, Starkweather. We'll get there."

"Domn if he don't, H.H.," added McCann. "And soon."

"Very soon. Too many streaks of rust in the South instead of real
railroad service. Bourbon, if you have it."

"Kentucky prime, Kingston. There is no other as good."

"I'll swear to that."

The three men held their glasses up against the gaslight fixture
above them.

"Gents," said H.H., "to a good dinner."

"To your hospitality," said Kingston.

McCann just nodded and took a small sip. He seemed amused at
these two men, smiling, tasting their whiskey, eyes meeting over the
rims. Howard had been carefully studying Enoch Kingston from

251

the first moment he had come into the study. If legends—scurrilous gossip—were later to distort the Westerner and his projects, actually he had in common many traits and drives that so many of the early railroad creators had. Men Howard knew—James J. Hill, E. H. Harriman, Henry Villard, William E. Rockefeller, Collis Huntington. Names that the grandchildren of Howard Starkweather—or the average citizen—would hardly know.

The railroad world was already at its peak and full of problems. The St. Paul and Pacific, Minneapolis and Manitoba, Southern Pacific, Great Northern Railroad, Illinois Central—all were coming into major phases that called for reorganization. Nothing was yet fully settled as to control of many of these rail systems, and men like Enoch Kingston were still violently fighting to hold, grab, and extend the rights-of-way—steel rails on wooden ties—in places where, as Kingston put it at dinner to a question of Katie's, "the hoot of a train whistle had never been heard before."

It was a fine dinner—Chauncey had seen to that; the butler, Brookton, had trained help from the city. The chef, Louie Bacota (once the pride of the Antlers in Denver), had done wonders with crab and shrimp in a hot sauce, to game birds, sweetbreads cooked in champagne. Poured were several proper wines St. Mars had recommended: Château Maucaillou, Château Fortra, Châteauneuf-du-Pape.

Harry studied the man from the West. He saw much more than his father or even St. Mars did, perhaps. Donald McCann also had had a hint that what all these new giants were like did not appear in their social actions. There was a kind of rush to fulfill dreams never uttered or explained, McCann thought. These men who had settled into (seized?) control of the far-flung rail lines under the tall trees—trees falling soon to the ax in a hunt for railroad ties to lay more rail, to cut more ties, to . . . and so on. . . . They were not, Harry decided, men like the sleek and groomed people who controlled the Pennsy, the New York Central, the anthracite routes of the Philadelphia & Reading. No, the Kingston types were untamed and aching, almost in pain, to achieve—yet their features were often set into masks. They had to come east to face the men of the Street who manipulated their lifeblood, the shares and bonds. Investment bankers who took their share off the top and were slowly but surely becoming the controllers of the rail systems.

Kingston caught Harry's study of him across the crisp linen and between the Sung and silver bowls of hothouse fruit. He smiled. "Why don't you come out to see us someday? Cross the Big Muddy, see the Rockies. I've this railroad car—lots of times it's loafing on a siding. You and the wife can feel free to use it, see the West. Been there much?"

"Thank you. My brother, Charles, he spent summers on ranches."

The opera singer turned her pleased smile on Kingston. "You Westerners, such *de luxe de grandeur.* You remind me of Australians I once knew."

"Big fellows, aren't they? Hope you still like them. How do you remember all the words and tunes in an opera?"

"Arias, Mr. Kingston, not tunes." She delightfully pressed her fingers into his arm just above the elbow to make the point. *"Très drôle."*

"You'll forgive me, Madame Nassenda—but I'm like President Grant was when it comes to serious music. Grant said once, 'I only know two tunes. One is "Pop Goes the Weasel"; the other isn't.' And he was not, as a type, *très drôle."*

"Touché, Mr. Kingston."

The baked Alaska was being brought in. The gaslight had been lowered. Bowls of cherries jubilee flames leaped up, blue brandy fire reflecting as secret cold fire on the jewels of the ladies. . . .

Later, after the guests were gone, Howard sat in the darkened study, just some ash with red glowing centers in the fireplace. The drapes drawn back on the bow window facing the river. A moon nearly as bright as day picked out trees and trimmed hedges, the slope of the lawns down to the diver. There was a tap on the door and Donald McCann—a weekend houseguest—came in; in a nightshirt, red bedcap on his head.

"Couldna' sleep. As I grow older, I dream of footsteps on stones, steps of people I shall never see again."

"Should have kept your opera singer as a bed warmer."

"Ah, Nalda had early-morning rehearsal sessions in the city. Also she is taken with that Kingston. I'm sure they've arranged last night a 'rendee-voo.'"

"Never mind, Donald, you can buy her back for another necklace. What do you think of Kingston? I mean in a business way, not as a stud."

"To be had for ourselves is often our only strength. . . . King-

253

ston? You tell me, H.H. You had him in here for an hour after dinner. By the way, the sauce with the pheasants was a bit *too* rich. I feel it *here*. What you and he talk about as to the railroad?"

Howard turned up a gas jet. "He listened to me. He's a good listener. I suspect talkers, but I feel listeners have splendid character when they hear me out."

"Will he go into any railroad combine you're thinking of?"

"Don't know, Donald. Just don't know. Kingston doesn't leak information exactly. He's been listening to Morgan and his men. He's damn well informed of what Southern lines are close to bankruptcy. And he's aware of who is top dog on the Street."

"He's a domn fox—balancing you against Morgan, Morgan against you."

"I think so. I've decided not to push. Let St. Mars handle him for the rest of his stay in town. St. Mars is smooth."

"Very, I've observed. Like a pebble that's been a long time in a running brook."

The week was a busy one at Starkweather & Company. A time of interacting pressures and tensions. It was clear that a great combining of railroads would have to be made to save at least the third of the nation's systems that were in trouble. Enoch Kingston was considered one of the men who would head a combination of many of the Southern and Southwestern roads. He was seen about town escorting an opera singer, was found by a reporter half asleep in a box at the opera during a performance of one of the *Ring* operas. The reporter asked him what he thought of the opera. Kingston gave a small smile. "I have to agree with Mark Twain. 'Wagner is better than he sounds.'"

Later that week it was rumored on the Street that he had left in his private railroad car, was headed west with Madame Nassenda as his guest in the big silver bed.

Howard sat in his office pitching playing cards into his top hat set out on the floor. It was a way he had of trying to remain calm while waiting out a project, some ostensible consequence.

Chauncey came in and watched Howard miss three throws. "You're pitching too tensely, H.H. Why would Kingston run off with the lady just now?"

"Chauncey, there is sometimes the moment in people when two experiences touch. What else is new?"

"There is something on the boil across the Street."

"Yes, Morgan drove down early today from his Fifth Avenue place. He's deserted Long Island. Not like him, this time of the year."

"He had a long talk two days ago with Kingston there on Fifth Avenue. Showed him his art treasures."

"Yes, he owns a very fine junk shop. Been there a couple of times. I got the feeling it's J.P.'s way of saying, 'God, look at me.' "

"What do you think, H.H.?" When H.H. got quietly sardonic like this, he was like a jammed steam valve.

Howard flung the cards into a corner and shook his head.

"Kingston may be playing us one against the other. Then maybe go to the Jews. Belmont, Kahn, even the Rothschilds. We can only wait and—"

The door opened after just one hard knock, and Charlie came in wearing his tan bowler hat on the back of his head, his silk-faced frock coat unbuttoned, his waistcoat half so.

Chaunce asked, "You been in an accident?"

Charlie exhaled, banged down his cane on a corner of Howard's desk, then slumped down in a chair. "These damn trains the Central runs, I've eaten a half pound of cinders since leaving Canada."

Howard stared at his son, expressionless. "The Bank of Montreal in good health?"

"Splendid, happy as grigs, H.H. They're deep in St. Paul, Minneapolis and Manitoba. Backing railroad shares. I also got some sweet news. You can forget Kingston and the Southwest systems reorganization. It's been in J.P.'s pocket across the Street for a week."

Chaunce addressed the ceiling. "Sonofabitch Kingston never hinted."

"How was it done?" Howard asked, leaning back in his chair. His voice had, Chaunce thought, a false tranquillity.

"St. Mars, the bastard, sold us out. Montreal had private information. Besides details to go ahead with the St. Paul project, they got notes showing St. Mars has been working out for across the Street."

Chauncey kicked over the hat on the floor. "I'm going to shoot the bastard on sight. That's what I'm going to do!"

Howard held up a hand, shook his forefinger at the angry man. "It had to come, I suppose. I didn't expect it for a few years. St. Mars wants to be big. Bigger than he'll ever be here. That's the bad

255

Chesney blood coming out in him. So it's clear he's been advising Kingston. Morgan was the better company for him to reorganize, issue new shares, rebuild the railroads and control rates, routes. Well, you know what profit there is if you control a few thousand miles of railroad and all the gravy of free federal lands turned over to you."

Charlie opened his tie, rubbed an unshaven cheek. "We overlooked the fact that Mrs. St. Mars Chesney is related to Mark Hanna, the political boss—and he's a Morgan-Rockefeller man. They'll make St. Mars a partner over there—I'll bet my last silver dollar on it."

"In time, in time," Howard said. "But right now he'll just assist in the Southern road mergers." Howard stood up. "Well, boys, we lost a big one. Very big one. Chaunce, get started buying up stock and shares in every troubled road in the Southwest and South. Morgan is going to make *us* a few million as a consolation prize. When this thing gets out, prices will go up on those limping halfpenny rails when it's found out Morgan is taking over and Kingston will run them. Yep."

"I've an idea," Chauncey said. "The shares, they've *already* been bought up, pledged with Morgan. Are in big bundles in the safes across the Street."

Charlie stood up, patted his father's back. "Got to shave and bathe, need a good rubdown in a Turkish bath. Sorry, H.H."

"All I want now is St. Mars' head mounted on the wall. Let's celebrate something. . . . We'll go see Weber and Fields tonight. Chaunce, get us a table at Delmonico's after the show." He inspected his hand as if some message were there, held up some fingers. "A table for four." He looked up. "You know I could have taken that opera singer away from Kingston. But I was loyal to Donald and, well—she talks French while in the hay, I'm sure."

Preparing to retire for the night, Harry was gargling. Susan had always impressed on him, since early childhood, he had a weak throat that needed close attention. He rinsed the taste of the gargle from his mouth and went into the bedroom. Katie, having fed the baby—and seen him removed to the nursery—was relaxing half asleep on a rose-colored pillow. A bowl of muguets—wild lilies of the valley—filled the room with a pungent odor.

Katie said, "I don't see what all the gloom is about. It isn't as if your father were as poor as your Aunt Drucilla."

"Aunt Dru isn't poor. She has millions. H.H. says she's just a bit bent in the head—a miser and a really good speculator. I could have predicted St. Mars' turncoat act. But they don't read my reports in detail. Katie, we're moving out of here. Out of Shad Point."

"Why ever?"

Harry began to wind his watch. "We'll take a house on Fifth Avenue up near the museum. I've enough stock I can get a loan against for a really fine place."

"But why, dear? Your father will—well, your father will just blow up and roar."

"I'm going to prove something to myself. That I can live as an individual with my wife and son. Do my work and not be under H.H.'s thumb when away from the bank. We're going to be somebody in society. Rise on our own. Charlie doesn't care for social position. H.H. is too numb to it. But we, our children will be up there with the Astors, the Vanderbilts, the rest. . . . Oh, damn, I've overwound the watch spring."

"Child. Not children."

"We'll have more. We're young, ardent. Katie?"

"You think it's all right?"

"Andy is three months old." He held the watch to his ear. It was ticking.

"Well, if. . . . "

(Lillian Minerva Starkweather was conceived that night; the same night the young Starkweathers started to climb into high society. Many years later Lillian gave the great ball at Sherry's that caused many of the best families to beg off an Astor event and come to hers. She was at that time married to Sir Henry Denton-Upshaw, of the Hampshire Denton-Upshaws. Later she divorced him and married a cousin of the Morgensteins who, like the original American Morgensteins, had been converted from Judaism to the Protestant faith. Lillian was one of the leaders of the woman suffrage movement and was twice arrested, in 1913 and 1915, for battling with police during marches demanding votes for women.)

36

Howard Starkweather had the habit of walking about on his land at Shad Point on those nights when he could not fall asleep. As he grew older, sometimes the sleep did not come easily. Now wrapped in a great wolf-pelt coat Charles had brought back for him from one of his stays in the West, he was walking along the riverbank, beating the wet wild grass with his cane. Early that day he had seen a V of geese spearing across the sky. Now the night was heavy, dark like his mood, the air still but for the purling run of some little stream close by making its way to the river.

Howard had accepted his defeat by the House of Morgan, had made a bitter mouth about the treason of St. Mars Chesney. One lived with no esoteric metaphors. Aware in a world of incertitude no man can be always proved loyal, and no condition in the hostile environment of existence could be forever depended on.

He beheaded a clump of daisies. It hurt, the betrayal and defeat, but as he walked along on the night-dew-damp grass, he knew he would accept the event and go on. It just shifted perspectives and brought on some new awareness. Older, but no mellower, youth was gone, middle age slipping by. He had done much, hoped to do more.

There were some night colors on the river. Little yellow bowls of lantern light; a few feet of highlighted sapphire-blue river the light picked out. Night fishers, boozers, other lives perhaps almost too poignant to think of. He got a dose of insight—a sense of lonely life in others. He thought of the sea he had left as a young man—and had no regrets. The sea was a hostile place; however, there nature, not men, menaced you. Harry, with his education, had said to me once that we all came from the sea; the sea was once the mother of the whole living process. Think of that, sailor. Ha. He stooped and turtled his neck deeper into the fur collar. It was too damp to light a cigar; the wind was rising from down the bay. And he was alone. Even if he had good sons, and Charlie was a comer. Starkweather & Company was a bank to be reckoned with, and he had plans, yes, plans, a pocket full of plans, a head full of ideas enough to amaze the Street. All these plans needed were his tenacious application. Yet he was alone, walking on the riverbank. He had come a far bit this night in his walk; to the east just over the knoll was the private burying ground where the remains of his first wife lay. Amy. Lay. Not rested. Nothing is as gone from us as the dead.

I have no regard for any idea something survives after we kick off—anything that is like being alive here. No use going to look where she lies, just muck that once was living beauty, a hump of grass-covered earth, a gray slab of stone with marks on it.

I loved. In indulgent serenity, *we* loved. Now I don't find it possible to love (the way one should) one's children. I don't feel close enough to Charlie or Harry, his wife, their son. What the hell kind of barrier separates me from them? I may admire or be kind or be solicitous. But why no deep blood-pumping love? But for one person.

I love Chaunce. He's closer to me than my own. I love him not in the physical sense—for each other, the love of sailors belowdeck. For that I need frivolous, elegant women. But for the deep true love of one human being for another, Chaunce, he's closest to me. It's not true, as Amy once put it, "He's the son we'll never have." No, I have sons, have a grandson, will have more. Somehow Chaunce and myself are shipwrecked sailors alone on a raft that will never reach any shore, just drift, we to fish and catch rainwater, see the curtsying horizon always beyond our reach. *My* reach. Don't speak for others, old man.

He stopped, breathing hard from the effort of walking, vapor visible as he exhaled, stopped near a stone wall raised by some colonial farmer, stones now moss-flecked and bone white like a collection of skulls revealed by the moonlight scudding through lacy clouds. He got out the leather-bound flask and took a good pull of brandy. It was a night cold and damp and would soon be growing darker as the moon took on more veils. There was a movement, a crisp crushing of fallen leaves to the left, and he saw a wet mass of reddish fur and the sharp point of a black nose. It was a fox, a vixen by the heavy belly on her, looking miserable and damp. The first he had seen on the place. In her mouth she carried the corpse of a chicken, one of his prize reds. She was cornered in a break of the stone wall. He lifted his cane, the heavy blackwood stick, to strike her hard to kill. Then held back the blow. The vixen twisted away, free, and ran off, the chicken still in her mouth, into thick bayberry bush. Howard Starkweather lowered the stick. One does not, he thought, strike down a survivor.

BOOK VII

The best way to prevent stealing is to give
the thief what he wants before he steals it.
Honesty is not the best way to make money
but it is the best way to keep it.
                    —C. NORTHCOTE PARKINSON

37

In the archives of H. H. Starkweather & Company there exists a scrapbook kept by Tyler Starkweather when he was a boy. The Sunday *Times* in the early 1900's was printing every week what it called a rotogravure section, which consisted of the use of a dismal brown ink to reproduce photographs of the week's events; social doings and the posed features of prominent people, also the arrogant grace of race horses at Saratoga. To have one's image in the rotogravure section was social status to many. "It didn't show," said Donald McCann, "the flaws in the idyll of a factual world."

Under the date of April 18, 1911, there is a whole page pasted in headlined

CORNERSTONE LAYING OF NEW STARKWEATHER & COMPANY BUILDING. WALL STREET SALUTES EVENT AS HOWARD HARRISON STARKWEATHER, FOUNDER OF GIANT INVESTMENT BANK, BREAKS GROUND WITH GOLDEN SHOVEL

The shovel was actually only painted with gold radiator metal paint, as Tyler saw at once. Howard, at seventy-four, looked rather displeased in frock coat and top hat, leaning on one polished and spat-clad shoe on the top of the shovel, its point placed in a shallow hole prepared for it. Certainly no suggestion of decorum or reverence.

Founder of the famous Wall Street bank turned the first shovel of earth in the groundbreaking ceremony of what is to be the newest bank building on the famous street, nearly across from the House of Morgan.

Another picture taken at the groundbreaking is identified as "Sons and heirs and family look on at historic moment."

Charles and Harrison Starkweather, sons of Howard Harrison Starkweather and heirs to the investment banking empire, and rest of family. Left to right are Mrs. Harrison Starkweather (*née* Van Rogen), daughter Lillian, sons Andrew, Joseph, Tyler, and the youngest daughter, Pauline.

The brown tones of the reproduction do not do justice to the family group; missing its color, the details of lace on the girls' garments, the red waistcoats the boys are wearing. Andy, proper teenager, trying to look bored, Joseph smiling, a cigarette out of sight in his fingers behind his back. Tyler, the most serious, as if trying to pump himself full of the importance of the event.

Both Harry and Katie are impressive in size; in their early forties, they have weight and dignity. In the background, in a long black coat and tiny feathered hat, is Drucilla Brooks scowling.

There is a small oval picture:

EXECUTIVE VICE PRESIDENT, CHAUNCEY WILCOX

Mr. Wilcox is the only member of the firm who was with Mr. Howard Harrison Starkweather when the firm was founded as a small establishment during the Civil War, in 1863.

Under most of the scrapbook images, theater programs, picture postal cards, Tyler had lettered titles or comments in blue ink, not too neatly or spotlessly.

Gee, what a great DAY. GRAMPS took us all to the Waldorf. Dad gave each of us a gold watch with lettering: GROUNDBREAKING DAY, APRIL 18, 1911. H. H. STARKWEATHER & COMPANY

There is much of interest in the scrapbook, which was kept from 1910 to 1917, when Tyler discarded it as a childish thing. It gives some clues of situations, family history that is not distorted, as was the official history published in 1963. *A Hundred Years on Wall Street: A Century of Starkweather Progress.*

Tyler's pages contain one of the first aerial photographs taken from a Wright brothers flying machine; this picture is of all of Shad Point, showing the river and the vast acreage of the private Starkweather world. The huge mansion of the founder with its stables, early garage, its rose gardens and lawns, the enlarged boathouse. Winding private roads, neatly hedged and landscaped. The Harri-

264

son Starkweathers' summer home on the lip of the river. Also a house with wings added in 1909, set among trees and a small lake, the residence of Mr. and Mrs. (Sunny Starkweather) Rolf Arlington; here there is a tennis court, a play area for their three girls, a small gravel track for Rolf (a racing-car buff) to try out his Mercer 35J Raceabout, with which he hopes someday to humble other society racers. The house is of red and yellow brick and suggestive of a French château.

Near the northern end of the estate is the Art Nouveau white-walled (lots of glass) home of Mr. and Mrs. (Phyl Starkweather) Fiore-Brown. The Fiore-Browns are childless. They have both a lily pond and a swimming pool. They raise collies; the kennels are plainly seen in the picture. Weekends they serve cocktails to people who come in early motorcars—Simplexes, Pierce-Arrows, Stutz Black Hawks—and some even in a flivver or Tin Lizzie built by someone called Henry Ford. "Very *soigné* types," is Tyler's lettering over the house.

Lillian, the oldest daughter, does not live at Shad Point even if her grandfather has set aside fifty acres for her. There is also a boarded-up cottage that was built for Christine, the youngest daughter of the Howard Harrison Starkweathers. But she is hardly ever mentioned in front of her parents or grandfather. She was a bright and cheerful girl, a skilled tennis player, a small-boat sailor of merit, at first consorting delicately, then engaged to J. Brewster Wilson, a sportsman, serving his first term in Albany when he went off to Cuba in '98 as a volunteer in a black regiment and died at Sagua la Grande of spoiled Chicago canned beef. Christine neither mourned in public nor let people pity her. Instead she became an Anglican High Church convert and took vows as a nun in the Order of the Sacred Heart of Mercy, a Canadian order. It is doubtful if H.H. actually said, as was gossiped, "I'd rather see her a Democrat than Church of England."

Tyler had labeled this bird's-eye view of Shad Point: "If I were a bird, this is what I would see. Tweet. Tweet."

Not pasted, but folded in between pictures of the Harry Starkweather boys playing croquet and H.H. seated in his first auto car, a Stevens-Duryea, with Chauncey, both goggled and in white linen dusters, is a copy of a front page of the New York *World*.

GIANT LINER *Titanic* STRIKES ICEBERG AND SINKS: HUNDREDS FEARED DROWNED!

It was a newspaper page that many of the best families were to save, and in time, as Tyler was to discover, to have a relative go down in the White Star's "unsinkable" liner became a social-status item to bring up casually in conversation.

In a later edition of the newspaper Tyler had drawn a red crayon line around a retouched photograph of Charles Starkweather.

HEIR TO GREAT WALL STREET BANKING HOUSE AMONG THOSE LOST AT SEA

Charles Starkweather, forty-one, among those listed as having gone down with doomed White Star luxury liner. . . .

Even with the heavy photo retouching and the coarse grain of the reproduction, Charlie's fine head, with long, thin uptwisted mustache, a diamond stickpin in a foulard tie, a touch of a small flower in his lapel with a tiny sliver of ribbon of some honorable order never identified, came through. There were rumors he had a wife or mistress in Germany, where he had set up mutual banking interests with Oberbeck, Longstrasse und Von Zellern Deutschebank of Berlin as representatives of H. H. Starkweather & Company in Central Europe. The rumor of the wife, mistress, even of a child, could not be traced by the family, as in the next half-dozen years there was a war and after that a postwar chaos.

The nation was not yet anti-German, but the Street, as J. P. Morgan and Starkweather & Company became by 1912 the two most important houses to arrange vast European loans, would in the near future back the Allies.

The several scrapbook pictures lettered GRAMPS show H.H. not too happy to be shaking Woodrow Wilson's hand, or smoking cigars with a top British embassy official behind a hedge at a Long Island garden party. Of historic interest is a now-faded snapshot—never reproduced—made with a Kodak box camera of H.H. and J. P. Morgan seated on the terrace of the yacht club in white wickerwork rockers. Two old men in black broadcloth, smoking their Havanas and both looking rather expressionless. Tyler was to think the picture was taken late in 1912 or early in 1913. It was the last meeting of the two men. There is already a hint of death about the too-large man, the body of Morgan overrelaxed, the eyes like those of a sick hawk. A Roman, Tyler was to think later, of the Aurelian period; massive, a belly curved like a cello.

266

Howard knew very well when the snapshot of himself and Morgan had been taken. As they both grew older, the two men, rivals in the eyes of the Street, liked to meet once a month some afternoon at the yacht club and, against doctor's orders, after escargots and pepper steaks, truffles in pâté maison, sit, drinks in hand, exchanging small talk; the real estate market, the American cup races. International money, the coming Pujo investigation, the political scene. They never seriously talked of investment banking, that is, but on the day that picture was taken by the barman of the club, an Englishman who had once been a jockey and claimed to have ridden in the derby the day the American jockey Tod Sloan had pulled the king's horse for some gambling syndicate—and since then all American riders had been banned from British racetracks. The barman was so pleased with his picture of the two money nabobs, as he called them, he gave H.H. a print. "It ain't art, Mr. Starkweather, but it's the two of you very solid, now ain't it?"

H.H. had to admit it was.

The night before the meeting with J.P. he was staying in the city in his hotel suite; it had become a sort of ritual the second Tuesday in the month if he were in the city. H.H. couldn't sleep. As he grew older, since passing his sixties, sleep had become a problem. And now the talk of war, of trouble in the Balkans, even a European war—that was unthinkable in a modern world of progress, solid money, international credits. It all kept sleep away. Not the warm milk or six pages of Emerson, a hot bath brought sleep. Ten minutes after he had extinguished the reading lamp, he shifted his position in bed, and a half hour later his tossings had made a tangle of the blankets. It was no use; he couldn't fall asleep.

On the worst of his insomnia nights H.H., if in town, had a sovereign remedy. He would get up, dress in comfortable clothes, and wander until after dawn among the city's markets. With sleep impossible, he turned on the light again, threw aside the blankets, dressed in a tweed suit, and went out through a deserted lobby onto the streets in a cold dawn.

He had a wide choice of markets to visit. He could pick his way under the great spanning bridges of the East River that arched over to Brooklyn, or he could go to the waterfront at the foot of Fulton Street. There, under the light of flares and bonfires, he could lose himself in the busy life of the market which had been established years ago "to supply the common people with the necessities of life at a reasonable price." Before daybreak he could see tons of fish lifted by cranes and by hand from the holds of trawlers and draggers and from refrigerated trucks. He could watch men in rubber boots to their hips clean, bone, ice, and pack deep-sea fish that slithered in dripping stalls. It reminded him of his own hard years as a sailor.

He could go to the large market. There he could look into a huge cornucopia of fruits and vegetables, the harvest of orchards and truck gardens, trainloads of Idaho potatoes and strawberries in and out of season, and apples and cabbages and celery and lettuce and talk to his friends, the commission merchants, dealers in cantaloupes and apples and lemons and oranges and grapefruit. Enjoy their quick, decisive bargaining and understand the subtle inflections of their voices as they described their produce. His eyes could find pleasure and restfulness in the color and composition of the heaps of carrots and spinach and cauliflower. His mind could find peace amid all the chatter and rapid calculation.

He decided to go downtown to the Washington Market, bounded by West, Fulton, Washington, and Vesey streets. He, in a taxi, rode down past the Gansevoort Market and saw through his cab window a milling crowd of grocers, pushcart vendors, and restaurant buyers around the farmers' trucks. They were digging arms into baskets of fruits and vegetables to ascertain quality. Here and there a derelict bent down to pick up a vegetable that had rolled to the curb. Two nuns stood patiently waiting for a contribution of money or food for the destitute. A Wall Street of food, he thought.

H.H. dismissed his cab at Greenwich and Barclay streets and walked one block west and one south. The glow of lights from the farmers' trucks threw grotesque shadows among the jostling buyers. Marvelous odors made him distend his nostrils. Cheeses and hams from Holland, kippers from Norway, partridge quail, pheasant, and wild duck from England made him sniff with delight. He saw freight trains discharge their loads of beef, lamb, and pork, of swordfish, tongues in cellophane, pompano, venison, and crate after crate of cackling chickens. His roving eye took in vats of butter stacked like a lesser pyramid and tins of lard and eggs by the hundreds of dozens. He wished he had the appetite of his youth. *Christ, can any city devour all this?* His feet scuffed through discarded cabbage leaves and the droppings of heavy-rumped draft horses. All around him were warehouses and storage buildings that were packed with sides of beef, gutted pigs, and sheep slung by tied legs on long racks.

All night the trucks, he knew, had been coming from Long Island, from the South and the West, grinding steadily past sleeping towns, moving along the roads in moonlight, heading for the hungry city. They carried sacks and crates and boxes and barrels. Some were loose-piled with oranges, some with basketed pears and peaches, some with rolling cabbages, watermelons, and eggplants. Others rode lightly under a large load of greens to which clots of dark earth still clung.

Across from the Jersey shore long sections of freight cars were being ferried while tug whistles moaned. Some of these cars had come from as far away as the High Sierras and through the long passes of the Rockies. He thought, They've traveled, gathered red dust in Kansas, chalk marks in the freight stations of Chicago. Some of them had been started in New Orleans and had come up along the Atlantic seaboard, dropping cars and coupling with others as they rolled northward. One could develop a hotbox in New Mexico and another be sidetracked in Wyoming.

Cutting across the rippling wake of the train ferries were barnacle-crusted tramps and freighters from the food ports of the world. They carried citrus and bananas and boxed luxury foods. Their holds were full of beef and the drawn and quartered bodies of smaller herbivores. The ships docked, and clutching steel hands in the shape of hooks at the end of the long arms of cranes lifted food to the docks. A line of trucks moved forward and carried it all to market.

H.H. walked down Washington Street, taking it all in, stopping for a moment to watch a florid man lift a side of beef to his shoulder, and noticed how the man's cheeks matched the color of the bloodred meat. Presently he came back, adjusting the square of burlap that lay over his shoulder as a pad. He leaned against the lowered tail of the truck and wiped his face. Another side of beef was slid over toward him, and again he leaned down to take it on his back and carry it up an incline to the elevator in the storage building.

"Fine beef," H.H. said to the man when he returned.

"Kansas City firsts," the man replied. Another side of beef had been hooked and pulled toward him. H.H. moved on among bales and boxes and loose heaps of produce. The gasoline flares and the

269

clusters of electric bulbs were giving up a losing fight against the coming dawn. Slow-gaited horses were pulling empty carts and wagons toward West Street and trucks were starting for the ferries and tunnels. The stock market would open in four hours.

He listened to a boss of a gang of market roustabouts who were unloading crates of berries in a chain by passing them from one to the other down a line from trucks to warehouse.

"Come on, you lead feet! Faster! This stuff has to move or else she'll spoil. Pick 'em up and pass 'em on! Don't bash those crates! They're going uptown. Careful, or they go to the pushcarts at cut rate!"

So much food and so little waste, H.H. thought as he wandered on, for a hungry city. In a few hours it would begin to stir and demand oranges and prunes and grapefruit, cereals, and eggs and butter and ham and bacon and salt and sugar and tea and coffee, tons and tons of coffee with which to start the day. And those long glass-lined milk trucks that brought thousands and thousands of gallons to the city each day could now go back to the dairy farms and wait for the cows to provide them tomorrow's loads. Bottles of milk and cream stood already in doorways. Fresh bread had already been delivered, and in pantries there were jars of jelly and marmalade and honey. The city could do nothing until it ate.

The nicotine-colored sky in the east was turning to a gray-gold. Flares were snuffed out and electric lights dimmed. The streets suddenly lost their vitality; they were littered with crushed fruits and vegetables. Lines of casual workers were being paid off for their brief but heavy labors. The market was getting scrubbed before its daytime sleep. Street cleaners were stretching lines of flat high-pressure hose. Water from hydrants would soon fill the hose to roundness and wash the market clean again.

H.H. walked one block north and then one east, and following that zigzag pattern, he reached Sixth Avenue and looked up that street lined with the shabby buildings, the elevated structure. A bus came along and H.H. boarded it. All the seats were taken by men and women on their way to work. He held no bleeding-heart regard for the poor, the workers. They were human beings to him. Good or bad, decent or scum. He judged men by their actions. Was not starry-eyed over hopes of political change to make a perfect world. They held tin lunch boxes in their laps and some of them were rubbing the sleep out of their eyes. At Fourteenth Street a

270

number of passengers got off and H.H. found a seat. For the first time he felt fatigue.

When he stepped off the bus within a block of his address, he yawned and stretched. He went into a cafeteria, picked up a tray, knife, fork, spoon, and napkin, and shuffled onward to the counter. He ordered a large glass of orange juice, scrambled eggs, coffee, and toast. He ate with voracious appetite and felt revived. With long strides he walked the remaining distance to his suite and waved cheerfully to the clerk on duty as he passed through the lobby on his way to the elevator. In a few minutes he would be in bed. Harry would ring if there was a problem at the bank. Now all he wanted was to sleep, yep.

These were the lonely years for Howard. He had no wife (Susan had politely died in 1907 over a whist table in Newport). The latest of his mistresses, a windblown Texas widow, he had left in Denver, becoming bored with her, and he had not yet replaced her. The itch for sensual games of the flesh, for the pattern of the two-backed beast, was still with him, even at seventy-two, but it didn't spur or drive him the way it once had. He was beginning to wonder if the sexual act wasn't dreadfully overrated. Still, he thought, later that week, sitting on the veranda at Shad Point—a porch festooned with morning glory, honeysuckle, and clematis—still, for all that, where the genitalia lead a man, a man must follow.

Tyler, young as he was, had a remarkable ability to understand some of his grandfather's moods, even emotional reactions. With the loss of Charlie, H.H. seemed far away, and yet he had to pull himself away from brooding; there was the serious business of the bank. Very early Tyler learned you always thought of the Bank with that big letter *B*, unless you thought of it as THE BANK. As a small boy he had sat watching the floor of the Stock Exchange charge into the day's business, had learned to read the business section of the *Times* the way his schoolmates read *Starky & Company* or *Call of the Wild*. When *they* talked of buried pirate gold or running away with a circus, Tyler noted the dealings in steel, what hog bellies were doing, and figured the bank was bullish on the motorcar stocks, always a gamble with everyone trying to push Henry Ford out of his top position.

He would never forget the day he was permitted to be a board

boy and walk around with chalk and change the prices of corporation stock as they came in over the ticker. He busy with a strip of
paper marking up the fall or gain in copper, processed foods, train
systems, the shares in banks, holding companies. The summer he
worked two months as a board boy was better than trying to be an
Eagle Scout. H.H. patted his shoulder and sneezed at the chalk
dust. "A damn little broker here. Have to take him to the Bankers
Club for lunch."

"Thanks, Gramps, but I'd rather go to Max's Busy Bee and have
corned-beef sandwiches with some of the other board boys."

H.H. understood and give him a ten-dollar gold coin with which
to treat the boys. "To all the trash food they can eat."

38

COFFEE

Coffee futures were higher Monday. Tight supplies of green
coffee in the New York market, which are suitable for delivery
against the Coffee C contract, attracted demand for futures
contracts.

Today was first-notice day for the 1912 new delivery. Market quarters said fresh delivery notices were issued against the
nearby September contract, and all of them were reported
promptly stopped.

Roaster demand for green coffee was slow.

Coffee spot Santos No. 4 ex-dock closed at n64.

Howard set down the report; how could he care about anything
with such a personal loss? How could he ever get over it? One did,
everyone said so.

Charlie's loss had been a great blow.

J.P. Morgan had his son Jack prepared for it, taking over. With
Charlie lost, Howard had felt he had aged ten years. The agony of
the first sea-carried wireless messages coming in, and people gathering in front of the offices of the *Sun*, the *Times*, the *American* for
the hasty-lettered or chalked-up tragic news. Charlie gone? That
wise, happy, life-loving body lost forever in the icy North Atlantic.
Food for fish, my son's bones left to turn to coral on the ocean bottom. I have always hated the sea.

Howard wore a mourning band—and he told himself: One survived. Survival was all. Harry had turned out fine. In his damn high-toned society manner and his frozen turnip of a dinner-party-giving wife in her voluminous skirts, disquieting smile, the line was going on. Harry was not given to showy action, but he had self-assurance, a Starkweather head on his shoulders. He'd do fine. Not as well as poor Charlie would have done. Charlie, my Charlie, he thought, rocking on the veranda at Shad Point. Raised him from a pup to run the whole shebang. But one takes all blows on the elbows, as Jim Corbett says.

There were grandchildren. Harry's (and Katie's) three boys. Andy would be in time a replacement for Charlie. He had the same grace, a supple copious mind, but needed a little acid in him, a growl, a way of taking life in a tight handshake. Not collecting—what the hell was it? Rare stamps, Goya etchings. Well, there were reserves, Joe and Tyler. Maybe if Joe stopped lifting skirts and could hold his liquor better, he'd make a fighting head of a department floor manager with a seat on the Exchange. Ty? A bit of a tad yet; those big eyes full of awe and wonder, with the pale skin of a Chesney; was there no end to *their* damn bloodline, a hope of it petering out? It's not just what genes a marriage gives you, as to what it doesn't take away.

After a while he slept better nights. He'd wake, order up kippers, and near noon on a Sunday order a Kansas City steak if he were staying in his city suite. And at times add a pitcher of Pilsener. He was eating such a steak, reading the *Times'* weekend stock pages, seated in his bathrobe, when Chauncey Wilcox came in carrying a smoked ham wrapped in brown paper.

"Morning, H.H. Wait till you sink your teeth into this ham. Peanut-fed—not city slops—smoked in the Virginia backcountry, smoked in smoldering hickory shavings, six months."

"You look as if you've been eating a lot of it."

"Come off it, H.H. Maybe I've put on a few pounds here and there."

Chauncey had filled out in his middle age. He was no longer the slim young Indian type, but a beefy, too-beefy man, too red-faced, too much pugnacious chin, wry quizzical eyebrows. But the hair still oily black (Did he color it? H.H. wondered). Chauncey was dressed to the nines, as the fashionable dudes put it. Real Savile Row tailoring; banker somber, dark-toned thick material. Just some loops of gold watch chains, a diamond on one finger.

"Sleep well?"

"All morning. Ring for coffee, Chaunce."

"Not for me. I've packed it in early. Week's market very good. Somebody is stockpiling steel, copper chemicals."

"The damn Germans," said H.H. "But there will be no big war."

Chauncey speared some french fries from H.H.'s plate. "Too civilized a world, eh? Mankind, you feel, has come down from the trees and out of the caves. Personally, me, I'm buying Du Pont, McCann Steel, Anaconda."

"Donald wouldn't like his steel used for weapons."

"What does he think, H.H., it's used for? Garbage cans, making toys for kids? Since he set up the goddamn McCann Fund, you'd think he was working to get his wings and a harp from St. Peter here on this earth."

"That's what comes of getting to love opera." Howard put down the newspaper and reached for a cigar.

"And opera singers. I'd rather get into bed with a suffragette. Oh, sorry, forgot about your girl Lillian."

"The Turkish-Balkans war can explode Europe."

Chaunce nodded. "Talk of some U.S. special officers training group; if we do have trouble, it's my last chance since my relatives on my mother's side got Custer. But the Balkans—hell, nothing there."

"Need you in the bank. You're way overage for a soldier. . . . Order my car. I'm going out to the yacht club."

"Give my best to J.P. Whatever happened to St. Mars? Thought he was going to be a big man there."

"No. J.P. put in his son Jack, J.P., Jr. St. Mars is out in Shanghai with the Sassoons, I heard. Says Asia is the future; China will dominate the world. Always had a good opinion of himself as a thinker."

Chauncey said a dirty word about St. Mars and phoned down for Mr. Starkweather's car.

They sat sipping Pilsener, H.H. and J.P., sure of each other, close at times without talking. Yet both aware there had been great changes, and the best years of achieving and endeavor were perhaps behind them.

The yacht club was enjoying a season of good weather.

"That the way you see it?"

"It's best to see it could be that way."

"Christ, it's Europe, it's what they call civilization, all the high-toned malarkey about science and progress and—"

274

"And the whole shooting match may go up in flames."

"Hard to take, J.P. The world setting fire to its pants."

"Just talk maybe. Saber rattling."

They were seated on the wide terrace of the yacht club, and before them the Long Island Sound dimpled and dipped in polite swells, pure silver. The white wings of sailing craft were making sharp sudden turns as they tacked. Off by the club float some young girls were splashing around in the diving area of jade-green water, laughing, their young bodies limber, arching, and moving about. Both old men watched this water play with mellow interest; both were hedonists who had known many women. Their emotions stirred like restless sleepers at the sight of the young bodies.

H.H. took his eyes off the water girls. "Europe can't afford a big war. This Turkish-Balkans thing is a conflict between half-wits."

"Europe doesn't have to *afford* a big war, Starkweather. Just *want* to fight one. That bastard Willy, the kaiser, feels the Germans can lick the world."

"You think the English will try to keep things calm?"

"England is the last honorable country in Europe, Starkweather. A trustworthy people."

H.H. said nothing, just enjoyed the cigar. J. P. Morgan was a well-known Anglophile and cocksman; had been keeping an actress in some castle in Britain. As McCann had said of such situations, "Where a man's genitalia find perfection, there, too, his heart usually is."

Morgan leaned forward with effort; the chair creaked. He was old and large and would not last out the year, Howard thought. "My son Jack knows my idea. The House of Morgan will seek extended credits for the British Empire. We shall arrange loans to supply her with the wherewithal to exist and fight in case of war. Now, Starkweather, to keep the peace of balance of power, I'd like to hear you say you'll join us and help to take care of, say, the Italians' needs, credits, loans."

Howard laughed and shook ash off his cigar, the wind scattering it. "I'd rather have the English as creditors than the others."

"Oh, you'll be a partner. I'm also working things out with the Rothschilds, others, so there will be some sharing and dividing of the business. I don't give a plugged shilling, a good goddamn about the right or the wrong. I don't want to see England and whatever allies she'll have lower her banners."

"Like a tart her drawers?"

275

"We're old men yammering, Starkweather. Peace *will* hold. No country in Europe can fight a war of any prolonged length without outside help. The Germans depend on the Scandinavians for steel and chemicals. They could seize some of Europe outside their borders, what they can for coal, iron, foodstuffs. But French élan, the English bulldog strain will make them think twice about making war."

"How long do you think war could last?"

J.P. gave a sour smile. "I'll ask my horoscope reader."

The girls were coming out of the water in a rush of limbs—legs, arms shiny wet, heads tilted back, teasing and jesting among themselves, running across the short stretch of lawn to the dressing rooms. The old men unashamedly enjoyed them like some instantaneously rendered dream.

Howard leaned back in his chair. "Mark Twain was right, you know, J.P., when he said he'd rather see Lillian Russell naked than General Grant with all his medals on."

Morgan grunted agreement and shut his eyes to the sunlight.

How calm and packed away in time most of the items in Tyler's scrapbook were to seem years later, looking back at 1912, 1913. A tennis match photographed at Shad Point. Andy taking flying lessons summers in a Wright brothers pusher flying machine in a Long Island meadow; Aunt Dru (a short item) denying she had forgotten to pay for a bar of soap and a box of carpet tacks at a Woolworth's five-and-ten. H.H. dressed as a pirate at the birthday party for his granddaughter Pauline, looking very amused and yet menacing, a black patch over one eye, a hat with skull and crossbones symbols, a cutlass in hand. (Later the radical *The Masses* reproduced it in 1917 under the title "The Great Pirate of Wall Street.")

The spring of 1914 is represented in the scrapbook by some pages torn from Ernest Thompson Seton's *Scouting for Boys,* also a reproduction of an Arrow collar ad of a young dude, to which Pauline had added a blue-ink mustache and the words "Be my Valentine, Ty—guess who."

In July of 1914 J.P.'s heir, Jack, found himself not only the head of the House Morgan but in the position that if war came—and it certainly would if all signs were right—the Street would become the very active agents for the European powers in arranging for credits, loans, and the buying of supplies.

Jack Morgan turned to H.H. for some talks on what had to be done. He called, at H.H.'s advice, a meeting at the House of Morgan of the heads of the major investment banks on Wall Street. Almost, Harry felt, like a high prelate bringing together a historic ecclesiastic conference.

Jack handled himself well in his father's old meeting room. Large, rather shy, middle-aged, a son kept too long in his father's shadow, he was rather ponderous.

H.H. rose and explained what was ahead. "I'm sure J.P. himself, were he alive and wise as always pertaining to money, would agree that it might be a good idea to close the Stock Exchange for a while on the declaring of a general European war—I suggest a four-month closing."

"Damn it, H.H. Why?"

"Close the Exchange because they're scrapping!"

There was muttering around the big polished table. H.H. just smiled. "There is a bigger problem, gents, perhaps."

"What!"

"Do we suspend gold payments to Europe during the period of a war or threat of one? Huh? Jack, what is your opinion?"

J.P., Jr., a paler version of his father without the diseased nose, a milder person, but now firm enough, it was clear, as he spoke of the proper business of investment banking. "My father always felt it's the bankers' prime duty to maintain the market in money. I say we must—have to—continue the gold shipments to Europe. We shall here. But I leave it to you gentlemen to decide for the Street."

H.H. looked over the dozen men who were the Street. Anarchists of money? Jesuits of credits? Or just snake-oil salesmen doing a brisk business? "Raise your hands if you agree."

It was decided to continue gold shipments to Europe.

H.H. was pleased. "Cash flow, don't ever forget it, is the lifeblood of the world. Without it you have a planet to give back to the apes. No wheels turning, no food being shipped, ores mined, cities fed, wages and taxes paid. Christ, just this morning the City of New York owed a hundred million in gold abroad and didn't have it. Morgan and Starkweather and Company arranged to finance the loan."

There were top hats worn and the bankers donned theirs and departed. In August the Great War began. The Street was more active than it had ever been. Howard, Harry, and Chauncey sat in the biggest of the new offices in the new bank and looked over cables from abroad. Hard to believe, Harry felt, that men were actually dying in the wheat fields, among the poppies and in the apple orchards of Europe.

Chauncey riffled through some charts. "I think we've picked sides, eh, H.H.?"

"I'd say so. Unless you want Germans with their spike helmets playing tennis at Shad Point and ruling the world. Of course, they're all guilty of pride, flag-waving, heating up the yahoos."

Besides watching the turmoil rising in the world, Tyler was also discovering his own body, and if Joe kept him from running with his crowd of young smut hounds and their telling of juicy stories, he would explore on his own. He had this dream of a dark girl, very well shaped, perhaps a bit big in the rump (the age of Lillian Russell was still there). But somehow she had to be Latin. In his dreams she was from another world than the Starkweather world. Her skin was hot to the touch, and what was inside of his schoolboy pants became agitated and troublesome, but still was pleasant.

Alone it wasn't so much. But the dreams, the daydreams leading up to it, fine. He began to sniff at women as they passed. They had this fine odor of powder and armpits protected by dress shields. And the flesh, yes, the flesh, he liked the words, "the flesh." He could imagine them naked, the friends of the family, the ladies who played whist. See with X-ray eyes the damp moss of their pelvic *V*, feel the smooth skin of their grand spreading asses, run his tongue up their hairless legs, lick them behind their knees. He found the usual schoolboy sources of words or missing words, not in the dictionaries, burrowed in stray medical volumes. All that intricate network of veins, muscles, organs. One put it *there*; it went in *there*. It was shaped like *this*. And what else could one do with the reality behind the drawings for med students, the diagrams? He had heard of French picture postal cards and dirty funny papers. And of harems and flogging of *nates* in British schools. But he wanted reality, *not* print.

At Shad Point there was a Mexican gardener who cut flowers for the vases and bowls of the big house. He lived in a hut behind the glass hothouses with a fat wife who raised red hens, and they had several children. The only girl was called Carmen, a girl who scratched her head (with need, he supposed) and chewed gum, and whatever her age—twelve? fourteen?—she was, as one of the horse grooms said, "some built."

278

Carmen wore a little gold cross and got cuffed by her mother when she didn't go to Mass in the village. In season she went hunting mushrooms along the river meadows and woods. One afternoon Tyler, pitching flat stones into the Hudson, saw her cross by the bushes where there was a foxy smell and mud turtles were often found in dead tree stumps.

"Ha, you wanna come help me find the 'rooms?"

"What?" he asked.

"The mushrooms. I get my ass kicked I no find a lot."

Always helpful, he followed the girl, she barefoot, in a knee-length garment and nothing else he saw—followed into the woods, where the mushrooms grew thickest. It didn't take long until they had a full basket and they sat against a fallen ash tree and chewed on sour grass.

"You ever see it?" she asked.

"See what?"

"A girl's thang."

"Huh? Oh, sure."

"I seen boy's thang. My brudda's. You got a big one?"

Tyler shrugged. "I don't know."

"Let's see him." She was bold enough to reach and Tyler was willing enough to help. There was really nothing under the garment but naked girl. The reality was better than the medical books. It was soon all panting and hugging and handling. Busy fingers, grasping hands. *Very* satisfactory as he spurted. He might, he felt, have had all, full entry, but the tree trimmers were coming along the river to cut down the extra oak boughs and trim the evergreens. Carmen stood up, wriggled to lower her garment, sniffed her hand, and ran off quickly, hooting like a demented owl.

Tyler sat for a long time sucking in breath. It was really a delightful world, and they hadn't lied about men's and women's parts. There was a lot he didn't know, but he'd spend a great part of his life, he hoped, finding out. Yes. He buttoned up and he, too, sniffed his fingers and went home whistling, suddenly very hungry.

He twice more, before going back to school, met Carmen in the woods. They built a little shelter of fallen branches, covered it with leaves, and made what Carmen called *luff*. There was one demand she made: *no putting in*. That was big *sinful* and Father Manuel had impressed on the girls at confession it was the big sin and Hail Marys could never make up for a husband finding his wife had permitted someone else to put it in. There was, of course, a lot more that, while also a sin, could be confessed to and given Hail Marys and promises to try to resist in the future. But the flesh was weak and randy, and God was a man and he understood men did things to women's blood.

That fall in school Tyler had a wise look when the chaps talked of their adventures with their mothers' maids, waitresses, nannies, and two boys hinted of actually having contact with whores. But they were liars, Tyler felt. He made some small confessions, acting as the expert to several doubters as to anatomy and games. But it was clear to him that someday a marvelous dark girl with a knock-out body would come his way, and *luff* would be complete and *putting in* would be very heaven.

39

Harry Starkweather tapped a pencil against a cheek at one of the daily meetings in H.H.'s office. He looked earnest and a bit thinner. Since the death of Charlie he had moved—like a chess piece moving several squares—to assume a greater part in the routine of the bank and had shown such a firm understanding and determination that H.H. wondered if his second son had the brains to go with his get-up-and-go. Harry seemed in some sort of doubt this morning. The Germans were still advancing. "No one seems to understand the costs of a modern war. What the Allies will need in machines, arms, food, clothing, gasoline, paper, steel, a half-million horses, mules, medical supplies, machine tools. We, who offer the resources of our nation, may be betting on the wrong side."

Chauncey laughed. "You mean the Allies could lose the war?"

"Yes, if it is prolonged. The Germans are on the Marne. Even if the French hold, what if either side can't come to a quick—"

A young male clerk in a high collar, very narrow pants, put his head in the door. "Sorry, sir . . . phone . . . *very* important."

"Damn it, Wilkins," said H.H. "No calls."

"Yes, sir. But Sir Cecil Spring-Rice is on the wire—the British ambassador, calling from Washington."

Chauncey whistled. "Trouble, I bet. Maybe the Allies are beaten."

H.H. frowned, picked up the phone. "Yes, yes, speaking." He

lifted his eyebrows in a gesture of wonder. "Yes. . . . Ah, Sir Cecil. . . . Yes, of course I remember. Dined together at the Pedlocks'. What?"

The voice at the other end was cultured, a bit high, and the phone wires seemed to be muttering in a breeze. "I've had a phone conversation with young Morgan and he suggested, Starkweather, I explain the true British situation as of this moment. . . . Hello, hello? Are you there, sir?"

"Yes, yes. The damn line is buzzing, Sir Cecil."

"England is calling in all its resources, needs badly a great deal more of supplies and a banking setup that must come from your country. Now our purchasing programs of his majesty's government informs us we are paying too-high prices, and the service has been very bad. Oh, very. So it seems you gentlemen, who are the major bankers, would, we are told, perhaps act as our purchasing agents for all we need here, under the control of yourself and the House of Morgan. That is the suggestion."

"I see, Sir Cecil."

"We've been mulched, had badly by your chaps in trade, so far. We've been paying as high as nearly eight percent in commissions. Now, if we could lower that—cut out all our agents. . . ."

H.H. said, "How does two percent strike you, Sir Cecil? Does that feel fair? I'm sure the House of Morgan would agree. We'd pay all costs of handling. You think Lloyd George wouldn't bitch over that?"

"I'm sure he'd accept with delight. . . . Of course you people—as neutrals. . . ."

"Oh, yes, as neutrals." H.H. held back the laughter in his throat. "My son, Hal—Harrison—will handle our end of it. How are the French handling this?"

"Morgan, Harjes and Company in Paris have, I'm sure you are aware, just gotten six million in gold from the Bank of France to open accounts in Wall Street."

"Yes. Over here you're going to run into a hard shell named William Jennings Bryan, the Secretary of State. He'll scream it's not legal as we're, cross our hearts, neutral. But Wilson is a romantic, and worse, an idealist. We'll manage, Sir Cecil."

"If you could, sir, see the National City loan of ten million to France isn't held up, we'd be most grateful."

The conversation went on for five minutes before H.H. hung up

281

and said very seriously, "Well, this bank is in the war up to its ass. So is most of the Street. *But* the U.S.A. remains neutral."

"We'll get into the war ourselves over these damn loans," said Harry after H.H. had explained the gist of the conversation with the British ambassador.

"You bet your sweet dollar we could," said Chauncey. "But Morgan will be blamed—he's the radicals' symbol of money. Well, he'll get the biggest share of the commissions."

Harry said, "We could do as well."

H.H. was making notes on a sheet of paper. "The Street, through Morgan up front, will arrange a half-billion-dollar loan through an American bank syndicate—to aid England, the French. To be used only for the buying of supplies in the United States. Not a red cent leaves our shores or, as they say, maybe a pittance."

"Half a billion," Harry mused. "Hm, that's rather shooting for the moon."

H.H. tore up his sheet of paper and put the bits into a jacket pocket. "If the war goes on, maybe a year or two more, three billion will come from American loans to the Allies. File that in your noggins. Now I need my lunch."

Harry sat doing sums in his head. "Whoever handles the major loans will make fifty million a year on commissions—gross income for handling purchasing."

"Like all bankers," said H.H., rising, reaching for his square-crowned derby and cane, "I have always believed in making a profit. I'm not greedy, but we do perform a needed service." He shook his head and thrust his cane at Harry like a sword. "The bastards who made this war, if they had all their marbles, would know all this money could have been used to make their rotting cities better, take care of the poor—hell, the men are five feet tall in the London slums—underfed—the middle class needs better education. So? Europe will have fireworks instead. Yep!"

"Doesn't make sense, does it?" Harry said.

H.H. shook his head. "Because man is an undomesticated animal. Man is wolf to man—that's some old Latin motto, isn't it? Donald McCann thinks these times he'd like to resign from the human race like, he says, from a club. Let's go to lunch."

If H.H. expected the House of Morgan to be blamed for getting the United States into the Great War, he was only partly right. While "the Morgan loans" were the core of the radicals' blame for the United States' entering the conflict, the Starkweather loans were also listed as a pressure, and a fact in the balanced judgments of some later historians as also pushing Woodrow Wilson into the war. Aided by the Germans' reaction with their usual senseless fury to the supplies being ferried across the Atlantic. Even serious students of economics, Howard said, were divided on U.S. intervention; between the German blockade of England and the sinking of American ships and their war cargoes, the taking of American lives. He didn't ignore the Morgan and Starkweather loans for directing Americans into a war under a slogan popular but, he thought, rather banal. "The war to make the world safe for democracy."

It was Donald McCann, spending a weekend at Shad Point, watching one morning the grooms exercising the riding horses, he and H.H. leaning on the whitewashed fence, who commented, "You must be daft, H.H., to allow such a slogan. Nine-tenths of the world want food, not freedom. Anyway, democracy is often not liberty or freedom at all, it's a way some rabble-rouser fools the natives to elect him to office, a soft job and a bank account."

"Why so sanctimonious, Donald? McCann Steel Company is going to buy you more and bigger opera houses to give away, more young opera singers to educate, more composers to make more noise by scraping horsehair across sliced cat-entrail strings or to fart sound through a brass horn. Why, posterity will smother you in praise while your steel wipes out a generation. I think it is a way we old men show our hate of youth."

"I know you've done fine handling my shares. You always had a mean mouth, H.H. Yes, yes."

"Damn right. In 1913 McCann Steel shares were earning eleven dollars, four cents a share of common stock."

"I was satisfied!"

"Like hell. Now it's earning forty-eight dollars and fifty cents a share."

"Suppose, just suppose, H.H., there is a Judgment Day."

"If you control the Street, Hell would be apple pie to take over."

The grooms were riding a gray hunter and a Moran red around the half-mile track. "Donald, it's all a matter of taste. Now, I prefer horses to any opera singer I ever got down on her back."

"You've feeling for the wonder of women. I didn't know you knew opera singers, with your carnal nature."

283

"I did. If I could stuff a pillow in their mouths when I had them in bed. Remember the one Enoch Kingston, the railroad king, took away from you? Ha!"

"She's back. An old biddy now. We're all old now, aren't we, H.H.? At least the McCann Fund does a public service. All the opera houses I've built and given away. Why, I've spent more than Rockefeller and his domn foundation, or Rhodes and his buggering scholarships, and Carnegie and his free public libraries; and what the devil have the rich Jews been spending on?"

"Helping artists and writers of promise. . . . I think I'll buy some Arabian mares."

McCann chewed on an unlit cigar; doctors had forbidden him tobacco. "Hum. . . . As if we need more scrawls on walls or spoiling good paper printing dirty little stories of dirty little people. Let them listen to good voices. Yes!"

The thin groom rode up on the gray hunter, bred from a Narragansett pacer. "Stock been gettin' a bit heavy, Mr. Starkweather. Too much winter feed."

H.H. patted McCann's paunch. "Haven't we all?"

As the two men walked away from the exercise track, they were silent. McCann had grown into a kind of ghost, H.H. thought. Bent and aged, the old ferocity to control and own cut down. Seemed to be glancing into a world of fantasy. Judgment Day! Be sniveling to a priest to build a salad of oil and ash on his brow soon. H.H. was generous but McCann felt wealth was sin. McCann was shoveling it out in his McCann Fund all over the country. Sponsoring classical music, forming symphony orchestras, and for a town that could not support an opera house, at least a town hall for choral groups, glee clubs, even barbershop quartets. "The burden of great fortune" is what McCann told interviewers.

"What are you going to do with your money, H.H.?" It was a direct question and McCann waited for an answer.

H.H. seemed to weigh his answer. "As easy to lose your money as make it. I'm only sure of one damn thing. I'm not getting buried with it in my private graveyard on this place. Donald, could I reserve you a nice ten-by-ten plot?"

McCann shivered as they entered the house. "Don't be talking of death like that. I'm afeared of dying. But answer my question."

"All right, I'll put all cards face up on the table. Charity ruins the people taking it. Bread and circuses ruined Rome. I'm going to build a dynasty. Is that so bad? Bankers do serve a nation, the world. It's not a perfect system, by no means. In fact a lot of our ways of doing things stink. But show me anything that's perfect or a system of justice that is fair to all. So Starkweather and Company will grow. I have plans for my son and grandchildren. Maybe a whole raft of Starkweather public banks, a hundred, two hundred. For the day is coming when we'll be forced by Washington to go in for the banking and trust business like any other savings bank, loan or trust company. Yes, go public and sell shares. But the control will be with the Starkweathers, Rockefeller, Morgan. All of us will someday have to play the game that way."

"It's a dream, H.H. Pride goeth before a fall. You'd have to live to be two hundred years old to see it all done."

H.H. slapped McCann on the back. "Barkis is willing."

"You're reading novels again," Donald said as they entered the dining room for lunch.

"It's something to do as you get older."

Tyler Starkweather's scrapbook contained none of the information of the activities, feverish bustle, and late hours in 1914 on the Street when the European war actually burst out in August, and J. P. Morgan had been dead more than a year. "Died in Rome," H.H. said to Jack Morgan, "like a Caesar." There are pictures in the scrapbook of troops marching and the kaiser in cape and silver helmet, fishhook mustache, looking like something out of a demented Wagnerian opera; also the lines of tired British regulars, bloodied and muddy, on the road back from Mons; paintings of Frenchmen in long horizon-blue tailcoats and baggy red pants, needle bayonets held forward on the charge and mouths open to cheer themselves on. And the dead, bloated horses among them, ruined churches in Belgium, cartoons, drawings of rapes, shooting of civilians, babies speared like sausages held on Hun bayonets as if to be cooked. The word "Hun" is used very often in the titles of the clippings Tyler pasted in his scrapbook. It was all presented as if the war were a rite of purification and manly fun. ("If you know a better 'ole, go to it.")

Of a personal family nature there is a picture of a row of young male faces at the rail of a ship.

AMERICANS SAIL TO FLY FOR THE ALLIES

In purple pencil an arrow points to a face under a checkered cap, and above are hand-printed words: "Andy sails for Europe to be an aeroplane man." Not the RAF but the Lafayette Escadrille.

Andy was nineteen, had left Yale, mathematics, and natural sciences, left classmates, and now was off to "save civilization," as some claimed.

By late 1915 Andy's picture with two others is on a postal card taken in some Paris shop, Le Blanc's on the rue Scribe (9ème arr.). Andy very handsome in his British-made military tailoring, boots, Sam Browne belt, peaked cap, swagger stick, the uniform of the Lafayette Escadrille. In ink Andy had written on the card: "Me and friend Raoul Lufbéry. Paul is from the 12ème Groupe des Escadrilles de la Chase. . . . A jolly good chum. Yr. brother, André."

It was the signature "André" that baffled. Andy to André?

The Street kept late hours, and handsome French and Italian officers, wounded, with an arm lost or limping, aided by a cane, came over to seek aid for their brave nations holding the beasts of the *Nibelungenlied* at bay.

Tyler's scrapbook contains a clipping from the *Ladies' Home Journal* picturing his mother, Susan, wearing a Red Cross headcloth, standing in front of a statue of Lafayette someplace with a group of maimed French officers in full uniform.

MRS. HARRISON STARKWEATHER HEADS RED CROSS DRIVE TO AID
VICTIMS OF THE GREAT WAR

A clipping from the Norton-on-Hudson *Daily News* shows Tyler in a Boy Scout uniform of the period, wide-brimmed hat, leggings, ill-fitting jacket, lugging a grocery box filled with peach pits, aided by his sister Pauline.

SCOUTS AND FAMILIES DO THEIR BIT

Tyler and Pauline Starkweather do their bit collecting peach pits that will be carbonized to make filters for gas masks.

Another clipping, from the *Wall Street Journal,* shows a portly and sweaty Chauncey Wilcox and Richard Harding Davis, both in uniform, lying behind a machine gun on a tripod and acting for the camera as if they were firing it. There is no ammunition belt.

Chauncey Wilcox, a vice president of H. H. Starkweather & Company, the grandson of Sitting Bull, and Richard Harding Davis, famed journalist, setting an example in preparedness just in case America should enter the conflict now raging in Europe.

Chauncey—he had lied by fifteen years as to his true age—never did find out who had issued the false information of his being related to Sitting Bull; he did lose ten pounds in two weeks at Plattsburg and was often photographed in uniform. ("This country does not intend to be involved in this war. It would be a crime against civilization"—Woodrow Wilson.)

H.H. remained a staunch Republican, but Harry came out for the election of Wilson; there is a blurred picture from *The Literary Digest* of Harry and Katie standing with President Wilson and Senator Lodge in front of a billboard that announces, among other things, VOTE FOR WOODROW WILSON—HE KEPT US OUT OF THE WAR—HE EXTENDED THE PARCEL POST.

H.H. went to bed on election night—"Democracy can at times be more dangerous than trench warfare"—hoping to see that Charles Evans Hughes had beaten "that pious son of a bitch of a randy schoolteacher." But by morning the results from California, coming in late, showed Wilson had been reelected.

There is in the scrapbook an invitation to Mr. and Mrs. Harrison Chesney Starkweather to attend the taking of the oath. However, the inaugural ball was canceled. There is no record that they went to Washington. The bank was busy arranging British and French loans. H.H. didn't care to do business with the Italians. "What are they doing in a war? A fine people—they sing too much, eat the pasta, and make bambinos. They shouldn't ever go to war."

The world spun on. Harry Starkweather kept three eight-hour shifts of telephone operators on the switchboard. It was a time of big money, and the bank was on the way to get the biggest. Even Harry carried his black leather portfolio back and forth from his office at unreasonable hours.

War held the world, and with a thousand threads and sounds and messages and whispers it marched through the doors of the bank. Orders were piling high these days and men hung on H.H.'s words.

When the day's business had run its course and the workers had gone home for the night, Harry sat at his desk, writing long pages of digests, calling Europe and South America on the telephone. His eyes red-rimmed and his head shaggy, he would pour himself a stiff drink of brandy and sit back to take stock of his world.

H.H. had told him; it was a strange world at war. The last quarter had added six billion dollars to the value of New York Stock Exchange securities. The average on sixty industrial leaders was a pleasure to behold. Bethlehem, McCann Steel were skyrocketing. True, peace scares were already threatening to disturb the rising averages, but these could be turned, said Chauncey, into money, too.

Copper and grain would have to be watched. Right now the powers were holding off a bit with their purchases, but they would buy, all right, and be glad to get them. Chemicals, pipelines, textiles, and rail equipment were being bought.

It was a world for big money, a business world, tough and skeptical. Put your cash on the barrelhead and you could buy anything, and you could sell anything, too, whether you had it or not, if you had the right connections in the right places.

The Germans were dropping out of South America. Legislation was going through or being stifled on command; the machinery was freely oiled. Glafkos Gerasimopoulos, the peripatetic Greek, was in Peru, looking over motor roads, rail lines. The bank was prepared to sell options to petroleum, gold, copper, sulfur, mica, limestone, nitrates, borates, deposits of alkaline salts. As agents—getting their commissions. Harry and Katie had no time for too many big dinner parties. Went to the opera only rarely.

H.H. began to depend on Harry more and more. The British Navy had just intercepted a ship loaded with the kaiser's personal coffee barrels. The Hun emitted new blasts against Albion. European clients of the bank were watching their investments all over the world in holding companies, and their life-insurance premiums, payable in almost every coinage of the world, would go a long way toward defraying the national debt.

Geneva was firm—war was profit.

In Berlin and Frankfort and Munich women stood in the slashing rain for rancid lard, moldy potatoes, and small cuts of horse-flesh. Men worked fourteen and sixteen hours a day and with no right to protest. Unionism was a relic of a forgotten day. The Junkers were running things now. Workers were for work.

The French franc, at 2.26¼, Harry noted, was off a quarter. The belga was 16.64. The Swiss franc was at 22. South American currencies managed to hold their own. In New York the gold imports were increasing daily. More gold was waiting to be delivered, but the seas were armed and dangerous. The American soil held the biggest lump of yellow metal ever gathered together in one spot. Hawthorn blossoms grew over great vaults. Alert guards drove flower lovers away.

Everywhere the earth was giving up wealth to produce a crueler war. The peons were, as Howard knew, checking his reports, busy. Busy laborers, the barley buckers, the bindle stiffs, the pickers and setters of seeds and plant shoots were tired and their backs ached. Rubber gatherers, miners, breeders, herders worked to keep the world supplied. H.H. could see it all in a steadily moving panorama, not nearly so complex as it seemed because all of it had one motivation: profit.

Futures in cottonseed oil, coffee, sugar, hides, tin, black pepper, zinc, wool were rising. One had to keep an eye on everything. Time loans, commercial paper, bankers' acceptances, clearinghouse exchanges—these, too, had to be scrutinized. Bullion was fixed by the Bank of England, but the black exchanges were doing business in cellars and in the back rooms of cafés, and their dealings, too, had some effect.

Everywhere men like H.H. were stirring, alert to catch profits. Gold and diamonds were being sold; bills were exchanged, deals consummated, promises projected into a near or remote future, and always for that difference that represented profit. That was the universal law of the Street.

Raw fur prices were up, twenty percent on skunk, ten percent on silver fox. "Wars do that," H.H. said. "My lady must keep her ass warm."

Ships sailed the seas, but not boldly; they were convoyed by battlewagons. In all the ports of the world tramp ships were waiting with their loads to sail for war profits. Even H.H. began to wonder when and how this all-consuming era would ever end.

40

Howard Starkweather was taking the six-member British purchasing mission in to lunch at Shad Point. Harry was on the West Coast seeing to the hurrying up of the building of some of the sixty thousand airplanes on order (none ever flew in combat in France).

The butler was waiting. He had a cable in his hand. "It was just delivered, sir."

Howard turned a worried face to the offered envelope. "Andy! I have a feeling it's about Andy," he said as he tore it open.

> CAPT. A. H. STARKWETTER [*sic*] SHOT DOWN.
> HOSPITALIZED. CONDITION SERIOUS.
> RAOUL LUFBÉRY. LAFAYETTE ESCADRILLE
> BASE 47A FRANCE.

Lieutenant Andrew Starkweather had become an ace, very effective against the Fokkers. He already had, as a flier *extraordinaire,* the Médaille Militaire and the Croix de Guerre. He was flying this gray day his Spad between Crévecoeur-le-Grand and Lassigny, in protection of a lumbering camera plane, watching for fast Jagdstaffel interceptors above the black smoke puff of Archies, enemy antiaircraft fire. He lived now like an old hand—an exhausted swimmer, rising each morning moderately manic-depressive.

He was seeing a girl, Sidonie d'Argreste. The family was Balbac, D'Argrèste et Cie. (steel). A special girl on his leaves in Paris, and his French was improving. Not at all like the college French. He liked the French; the Paris branch of Starkweather & Company had seen to it that he met the haut monde of society. Later, when he read Proust, in French of course, and was a French citizen with a French family, he was pleased he had decided to change over; Andy becoming André, as he was already being called by his future in-laws. He was not a snob or a prig, but had a diffident skepticism about America. He belonged (Tyler later decided) to a way of thinking, feeling, of those who were born during the period of Henry James' characters who were seeking a purposeful narrowness of passion in a polite society. Those well off, feeling America crude, who fled to Europe just before the turn of the century. Andy was the tail end, the last of these escapees from the strenuous, too-strong life of an expanding nation, a retiring, as Donald McCann said, to Old World museums and Louis Quinze sofas.

André was thinking of this as he lay in a first-aid station after being shot down while hunting *Drachen*. German captive observation balloons on their long ground-tied cables. Lord, what a day. He had gotten three of the damn gas bags on the Meuse, socking home his incendiary belts from the Lewis guns. Coming down through dreadful Archie fire to get the first, then the second, it drifting off in a rose of flame, the observer jumping in his parachute as the ground crew tried to wind down the leashed burning globe.

Andy—Capitaine Starkweather since his promotion—got the last *Drachen* at dusk as he felt the Spad shudder and his guns, firing through the propeller controls, bang home the last of the incendiaries smack into the collapsing bag. He saw the observer fall, thrown from his basket, no parachute opening. Then Andy got a blast of hot oil in his face over his goggles. The plane seemed to sit on its tail and drop off into a spin. He had been living on brandy and milk with an egg beaten into it, dreaming of the Boches' Pfalz scout planes. His nerves were frayed; solid food couldn't stay down. Now in the spin, he vomited a spray of brandy and milk all over his instrument panel and tried to baby the badly shot-up ship eastward and home. But he knew he'd not make it back to base. The rudder controls were too loose or gone, and his right wing looked as if giant termites had chewed it. Someplace nearer, the Storks—Les Cigognes—had a French flying field. But where the hell—*where?*

Canadians in the line were someplace west of Murvaux. There was a field there, too. Brier's Farm they called it. The plane leveled, shook—died in midair. He crash-landed in the wire of the Princess Pat regiment, on duty in the sector.

A corporal and two privates crawled out to get Andy through the wire as he sounded his Klaxon. "Keep your pecker up, old cock, we'll see you through."

They took his presentation watch from H.H. and the three thousand francs when they left him in the field station. As the corporal put it to the two privates, "The bloody fuckin' frogs will only lift it off the poor bloody fuckin' officer. He'd want to reward us with a few pints of 'arf and 'arf if he were conscious—don't you think, lads?"

291

The French doctor, a short fat man with no neck, it seemed, and very black whiskers, turned from a bandaged *pilote de bombardement.* He removed Andy's leg just below the knee, muttering, "Do not worry, *mon cher,* you are thin but healthy, and I am *écrasé de travail*—and all the vital *amour* parts not touched. *Bonheur."*

Andy was too fogged out to answer or know much. He had a sense he was smelling butterfly ether, with which, when a boy at Shad Point, he and Joe killed the insects they caught, mounted on pins; there was a hard light in his eyes. He felt wet and his groin ached. He was in a jolting Ford ambulance moving on a badly shelled road, and some stitches in his stump had given way and he was bleeding. All he felt was very weak after that, and at the railroad junction on the Red Cross train they didn't expect him to live because of loss of blood. A chest infection ("*C'est tout autre chose*"); he had water in his lungs.

It was not at all the noble wound on the war posters, a handsome head bound around with bandages and a small crimson spot the size of a dime, like a hero's red badge. No, he stank. God, the smell of flesh rot. The knee kept throwing off bone splinters; his fever went to 104. Then one day, damp in his own sweat, Capitaine Starkweather opened his eyes to find himself in a huge room, whitewashed walls, and sitting by the bed with a bag from which protruded the necks of wine bottles, the heel of a crusty loaf of bread, was the girl, Sidonie, he was going to marry. He began to weep with delight (*"Nous maintiendrons"*).

Tyler's scrapbook (it had once belonged to his brother Joe, who kept baseball scores in it) fills some gaps, but not all, in the Starkweathers' war years. There are clippings of the sinking of the Cunard liner *Lusitania,* by the U-20 commanded by Kapitänleutnant Schwieger, in which 1,198 men, women, and children lost their lives. Because 128 of them were American civilians, Americans' dislike of Germans moved from a passive relationship into demands for direct action. The news reports Tyler pasted up stated the ship was unarmed and carried no munitions of war.

However, Howard grimaced at Aunt Dru when she came to his office to talk of "the brutal Hun, the innocent ship on its trip of peace and mercy."

"Innocent ship, trip of peace and mercy, hell, Drucilla! It was slaughter of the innocent, I admit, but the damn ship carried over ten thousand cases of Remington Arms Company cartridges, over twelve hundred of shrapnel from a McCann Steel foundry, consigned to the British ammunition stores at Woolwich."

"Lies, lies, H.H.," said Aunt Dru, sitting down, having tea in Howard's office, gobbling cookies Howard's staff served for tea every afternoon. Drucilla Brooks was, as usual, in shabby black, her hair now all white, pulled back on a weathered skull, features birdlike. Almost a hawk's head, Howard thought as she waved a cookie in his face, a cookie held in gloves much darned. "Lies! Oh, the irrationality of the world."

"No lies, Drucilla, Starkweather and Company arranged the loans for this shipment. Donald McCann has been working his mills day and night to fill war orders."

"It means America in the war," shouted Aunt Dru. "They'll not get my Nick to be a soldier boy. It's all in the prophecy of Nostradamus—the last great war. But not with Nick."

As Nick Brooks was now middle-aged, bald, with a badly fitted bridge in a thick-lipped mouth, still bowlegged but with a sturdy enough body, he was not soldier material. Frugal meals had kept him from getting fat. He was sly, not gauche, and was as keen as his mother in knowing the stock market. While he wasn't permitted to speculate on his own without her permission, the son and mother respected each other, understood their mutual distrust of a scurrilous world. They were among the strange but interesting characters on the Street. Familiar sights in their worn clothes, but of good make, the thin tall woman in black and the little feathered hat (the original egret feathers, some said), accompanied by the rather mature shorter son, in derby and loose-hanging serge suit, shoes never shined, buttons missing off his gray spats. Shrewd bargainers, they studied the stock reports, not the news of Passendale and Gallipoli.

"No, Nick will not carry a gun. I'll buy a substitute."

"Not in any coming war, Drucilla, I fear. He's too old anyway and physically, well, his legs."

"His legs are fine. A gentleman's legs. . . . How's that auto-car company McCann, the old lecher, is backing? What's the Scarlet-Duck Motor stock doing?"

"The Star-Falcon Motor Company, and he's a major stockholder. The Detroit plant uses his steel. I'd say with war coming, maybe over this damn ship sinking, it will be busy producing staff cars and the Red Devil truck planned. It's quoted at seventy-eight a share to-day."

"Was seventy-two last week. Buy me one hundred and twenty thousand shares."

H. H. Starkweather & Company had in 1910 floated the issue of the Star-Falcon Motor Company (a Delaware corporation, now that President Wilson had reformed New Jersey's once easy and loose corporation setup). The bank had marketed one hundred twenty-eight million dollars' worth of the stock. Donald McCann held twenty percent of the stock in the motor company, Starkweather & Company eleven percent. The popular roadster, the Red Falcon, was a huge sporting machine with an oval gas tank set on behind the driver, a vast hood held down by a leather belt and brass buckles. It was the sports car of the young well-off sporting set, the young men. So low was the seat that one drove it almost on one's back. Chauncey Wilcox had two, the super Rex Racer and the war-time Falcon Road Runner (also being bought by the army). The Road Runner had rear seats and a canvas top, mica snap-on side curtains for foul weather. The new truck, the Red Devil, a recent addition, had solid rubber tires, chain drive, and was rugged, if not a thing of beauty. With a canvas top added, the military was testing it for squad transport at Fort Dix.

Aunt Dru had the keen eye of a seer for bad news. The British exploited the sinking of the *Lusitania* and released a certain Zimmermann cable the Germans had sent to their embassy in Mexico, having broken the German's secret code early.

The cable spoke of plans to back a Japanese army to be sent to Mexico and to get Mexico into a war; mount an invasion of the United States to get back territory in Texas, New Mexico, Arizona, California; never taken seriously by historians. But President Wilson began to think of declaring war on Germany. McCann told Howard, "Wilson is the godhead of some silly esoteric itches and fears."

Wilson was to ask for war in an address to both houses of Congress, ending with words H.H. always felt were ironic and not at all fitting to any actual conditions of the world: "We . . . dedicate our lives and fortunes, everything that we are and everything that we have, and with pride of those who know that the day will come when America is privileged to spend her blood and her might for the principles that gave her birth and happiness, the peace which she has treasured. . . ."

294

H.H. almost chewed his cigar in half. "*He* dedicates *our* fortunes, this patch-pants idealist! Why, I bet he doesn't own five hundred dollars' worth of secondhand furniture."

Harry looked up from the morning *Tribune*. "I understand he went back to the White House and wept."

"Send him a dozen crying towels."

Howard disliked the idea of America in the war. Yet knew it secured the American loans to the Allies. McCann was ironic: "Rule, Britannia; save Wall Street." The Americans would make the difference in the stalemate in France that kept ten million louse-bitten men dug in underground—among hundreds of thousands dead—from the channel to the Swiss border. "Human beings dying in a stench of their own muck, drowning in mud" (Donald McCann was very expressive, a dour Calvinist). Murderous generals were wiping out a whole generation in frontal attacks to gain a few dozen yards. "And it will be dressed up in the zenith of respectability as a great crusade."

Howard's controlled rage was expressed in a talk he had with Chauncey Wilcox the morning after war was declared—at breakfast in his suite. (He was hardly ever at Shad Point weekdays during times of turmoil.) Chauncey had eaten grilled kidneys and bacon, had two cups of strong coffee. He leaned his elbow on the table, too cheerful, like a child with a secret to reveal.

"H.H., I've joined the army. Going to take the quick officers' training course. I'm off to the war."

"Christ, Chaunce, you're a fat middle-aged man."

"I lied about my age. By fifteen years. I'm middle-aged, sure, but all muscle under the blubber. I've been in the reserves for seven years. I've trained summers, I've had Plattsburg. Damn it, I'll make a good Yankee-Doodle officer."

Howard pursed his mouth and the coffee tasted bitter for all the two spoons of sugar his doctor forbade him to put in and which he put in.

"Look, this war isn't going to settle anything but who's top dog for the next decade or so, then it will start again. A gouging rough-and-tumble by leaders who love kicking whole populations around. It's a dogfight that will last the rest of the century. Maybe beyond."

"H.H., you been going to ol' J.P.'s crystal-ball reader. Still, I'm going to be a soldier, H.H. Truth is I hate the Street since the Ivy League has moved in. Up to its ass in college boys."

Howard just held the cup to his mouth, but didn't drink from it. "Hate it? Like the devil, you do. Don't bullshit me. You're a plunger and a damn good man, at times, on the Exchange. You put Star-Falcon Motors over."

"Yes. McCann presented me with two cars, too. But I get so bored. Everything, booze, women, poker, more booze, more quiff, and just numbers added on my bank balance. H.H., don't you sometimes wish you never left the sea?"

"Christ," said H.H., getting up. "I thought at least you understood the world as it is. In life, I've come to think, there are just two things you can bet on. That there will be good men and there will be bad men. And the good have so far, maybe, kept a small step ahead of the bad men. The other thing is flux, chance, luck, constant change. You can't pee in the same water of a river twice."

"And all the rest?" Chauncey chewed on a slice of bread and marmalade.

"The rest is wind, fancy talk, little intricate games we play, on paper mostly. Look what liars writers are. The better the writer, the bigger the lie."

Chauncey licked a finger. "You hate the idea of dying, H.H.?"

"Death is a senseless thing and with a nasty mess usually at the end." He laughed suddenly. "It's not being dead, it's the dying that's lousy, a rotten way of doing things. Chaunce, tell me square, you sort of want to die, don't you?"

"Shove off, H.H., I'm walking out of this war, a guy with a chestload of medals and the most expensive case of clap in Paris or London."

Two weeks later Chauncey was in uniform and six weeks after that a captain of supplies, a hastily made captain. (Starkweather & Company had friends in high places.)

"I'm a good officer, a real iron ass," he told Tyler when Chauncey came to Shad Point one weekend to say good-bye.

"It's a raw army, Ty, and hicks from the hill country and cornfields who never ate white bread before. But damn it, it's full of brine and vinegar."

"If it lasts and I get in, Uncle Chaunce, I hope you'll ask for me."

"Sure, Ty, you can drive my staff car. But don't do anything dippy like enlisting before you're eighteen."

Chauncey Wilcox was off, after a last meeting with Howard in the study that lasted an hour. Chauncey came out blowing his nose, and Howard, after the big man left, was a little red-eyed at dinner. He said to Joe, "Chaunce told me he gave you his Red Falcon. I forbid you to drive it. I'll break your tail. It's a hell of a powerful auto and—"

Joe said, "Gramps, I've been driving it for a year now, every chance I had. Chaunce taught me himself."

"Oh? I'll try to finagle you a license."

Tyler smiled. "Joe's twenty, has a license. I'm seventeen, Gramps."

The old man looked up from his hot apple pie and wedge of cheese. "God damn it, I'm seventy-seven!" He gave an open-mouthed smile. "How did I get here? Let it be a lesson to you whelps. If you're not careful, you'll wake up one morning soon, look around you, and you'll be eighty years old. How about more pie all around?"

Tyler's scrapbook brings back the excitement and the tempo of America, of New York in coarse cadence, cheerfully going into the war. It was Tyler's rat-pack period when he was collecting song sheets, cartoons from the *Review of Reviews* by Partridge, Kirby, Raemaekers, motion-picture stills. And planning to get into the war. Living in the fear he would be denied participation—it would all end before he could put on a uniform, wear a Sam Browne belt, boots, even spurs. He had been for some years past reading a series of books called *The Boy Allies,* and he and Joe had war maps tacked to some of the walls. They kept moving red and black pins around on them. Everyone literate around them had read *My Four Years in Germany,* by an American ambassador, and *Over the Top,* a trench memoir. But now Tyler felt as H.H. did: It was a new war, an American war. As he wrote in an essay at school, "To miss it in uniform would be like not going on the First Crusade to the Holy Land or Columbus turning back."

As for his personal private dreaming of the proper woman, he had become a kind of researcher. Not merely reading Havelock Ellis, dabbling in early volumes of Freud. But as the decent sensual young man he was at tea dances, college proms, social events where the young daughters of the *Blue Book* families gave balls for debutantes. He had developed what was called a line. But all charm, he never did the wrong thing with the wrong girls. Nor did he move in on waitresses and shopgirls, as some of the Princeton youths did.

He was no virgin, but he was no sexual adventurer either. The few discreet affairs had been with older women (as decent and sensual as himself was the way he thought of it). There was never any exchange of money, nor did he accept gifts, but he did buy small flasks of perfume at times, a Mark Cross overnight bag in good pigskin.

No, he was not going to fling himself on any passion but the right one (again his version of himself) unless he was to die in the war. Somehow that seemed proper and the thing to do if one had to make the sacrifice. Not that he expected to die in battle. Someday *he* would be the bank; it was a good dream, like being a great explorer, an inventor of some remarkable process, painting pictures like Rembrandt, only more up-to-date of course. Hardly likely to come true in most cases, he knew. But it was pleasant to dream, to go well tailored to an afternoon tea dance with some sweet young thing (years later he wrote, "I knew all the Daisys Scotty didn't").

41

A letter from Tyler to his brother André, July 8, 1917:

Since President Wilson asked Congress to vote a war with Germany, the United States is also at war with the Central Powers, including Austria-Hungary and Turkey. Lots of excitement, the whole country is excited. Federal agents moved in to seize eighteen German ships, five of them anchored in the Hudson River, one just off Shad Point. A steel net is sunk across the narrows to keep out nosy U-boats. And New York has become the port of embarkation for the AEF (American Expeditionary Forces) to sail for France, of course singing "Over There," by George M. Cohan. Tugboats and minesweepers are active, exploding floating mines off Sandy Hook, laid there by the U-boats. All the big liners camouflaged in patches and shapes—ships to carry supplies and a million Americans to fight in what now is relabeled the World War. Gramps sees it all as "a wartime city grown raucous, greedy, and enjoying entertaining officers and men, creating profiteers by the thousands." Gramps is busy, fully active, even if a bit brittle. Dad is trying to put down a not-so-secret underground stock exchange that deals in sugar, flour, cloth, gasoline, steel, down to silk shirts for the shipyard workers. One

firm—*not* H. H. Starkweather & Company—last year cut up
schoolroom chalk and sold it—two million boxes of it—as as-
pirin to the Czarist Russian Army. There is continued danger
of German agents blowing up New York's utilities, water
plants, power generators. Bridges in the city are guarded;
there is fear of subway explosions.

I hope to get to France myself soon. Save me a large-boned
ardent Latin type. Is your wife, Sidonie, a redhead? Sounds
like one.

Among the clippings in the scrapbook was an unidentified cutting. "The only war I have ever approved of was the Trojan war: It
was fought over a woman."

The other clippings showed the Hun was a dastardly swine. Poison gas, flamethrowers, nun rapers, inhuman ways of destroying
mankind.

Tyler writes to his brother André in Paris, January 10, 1918:

We are short of coal; the offices are freezing. I've dug up
Grandpa's old wolf-pelt sled robe. The New York shops are
featuring smart black for young widows of soldiers. . . .

Tyler to André, November 12, 1918:

On the seventh there was a caterwauling in the streets and
all over Fifth Avenue, fit to burst your eardrums. Armistice:
trucks being overturned, pots and pans banged. End of the
war: Yahoo! Everyone yelling and the cross streets down to
Times Square, Thirty-fourth, like the Johnstown dam burst
again. Everyone running in all directions with flags. Joe says
Wall Street, Union Square, the same bedlam. You could get all
the free kisses you wanted on Fifty-seventh Street, and at Thirty-fourth and Fifth Avenue the snake dancing holding up everything, everybody—ear-bursting noise. Every office in New
York was getting rid of its wastepaper, other things being
thrown into the streets. Uniform meant you were a hero, and
you could hear the tugs and riverboats blasting their sirens,
honking of Klaxons enough to make a cat faint. All for nothing. We were drinking champagne at Starkweather & Company. The Street going into a St. Vitus seizure, when it was clear
there was no peace move at all. Some fish head had started a
rumor and passed it on. Was the last of a case of Gramps' good

299

champagne in the office, so we finished it. As you know, four days later it began again; bells, horns, and tug whistles—noise from the Jersey factories across the way—and this time it was real—Armistice! This time the butler made us all hot toddies and I stayed indoors. Jesus, I missed it all. The war, the excitement. Do I sound callow? And you with a leg gone.

Tyler to André, January 10, 1919:

The flu epidemic has been big here now for two weeks. Dr. Bolton calls it Spanish influenza. But why blame it on the Spaniards? Aunt Dru says it came off the docks from those rundown people coming over from Europe. I'll murder the next person telling the joke, "*I had a little bird and its name was Enza. I opened the window and in-flu-Enza.*"

Aunt Dru, staying at Shad Point, was down with it, chilled and feeling, she said, her spine was made of gruel, beetles dancing in her eyes and ears. No sense of balance and coughing so you'd think she'd end up in Denver. Some jackass, the city's health commissioner, has issued a statement: "The city is in no danger from an epidemic." That's a time to worry when officials get cheerful as your ship sinks under your feet. Hospitals are filling up, and there is talk nearly a thousand people a day are dying. You can't get central on the phone, and the cops and the fire boys are also hard hit by this plague in a modern city. Gramps says even the Street is badly affected. If I go into the streets, I wear a gauze mask. The shops reek from people who are dosing themselves on garlic and wearing little bags of camphor, and what was the smelly stuff we wore as kids around our necks when scarlet fever was around? Gramps says a petrified horse chestnut is a sure charm; he believes in nothing. Joe sits around reading the funnies. Abie Kabibble and Mutt and Jeff, filling himself with gin and ginger ale. He also reads me items like the Germans, the swine, when they lost at sea, sent their last U-boats to plant the flu germ among us. I think I'll try some gin and ginger ale to cheer myself up. Hard to believe you have a son named Jules Marcel.

Regards, best wishes to the mother, Mrs. André Starkweather. H.H. insists Marcel is a girl's name.

The last item that Tyler pasted in the scrapbook before he discontinued it was a black-bordered notice inserted in the *Wall Street Journal:*

300

```
┌─────────────────────────────────────────┐
│                                         │
│   H. H. STARKWEATHER & COMPANY          │
│                                         │
│      sadly announces the death          │
│                                         │
│                  of                     │
│                                         │
│      CAPTAIN CHAUNCEY WILCOX            │
│                                         │
│        68th Division, U.S. Army         │
│                                         │
│                 and                     │
│                                         │
│       SENIOR VICE PRESIDENT             │
│                                         │
│                  of                     │
│                                         │
│   H. H. STARKWEATHER & COMPANY          │
│                                         │
└─────────────────────────────────────────┘
```

We have just received word that our associate of long standing died during the influenza epidemic in the embarkation camp at Cherbourg, France, on January 28, 1919.

His loss is that of a remarkable man, a faithful friend, one who also was with the founder of this firm, which he always referred to as "The Bank," from the first day it opened its door in 1863. To say he will be missed is not enough; no words can express his tragic, untimely loss to the firm and to lifelong friendships.

HOWARD HARRISON STARKWEATHER
Chairman of the Board

HARRISON CHESNEY STARKWEATHER
President

BOOK VIII

Education is a fiction. It is merely acquiring the capacity to live in the society of people similarly educated.

—EDWARD WELBOURNE

42

In later years Tyler never could fully understand how he found his dark Latin dream and lost it. Never could fully, clearly bring himself to think of how it had faded out or, rather, been brutally torn from him, broken, fallen away. He used *all* those words in thinking about it. All those marvelous months on months of Margo and him. The lovemaking, the being sure, *so* sure it was the only drama of his young life that had the sense and the beauty of something as perfect as a Greek vase (not that he knew very much about Greek vases, but it had a good solid sound).

They had fought, of course. Margo had shouted, "Your goddamn high-set family—you think they will ever untie the apron strings and let you marry outside of their fancy nose-picking damn mob of snobs!"

"Oh, hell, I want it right for us. I want it all, you, the family, the things the bank can give us."

"Shove gold dust up your navel."

They were in bed; now their worst fights and making up with love play were coming closer and closer together. Yet he felt so sure everything would work out, everything would come around, as so much had come around in his life. It wasn't just being a Starkweather, not that he felt that such a bad thing, it was that he was sure Margo was held to him by the bonds of their sensual skills, her love beyond reason. And love was love, as he put it to her.

It was clear to her at last he had no idea of their true situation, no idea she would move out of his life suddenly, and on his part, to his amazement, he would be marrying someone else. It didn't happen that way in novels and the movies. The right boy got the right girl and they lived a full happy life after page 400 or at the end of reel six. But Margo hated novels and never went to the movies.

As Tyler stood in the church under the stained-glass windows designed by Burne-Jones, Milly in a Courtney heirloom wedding dress, holding onto his arm, he felt a silent trembling, a peculiar reticence. He told himself, nonsense, he was completely happy; it had been over a year since he had seen Margo Crivelli, his Italian bohemian girl, was free of that state of perpetual inquiry of hers. The organ was playing the last strains of some music rather familiar, and now the sound was petering out. Tyler stood facing the pleasant-looking, round-faced man with a fringe of gray hair over one side of his forehead; the rest of the face was Mr. Pickwick's from a picture in a book Tyler had gotten on his twelfth birthday.

As he turned his head, he saw the Courtneys were starched, properly attired, in six pews to the right. The Starkweathers were to the left, quiet as if at a séance, all in their best bib and tucker, gray-striped trousers on the men with fawn-colored waistcoats and violet stocks, the females in various discreet models of expensive gowns. Harry and Katie looking as if shined and waxed. Joe, after last night's bachelor party, happy, at ease with three drinks— potent stuff called horses' necks—before he entered the church. Aunt Dru and Nick—he gave them a smile—in fairly decent clothes. Aunt Dru's mouth twitching a bit as she looked over the famous windows, a gift of the bride's grandfather.

Yes, Tyler decided, I have come a far way from the young and foolish boy; I have come to exist properly in the world of my family. And I love this dark-haired girl, always, even now, seeming to stand on her toes, and her lower lip protruding somewhat, and I'm marrying her.

Marrying her. Yes. Why was he looking about as if expecting some late, important guests? It could be he was thinking of Uncle Chauncey Wilcox, whose body had been brought back from France

306

and buried in Gramps' private cemetery at Shad Point. At least, H.H. said, he hoped it was Chaunce "and not the remains of a French horse."

Tyler stopped sneaking glances from side to side.

The Reverend Pickwick spoke, the halo of a mullioned window behind him. "Dearly beloved . . . we are gathered here. . . ."

The organ made low background sounds like those of a flageolet and flute.

Somehow it all went well and Joe, best man, found the ring first try, Milly lifted her veil, and Tyler found her lips cool and delightful. Joe made a jest on the coming acts of procreation. Then to the waiting Cadillacs and Pierce-Arrows, to Cambridge and the wedding meats, which turned out to be a huge buffet catered by the staff of the Ritz-Carlton in Boston. Music by a sedate group of middle-aged musicians who began with Purcell virginal music and progressed to "Alice Blue Gown."

Howard was trying to seem pleased with the Courtneys' lesser relations from Pittsfield who were recalling other weddings among the best families of New England; Emerson was mentioned and Howard had an impression so was Bunker Hill, but wasn't sure, as he had turned to take up a glass of brandy.

Harry and Katie were properly at ease—after all, the Courtneys were old English Protestant stock—and Aunt Dru was talking earnestly to Joe, who was chewing on a slice of rare roast beef and sipping a double martini.

"I'm sure, Joe, vegetarians are the only healthy people."

"Now, Aunt Dru, I remember you eating a steak at Shad Point so bloody the cow still mooed."

"I'm living on vegetables. So is Nick. But really. For the true order of nonmeat eaters: Ovolactarians eat anything that doesn't have a face; lactarians, no eggs, but permitted are milk, cheese, yogurt; vegetarians, grains, nuts but no vegetables, for if the 'host' plant dies after the crop is harvested, it is *verboten*. A tree or bush, you see, remains after fruit and nuts are harvested, so—"

"Aunt Dru, Nick has just finished his second whole lobster."

Tyler and Milly slipped away at five o'clock. Three Yale men had to aid Joe back to his hotel on Copley Square.

In after years Tyler would come around to thinking that it was he who had broken with Margo because of her rages against his

307

family, the bank, the Street, so his loyalty to his family had in the end led to the breaking up of the love affair and turned it away from marriage, not any commiserating over compromises. A marriage, he'd insisted to Margo, would take place *if* he had had time, time to get the family to accept her.

In fact it was she, in flagrant disenchantment, who had made the final break after one more sad and dismal weekend in her studio. Making love, shouting at each other, critical of personal idiosyncrasies, loud threats tossed at each other, hers often in obscene Italian.

Facing each other that last Monday morning, seated in robes over a vile pot of coffee, he heard his basic deficiencies; Margo, tossing from her forehead her uncombed hair hanging over her eyes, had shouted, "You shit! I'm leaving tomorrow for Mexico. I'm going to help paint murals."

"Murals?" He was getting strawberry jam on his fingers trying to prepare a stale English muffin for breakfast. "Mexico?"

"Yes, Mexico. I've had it with you up to *here*." She indicated the spot on her neck with the side of a hand. "I'm joining a crew helping this fellow Rivera, who's frescoing some damn official building down there."

"But we're so close, I mean—"

"You mean you, you goddamn Episcopalian!"

With that she had gone into the bedroom, the latch clicking, and he sat, strawberry jam dripping down onto his bare leg exposed by the open robe. He did not think she would go, break up all they had planned and held onto for so long. It was love, LOVE, a symbol, a word he respected, a state of emotion he felt was vital and paramount in his life. With her, in her, through her. He remembered a Latin tag from a Princeton class: *Materia appetit formamut virum femina.* (Matter seeks form as woman seeks man.)

He felt betrayed, for all the good fat Latin truth. Also guilty, for the family had softened a bit. Gramps had said only the week before, "If you want the damn girl, wait until your sister Pauline has her debut. But don't expect me to give you a public wedding or any approval."

Wasn't that a weakening of the family position? And Mother had wiped her nose with her tiny lace hankie, her way of weeping dryly with taste and discretion. Tuesday at breakfast she had looked up from the pages of the *Tribune* opened to the society section. "I don't suppose we'll ever see *your* marriage announcement accepted, Ty, as an item in the *Tribune*,"

Now, now he sat and the bedroom door was on the latch. He sat feeling the jam drip and, unaware of what he was doing, he lifted the jam from his leg with two fingers and licked them. It was, he told himself, just one more crisis in their relationship. Another Italian exposure of shrill temper, he thought. Like all the others, it would pass. They would be back in bed again. It would pass.

It didn't. She never unlocked the bedroom door while he was there but for a moment to toss out his clothes and shoes, gold tie-pin, key chain. He dressed and sent her twelve dollars' worth of yellow roses from the Waldorf flower shop, charged to the Stark-weather account. He felt anesthetized and distraught. How could she live without him? The janitor told him next day when he came dragging his tail, desperate, with two tins of caviar and a half dozen of her favorite Mumm Sec, that the artist lady was gone. "Had them two big leather cases and took a cab and just went."

"Any forwarding address?"

"Jus' said Mexico and that I could have the stuff in the icebox, and the vacuum cleaner. The janitor winked. "She said you had the extra key."

Tyler, feeling a numbness and a kind of icing of his spine, took out his key ring on its chain and with some difficulty removed the right key, handing it to the janitor with a five-dollar bill.

"Be seein' you, Mr. Starky."

Tyler shook his head and walked off. The pain, the full pain wasn't hitting him yet. Just he was dying from the inside out. He wondered how everyone in the street could go about his business while he was bleeding inside, in agony. Couldn't they see? Weren't they aware of his suffering? How damn callous the world was. He went over to Moriarty's speakeasy and had one bad scotch. The strongest man must stand alone. Yes. Romantically one got drunk at such times. But he felt no desire to get boozed with the motley crew (a Princeton lit. word, "motley"), the motley crew of newspaper bums, unemployed actors, and just loafers waiting for the day to proceed and become night. At his second scotch (just a bit more to brighten his outrage) he wondered if he should go right down to Mexico, punch Rivera right in the mouth. He told Jack Moriarty, "This painter, he's that big fat guy, paints peasants with dirty big feet—feet bigger than their heads . . . paints it all. Very sym . . . symbolic of the earth—"

"You don't say, Mac."

At the fourth scotch they sent Tyler home in a cab. Moriarty's was a very respectable speak. Tyler was an old client, going back to his first year at Princeton when he'd turned up in a raccoon coat for some goings on in town with some of his classmates. How young and innocent he had been. Love is a false ecstasy, merely a trap to propagate the species.

Tyler didn't drink much after that. Didn't go to Mexico. Didn't seek out friends to tell them of his painful sadness. Did his work at H. H. Starkweather & Company. In fact his work improved as he threw himself into studying in greater detail the situations in post-war Europe. He was proved right about the inflation of the German mark and so later on the firm avoided becoming involved in some sticky monetary problems with their Middle European representatives, such as the issue of the reorganizing of clients in Krupp holdings.

The family didn't ask questions of Tyler. But they seemed to have figured out the Italian girl situation, and when his sister Pauline returned from the Grotanelli School in Siena, Italy, he attended her debutante coming out at the Pierre, dancing with a lot of girls he felt were too young for him.

He was still a young man suffering from female cupidity, he told himself. He had an affair with a married woman, an interior decorator on Madison Avenue, whose husband was a fashion designer. Tyler retreated when it became a threesome, the designer also wanting to take group photographs. Tyler was actually horrified at the decay of decency, the decadence of life in a big city. To recover from his efforts at depravity, he went up to Dartmouth, at Hanover, for the Winter Carnival and sprained his ankle. He came home with a cane, and in the spring a sodden young man with brass-colored hair in a speakeasy, pounding on the bar and singing, was introduced to Tyler by the barman as the author of *This Side of Paradise*. Tyler said he already knew the writer, had avoided him at college as a Western hick running with Bunny's literary crowd.

He went to a horse show in Boston, not that he liked or disliked horses, but to meet with Mr. Abbott Adams Courtney on a project of the insurance company that Mr. Courtney's father had founded, a firm so bloated with assets it was seeking ways to invest its surplus.

Mr. Courtney had been Book, Snake and Zeta Phi at Yale. He invited Tyler to dine at Courtney Manor and meet their two daughters, Mildred and Linda. He first picked Linda as a target, but she spat a bit when she talked, not much, but it was clear she was wet-mouthed when vocal. He took Mildred Elaine Courtney to a Canadian hockey team game playing in town. She promised to come down to New York and call him when she did. She had heard of this funny man in the *Follies* who chewed gum and whirled a rope and was side-splittingly funny.

Tyler didn't expect her to call him three weeks later. She did, and he took her to Moriarty's, dinner at the Ritz, and to the *Follies*. Tea dancing the next day. Milly was staying with her Aunt Gertrude in Murray Hill, and Aunt Gertrude smoked cigarettes in a long green jade holder, collected chalcedony *netsukes,* and had paintings by people like Braque and Duchamp on her walls. She knew Natalie Barney and Edith Wharton in Paris. She served him gin while Milly changed upstairs, and she asked, "What's your intention toward our little gal?"

Tyler said, "Social, very social. I'm taking her to the crew races—Harvard-Princeton. My father rowed for Harvard, you know."

"Boy, am I impressed," said Aunt Gertrude, and put a fresh Camel in her holder.

They were officially engaged by the time Milly went back to Boston. Both families were delighted with the idea of the marriage "of the two children," as Katie put it. Tyler was not displeased with the idea. Milly was fun, with her bobbed hair and waistless gowns, long fine legs, and her ability to match him in the latest dances. She was warm, emotionally direct, and simple, so far. There was none of the arguing and rages as with the Italian. None of the hand wringing, glass breaking, no voices raised in Italian oaths. No danger of the closeness to physical violence that seemed always to be near with his first deep love. Margo, the paint-stained bitch, and her deception and betrayals.

Tyler took Milly to bed after a Princeton-Yale football game, in a discreet flat loaned from a classmate writing advertising copy; a flat on West Seventy-second Street. It was a splendidly satisfactory copulation, satisfactory to both. He had never deflowered a virgin (it all seemed a line from a novel); he had been ardent and tender in turn—took the weight of his body on his elbow. She wept later, delighted, on his naked shoulder and said he was the most wonderful man in the whole world and their life together would be just marvelous. She called him lover as they dressed and later discreetly dropped the bloodied towel they had brought away into an ashcan on the corner of Seventy-second and Broadway.

311

The only bad moment Tyler had was when he saw a photograph in the *Literary Digest* captioned "Mexican artist completes work . . . largest mural in Mexico." The photograph showed Margo in overalls, by the artist's side, mixing paint.

Mr. and Mrs. Tyler Starkweather, after a Bermuda honeymoon, took a small flat on Park Avenue just above the Grand Central. It would do until their home at Shad Point had been built, a gift from H.H. Tyler had seen a book of pictures in an artist's studio of the work of Frank Lloyd Wright, and he envisioned a low flat house of boxlike design, hugging the riverbank, living in its purely native stone a geometric existence as part of the landscape. But Howard had shaken his head.

"Oh, he's fine enough, a designer galoot—don't deny it—this Wright. But a freak. Mule barns are what his houses look like. Knew this fellow outside Chicago, had a Wright house and the damn roof leaked on him when he sat in his living room. He called Wright on the phone and Wright told the fellow, 'Just move your chair.'"

The end result was the Tyler Starkweathers got a glorified Cape Cod cottage with several Dutch-tile fireplaces, a planting of birch trees, and a terrace facing the river. They kept the Park Avenue flat and spent about half their time in the city. They were not aware it was to be called the Roaring Twenties and the Jazz Age. They went to the theater, drank in speaks, visited nightclubs. But years later they wondered where they had been when all those events and dramas that were being written of as the decade of Flaming Youth were going on. They had merely lived the lives of their social status. If they had a disappointment, it was that Milly didn't get pregnant.

43

Tyler after his marriage grew closer to his grandfather. H.H. was from a different age, a survivor, he saw, of other eras. The old man didn't object to change. "Christ, Ty, we in our time created more history than we could eat. So why not your times?"

Howard would observe the changes; he enjoyed the city in nearly all its aspects. And he did not expect the human race to get any better or become any happier; he was not, as he said, "a reformer, no, an observer, yes."

Postwar New York was not in the 1920's a city of society's Four Hundred or Stanford White's naked girls on a swing. It was a new kind of hurry, he felt, and a change in the old town, with only memory connecting it with the past he had known—of the Edwardian polished brass doorknobs, the genteel Washington Square houses, the placid walks in Central Park, the manly sanctuaries of the Hoffman House, the Ritz Bar. The saloon of the middle class was gone. Prohibition was a tradition, he told Tyler, not a law to the city. "While the boys were over there fighting, they snuck it in." The young clerks in the bank, on the Street, were often returning doughboys of the AEF, had tasted sexual liberty overseas or lied about their French clap. The bank now had female help. The flapper was in. A New York girl (Harry and Katie said) no one had seen before. Slimmer, hair bobbed or shingled, spit curls à la Clara Bow, the It girl of the movies. The lessons of misread Freud were strong, Harry insisted, and at NYU there were copies, he was told, of his work in translation.

"The vile speakeasies," said Katie. "Vile. Remember, Harry, the night the orchestra at Delmonico's played 'Auld Lang Syne' and that was the end of its existence?"

Harry said, "There were a few moist eyes among the diners."

It was clear to Howard his son and daughter-in-law were not accepting change, not the way he was willing to observe and be amused at a lot of what was going on. As he told Tyler at the bank, "There's this damn Chesney horseshit in Hal about tradition and being better than most people. I get this feeling they're not going to have a happy old age."

Tyler and Milly had their own set of friends from college, from the Street—some new people named e e cummings ("He hates capital letters"), Bunny Wilson. Some went to Paris to bring back tidings about people called Sylvia Beach, Gertrude Stein, joined with names like the Cole Porters, Zelda and Scotty, the Murphys, Redtop, Josephine Baker, and hundreds of thousands of Americans, as Joe put it, "unknown to fame."

Tyler and Milly went over to visit André and his growing French family. They went to see the Garde Republicaine in the rue de Rivoli.

The most fashionable sailings were those of the French Line's *La France*. Their friends attended their leaving with baskets of Sherry's, Park & Tilford goodies, bootleg bottles. Most in formal evening attire, top hat and cane; bead-decorated gowns. They partied until the *hoot hoot* of the sirens sounded and stewards tapped on doors, announcing, "All ashore!" One Yale fullback didn't leave and was carried to sea, to be taken back in the pilot as the choppy Atlantic met bay water in the Kill Van Kull. And Milly said, "I'm going to be seasick."

"Please, not on deck."

The more sedate travelers took the British boats. Harry and Katie liked the stately Cunarders. "Everything neat without that gaudy French touch."

It was clear that Andy, turned into André, had broken all American ties but for representing Starkweather & Company's interests in Paris. He belonged to the Jockey Club, ran some racehorses at Auteuil and Chantilly, and deplored "the *outré* type of American who came to drink and try to write and paint." He was rather a gallant figure with the hero's limp caused by the loss of a limb in the war; decorated, he wore the scarlet sliver of the Legion of Honor in his lapel. "It isn't just how crass America has become," he told Harry and Katie at the dinner he and Sidonie gave them at Lapérouse. "You're destroying, *très gaiement*, centuries of culture, inbred beliefs." Harry and Katie couldn't communicate very well with their four grandchildren; very neat, too pale, overpolite, dressed oddly, or so thought *Grand-père* and *Grand-mère*.

H.H. just said, "Andy sounds like he's turned into a horse's ass."

With Andy lost to the Street and family, his tasks in Paris were minor; he actually drew a good income for doing little but drinking a glass of Hospice de Beaune once a week as he listened to some branch manager give him some figures or offer him a document to sign.

H.H. had also given up on Joe. Joe enjoyed his bohemian life in the Village, his drinking, his tacky women with their stringy hair, loop earrings, sandaled feet, and talk of Dada, five-year plans, and free verse; stereotypes really, as H.H. and Harry saw them. Joe was the radical press' rich man's son who had turned against his family's way of life to free the sweated workers, make a better life for the toiling masses, the dispossessed, the sharecroppers.

Harry wondered at his son's taste to show up at Shad Point in a brown workshirt, gray wrinkled tie, unpressed suit. And with a couple of what he called "Jewish sweatshop girls," who sewed, as they said, "cloaks and suits." They were given to saying "Thoid Affnue" and "Long Hiland."

314

Joe had left the bank, cashed in his seat on the Exchange for over one hundred thousand dollars, and had joined the American Communist Party. It wasn't, he confessed to his grandfather, that he was a fully convinced Marxist. "This next weekend at Shad Point, if I could, I'd like to borrow the grounds for a rally of striking Paterson silk mill workers. Now, H.H., just think of the publicity, the family's exclusive estate and these workers—all the pressers and street sweepers, mill hands, plumbers' helpers—among the trees. Make every newspaper in the country."

Howard saw the sardonic grin on Joe's face and lowered his cane and laughed. "You addle-headed pup—I thought you were serious. What are you going to do when your money runs out?"

"I'm putting out a little magazine, *Whole Truth*. Like the title?"

"Yep. It's nice to know you think you know the whole truth. I'm an old man, and I have never found anybody had the truth by the tail; most wouldn't know the truth if it bit them. And you—all you do is sniff around like a dog around a bitch in heat and yet know you're close to it, the truth. Well, it turns out usually not to be the truth at all. Joe, what's the matter with working hard, living well, dressing clean, and getting your money's worth for what you spend?"

"I'll lend you *Das Kapital*."

"Christ, Joey, I knew what the old Yid was writing about maybe before he did. Joseph Pedlock knew him, you know. And old Pedlock said what it all comes down to is those who have are envied by the have-nots, and when you reverse the situation, the have-nots are just as big bastards and exploiters as the haves. Come on, you snot-nosed know-it-all—people act like anyone else, not like saints."

Joe didn't argue with his grandfather. The old boy had a good head on him and was a robber baron—as Joe's radical friends put it—and exploiter, a merchant of death, a believer in organized godheads, strikebreakers. Also in colonialism, a high tariff, and, as a girl he once lived with said, "A goddamn white Protestant Anglo-Saxon bigot." Joe didn't believe all this; it was just that the old man was blind to the changeover in history. Hadn't Lincoln Steffens just lectured on Russia and repeated, "I have seen the future and its works"? But H.H. believed the lying stories about the starvation and death of millions of Russians in a great famine and lies of a Red Terror, of a secret police. The old man was hopeless. When Joe was leaving, his grandfather asked, "Who sends me to the wall when the revolution comes? You, Joey?"

"No, one of your clerks most likely, boring from within."

"Hell, no, they all want to be vice presidents, own a two-story house in Queens, and yell about their income taxes."

Joe wrote an article for the *New Masses* on "the traumatic shock of ancient belief destroyed." He was photographed with Emma Goldman.

Tyler's sister Pauline was twenty-one years old in 1923. Harry and Katie had felt their youngest daughter should have special advantages and she had been outfitted by Roue of London, boarded at the Kilquahanity House School, Castle Douglas, Scotland, and then attended a Swiss school, an Italian one (very highly recommended), where she met the daughters of rich American Catholics related to the Ryans, Murrays, Cudahys, McDonnells, and Oelrichs. And learned of the gooey drip of Protestant cant.

So when she returned home it was only natural she would be invited to parties on Murray Bay, a title invented for the section of Long Island where the Irish bankers, contractors, and political figures had built homes. Here Pauline Starkweather met the O'Degans, particularly Johnny Thomas O'Degan, son of Matthew "Buck" Joseph O'Degan. Pauline fell in love, insisted she would marry Johnny *"even* if he were a Jew."

At breakfast one morning she boldly announced her engagement.

Harry and Katie shook their heads in incomprehension and mild hostility. "But, my dear girl," said Katie, "you remember all the problems we had when Tyler wanted to marry that Catholic girl."

"She was Italian, Mom. The O'Degans are Scotch-Irish."

Katie felt this most awkward predicament gave her a need for smelling salts. "It's not that I am against them turning from shanty Irish to lace curtain Celt in one generation. But they all drink *so,* and they'll never get into the *Social Register.* Oh, Pauline darling, you're so naïve and imperceptive. Think it over. H.H. is going to raise the roof if you persist. Your grandfather has always felt everyone in the family must think of the bank in setting a life-style."

Pauline rose; small and slim with gray-green eyes and a tilted button nose. She had, when upset, a slight speech impediment. She now gave an answer she had learned at the very fashionable Swiss school from the gossiping group in her wing of the place. "Grandfather can go piss up a rope."

* * *

316

The wedding was held at St. Thomas More, the O'Degans feeling, as most of their class did, that "St. Pat's had no real class." One belonged—if monied *and* Catholic—to St. Thomas More, St. Ignatius Loyola, or St. Jean the Baptist. The tops, Mrs. Matthew O'Degan explained to Katie, for an important churchgoer in New York.

Johnny O'Degan was a proper and lively, decent young man, educated at the Portsmouth Priory prep school, graduated from Georgetown. Mrs. O'Degan felt Holy Cross and Fordham rather second-class schools. Johnny had dark hair, a pale face often showing ambiguous contradictory emotions. He had slightly protruding teeth and was a kind person and lovable. Howard put in an appearance at the church—told Tyler, "This Johnny, he looks like a white-bellied fish."

"Now, Gramps, he's a handsome boy and he loves Pauline very much and, if it means anything, his family have money and social position."

"Yep, his father is Buck O'Degan, the biggest son of a bitch of a city contractor—grafter—and once was running a bucket shop on the Street with that bastard from Boston."

There was no getting away from it, Tyler decided, H.H. was bigoted, old-fashioned, and you had to allow for his age. He was old.

Buck O'Degan, high in Tammany and the national Democratic Party, had hired an entire floor at the Plaza for the wedding party after the church ceremony. Buck and Mary O'Degan were happily greeting guests; there seemed to be no end of McDonnells, Murrays, Farleys, Schiffs, and Lehmans to greet. And "the big boys, the Tammany officials," said Aunt Dru to Ty, "all with their wives and children and there's the cardinal himself."

"Yes, in proper crimson and his plump foxy face all pleasure."

"Why, just like anybody at all, and holding out his arm with the ring." Aunt Dru was seeking a solid faith, but the cost of joining a proper, well-thought-of creed appalled her.

The young couple went to Europe on their honeymoon and Pauline was presented at court, and in Rome they had an audience with the pope, who made Johnny a Knight of St. Gregory, of which Johnny said, "It's nothing much, just a notch ahead of being one of the Knights of Columbus."

"Oh, no, Johnny, it's an honor." Pauline was delighted with mar-

317

riage—it not only made proper one's sinful desires but it was a sampling of O'Degan warmth, so missing among the Starkweathers.

"Pop now, he's a papal marquis, Pauline, a Knight of Malta."

Pauline said never mind and they went to hunt up antiques for the house Howard was building for them at Shad Point.

The O'Degans, for whom family loyalty, possessive warmth came first, had wanted to offer the young couple an apartment on Park Avenue, but thinking of what was "best for the kids," felt it was better to bow to the wishes of H.H. "The crusty auld bastard—after all, he is taking Johnny into the bank."

If Howard was prejudiced against the O'Degans, he was also still able to recognize ability; Johnny was bright, had a feeling for the stock market, and was neither loud nor given to drink, which Harry feared as the "Irish curse." Johnny was the perfect husband and brought Pauline back, after three months in Europe, pregnant, so that in time she produced a daughter (she was to have four more daughters and a son who died at the age of two). It was to prove a long and happy marriage.

Johnny settled in well at H. H. Starkweather & Company, and some of the vast church business in land, housing, stocks, trusts, donations came to the bank. Most profitable were the trusts and some of its portfolios of shares and investments. Buck O'Degan often dropped in to visit at the bank, offering cigars and running a hand over the wood of Johnny's desk in Overseas Investments.

He'd visit with H.H. and sit sipping the good bourbon, having a little trouble crossing his legs (being paunch-proud). Howard grew to like the red-faced, foulmouthed individual; wise from the gutter, clever as a power in politics, a proud family man. "I did as you did, H.H., begun on me own; me folks died in the potato famine in that shitpoke Ireland. Bad fess on the damn sod, and I pitched horse manure as a boy for the quality in Philly and drove a horsecar on Canal Street in rain and storm on the open platform. You knew Tweed himself, didn't you?"

"I met him."

"Yes, well I was one of his young gilhoolees and worked for the contractors, collecting the boodle for the hall's share. And soon had contracts for bricks and paving."

Howard smiled. "Something for everybody was Tweed's way."

"City contracts, lovely things, and during the war O'Degan Construction Company built the piers at Hoboken and the camp at Yaphank. It's brick and cement I love, solid material. Brick."

"You used to throw them, I remember, in the riots of sixty-three; they were called dominicks. Now you're smart enough to make and sell them."

"And invest. I'm after a dynasty like Joe Kennedy or Kelly in Philly. I own some bank stocks I want you to look over, and would you recommend this radio thing as worth a gamble? This RCA that Goldman, Sachs is boosting? It's just noise farting in the night; radio."

"My son, Hal, thinks radio is going to be so big it will do away with the stage and even hurt the movie business."

"Well, films I leave to Kennedy. I hear he's stirring in them and sniffing the actresses' skirts. I like something in business you feel is needed. Well, like a brick. I'm moving all my accounts over with you, H.H."

"Why? You're with a good firm now. O'Donnell and Flynn."

"Well, it's family now, isn't it? It's for the kids—Johnny and Pauline and little Mary."

It was an impressive account, the O'Degan portfolio—and Howard kept silent about it. Johnny O'Degan worked well with Tyler, and when Tyler came up with the idea of putting brokerage offices on the great ocean liners crossing the Atlantic, it was Johnny who had the political connections (through his father and the Harbor Commission) to put branch offices of H. H. Starkweather & Company on the *Berengaria, Bismarck, Leviathan,* and the *France.*

The John Thomas O'Degans named their first daughter Mary Margaret and their second one Maureen. She was born in England, for Johnny (and his family) soon was with Starkweather & Smollet, Threadneedle Street, the London branch. . . .

Tyler became fascinated at the daily routine of H. H. Starkweather's handling of the buying and selling of stock. This afternoon the market moved forward in flurries. A cold ferocity drove the tickers. The AP wires clattered away with news too commonplace to stir a crisis. The customers' room was packed. Every chair was taken. Staccato noises filled the air. Thick smoke hung in layers about the room, and the board boys tore tape off the clicking tickers and changed numbers, working quickly to keep up with the market.

A shabby little man in a bowler hat had finished some sandwiches and washed them down with big gulps of ice water from the cooler.

319

He was now comparing his order sheets with figures in his leather-bound notebook. He had bought more than he intended and was now wondering how to reconcile his commitments to his day's plan of action. He wiped his face with an old gray silk handkerchief and hastily added a few figures on the loose-leaf sheet in the hope of finding a solution to his mathematical problem. Tyler smiled at the little man.

In the shadow of the board stood Tyler, patiently explaining Brazil 4s, Brit Vic 4s, and Benigno Crespi 7s to an old lady who clung to a lapdog. One of the other customers' men was busy at the phone, talking quietly but confidently, with one fearful eye on the clock. He expected a landslide of profit taking before the Exchange closed at three.

Everyone watched the board. The room was full of buyers and sellers: a man who bought U.S. Governments exclusively, men who came to use the red leather chairs, shopkeepers, manufacturers, night workers, politicos, and hangers-on.

Old Maryatt at the margin cage was slowly reckoning his margin accounts to be sold up. Desmond, head of the runners and board boys, was having a fit about some Amerex Holding Corporation bonds that had been delivered to the wrong address. He was swearing prodigiously, driving the runners with the whip of his tongue as he bullied them.

Joel Brown, the room's wit, his broad smile stretched to the tearing point, was overhearty. He was carrying a batch of orders and winking at the bookkeepers bent over their cumbersome machines. Breezy generosity oozed from him. Pleased with himself, he slapped the customers' men on their backs, waved to the shabby little man with the bowler hat green with age, and then sat down behind the man who specialized in U.S. Governments. With gentle, happy cunning, Joel leaned over and inserted an open book of paper matches into the specialist's shoe sole next to the uppers.

Carefully—half the room watching him with suppressed interest—he set fire to the book of matches, and when they flared up and the victim suddenly yelped and shot up from his seat slapping at his feet, Joel wiped the tears of joy from his eyes, slapped his dupe on the back, and only half listened while a white-haired old boy asked about certain oil stocks in an incoherent voice.

Joel looked down on his own gray suede shoes and said, "Ha, ha! Did you see his face when the matches went off? Oil? Hell, I guess about two hundred and seventy-five million barrels were shipped last month. How would I know? Ask Tyler. He knows everything. Pennsylvania and Appalachian wells have over ten thousand barrels a day flowing. Me? I like the East Texas fields, about two hundred and seventy-five thousand barrels refinable a day. No hard feelings?" He slapped the chagrined specialist on the back.

Tyler watched the customers' room settle down to business. The board numbers were changed, the customers slid lower into their red leather chairs, and the phones rang more insistently. Selling for profit taking had set in. Some were selling, taking their profits and getting ready to worry, take on tomorrow's market. The ticker clattered on.

The Gold Room chief passed on his way out, his neatly rolled black umbrella on his arm, his black bowler hat sitting serenely on his head, his face a study in detachment. He nodded good-bye to Tyler and waited rigidly until the elevator door opened. Joel winked at one of the telephone operators. "I wonder if he has blood in his veins or twenty-two-karat liquid gold?"

Tyler, checking freight loadings, felt a deadly hum now set in. Everyone began to move a little faster and watch the clock closer. Girls went running on slim legs from typewriters to officers' desks, piling up letters to be signed and sent through the stamping machines. The adding machines clanked on. The ticker tape was in its final spasms. Last-minute sales were being given. Wire-service rolls were unwinding with summaries of market trends in *bourses* long since closed in Rome and Berlin and London.

Three o'clock! Exchange dealings closed.

The girls relax at their typewriters. The clerks yawn. The customers' men write last orders slowly, pin together their memos. The margin cage sifts the wheat from the chaff, and the open files and safes wait for their ledgers and accounts. Tyler locks up his data.

Old Maryatt sips water from a tall tumbler and shakes his head. He tells Tyler the colossal effrontery of all this trading is something he will never understand. "Everyone so busy selling and buying. Selling and buying *what?* Paper." He shook his head again and finished his water. It was altogether too much for him.

He looked at his heavy watch. After three. He blew on his glasses, wiped them until they glistened, and ordered his clerks to begin moving the ledgers to the safe. The day's totals were coming in over the ticker.

"Record day, Mr. Maryatt."

"Yes, indeed, Mr. Tyler."

Yes, indeed, Tyler felt, the bull market is ruling the Street—the nation.

Some few times, very tired after a hard day in the market, going home in the taxi, Tyler thought he was going to Margo's studio. They would make a night of it, eat, drink, go to bed, raise high jinks. It would be good to be with Margo. Lord, more fun than a crate of monkeys, his Latin girl. It was a shock to find he had been half asleep in the taxi and it was now drawing up to his address. Milly. Good old Milly. Christ, he must have been real bushed to be thinking of that disordered studio, the damn cat, Margo.

He'd have to keep a tight control of his daydreams. He didn't want that old way of life. No, of course not. He had everything. Milly among the dining-room crystal and the table set right, and the scotch and water ready. No martinis for him; that was for the five fifteen crowd.

"Good day, dear?"

"Damn good day for the market, the bank. We going out?"

"No, I feel you work too hard."

Nice of her to care. A good wife is above rubies, or whatever the hell somebody wrote. The dinner was good, not heavy; they had to keep their figures. The couple, the Swenskies, Alvida and Thorsten, kept the place neat, spick and span; the cooking was healthy, rather tasteless, but then he usually had a good lunch downtown.

One day on Fifty-seventh Street he saw Margo, her back to him, staring into a window at a Degas painting. He followed her, the tight hat, the pale fox collar. And at Fifth Avenue he felt, What the hell—it's a long time gone and we could have a drink. He put a hand on her shoulder and said, "Well, what do you know."

She turned around and it wasn't Margo at all. Not when you saw the face. The woman said, "Is this a pickup?"

"I thought you were someone else, an old friend."

"I don't mind."

He lifted his homburg in a polite salute and walked away. No, it wasn't Margo. Margo would have kicked him in the shins.

"Watch it, old boy," he said out loud. He went around to a speakeasy and sat at the bar nursing a drink while the bartender marked a racing sheet. He had one more and forced himself not to think of Margo. It worked pretty well, and for Milly's birthday he bought her emerald earrings and talked of adopting a child.

322

44

The legend of H. H. Starkweather & Company's great battle in the middle 1920's with the New York Stock Exchange has gathered so much myth that one must go back to actual records and company reports, the files of the Exchange itself, to discover the basic facts. Howard Harrison Starkweather is usually credited with leading the stock battle of Star-Falcon Motors against the speculators, the brokers entrenched inside the Exchange itself. Actually, in 1925 Howard was over eighty, and the conducting of the affair was in the hands of his son, Harry, he at his prime, age fifty-three, aware of the broad implications, the formidable dangers of going up against the men who ruled the Exchange.

It all began simply enough. Donald McCann, health failing fast, had retired to a nursing home outside London. Talk of his being senile was denied. But he was old and confined to bed, and teams of medical men fought to keep him alive, if not conscious. His vast holdings were mostly in the hands of committees that ran the huge and rather bizarre McCann Fund. McCann, during the war years, had personally acquired control of the Star-Falcon Motor Company of Detroit, reorganized it, and H. H. Starkweather had issued new shares for an aggressive program of new models and expanding facilities. Both Howard and Harry held a great number of shares in Star-Falcon in their own names, as did the bank and many of their clients. The Star-Falcon was jestingly called the "Starkweather auto."

The report that Harry had prepared with Tyler, aided by their accountants, Beck, Ott & Tanney, indicated that profits for the next year, if following the pattern of 1924, would be twenty-five million dollars.

"It's a pretty auto," said Harry, filling his pipe, when the first copies of the report came out. Tyler agreed. The red and yellow image of the Star-Falcon sports roadster in the *Saturday Evening Post* full-page color advertisement was drawn with a bit too much increase in size, but the trademark—pale blue letters under the crimson hawk flying against a great shooting-star background—was impressive.

"I think, Dad, it's going to be a big year for the Star-Falcon Road King," said Tyler. "I'm a little scared of letting Milly drive it. Too much power under the hood."

"I hope it's a good sales season. The stock is selling for one-oh-one; it should make a few points from time to time."

"I see it opened this morning at one-eleven."

"What?" Harry frowned and stopped, a lit match halfway to the Dunhill's bowl.

"Is that bad, Dad? It's damn good."

Harry waved out the match and sucked on the unlit pipe. He pressed the tips of his fingers together. It was about as much of a gesture of surprise as he permitted himself. He sought a life of complacent gentility. "Bad rise for a single day's trading. I think S-F may be the football of speculators, manipulators."

"What can they do?"

"Force up the stock beyond its worth. Then, the shares over-priced well, they sell it short, contract to deliver when it's dropped low. Leave us in a rather exposed position with overpriced shares."

"But the cars are selling like penny candies."

Harry was off on his own train of thought. "At this point, if I'm guessing right, the actual sales, the physical conditions of factories, and S-F prospects become just toys for the speculators in the Street's game."

"The Stock Exchange could stop this."

Harry looked at his son as a teacher to a pupil. "My dear boy, the Stock Exchange is *part* of the game often. It's a gambling den like Canfield's tables at Saratoga. Did H.H. come in this morning?"

"I heard him growling that somebody moved his wastebasket to the wrong side."

"We'll put this Star-Falcon thing before him. He's old, I know, but it's perhaps a major problem."

Howard came into the bank only about twice a week. Except that his breathing was hard at times, and there was some slight tremor in his hands, he appeared as alert as ever. However, he felt Harry and Tyler needed to be left on their own to face at the bank its daily patterns, its problems and controversies. His own time was spent working out the organization of transferring most of the purely banking assets of H. H. Starkweather & Company into a public bank with branches—the Starkweather-Unity Bank & Trust Company—and selling its shares to the public.

Now in the most comfortable black leather chair in his office, which he refused to have reupholstered—as with his office, he had said, "Too many goddamn sissy decorators," and refused to have it modernized—he listened to Harry and the details of the rise, a too-

324

high rise in the stock of Star-Falcon Motors. He was not shocked—he had long since lost old pieties about the world, the supposed fundamental ideas of business. "Somebody has a lot of the stock by the ass and isn't letting go. Wait a day or so, Hal, and try to see who's behind it. My guess is it's the Stock Exchange ruling mob, the clique. Lots of Harvard dudes and Ivy League snobs."

"It's not like it was in the old days on the Street," said Tyler.

H.H. gave a short barking laugh. "It's *always* been this way. Don't wear any rosy glasses, Ty. If the Star-Falcon stock keeps going up and they can't stop it from rising, then we'll have them over a barrel. To cover their short sales, they'll have to buy S-F at very high prices."

Harry was again sucking on his unlit pipe. "Yes, and if it doesn't stay up, this raid can wreck our position, Father. Our heavy position in Star-Falcon."

"It could," said Howard. "I've been through it a dozen times. Well, at least half a dozen. To fight it, you buy up all of the stock you can. Never mind the price maintaining its rise. The shorts will be forced to keep buying to cover. Contracting for *our* stock to cover, and when they can't cover their contracts, we have them." He showed a closed fist, the back of the hand studded with liver spots. "You'll have the speculators' balls in your hand to press, *crush*."

"We'll need cash," said Tyler. "To buy all that stock that may be offered on the rise."

"Borrow to the hilt. Borrow. Our credit is good. Chase, Manufacturers Trust, wherever we can. God damn it, Hal, light your pipe—you sound like a horse windy with green-corn colic."

Star-Falcon Motors opened the week at 134. And as the bank watched, reacted, a month later it was at 246.

Howard seemed calm enough—only biting through two pipe-stems. H. H. Starkweather & Company was now committed to millions in short-term loans.

Howard winked an eye. "When it goes to three hundred, a lot of the buyers outside the plot are going to grab for their profits without holding on. You, Hal, buy all that's offered."

"But at those inflated prices!"

"You've got no choice," said the old man, winking again at Tyler. "Has he, Ty? They have our heads on the chopping block."

"I don't know. It's just the stock moving at this damn furious im-

325

pulse isn't worth three hundred dollars a share. We'd have to be General Motors and Ford combined to be worth what it is selling for this morning."

"Watch the short sellers, who hope it will break and drop like a rock when it hits over three hundred and profit taking moves in. They're damn sure the price has to collapse."

"Aren't you, H.H.?" Harry asked. He had taken to chewing gum, trying to conceal a habit he considered nasty.

Howard walked slowly to the window of his office and looked down at the Street, his hands clasped behind his back. It was one of his window-gazing moods, Harry saw—and it was no use interrupting him until he had to decide something. It was a good five minutes—the little black marble clock under the picture of *Sea Witch* ticking away—before he turned back to face his son and grandson. He seemed to have come to a lucid assumption. "I'd say they'll sell short, in a vast attack on the price, after it goes over three-twenty-five. They'll have to have contracts for stock to cover. And as we own most of it now, they'll have to buy it from guess *who?*"

"Those people who have it," said Harry. "Us."

Tyler frowned—it was becoming *Alice in Wonderland* to him. "But, Gramps, haven't you always been against cornering a stock issue? I mean—"

"Sure as shooting, Ty. Of course I'm against the cruddy idea. I'd never, in ordinary conditions, go crazy enough to set out to capture a stock. But we're forced into this poker game, deuces wild and a cold deck with marked cards. The problem is when you keep buying under these conditions, you may find you own more shares than actually exist. We'll own more than one hundred percent of Star-Falcon Motors if the shorts go on making contracts."

"I give up," said Tyler.

"You may, but H. H. Starkweather and Company can't," said the old man. He poured himself a glass of water from an ornate silver-rimmed container, added two blue pills, and slowly sipped. "Damn short of some digestive juices, the sawbones quack says." Tyler noticed the slight tremor in his grandfather's hand.

"Christ, I wish I were fifty years younger and had some of the real rough-and-tumble galoots with me. Jim Fisk, Chauncey Wilcox, they were roaring Comanches, could swallow the Devil for breakfast and eat his horns for dessert."

The old man beat a fist on his desk top. "But it's another world, isn't it? I mean I'm too far along, too creaky, and my plumbing and wiring are out of whack."

"Now, H.H.," said Harry, "don't poor-mouth yourself."

"No, no, Hal, you're going to have to take on the fight." The old man sat down and smiled. "But the old head is still on my shoulders. I've got ideas I haven't used yet. Need dusting off, but they're good ideas—yes."

Tyler felt H.H. was playing a road-company wily Ulysses.

Howard closed his eyes and seemed to sleep. Tyler looked at his father, who shrugged his shoulders, and they left the office. In the hall Tyler said, "He fell asleep."

"To be most subtle, act the most obvious. Also he rests this way at times. He's usually as keen as ever upstairs." Harry tapped his own head. "It's just he's a bit weak in the limbs and at times he's a bit deaf."

Star-Falcon Motors hit 332 in a week and ended up at 355. H. H. Starkweather & Company continued buying and also lending stock to short sellers and buying it back. To Tyler it was all a sense of foolish urgency played out on a treadmill.

The Street was, of course, fully aware of the fight and knew of the entrenched members of the Stock Exchange who were working on shorts to bring the price of Star-Falcon down to ruin to cover their short sales.

At 360 Harry knew the bank had won. The short sellers would have to buy back the stock they owed the firm and at the top price.

Tyler told Milly at dinner, "They'll be ruined, could even be outlawed for breach of contracts."

Milly said, "I don't understand any of it. Shorts, longs, bulls, bears."

The first sign of trouble in the settlement with the bank was Aunt Dru barging into Harry's office, screaming, trailed by a wary but amused Nick. The two coming past secretaries and clerks, banging into Harry's private office with a rush. Aunt Dru was waving a shabby man's umbrella she always carried. She had a great capacity for making scenes—more a presence than a rational person. She had, over the years, become a caricature of herself; seemed to enjoy her notoriety on the Street.

"Outrageous! Indecent! A massacre!"

`Harry looked up from his desk and warded off the menacing umbrella with a lifted hand.

"Aunt Dru—really. . . ."

"You've ruined me! Ruined us! Nephew!"

"Oh, come now, Aunt Dru. . . . You're so full of vagaries."

"Vagaries!" She shouted at the ceiling. "He talks nonsense and I'm down two million in shorts on Star-Falcon Motors!"

Nick stood very still, enjoying the scene.

"You've made millions, Aunt Dru, in the past. And we warned you not to—"

"Don't tell *me* about how to buy and sell on the Street! I was active when you were still wetting your bed! I was aware of how the market works before you were through filling your first diaper!"

She swung the umbrella again. Nick grabbed her weapon arm. "Mum, we came here for a purpose."

Nick in middle age was just as smart as his old mother; but Harry suspected he was a lot saner. (H.H. had said, "If the old crow were not the notorious Drucilla Brooks and suspected of having holdings of millions, they could have put her in a bag, hung her on a wall long ago.")

Nick seemed at times to act as her balance wheel; portly, bald under his dusty derby, a bit of a waddle to his walk, an overlarge mustache straggling into his mouth, he did have a kind of vitality, an ability to curb his mother's fury, unless she was really "running past" what he called "danger signals." Then he could not calm one of her rages, her voice rising, as he thought, like a great organ toccata.

"Mum, you'll get heartburn again. Get to the point."

"Point! *Point!*" She tucked the umbrella under one arm and held up with her two hands a handbag made, it seemed, of an entire baby alligator, a receptacle she was never without. Slept with it, some said, under her pillow.

"Nephew! You're not going to hold me to those contracts if the stock stays up!"

"Now, Aunt Dru, H. H. Starkweather and Company is a publicly owned chartered institution . . . and—"

"You forget I'm an owner here, too! I have some part of poor Susan's share, handling it for her girls. And I've my own small share H.H. put me down for a long time ago. Ha!"

"Then you can surely see we have to protect you. I mean the stock you hold in H. H. Starkweather and—"

"Tell it to Sweeney!" The umbrella was lifted again, the voice rose in a merciless crescendo. "You listen good! Nobody who does

328

this to Drucilla Brooks escapes my curse! Nobody can make a fool of me. . . ."

It took Nick and two clerks to remove her from Harry's office, she fighting, uttering threats, exposing clean but tattered petticoats. Harry mopped his brow as Tyler came in, excitement on his features.

"They're dragging Aunt Dru through the halls!"

"She's utterly mad. Should be locked up. Must talk to Nick. Yes, I'll talk to Nick. If we can get three doctors to certify her—"

"Nick will never agree. She trained him in her style. And he's like Aunt Dru. Well, of course, better adjusted, and he's drinking and keeps a harem, I hear, someplace out of Aunt Dru's reach. When she goes, he'll maybe inherit seventy-five million."

Harry adjusted his tie, wriggled a finger around in his tight collar. "Oh, I wonder if it's that much. Fifty million perhaps. She's been sold up before when short. Not often, she's a wily wise old speculator. Star-Falcon is at three-sixty-five."

That afternoon the men who controlled the Stock Exchange, and among whom were the speculators who had sold Star-Falcon short, sent Harry Starkweather a note: "The board has voted to ask for your appearance before the Business Committee of the Stock Exchange at ten tomorrow to explain the actions and activities that have taken place in the dealings in the stock of Star-Falcon Motors."

This was no discreet action, but a blow with power behind it.

H.H., when he was gotten to the phone at Shad Point, said, "What? What? Speak up. An appearance before that board of sharks in spats! You'll be facing the cocksuckers who have been selling us short. Go? Of course you have to go. But remember we practically own every share of Star-Falcon ever put on the market. . . . Yes . . . well, be firm, Hal. Hard. Rock hard. . . ."

"But there's no moral or ethical justification for them to—"

"Hard, Hal. Like a rhinoceros' nose."

It was a mistake to take the hard line with the Business Conduct Board, Tyler felt. His father displayed a fraying sensibility under pressure. If H.H. himself had been there, things might have gone somewhat differently. As it was, in the paneled room in the Exchange Building, Harry in a crisp gray suit and attended by Tyler in blue, carrying a dispatch case of records, faced the half-dozen

329

men around an overpolished table, some of them with strong faces, and some, Tyler found, despicable, knowing their records—mostly they were there because of their inherited status on the Street and their abilities to make money.

The first exchange between them and Harry was polite, but crisp. From there on it became "Let's get to the matter at hand."

"You must see, gentlemen," said Harry, "the problem is over those members of the Exchange who are now caught in a situation they made themselves. I didn't make it, H. H. Starkweather and Company didn't. There can be no quixotic expectancy from our bank."

"This is official Exchange business," said a soft-faced man with a voice, Tyler felt, that could have been dipped in olive oil. "We are members of a gentlemanly group; there is a code—oh, not written into our bylaws—but it is a code of the Exchange."

"You mean will H. H. Starkweather make it easy for some of the speculators to escape their obligation?"

The soft-faced man took on a brusque manner. "You can word it *any* way you want."

Harry said boldly, "We as investment bankers are offering to sell those caught in the short sales, enough shares so they can meet their commitments."

A wide man with a gray up-curled mustache licked his teeth. "At *what* price?"

"At the price originally paid?" asked the soft-faced man.

Harry said, "Three hundred and eighty dollars a share. We have huge expenses, bank interest, bookkeeping, staff costs."

The chairman, a sportsman, deeply tanned, recalled from his South Carolina stock farm for the meeting, acted as if hit by buckshot, looked up.

"For Christ's sake, Starkweather. We feel *your* firm is the guilty party in this whole frigging mess over Star-Falcon Motors."

"I resent that!" Harry's face flushed and Tyler sensed his father was taking too shrill a tone.

"We are, Starkweather, considering removing Star-Falcon stock from the Exchange trading list."

Tyler almost stood to protest, caught himself in time.

This was a deadly bit of information, and Harry's face flushed a deeper red. Tyler himself felt a clamminess in his hands, a tightening of his scrotum as after a sudden plunge into an icy swimming pool.

330

Harry stood up quivering, but his voice under control. "This is a most serious threat. H. H. Starkweather is one of the oldest houses on the Street and a most respectable—"

"Please sit down—"

"If you intend to suspend Star-Falcon, we will have problems in getting a market for the stock and can hold the Exchange to huge damages."

Tyler had his father by the arm. Harry turned to the men around the table. "If you remove the stock from dealing on your board, our price will go to one thousand dollars a share."

They left, Tyler feeling they were both somnambulists lost in a dream.

Two hours later the Governing Committee of the Stock Exchange, on the advice of the Business Committee of the Board of Governors, "unanimously voted to suspend dealing in the shares of Star-Falcon Motors."

The evening New York *World* reported that when the Exchange president was questioned by a reporter if the move to suspend Star-Falcon was legal, he had answered: "The New York Stock Exchange can do anything it wants to do."

45

H. H. Starkweather & Company was in serious trouble. The holdings it had in Star-Falcon and those shares it represented for Donald McCann—he now slowly dying in an English nursing home—the proxies of some of its clients, all added up to just about a majority of the stock of a motorcar company now outlawed by the Stock Exchange.

Howard rose once more to do battle, gave up spending some of his time at Shad Point, and moved back into his New York suite. Here he met with Harry and Tyler, appearing to his grandson as an old lion ready to roar again, a shine to his age-bracketed eyes, the remains of his white hair in disorder. Striding about in a dressing robe, barefoot, he paced the floor, Harry and Tyler watching him as he waved his arms, one hand holding a glass of bourbon and water slopping onto the rug.

"Christ, this is trouble. It's gut deep and we're bleeding. We've been borrowing millions from banks to buy the stock at high prices and those loans are due in a couple of months."

"Yes, they'll call the loans unless they favor our situation."

"Banks are banks, Hal. Not human hearts. One asset we have is that the cars are still selling at a nice clip." Howard picked up a paper from the fireplace mantel. "Yes, good sales, and we're making money on them, on every damn spanking car. Get Bonely and Rashe, our lawyers, to begin producing legal signals against the Exchange—talk of taking it to the Supreme Court."

Tyler said, "As long as the price of the stock keeps up we seem to be in good shape."

Harry shook his head and took out his gold cigarette case. "If we're not listed on the Exchange board, there's no scale of value to be put on the stock. However, we do have contracts with the firms representing the short sellers, and we can begin to demand they deliver stocks they haven't got *or* make payment for them."

"Yes, those contracts are legal—the Exchange can't deny them." H.H. sighed and took a deep swallow of his drink. Harry tapped a cigarette on his case, and H.H. set the glass down.

Tyler felt like the bearer of a gallows verdict as he said, "This morning I got word from an Exchange clerk I went to school with. He heard the Exchange is going to issue a statement that all contracts on the Star-Falcon stocks are to be held null and void."

Howard said softly, "I'll be goddamned."

Harry bent the cigarette he was tapping and threw it into the fireplace. "H.H., that means any failure to deliver Star-Falcon stock owned by us because they'll not be able to procure any is a failure to live up to contracts. They're off the hook."

"That's the rig of the jib," said Howard. "That's taking care of their own. Their goddamn Law Committee can tie the whole thing up forever."

Tyler said, "We can sue."

"Oh, sure, through the holes in our pants for the next twenty years. But the damn Exchange has been beaten in the courts only twice. Ty, get a message to the Exchange president—to be signed for—that we are willing to sell Star-Falcon shares—and willing to negotiate the price for the short sellers. Also that this is legal notice they *must* reestablish Star-Falcon Motors—list it again on the big board. Get a copy to every newspaper in town. Let the citizens get a dose of what the Street can do when it goes wrong."

The notice of offer from H. H. Starkweather was never answered, and in the next few days lawyers for both sides began to smile and prepare legal papers. The Exchange hired four lawyers, the most costly in the city. H.H. got three lawyers and their staffs to study the Star-Falcon matter. They began to pile up costs and hours, bent over law books.

"It's going to be a damn lawyers' holiday, gold-plated," H.H. said. He resigned from the Exchange, put up his seat for sale.

"What's the good of that?" asked Harry as they sat in H.H.'s office with a lawyer looking over piles of legal papers.

The lawyer, Mr. Rashe, was a small man with very large eyes, head too large for his body, ears that stuck out from his head. He kept turning a signet ring on his stubby finger. "With Mr. Stark-weather no longer a member of the Exchange, he doesn't have to obey its rules. He can now name publicly and to the press every one of the short sellers. He is no longer held back by any Exchange rule." He chuckled. "They outfoxed themselves on H.H. *Carper et colligere.* He's no longer held by any terms of secrecy. He can speak up about anything he knows of the Exchange shenanigans he's aware of. Yes, indeed."

Tyler said, "There's certainly a lot that hasn't been told about inside Exchange doings."

H.H. waved his arms. "I don't want to tell any damn privy secrets. I want the buggering tinhorns taught a lesson, that's all. And go on with our regular business."

Tyler said, "I've asked the New York *Times* Wall Street reporter up, and I've prepared a list of all Exchange officials we know for sure are among the short sellers, and others."

H.H. took the lists. "Yes, yes. Wilkins, Rosensweig, Hudson, Millstone, Kirby. Ah, Nicholas Brooks." The old man looked up. "That madwoman, Drucilla, too, of course." He folded the list and put it into a waistcoat pocket. "All right, let's give the whole list to the *Times.* That will put a wild hair up the Exchange's ass. Or put ours in a sling."

That night Harry heard the newsboys yelling extras in the street as he and Katie sat at dinner.

"Wall Street scandal. Wuxtra! Stock Exchange in plot to force Star-Falcon Motors to the wall! Wuxtra!"

The butler closed the windows and came back to the table. "Shall I serve the main course, sir?"

"Yes, Parker, yes. And get my car around to the front."

Katie studied her husband's face. "What can you do at this hour?"

"I don't know, my dear. But H.H. is down at the bank and he's

333

old. Tyler is there, and he's too young. It's on my shoulders, really. As our lawyer says, *Caret inia is et fine.*"

"Is it very, *very* serious?"

"It could just about mean the end of H.H. Starkweather and Company. We owe millions to banks. They're already pressing us, smelling out the situation."

"But H.H.'s holdings? Shad Point, the family assets? Some say hundreds of millions."

"Oh, that's a bit high and not all that easy to liquidate. What we shall need is cold hard cash. Besides, H.H. isn't going to sell Shad Point. And the McCann Fund can sue us, and so can the clients we've been buying for. It's an abominable, loathsome mess."

Katie said, "We could, my darling, modify our way of life. You know I do have an interest in my family's trust. We can still be fairly decently off. You'd still be able to smoke Dunhill tobacco—that's a jest dear. Oh, Harry, Harry, the Street isn't all there is to life."

Harry watched the roast duck being served. "Yes, of course, being just fairly well off is good enough for some. Myself, I'd get used to it. But H.H. isn't that timber. Father is rather a vindictive old man." He began to carve. "Besides, no one can tell how far down things can go if we don't fight. Criminal action, fines, even jail terms. So it's fight until we can reach some sort of agreement with the Exchange and the short sellers."

"That dreadful vulgar aunt of yours was on the phone this afternoon. She didn't make sense. Howling like a banshee."

"Aunt Dru has been among the biggest of the short sellers. Will you like some of the breast?"

"I'm not hungry, Harry." She turned her head away from the butler's view and began to weep.

The next mornng the short sellers named in the newspaper sent out statements that it wasn't true they were a plot-prone group. Their names, they claimed, had actually been "used to hide H. H. Starkweather's serious problems and troubles."

H.H. replied in an interview, flavored by oaths and whiskey, he'd "be happy to have a government investigation to look into the affairs of the Exchange, and also to study the shady way they made their own laws while regulating billions of dollars that trusting people put into stocks through a thoroughly private club called the Stock Exchange."

The Exchange issued statements: "We are not acting against

H. H. Starkweather & Company to protect short sellers. All actions taken against Star-Falcon Motors have been guided solely by a sense of duty for the best interests of the Exchange and the public."

As he read this statement, Howard did a little jig on his worn office rug. "They're whistling in the dark. Now, Ty, you'll please issue orders to call back *all* the shares in Star-Falcon we have *loaned* to the short sellers."

"But they can't deliver."

Howard patted his grandson's back. "Smart boy, oh, a very smart boy. We've done it all according to Exchange rules. Yes. No, they *can't* deliver. So we proceed—listen carefully—to bill the borrowers on the *other* exchange—the Curb Exchange on Broad Street. Tomorrow morning at ten o'clock. Give that to the newspapers."

Harry shook his head. "The Stock Exchange will not budge."

"Don't be so damn sure, Hal. Just keep your pecker up and be there at nine thirty at the Curb Exchange."

Hal wondered, was the old man sunk in self-delusion?

By nightfall the Street was buzzing with talk. Investment bankers, trust-company board members called each other or gathered in their clubs to talk over what was happening on Wall Street; one of the great old firms, H. H. Starkweather & Company, and the mighty, rather smug and exclusive Stock Exchange locked in battle, no holds barred. It recalled the embroilments, turmoils of the days of Drew, Fisk, Gould, Cooke, the early Morgan.

At nine o'clock the next morning Harry Starkweather left by the side door of his Fifth Avenue house, he hatted in a homburg, wearing a lounge suit, to go to the garage, where his chauffeur, an Irishman named Knobby Hayes, would be waiting to drive him down to the Broad Street Curb Exchange, where dealings were actually done in the street, out in the open. There still remained in Harry a residue of fastidious shyness, but also the determination to do his duty as he saw it.

Harry had slept badly, had taken little breakfast. Katie had not come down for the early meal. She did not want to rasp Harry's nerve ends or talk over the events. It always upset Harry to talk of the bank at meals; he would get those pains in his stomach and have to take baking soda in a glass of hot water.

After his bath and dressing he had looked in on Katie, still in bed, and said, "Good morning, dear," and she had said, "You, too, darling," and he had gone down to mess about with two soft-boiled eggs, nibble some thin toast, gulp two cups of coffee.

Harry walked down the alley between growing shrubs in white Italian marble urns, he thinking it was cool today, he should have worn a Burberry. By the largest urn, carved with nude figures of some forest nymphs and fawns, he saw a woman in black, crouched between two of the urns; he got the impression of a feral beast in a thicket.

The woman rose and shouted, "You have used me! You have felled me to the ground with your schemes!"

Harry saw a flash of fire from a black-gloved hand and then felt a mild tap of pain in his right shoulder, then something did strike him in the lower rib cage. He could only form the thought—*What an incoherent universe.*

The chauffeur, Knobby Hayes, rolling himself a handmade smoke as he stood by the well-polished Cadillac, heard the two shots and dropped the Bull Durham and the half-made cigarette ("Jasus—what's that now?"). As he ran off toward the house, he found Mr. Harrison Starkweather bent over, on his knees, his homburg fallen to the ground, clutching himself in the middle. The chauffeur thought he had heard footsteps going away behind the house, over to the other alley, which separated the house from the next place. He wasn't sure of the footsteps, for a bus was snorting on Fifth Avenue.

"Mr. Starkweather!" Dead? His first thought was to get a priest— then he knelt down and put a hand on Mr. Starkweather's shoulder. Himself was alive and he looked up, pale, calm.

"Hayes, don't alarm your mistress. Just ask her to ring up our doctor—urgent—and the Manhattan Hospital to send an ambulance. Quickly."

Activities had begun early at the bank. Tyler had been in since eight o'clock. H.H. hadn't even bothered to go back to his town suite. He had slept fitfully, muttering in his sleep; slept on his office couch, wrapped in an old red-fox robe, a robe left from the days when he and Chauncey used to take a fast cutter through Central Park over the well-packed snow. "Those were winters," he told Tyler on waking. "Why, I remember the big blizzard of eighty-eight. Every wire down—twenty-foot-high drifts. People frozen stiff on the el trains. But we sledded down . . . to keep the bank open."

336

He had awakened feeling lost in time. Wondering were the mobs out of Five Points attacking the Union Steam Works seeking weapons, or was it Jim Fisk giving him orders to buy gold? He recovered the present quickly, looked at his heavy gold watch. "Ah, yes, Ty. The Curb Exchange. Send down for hard rolls, a pot of coffee, sweet country butter—if there is any"

"Can they stop the Curb Exchange?"

"Hell, no!"

They sat sipping the coffee in large blue-glazed cups, the remains of a gift set from old J.P. in 1900. Tyler was tense, in a painful urgency; he felt ground glass in his stomach. His hair, oiled down, was in the fashion of the mid-1920's, his trousers very wide, the jacket belted, the Brooks Brothers shirt fresh. (When he was leaving that morning, Milly had said, "You look like a snazzy John Held drawing.")

"Well, Gramps. Ten o'clock today we know, don't we?"

"That's right." He sipped the coffee slowly. "It's like running the Union blockade with a quarter million in contraband, only now it's maybe a hundred million."

"Let's go to the Curb Exchange."

"Ty, you sit down. Harry will be there. Besides, I have to be on view here if some people come to call on me."

"Who?"

The old man winked. "It's nine fifteen o'clock. Have another cup of coffee. It's tepid but it's strong." He looked at the fireplace mantel, over which hung the oil painting of *Sea Witch.* The varnish had turned yellow; there were cracks showing on the heavily painted sea. Below it stood the small black marble clock.

"That little old clock was all I saved off *Sea Witch* when I had to abandon her in the buggering swamps. She burning, hull sieved like Swiss cheese by the Federal frigate's guns. Yep, I may end up with just a picture and a clock. . . . Kick my ass. I'm touched with self-pity. . . ."

"It was an exciting time to live."

"Christ, Ty, don't you find *this* morning exciting?"

"I do, but it's somehow different."

The old man sighed. "I used to feel maybe I'd like to go to my grave with a lifetime of work and family. Something worthwhile. But more and more I don't know."

Tyler was interested in family history, in legends about H.H. in

337

his youth. He wasn't just an old man in a tight, worried mood, flexing his jawline, a throbbing of the veins at his temples—yes, suggesting H.H. was under pressure. Life is a perpetual compromise, and fluctuations, contradictions.

The desk box buzzed.

"Mr. Starkweather, there are some gentlemen here wanting to see you. They say, urgently."

Howard looked at the little black marble clock ticking away. "Nine thirty-three. . . . Yes, *who* are they?"

"A delegation of the Stock Exchange Protective Committee."

"Oh? Send them in." He turned to Tyler, the tremor in his hands hardly under control. "You stay. We'll see what they want to say."

"They've given in."

"Don't be too sure. Only sure things are death and taxes, I hear. And nothing is sure about death as being final."

46

The delegation as it entered was most impressive. ("Like a gangster's set of pallbearers," Howard said later.) Four solid figures, two in their thirties, one middle-aged, a lean, elderly, ramrod-stiff figure with a long head, a dour mouth; the spokesman.

"Good morning, Mr. Starkweather," said the ramrod with cool, direct, and exemplary behavior.

"Morning, Nelson."

"You know the rest of this delegation."

"Of course." Howard waved a hand, trying to show neither rebuke nor ridicule. "Please sit down. This is my grandson, Tyler Starkweather."

The delegation sat.

Mr. Nelson spoke. He had a voice that seemed to be talking through pebbles lodged in his windpipe. "The Protective Committee of the Exchange has had a meeting, and it has been decided that a fair price should be set for the cost per share of Star-Falcon Motors, to pay back H. H. Starkweather what the short sellers owe the firm."

"How was a price set, gentlemen?" There was irony on Howard's surface felicity.

"Each man on the committee had a sheet of paper. On it he

marked down what he thought was a fair price for the Star-Falcon stock. That's the logical way to do it, don't you agree?"

"And?" The old man, Tyler noticed, had his eyes turned toward *Sea Witch*, not on the committee. He sat relaxed in his deep chair, low on his spine, his legs crossed, showing the elastic-side shoes he favored.

"The figures marked down were collected, added up, and from these an average was come to."

"*What* did it come to?"

"Four-forty-five a share. Is that acceptable to you, Mr. Starkweather?"

Howard stood up, his face expressionless. "Yes, it's acceptable to this bank." He held out a hand to Mr. Nelson. "Shall we shake on it?"

"Of course. Damn glad the damn thing is settled."

Howard shook hands with the entire committee; even Tyler shook their hands. It seemed a ritual to him, a truce taken in a labyrinth of deception.

"Of course," said Mr. Nelson, "your own seat on the Exchange is restored and the stock goes back to be listed on the board. The entire matter of Star-Falcon Motors is settled. The controversy is finished."

Howard waved off any idea of indignities felt on his side. "Will you gentlemen join me in a tot of bourbon?"

"Just a small one."

After the committee had gone, H.H. howled, "Great God Jehovah, they *knew* they had their cocks on the butcher block!"

Tyler sat back in his chair, legs spread-eagled before him. "Wow! Oh, wow! We've won!"

H.H. coughed. "Well, not yet, even if those sons of bitches gave in. We owe the banks about thirty million, and they'll be haunting us for payment. We'll have to press hard to collect what's owed us by the short sellers. But yes, it's been a victory. Wasn't it St. Augustine who said, 'God always writes straight but with crooked lines'?"

The desk box buzzed.

"Mr. Starkweather, it's the Manhattan Hospital."

"What for?"

"There's been an accident to Mr. Harrison Starkweather."

The afternoon newspapers featured the story of the attempted

339

assassination of Harry Starkweather in more space than they gave to the settlement of the battle between Starkweather & Company and the Stock Exchange in the matter of Star-Falcon Motor Company.

PRESIDENT OF WALL STREET FIRM SHOT

MYSTERIOUS GUNMAN SERIOUSLY WOUNDS

INVESTMENT BANKER

There were few details. No one had seen the would-be killer. The wounded man after the first emergency operation was in no condition to talk. The police had no clues. Harry was three hours in surgery. One slug (the police said it was a .38-caliber bullet) had shattered the right shoulder. The other had gone through some stomach tissues and was lodged near the spine, too close for the surgeons to attempt to remove it. They sewed up what severed muscles and tissues they had to and hoped there would be no peritonitis. Tyler and his mother and sister had only a brief glimpse of the blue-white face on the bed as Harry lay under a sedative. Blood transfusions were given. Harry Starkweather was in a very critical condition for four days.

To Tyler the fear of his father's dying—doctors' reports were ambiguous and contradictory—was mixed with thoughts that the bank's burdens would descend mostly upon him and an old man.

There were many rumors as to who had shot the banker. The police never did produce a suspect. Gossip was that Harry Starkweather, a most respectable married man with a lovely wife, had a mistress he had taken over from a notorious bootlegger and gangster with a grievance, and so Harry had been "burned" (Walter Winchell, New York *Mirror*) as a warning to give up the woman. Another irresponsible theory, popular at the Bankers Club, was that union organizers, "Communist controlled from Moscow," attempted the assassination as a warning they would not be stopped from trying to set up a union at the McCann Steel Company mills and at the Star-Falcon plants in Detroit.

Two weeks before Harry—thin, feeble, and answering no questions—and Katie left for Palm Beach, he in a wheelchair but with hopes of being able to walk again with the aid of canes, Drucilla Brooks, wearing her ermine tippet, was institutionalized at

340

McLean's Sanitarium as helplessly unable to handle her affairs rationally; in no condition to be permitted to remain free without some kind of restraint. Three doctors signed the commitment papers as requested by her son, Nicholas Chesney Brooks.

Nicholas never forgave the Starkweathers for insisting his mother be certified instead of letting her be kept as a guest in a private retirement home. It was made clear to Nicholas that Harry Starkweather would never bring public action against his mother, and he was left in full control of the one hundred and fifty million dollars of his mother's estate.

It was a time when some of the great investment houses of the Street became public banks or affiliated with some established bank they had always favored and held stock in. It was clear federal laws now in the offing would separate investment houses from public banking privileges. So a splitting and a separating of interests would have to take place. The House of Morgan would form a major division of interests by setting up the Morgan Guaranty Trust. The Rockefellers would become major stockholders in Chase Manhattan; and they saw to it that a Rockefeller ran the vast power of the family assets in the money market. H. H. Starkweather had long planned for the family to have a public bank of its own. So by 1927, with the assets of two new partners and merging with three smaller banks, stock was issued for the Starkweather-Unity Bank & Trust Company. The main bank to be an impressive building on lower Broadway, taking over branches of the two swallowed-up banks on Long Island, seven outlets in Manhattan and Queens, the Bronx, and Brooklyn. And with plans to creep upward to White Plains, Rye, Yonkers, out on Long Island to the Hamptons, and as far north as Albany.

Harry Starkweather had never fully recovered from his wounds. He spent most of his waking hours in a wheelchair, moving about painfully at times with the aid of two canes. He worked mostly at home in a hospital bed that cranked up to permit him to sit up at least three hours a day. The bullet had never been removed from near his spine, and doctors feared to probe for it, assuring Katie and Tyler, "The odds against its moving to damage the spinal cord are, well, conservatively, a thousand to one." Which Tyler thought was hardly medical phraseology.

The details of the public bank setup had been worked out well

341

and in full detail by Harry. But the burden of the final minutiae of takeover, stock issue, the salving of the state banking commission fell to Tyler and Nick Brooks, Nick being one of the new partners. Nick had inherited not only his mother's huge fortune of close to one hundred and fifty million but her shares in H. H. Starkweather & Company as well. He was also close to the O'Degan holdings—Buck O'Degan was the other new partner, a man deep in real estate, city construction companies, brick and gravel yards, pier contracts, harbor tugboats. Buck O'Degan and Nick each invested in ten percent of the two hundred thousand shares of the newly formed Starkweather-Unity Bank & Trust Company; Harry and Tyler were each set down for five percent of the stock. Howard Starkweather retained fifteen percent for the Shad Point Hudson Foundation—the family trust that was a lawyer's marvel of misty interpretations. It could be seen as a public foundation, a research endowment fund for social and national problems, as an educational source with scholarships. Basically it was created to keep the holdings of land and riverfront, the new bank assets, and the H. H. Starkweather & Company holdings under family control (H. H. Starkweather & Company would continue under Tyler and Johnny O'Degan—married to Tyler's sister Pauline—as a Wall Street investment business, also all under family control).

Harry Starkweather was nominal head of the family enterprises, but he was a failing man, too tired often for his former sensitive perception. Howard Starkweather was deep in his eighties, and there were days when he seemed to be talking of another time, except for those periods when he was his old self, a volcano; cursing, thinking, and projecting as he had done in his prime.

Tyler was still short of thirty years of age, so while he carried a great deal of the burden of the investment house and the new banks, he was just too young to be accepted by the Street as the center of the huge Starkweather interests. Johnny O'Degan, Buck's son, was even younger. None of the other sons-in-law showed any great ability or fervid assertiveness, so they were vice presidents, acting roles during short hours, but not aggressively.

Joe, Tyler's older brother, had almost disappeared from the family, gone into postwar radical causes. As a publisher, backer of little magazines with red covers, containing Gropper and Art Young cartoons of the Starkweathers, Rockefellers, Morgans as fat, top-hatted exploiters of heroic but hungry-looking strikers. It was

342

Nick Brooks to whom Howard and Tyler turned for help in running the Starkweather enterprises at their peak. Short of men at the top connected with the family. Nick (called Briney by some of his intimates because he lived mostly on a huge yacht, the *Mermaid*, wore a yachting cap instead of a banker's fedora) had turned into a brilliant handler, a skilled manipulator of money, credits, and the wildly profitable stock issues of the 1920's. He had his mother's ability to smell out money, to ferret for stocks that were dormant but could be alerted to move upward in a bull market. He did not have her madness, her irascibility in piling up fortunes, her perverted frugal ways. Not since he was clear of her physical presence.

Drucilla Brooks existed in a suite of rooms at a most private sanitarium. She was very happy. Unaware of the outer world, she collected twigs and dead flowers in the walled garden of the grounds, hoarded empty cigarette packs, pebbles, bits of gummed papers. These she kept in shoe boxes under her bed, counted and put into order, as her holdings in U.S. Steel, Du Pont Chemical, General Motors, RCA; she called them "my blue-chip issues." On the wall of her rooms she kept careful records of market gains, mergers, and stock splits (always a favorite of hers). As she read no papers, had no contact with the market, she insisted she got messages from the air and placed orders the same way. "Yes, yes, indeed," she said to her attendant, a burly Polish woman named Masha, who dunked her, protesting, into a weekly bath. "U.S. Steel up three points; I have a hundred and ten thousand shares."

"Goot. Now wash the feet. Don't eat the soap."

"RCA will go through the roof, Masha. Get in on it. Buy fifty thousand shares before noon, on margin."

"I do that."

Nick came to see her twice a year, brought her baskets of fruit, hampers of gourmet picklings and smokings: hams, caviar, truffles in brine, cheeses of pungent odors, smoked fish. Drucilla never ate any of this. Hothouse fruits rotted in her closets until attendants threw them out. The cans and cheeses, preserved meats, glass jars of rare fish eggs piled up under the bed until the twice-a-year painting of her rooms took place; then it was all carried off by the painters and the staff for their own use. As the walls were being painted over, she had to be restrained as she screamed, "You're destroying my bookkeeping, the records of my accounts."

She would greet Nick on his visits always with a smile on her thin,

343

gray-white face and wearing her ermine tippet, her little hat with the broken feathers. "Tell me, Nicky, you're not gorging on meat, are you? I'm very intolerant of deception."

"I have your list, Mum, pasted up on my shaving mirror."

"Good boy. What's with the market quote on United Fruit?"

"Doing fine. We've sent in the marines to run the plantations."

Nick always left the sanitarium feeling cheerful. Mum was in a splendid mood, happy in her phantom stock dealings, treated well. So much better than to have her roaming around the Street, being made ridiculous, and Mum a bit careless with a gun. Nick ate meat, kept two chefs, one permanently on his yacht, lived with a harem of girls—they all attitudes and no loyalties—whom he changed from time to time. Nick was his mother's boy; his main purpose in life was to increase his fortune and someday to take over the Starkweather holdings. . . . The old man was getting potty, Harry was a cripple, and young Tyler? Well, bright enough but not ruthless enough. It was men like Buck O'Degan, Johnny O'Degan's father, he'd have to work with; that damn mackerel snapper was an ass kisser of the Starkweathers, he so damn proud to be related. But greedy.

Tyler, more than his father, was intrigued by what was behind the daily market quotations. Not just symbols of mills, plants, but the commodities that fed the nation.

In Maine and Idaho the potatoes were in—great amber-yellow hills of them—knotted like the faces of old men, holding their good white meat under their dirty skins. On six million farms men worked and sweated, taking from the earth what it had to offer. Tyler wondered about them. He could never reconcile the lives of farmers everywhere with their importance to the living world. The men who grew the ingredients of bread would forever be incomprehensible to him.

In Minnesota, the Dakotas, and Montana the spring wheat was a six-inch stubble. At the great Marietta junction of the Ohio and Muskingum rivers and fields west to Red Wing, to the Republican River, to Wildcat Mountain, the corn was twelve feet high. Corn futures were higher, Tyler saw.

South of the James and the Ohio, cotton fluffed white over six states. From New Mexico to Galveston Bay countless fields, big and small, brought forth their crop. Landlord and sharecropper, bale

344

kings, chain-gang prisoners, slaves to the land or banks—all watched and appraised the fields. Tenant farmers hoarded their half bales in Tennessee, Crackers guarded their acres in red-soiled Georgia, and along the Black Warrior cotton would keep whole communities surviving. The bank was floating two hundred thousand new shares in the Prince Cotton Textile Corporation.

Tyler closed his eyes and he saw the land that was coal and oil and millions of cattlehides. Leather to go to Boston and Lynn and Worcester to be cut into shoes, to come out gleaming boots and slippers and good working brogues.

At Providence, Fall River, Bridgeport, the textile looms were humming with activity, their ingenious fingers weaving fabrics for the world to use. Omaha, Kansas City, Chicago, New York—the stockyards of 1928 were full to overflowing.

At Newark, at Gloversville, the tanning machines worked overtime in stench and fog. The great markets were bursting. The food came in on strings of cars over bridges of imposing grace. The mills and factories spilled out their products; the haulers and night trucks met dawns under a full load and were always waiting, waiting and ready for more. In darkness the seeds were bursting open; the roots were spreading, suckling from the soil. The earth was always giving . . . and Tyler awoke; he had fallen asleep at his desk doing some special chores for his father.

It was very late; the street traffic came muffled into the sleazy hotel room; the plumbing made indecent sounds from the bathroom; the door ajar showing just a sliver of light. Tyler moaned and sat up in the bed, the sagging spring protesting. The woman said, "How about a little light?"

"No, it's okay the way it is."

"Look, I'm not a bad looker, *boychik*."

"You're not Italian?"

"Does it make a difference in the dark?"

"I thought, well . . . it's fine, it's just the light hurts, in my eyes."

He felt her stir and her arms go around him. "You're a lover boy, let me tell you—and I'm not just saying that for the loot. What was that name you kept calling me? Some broad's name."

"I don't remember calling out any name."

"Masha, Molly . . . something like that. I think we both took on too much hooch. Where you going?"

345

He pressed a bill into her hand. She scratched a match alive and looked at the twenty dollars. . . . No, in the flare of the flame he saw he had been a fool again to think this whore was like her in any way.

"Look, stay the night. We got the room till morning."

He walked into the bathroom blinking his eyes, smelling the disinfectant and the bug powder.

47

Nineteen twenty-eight, according to business volume, was a good year for the nation, for H. H. Starkweather, for the Starkweather-Unity Bank & Trust branches. Harry seemed to have taken on more vitality under his new medical doctors, one a Herr Doktor Swengerin from Vienna, who was a world-acclaimed body manipulator. He had Harry up on only one cane, and he could stay out of his wheelchair for three hours at a time. Howard Starkweather had a new phone system installed at Shad Point that could put him in touch with Harry, Tyler, Nick Brooks, or Buck O'Degan (the latter two active vice presidents and major stockholders) just by pressing the proper buttons. H.H. didn't come down to the Street very often now or to the bank ("I'm drying up, getting ready to blow away like tumbleweed"). But he still was a voice to be listened to—a bit ambiguous at times—about the ways the Exchange worked. That he had had the board of the Exchange kowtow to him in the matter of the Star-Falcon Motors shares was already a Street legend. H.H. was still able to see opportunities he insisted most others didn't grasp. His self-assurance, self-confidence remained, but at times his memory failed.

The Starkweather-Unity banks delighted him. What he could not tolerate was an awareness of age, an acceptance of death.

"Damn it," he told Tyler and Milly—they were living that July in their summer home at Shad Point. "I'm as shiny as a new penny in my head, as I always was. Only I look in the mirror and it's an old dry hulk I don't know. Christ, Milly, you go break all the mirrors while you still have time."

He also wanted Tyler to hurry up and produce some grandsons. But so far the Tyler Starkweathers were childless, and not from lack of trying.

Tyler was potent enough, several medical men said. It must be Milly; "Some blockage of the ovaries," one Park Avenue specialist whispered to him. But Tyler never mentioned it to his wife. They got on quite well; they led an active social life and he never thought of his lost love, the Italian girl, Margo Crivelli, not *more* than once or twice a month after a particularly hard day at the bank over a predinner martini. She was sometimes in his dreams; he knew a smattering of Freud, enough to know that the subconscious belongs to another self, a kind of traitor.

Tyler, busy in the Street, was one of the few who worried over the prosperity of the times. Who believed the great bull market would ever falter? New York, Wall Street, the Stock Exchange had become all through the 1920's the Golden City of easy money, as "the common ordinary citizen" (Buck O'Degan's term), the store clerk, plumber, housewife, auto mechanic, read and heard of something called the stock market. Reports of how you put down a little on something called margin to play the game. Kelton, the head gardener at Shad Point: "Say ten percent of the value of the stock you buy. It's sure as shootin' bound to go up; it always has." And it did usually go up—until late in 1929. After all, of President Coolidge when in office, one wit had said, "He looks as if he were weaned on a pickle," and Nick quoted Cal as saying, "No Congress . . . on surveying the state of the Union, has met a more pleasing prospect than what appears at the present time."

Tyler commented, "So far."

Said Buck O'Degan, "Gloomy Gus. Why, it's like being given a wheelbarrow and they opened the U.S. Mint and said, 'Fill her up.'"

Joe wrote in his left-wing review: "Wall Street begins in a graveyard (Trinity Church) and ends in a river (East River)."

Tyler and Milly were invited to meet the new President, Herbert Hoover, who granted a press interview. "We shall soon, with the help of God, be in sight of the day when povery will be banished from this nation."

Milly elbowed Tyler when he whispered to her, "Of course, these days God is a Republican."

Harry didn't share his son's doubts. He found particularly significant the fact Hoover was a fine engineer. "The economic condition of the world is," said Hoover, "on the verge of a great forward movement."

347

Most of the New Yorkers Tyler knew—down to the bank's doorman—were involved in the stock market. He sensed that his grandfather agreed with him in part. The old man was, as he put it, putting his house in order. "My mind, I mean. I now know it was never just the damn money I was after. I was trying to prove myself. And in this world you prove yourself by piling up loot and kicking asses you don't like. They say it's an American sickness. Sickness, my foot. You take the Europeans, the Medicis, the Rothschilds, the Indian rajahs, the Chinese war lords; they're a million times greedier than we are. And the grubby French farmer—why, he'd let you cut his wife's throat for a gold coin. No, I think it was mainly for show and ass kicking I made the bank, beat the Street, formed the Starkweather-Unity. Oh, I enjoyed my howling at the moon, eating the fancy food, screwing the beautiful women. Don't you ever think power isn't fun, Ty. There's no guilt in me, however. I don't have to give to charity like Rockefeller, Carnegie, McCann, or the Guggenheims, all begging forgiveness. Still, still. . . ." The old man blinked his eyes and didn't go on with the idea.

"I'm selling some of my stockholdings, my personal stocks," Tyler said.

"Well, I've no crystal ball. You'll make a good profit, Ty. I haven't been paying too much attention to the market. 'The goose hangs high,' Harry keeps telling me. I hope it doesn't fly out of sight."

No use talking to Gramps, Tyler reflected (he isn't senile, just too damn old to care). "I've seen everything, Ty, and done everything but kiss boys. You may be right. Hal thinks it could be just a short reaction of the bears making a raid or profit taking ahead."

Tyler was half an hour late getting to the bank on October 24, 1929. The market had opened seemingly in its usual ever-rising good shape. Then a sharp drop and some brokers began to think of the margin accounts their customers weren't covering. But Nick agreed with Tyler not to press their clients. By noon there was a flood of selling orders. Harry said, "Anything done to raise panic at this strategic moment can start a cattle stampede." By two o'clock fear, even horror, had set in on the Street. The ticker tape was running half an hour behind, and the boys chalking up figures on the board were out of step. A man standing on the roof of H. H. Starkweather & Company was seen by some as a would-be suicide. Associated Press phoned Tyler about this slim mistake: "There's a rumor that a dozen ruined stock speculators have leaped to death or blown out their brains. We've had no such reports."

"No such things have taken place."

Police were moved into Wall Street to keep order; false information came in over stock wires and press reports that both Chicago's and Buffalo's stock and commodities exchanges had closed down.

Howard, dozing in the sunlight on his terrace overlooking the river, was not informed of the break.

When the market closed at last with fearful losses, Tyler sat in Harry's office with Nick and Buck O'Degan. The Irishman's face was a ruddier color than usual; he had been nipping whiskey at the office bar, but it seemed to have no effect on him. He appeared disoriented by events, as if his God had found him wanting.

"Did you see what Radio Common did?" he asked. "I mean it's chaos—that's all, a chaos."

Nick was marking up the back of an envelope. "I figure it's a collapse like we've never seen before. Let's begin to advise our clients to sell at the morning bell."

Harry frowned, wincing as he turned to face Nick. "Damn it, Nick, it's been a weak day, that's all. Our biggest clients are covering margin, not panicking—much."

"Dad," said Tyler, "Nick and I now feel the whole roof is caving in. Stocks have been and *are* overpriced. The problem is most buyers have only small margins paid down; the economy can be in deep trouble."

"Oh, shit," said O'Degan. "You can't sell the country that short. International Tri-State Brick and Cement—my family own sixty percent of it; it was one-ninety-three a week ago. You think I'm gonna lose three million dollars by selling at closing prices? Not on your tintype. I'm holding on."

Tyler tapped his fingers on the arm of his chair. "I've been selling a lot of my personal holdings for two weeks now."

"You bastard!"

Nick said, "Easy, Buck—it's Ty's right." The intercom buzzed. Harry picked it up and said, "Yes, yes. . . . Oh, I see. Well, we didn't want to bother you. You're sure you're fit. . . . I mean it's a brisk day and the trip . . . oh, of course." He hung up. "H.H. heard the late-hour radio news. He's coming down."

Nick asked, "What does he think?"

"Didn't say, just something about the Street has its balls in a sling."

O'Degan went to the bar. "Good, the old coot—he knows more of the Street's shenanigans than all of us put together."

H.H. appeared at dusk, wearing his wolf-pelt coat, having been driven down to the Street in his old Pierce-Arrow. He was in good shape, his eyes sparkling as he banged his cane on Harry's conference table, scarring its mirrorlike surface. He seemed revitalized by the crisis, as if coming out of an infinity of boredom.

O'Degan went off to see to his brickyards and contractors—to fire half his employees. Tyler and Nick were eating sandwiches, drinking coffee. Harry had lain down on the big sofa in his office. His back was very painful.

Howard faced them. "Well, mad-dog time and hydrophobia foaming out of the Street's mouth." He went off into hoarse irrelevancies, banging his cane on the furniture.

"Father, let's be practical. The Street must unite to stop this thing."

"You're damn right. I've alerted Jack Morgan. . . . Wish old J.P. were alive. We have to unite with Otto Kahn, Rockefeller, Jr.— people who carry the weight. This decline is something we have to nip in the bud before it turns on us and eats us, boots and all, spits out our bones."

Tyler nodded. "There's a hope, *if* the Street will unite."

H.H. got Tyler busy sending telegrams. "In bad times go to the top, Ty. Show confidence, act confidence, sell confidence."

As usual the stricken moneymen turned to the House of Morgan. But Jack Morgan was reported to be in Paris, in London, in Rome. Holding the bomb-scarred House of Morgan was the senior partner, Thomas Lamont. He agreed with H.H. there was need for a meeting. The investment bankers came secretly to a special meeting at Morgan. Lamont's plan, worked out with Howard, to stop the decline seemed to Tyler simple and direct: "Your banks hold six billion dollars in reserves. Gentlemen, form a pool of millions and begin to restore confidence in the stock market by buying, *buying!* Acting for you will be Morgan's floor manager, Richard Whitney."

H.H. banged his cane on the table. "We turn chicken now and I'll see you all on the Bowery free soup line."

The next day the visitors' section of the Stock Exchange was closed. After a good lunch Mr. Whitney, Tyler at his side on the trading floor, worked his way through a steaming, sweating mass of brokers, agents, clerks, runners, and up to U.S. Steel's post No. 2.

Tyler said, "H.H. insists we open big."

Whitney smiled, waved greeting. "All or nothing, eh?"

Several hundred thousand cutomers, the news was, were still pouring in margin money. Tyler said, "I smell fear."

"You smell *me*. Here goes." Whitney waved an offer. "Ten thousand shares, two-oh-five for U.S. Steel."

Steel, Tyler saw, was selling at 193½. A cheer went up. Morgan's Whitney was bucking the tide. The floor men shouted that the market was turning. Moving cheerfully about, distributing his orders, Whitney made offers for thirty million dollars' worth of stocks.

"How's it look, Starkweather?"

"Expensive. But it seems to be stopping the market panic."

"It also gives some wily stock owners a way of unloading their holdings."

When the bell ended the day's trading, U.S. Steel had lifted to 206. Tyler looked at his notes. "Nearly thirteen million of various other stocks have moved."

Whitney wiped his face. "I need a very large booze."

It was after eight o'clock that night that the stock tickers caught up with the day's dealings. Tyler hurried back to the bank. H.H., smoking a cigar, shook his head. "Montgomery Ward has fallen from eighty-three, gone as low as fifty before making a little comeback. Christ, it's going to be nip and tuck."

The next few days H. H. Starkweather & Company worked through the evening's late hours phoning clients for margin and *more* margin to protect themselves. Customers began to put up cash, sell assets to meet margin calls. But as second and third calls for margin came in and still stocks fell, Tyler saw the mirage fading.

H.H. slept in his office, drank, smoked, gave orders. "Sure, people having added thousands of dollars to their stock losses drop out, are sold out, ruined. You'll see millions of little people, well-off middle-class folks, workers and the elderly suddenly are real poor. Without a bank balance, without credit, usually in debt. But keep trying to keep *us* solvent. Survival is all now!"

Dark days followed darker days, more and more drops in stock

351

prices. The last margin calls went out from Starkweather & Company. H.H., unwashed, collar off, read the *Wall Street Journal*: "'The greatest stock market catastrophe of all times.'" He added, "Well, that's it, sweet and short. We like records in America, don't we?"

Tyler was pale, his stomach in knots. "A million savings gone, nearly one thousand business firms bankrupt, farm prices down to nothing, banks beginning to foreclose by the thousands."

H.H. said, "Remember my old friend Jim saying, 'Sometimes the bulls win, sometimes the bears, but hogs never.' So let's pick up the bits and begin patching."

It was H.H., Tyler, and Nick Brooks who met at the bank on a cold January day to survey the ruins and wonder at salvage. Harry was at home in bed, sunk in a deep disquietude; he was never to come down to H. H. Starkweather & Company again. The pressure on his spinal column had paralyzed his legs. He had developed an ulcer. Katie and nurses watched over him around the clock. He did not complain, just lay staring at the ceiling, muttering, "Fantastic, fantastic." He kept asking for his son Andy, but André, in his father-in-law's firm in France, was also involved in a battle for survival.

Buck O'Degan was under criminal indictment for some of his dealings with city contracts, bribes, faulty materials, dishonest engineering, a possible involvement with exposures of Mayor Jimmy Walker's City Hall. After the collapse of his cement and brick companies O'Degan lived with a squad of lawyers, fighting court orders, and the bankruptcy of his remaining assets. His holdings and those of his son Johnny in H. H. Starkweather & Company and the Starkweather-Unity Bank & Trust Company were fairly safe in some corporation controlled by his wife's relatives, and so unattachable. But even the value of these was in doubt.

H.H. seemed to have grown thinner and more active, needed less sleep, was more pugnacious. He sat in Harry's old place at the conference table. "Ty, you just sum it up for us."

"We'll survive. As you say, H.H., survival is all."

"You bet your tail on that."

"Our losses are, of course, very large. But we've retained a great deal, even if we've used up a lot of our cash resources. However, the Starkweather-Unity Banks have not failed. They're in good shape—relatively—compared to some."

Nick rubbed his bald pate and blinked his eyes rapidly as if to clear his mind. He had dark rings under his eyes; most likely, Tyler suspected, from the gossip-column reports (Winchell, Sobel, Sullivan) of orgies on his yacht, late parties at his Long Island estate. Nick had given up none of his hedonism, but he was brilliant in helping the company and the banks steer a dangerous route to safety; they were in better shape than most.

Nick said, "The Jewish All Nation-City Bank was in as good a shape as any, but the Christian-run banks drove it into receivership when it could have been saved."

"Dirty pool," said H.H. "Joseph Pedlock said All Nation would get lynched by us *goyim* if we ever had the chance to wreck them. Too bad. They were good Jew people. They helped us when we got into that Star-Falcon fracas."

Tyler said, "Yes, it was a nasty pogrom. But I think they'll turn out to be nearly ninety percent solvent when it's all settled. Why don't we make a bid to take over their thirty-five branch banks around the city and on the Island? Merge them with our Unity Bank and Trust Company?"

Howard looked up at Tyler, his bloodshot eyes wide open. "Ty, why not? *Why* not?"

Nick smiled. "I always liked a bargain."

Howard went back to Shad Point that night. He was feeling so tired now. Feeling his damn age; the burden of his bones, he told himself, is a mean load. He got into his big bed, drank the hot tea and rum the butler prepared for him. "I showed the young popinjays there's life in this old buzzard yet."

"That you did, sir. Now get some sleep. You're a bit flushed."

"Royal flush," muttered Howard. "Yes, it's a game—a game—the fun of flashing the right cards."

His burst of energy, the months he had directed the Starkweather assets through the first months of the Depression, salvaged what could be saved, made bold moves that had succeeded, brought other banks in trouble to join Starkweather-Unity—this had all left him worn down rather than serenely radiant. Just now *so* tired, indifferent. He no longer asked for daily reports on the Street, felt ground down on rising, activating himself somewhat with whiskey as the days advanced, he slowly walking along the riverbank—a river that retained the cadenced sounds it always had.

That year he was alone at Shad Point. Some of the family were in

353

Palm Beach; Harry had settled there permanently. Joe was leading marches on Washington, D.C., for Trotskyites, bonus hunters, Dust Bowl victims. The rest of the family—he could not keep track of them all—a half dozen were on the Riviera; dividend payments were recovering; grandchildren had moved to Santa Barbara, Carmel, Pasadena. No, he couldn't remember all their names. He had French grandchildren, too—some Marcels, Renés, other odd-named sprats.

Howard Harrison Starkweather was completely unaware of reality when the New York *Times* printed a headline story:

WITH A BILLION IN CASH

STARKWEATHER-UNITY BANK

EYES BARGAIN STOCKS

Hear this, Wall Street. The head of one of the nation's largest banks said it is interested in buying stock again.

Tyler Starkweather, chairman of the board of Starkweather-Unity Bank, the third largest nationally, suggested here that the time has come to take advantage of equity bargain values.

"We're starting to get interested in the market again," Starkweather said in an interview at Town Hall.

He said he could not speak for other big New York banks. But with personal and corporate trust monies under its management, placing it second only to Morgan Guaranty Trust Company as a money manager, a decision to increase its equity position could cause ripples in the stock market.

At present Starkweather-Unity Bank's cash position—the amount of money it has in short-term money market instruments—averages about 18–20% of the funds it manages. The rest is in trust funds, stock, and other securities.

Securities industry and financial analysts estimate that about $15 billion is still on the "sidelines"—being withheld from the stock market by big institutions reluctant to put it back into stock.

Starkweather said his bank was having as much trouble as any other financial institution in keeping its trust monies performing in an uncertain and often declining stock market.

He said that last year the bank's trust funds were eroded by about 20%. For the first six months the Starkweather-Unity Bank's equity holdings again dropped about 21% while the S&P index fell 11%.

354

"It's been a horrible year," said Tyler Starkweather, a personal friend of President Hoover and Governor Franklin Roosevelt.

Starkweather holdings and clients' accounts are mostly in Alcan Aluminum, Ltd., Montreal; American Electric Power; American Telephone & Telegraph; W. R. Grace & Company; Great Atlantic and Pacific Tea Company; Stauffer Chemical; Union Carbide; Consolidated Edison of New York; Phelps Dodge; Ralston Purina; Studebaker-Worthington; Westinghouse.

Tyler Starkweather said the family had income from American Power, American Telephone & Telegraph, McCann Steel, and Star-Falcon Motors stocks, U.S. Treasury and N.Y. Water District bonds.

48

Striding along in the new boots the village cobbler had made for him, the boy walked down the dusty pike. Under his arm was a bundle wrapped in muslin, tied with twine. It held an extra shirt, a rough towel, a bit of lye-ash soap, a bottle of liniment that his father had insisted when rubbed in was good for all aches and pains and whatever might torment a body. Also a copy of *Pilgrim's Progress*, half a yellow farm cheese, a pound of hardtack, half a fat slice of smoked ewe's tongue. Writing paper, a bone-shaft pen stuck into half a raw potato. Ink he would have to find. He was leaving home at twelve—with a badly spelled letter of introduction—to seek work in a relative's shipyard and in bad season perhaps go out to the Banks with the codfishers. He didn't mind leaving the hardscrabble, boulder-studded farm. As he walked along, the new boots taking on a bloom of dust, he looked up at the sky, a sky so blue, his now-dead granny used to say, "the blue of a Dutchman's pants."

The boy was happy, yet he was also apprehensive as to the future.

The old man could walk by the side of the boy—such innocence—and remember the cloth cap, with the earmuffs folded back, not needed in this spring weather. The old man could even touch the boy. But the boy was unaware of him, could not see him. It was unfair, the old man thought, this boy I can't warn; he's going off so free and foolish, callow and yet smart, too. A boy going to become me, and I can't thump him on the back, advise him of the potholes and the times ahead, of the ways of men; the world all wolf's teeth, also women with wonderful warm bodies and the juice of ripe plums dripping from their laughing mouths.

The old man's mind was as if overlaid with all the years he had memory of, but the chronological details did not seem to fit. He could not make himself known to the boy, get a response from the walking young figure. Yet the old man could ruffle like a little breeze the loose hair sticking out from under the boy's cap, even adjust the bundle under the arm.

Age is the time of flannelmouthed humiliation, he mused as his pulse flickered and the heart seemed to have a stone in it. He was an anachronism and knew it; past all things, past warm hope, cold-blooded jauntiness. He didn't fool himself. Neither grace nor God trapped in a stone church was with him. Just a feeling it had all been well worth it, but what *all* was he didn't much remember. Christ! No names, no faces (just the boy's), no events, no relationships or meanings. Just a hint of an idea to take life and pleasure, no matter how big the wound. To dominate one's work and environment, handle a 12-gauge over-and-under shotgun in a duck blind, corner gold, and to make sense where there is no sense. The family, the only trustworthy force, there, to stand up to all enemies. Loyalty—that's the ticket—the rigid rule. But, but, *but.* All are affected by time passing; time is passing even now, getting darker than goose turds.

No longer logical thought processes. . . . Do I wake or dream? . . . They are rolling the world from under my feet. He addressed the boy, Howie. His lips formed the words but no sound came out. The boy smiled. He had stopped by a fast-flowing stream below the Red Lion Inn crossroads. To lie prone, suck up cold water, mop his face with a red bandanna. Howie, Howie boy—listen. . . . The pulse grew slower, slowed, the heart gave a great stab of pain. And it was as if someone had stepped on a ripe fruit, pressing down to burst it under the ancient ribs, and at that one last moment the boy turned, wiping his mouth with the sleeve of his jacket, and asked, "Howard Harrison Starkweather, want to hear a riddle?"

EPILOGUE

Every man has room in his face for all his ancestors.
—EMERSON

Wine maketh merry, but money answereth all things.
—ECCLESIASTES 10:19

In 1945, after two years of negotiations, the New York State Highway Commission condemned two hundred acres of Shad Point, the private estate of the Starkweathers, for a superhighway through heavily trafficked routes to the north. In 1952, one cold clear night in January, the house of the late Harrison (Harry) Chesney Starkweather was saved from a brisk fire set by a drunken caretaker thawing out a frozen pipe with a blowtorch. The Harrison Starkweathers had not lived at Shad Point for many years, having retired to Palm Beach, he disabled by someone attempting to kill him.

Various grandchildren and great-grandchildren sometimes for weekends gave parties at one of the Shad Point homes still kept up by a crew of gardeners and caretakers. The boathouse and bathhouse were in use until the river was considered too polluted; then the facilities fell into disuse and the forty-foot sailing craft, the two motorboats were hauled up out of the water and covered with tarred canvas, where they slowly decayed into rot and rust, nests for the black river rats. The racing shell, the two rowboats, and several canoes were given to the YMCA, Norton-on-Hudson branch.

The fragmentation of the estate was to continue. Several of the private roads and blue-stoned gravel paths were abandoned. A romantic reporter on the New York *Post* wrote of "the *fin de siècle*" of the Starkweathers:

> The manor was finally finished the year a new wing was added when the autumn crash came in 1929. By July 8, 1932, the value of Big Board stocks had gone from a high of $87 billion, set September 3, 1929, to a depth of $15.6 billion. And the Dow, which stood at 381.17 before the great crash, sank to

359

41.22 in 1932—the year Howard Harrison Starkweather died and was laid to rest in the private burying ground at Shad Point. The final grave marker was not erected until 1946, being delayed by World War II, which prevented the completion and carving of the ebony stone on order from Italian craftsmen. In 1955 a red fox was found nesting in the boxwood hedge surrounding the plot. Caretakers planned to trap the creature but it disappeared and was never seen again.

The Tyler Starkweathers (he chairman of Starkweather-Unity and director of H. H. Starkweather & Company) never had any children, to their regret. As Tyler became more and more the active head of all the Starkweather enterprises he and Milly traveled a great deal, and she was written of (in *Vogue*) as an ideal *femme du monde* for the styles of Lanvin, Paquin, Vionnet: "Never too matronly. In exquisite corseting." Tyler and Milly took a sensory enjoyment in Rome, in Paris, London. They were always met, escorted, feted as representing the major Starkweather interests. Drinking the waters at Baden-Baden, facing a still life of *truite bleue* in places that the shiny-coated magazines listed as "fashionable preserves for the smart set."

It was in 1947 that Tyler Starkweather had what he always was to call "a touch of the male change of life." He was no longer young, but interesting-looking, walked with his muscled body held straight, yet he was aware it was soon to be middle-aged. It was that year, as December storms brewed in the Arctic Circle and came down from Canada to cover Shad Point deeply with snow and cause many accidents on the roads, that he told Milly he had to get to Mexico to see about some assets H.H. had left down there. It was only partly true, he told himself. There was a personal quest down there he had to fulfill, something he had to admit to himself even if he didn't want to think it out clearly.

In Mexico City he hunted for the old group of painters that had worked with Rivera, found out they had long ago broken up. No one seemed to know of any Margo Crivelli.

"The gringa women, they come and go, looking for the *macho*," said the Oficina de Inspección. Not even after Tyler gave him *la mordida*—the bite—the expected graft of a ten-dollar bill, was he much help beyond suggesting, "You can try the Migración Inmigración. They might know, *sí*."

360

It seemed a silly compulsion after all these years to stay on and eat *cuauhtemoc* with *frijoles*, get sick, and have the Aztec trots, still to go on. An art dealer trying to sell him some Maya pots—perhaps genuine—said as they drank, "Was she dark? Was she well made?" He drew with two hands a shape in the air. "Ah, Crivelli. Your wife, senor? No? Yes, yes, there was a painters colony of damn yan— of *norteamericanos* in Chapultepec, Trotsky followers, fresco painters, yes. *Bueno* drinkers all. Yes, she was there, but it's some years since. You have a picture? *No, es nada.* You go, you will know if she is there. No pots? The small one? Twenty dollahs. Stolen from a grave in Oaxaca."

When Tyler handed him an extra five, the dealer bowed his head and said, "*Dichosa la madre que te parió.*"

Tyler gave the pot to the hotel porter, and ill as he was feeling, his entrails still giving off spasms, but full of some chalky medical stuff a doctor had given him, he went on to Chapultepec. There was an art school of sorts in a shop off the *zócalo* and a large woman with brass-colored hair was in charge. She asked him if he was FBI.

"No, no, I'm just looking up an old friend, a Miss Crivelli, from New York at one time." He showed her his passport.

"New York? From there myself, donkey years ago. The damn Un-American Activities bastards ran me out, or just say I took it on the lam before they put me in the jug. Margo, eh?"

"Margo Crivelli. She worked on some fresco projects at one time."

The large woman nodded and smiled at him. "Those were the days. . . . Sit down. Great walls, great art. Now here it's all crap for the damn crooks in office who run this germ culture of a country. You *sure* you're not FBI?"

He handed her his card. She rubbed its surface with a thumb and hid it someplace in her smock. She produced a half bottle of mescal with only two dead flies in it, and they sat in the doorway drinking while men strolled by smoking brown paper cigarettes, and across the way a woman fanned a fire under a pot of beans and drove off thin, hungry pariah dogs.

"It was fine here, mister, until everybody began to come down to ball and booze and prices went up for *cerveza, el teléfono.* . . . Crivelli? She married somebody, I don't remember who. But it didn't last, I gathered. She was painting pictures to live on for some crumb-bum refugee dealer, a damn German, I heard.

361

In Villahermosa down in Tabasco. But they shot the dealer in some *cantina*. Then she stayed here at *El Farolito*—yes, that was the name of the fleabag joint. Left. Then? I don't know. Most likely she's dead."

"I hope not. I have to get back to the States. If you should hear of her, see her, give her my card."

"No message?"

He had been sipping from a fresh bottle of mescal, so he was surprised to hear himself say, "Tell her I still love her."

The large woman began to cry, belly and breasts shaking. "You wonderful son of a bitch." She hugged him to her, she smelling of turpentine, *chimaja*-root flavoring from her last meal. "You're a good john. Let's drink to love, I have a bottle of tequila here someplace. Can't not celebrate love, no how."

Tyler said no, his stomach wasn't really in working order for any more drink. Outside one of the scabby dogs had mounted a bitch and was mating with no great pleasure, judging by his expression. The woman cooking beans threw boiling water at the dogs; they howled and dragged themselves off. In the *cantina* next door the hour of *merienda* had started, and several drunks were making for it slowly. In the church up the street they were putting out red and yellow bunting.

"It's for the Feast of the Three Holy Kings tomorrow. . . . I just remembered something." She raised her huge body with difficulty and went away deep into the dusty shop with its poxed walls covered with charcoal sketches of peons and mules and women with very large bare feet. She came back with a tattered snapshot of several people waving bottles and standing in mock-heroic poses in front of a painted backdrop of Popocatepetl. She spit on a corner of her smock and wiped the surface of the picture. "Damn flies, no respect. That's Crivelli on the end there."

Tyler took the snapshot, yellowed and frayed. He was never sure if it was Margo under the fancy wide-brimmed straw hat with pompoms hanging from it. It was not a well-focused picture.

"You may have it, mister. That's me, thin, here at the left, well, not really thin but I was nice then, living with the *alcalde*. *Ojalá!* I was something special then, let me tell you. Weren't we all?"

She didn't mind the ten dollars Tyler gave her. She kissed him again and told him where to hire a car for the trip to Nuevo Laredo and not to overtip, as most jerks of *norteamericanos* did.

Once back across the border, Tyler looked for a long time at the tattered snapshot and put it away in his wallet with a postal card of the Zapotec ruins, a card on which someone had written in pencil, "*Evite que sus hijos lo destruyan.*" He had no idea how he had gotten the card, perhaps drinking too much with strangers. He tore it and the snapshot to bits and tossed the fragments into a litter basket at the airline terminal.

Six months later he had a letter from the large brass-haired woman in Chapultepec on ruled paper from a school notebook, written in pale brown ink:

DEAR T.S.:

How are you? *Qué tal?* I am not well, but I'll live.

About the lady you were asking about. There was a writer named Lowry, Malcolm Lowry, here—what he writes I don't know. Lives in the *barranca* when here, he says. I mentioned the lady's name as you were so understanding of me, and hell, you said something that touched this mushy romantic heart. *Bueno, bueno.* Lowry said, sure mike—he knew the lady; the lady, he said, went back to the USA three years ago. But you *will* find the lady someday sure. I see it in the stars. I am an Aries—you, too, says your passport. Our element, FIRE; quality, CARDINAL. Casanova was an Aries, Joan Crawford, St. Catherine of Siena. Astrological cross lines will bring the lady back to you. What is the lady's birthday and what is your birth hour and your mother's sign? Send me fifty dollars and I will have a chart for you and the lady by return mail showing *why* you will find her. I have this cough and am not long for this world. But I know you will get the lady back. You will both be *very* happy. Don't delay.

Hasta la vista,
NANA TRACKENBERG

Tyler sent a money order but no information and hoped never to hear from the large woman again. He didn't. He kept the letter in a locked drawer of his desk at the bank. His digestive system bothered him for some months, but in time it cleared up.

He and Milly continued a pleasant, well-ordered life.

They attended many weddings, Tyler in ascot and striped trousers, Milly in some new coiffure. They kept records of birthdays, anniversaries of nephews and nieces, even second cousins.

The Tyler Starkweathers got along well, their opinions, domestic

363

and public, those they expressed, could be reconciled. Tyler found his homelife pleasant if not exciting; proper meals, tranquil copulation, well-trained servants. His tasks at the office gave him all the work he could handle, and he liked his work, his duties, his responsibilities. He was spoken of as "one of the men on the Street in the know."

Sometimes they were happy they had no children; as when they saw the adenoidal adolescent features' of problem children before they were sent to Vassar, Radcliffe, Bennington, Harvard, Yale, Princeton, and later became scandals at the El Morocco, at Newport, Reno. As for Shad Point, it continued to be written up as being of "a Renaissance lavishness," when it was actually past its prime. But the press needed a Forest of Arden close enough to the city to excite readers by the way the upper-middle-class rich lived. And so the legend of H.H. grew.

The town house was the Tyler Starkweathers' social seasonal address. They attended the opera. Tyler could sing in the shower "*Là-bas, là-bas dans les montagnes*" from *Carmen*. Summers were often spent at Shad Point. Milly collected milk glass. She was a great reader of the newer writers; Dylan Thomas once pinched her buttocks at a publisher's party. Milly was not a snob, not at all a prude—rather brisk, bright, and contented. She never whined, and when she got her migraines before her menopause, she retired to bed with a wet cloth on her forehead and lay in darkness. Tyler was never unfaithful to her—in the city. On business trips there was some use of corporation call girls. He was a reasonable, sensual man.

They drank well, drank a lot at times, but neither was alcoholic. They did not gossip about the sexual aberrations or the pathology of their small tight group of friends. Milly had some big losses at bridge and gave it up. Tyler entertained schoolboys from St. Paul's, Exeter, Groton when some teacher brought them to the Street to see how their fathers and uncles (or trusts) made their money. The Tyler Starkweathers were generous with charities. At Tyler's insistence they bought and hung the first Jackson Pollock to be seen in a Republican living room. ("I used to mix with artists in my youth.") They tried to age gracefully, but did not desperately seek new diets, expensive quacks with injections of secret glandular extracts. The weaker of their friends began to die off, and Tyler laid in a

364

supply of black ties from Sulka's. He kept a dark suit in his office so he could attend a burial service, going directly from the bank.

After the burial, by his father's side, of Harry Starkweather in the private cemetery at Shad Point, the county passed an ordinance forbidding the interment of any more people on the six-acre site or its use as a burial ground. (The body of Katie was a few years later smuggled in to rest beside her husband.)

Milly Starkweather died in Rome in 1962 while on a visit there with Tyler, and she was buried in a Protestant cemetery in that city. Tyler when in his mid-seventies was the only member of the family who still lived permanently at Shad Point, in the house his grandfather had built for him and his bride so many years ago. When he spent a night in the city, it was understood by the couple who "did" for him that he stayed at the Princeton Club.

There were no longer any members of the Starkweather family or any of the in-laws connected with the running of the Starkweather-Unity Bank & Trust Company, by 1965 the third largest in the nation with its various branches and services. H. H. Starkweather & Company, the investment firm, by the late 1950's had merged with Wembler & Boskin, becoming Wembler, Boskin & Starkweather. Tyler retired—sold out his interests—a few years later when scandal hit the firm. He resigned in a handwritten note, enclosing without comment a clipping from the New York *Times*:

> One of Wall Street's best-known investment banking firms, Wembler, Boskin & Starkweather & Company, admitted it did not reveal significant information to investors in Western, Great Plains & Gulf R.R. in the months before the railroad filed the biggest bankruptcy in history.
>
> In court papers filed here Chester H. Wembler, president and senior partner, said he was aware the firm was selling commercial paper in Western, Great Plains & Gulf R.R. while it possessed nonpublic information indicating severe financial problems within the company.
>
> Commercial paper is a form of short-term investment used chiefly by corporations. Wembler, Boskin & Starkweather is one of Wall Street's largest commercial-paper dealers and sold hundreds of millions of dollars' worth of Western, Great Plains & Gulf paper.

After Western, Great Plains & Gulf went into reorganization, a number of suits were filed against Wembler, Boskin & Starkweather, charging the firm did not adhere to federal disclosure rules. At the time of its failure, Western, Great Plains & Gulf R.R. had $82.5 million in commercial paper outstanding, down from a peak of about $200 million.

The Wembler testimony is in a deposition taken in May. The suit revolves around the question of whether Wembler, Boskin & Starkweather possessed nonpublic information about Western, Great Plains & Gulf's financial condition which should have been given to its potential investors. The firm has taken the position, according to a Securities and Exchange Commission study of the Western, Great Plains & Gulf case, that it was only a dealer in the commercial paper and did not have the obligation to disclose information that normally falls on an underwriter of securities.

Throughout the deposition Wembler, a former chairman of the New York Stock Exchange who is regarded as one of the most influential persons on Wall Street, denied any day-to-day contact with the sale of Western, Great Plains & Gulf commercial paper. However, he said he was the "principal contact" with the company and was partly responsible for bringing the railroad's business to Wembler, Boskin & Starkweather & Company.

Wembler, Boskin & Starkweather & Company began selling Western, Great Plains & Gulf commercial papers after the Interstate Commerce Commission gave the company permission to issue $100 million worth. The limit was later raised to $150 million, then to $200 million.

Like H.H., Tyler Starkweather had come around to thinking that once one was comfortable and had no money problems the game was only a game. Unlike H.H., he didn't care for the use of power. As to kicking asses: When the subject was brought up at one of his clubs, he amused some members by stating he'd "rather kiss them."

As for the Starkweather-Unity Bank & Trust Company, Tyler resigned as president, lost control of Starkweather-Unity; and in 1962, when Nicholas Brooks and Johnny O'Degan made their moves to seize control during a merger with the Island-City Security Trust Company, Tyler became aware of what was going on when the *Wall Street Journal* sent a reporter to interview him at Shad Point.

"Were you aware, Mr. Starkweather, that the Shore-Export Corporation is controlled by the Brooks-O'Degan interests and they have been buying up bank shares and now control at least twenty percent? Your sister, Mrs. John O'Degan, inherited most of your late father's shares."

Tyler had hoped that morning to knock some golf balls around on the Shad Point private course of eight good holes. It helped dispel his moods of anger and skepticism about the way the world was changing. He was dressed in slacks, a pale yellow cardigan sweater, and wore a plaid peaked cap.

"I must say I've had some hints."

"Will this mean you will be replaced as president?"

"I suppose that's the big *real* red-hot question you have?"

"Yes."

"Frankly, I'd be a jackass if I didn't have a feeling attempts will be made to retire me. But the Starkweather Foundation holds enough shares; there are some of my aunts' estates with stock, H.H.'s daughters. Various people, grandchildren of the founder. I'd give good odds I'll weather the storm."

The reporter looked up from his notes. "Nicholas Brooks maintains the foundation owns very little bank stock; your grandfather Howard Harrison changed their assets to real estate, certain motor-company holdings. Besides, Mr. Brooks is a stubborn old man, and he claims there is a clause in the gift of bank stocks to the foundation that can be interpreted that it is nonvoting stock."

"That's legal crap for the damn lawyers to work out."

The reporter studied Tyler. He saw a man very polite up till now. Tall, white-haired, ruddy-faced, still on the slim side. (He'd write him up as "the last of the F. Scott Fitzgerald mob, a lone survivor—diffident, weathered.")

"I'm sure, young man, there will always be a Starkweather in the bank. It's part of the native scene, like apple pie and baseball."

He was not so sure as he practiced some approach shots to the third green. (What bullshit I gave that reporter.)

The next day Tyler went into the city and talked to his most trustworthy lawyer. Kenneth Walton Rashe II, the third member of his family to serve the Starkweathers, stretched his lips firmly on his overlarge teeth and looked at Tyler over his Churchill half glasses. He liked Tyler—one of the few old clients not tinged with misanthropy or fear of the welfare state.

"You can put up a good fight. You'll have a good proxy battle. It will also harm the bank stocks. Perhaps *if*. . . ."

"Oh, come on, Ken, no perhaps today. Well?"

"It will be a knock-down-drag-out struggle. You're a healthy man in your prime, Tyler, *but*. . . ."

"But I'm in my sixties, that's it—with a bit of blood pressure. So why put my tail in the wringer?"

Rashe II nodded and took a package of mints from a drawer, took one and offered the pack to Tyler. "Given up smoking. Will you have a mint?"

"No, thanks. I'm a pipe man. Have my father's collection. . . . Jesus—cockeyed, isn't it, to fight for something my grandfather and father built up with such hopes, and now those pricks are grabbing it."

"I must say Nicholas Brooks is not what I would call legally insane. Insanity, you know, is a legal term, not a medical. Frankly, I smell some kind of revenge motive in tying in the O'Degan family. . . . Well, his mother, I *hear*. . . ." The lawyer waved an arm vaguely in the air. "His late mother—an amazing woman—was a kook. And your sister, Mrs. John O'Degan, holds a lot of your father's, grandfather's shares. She'll vote with the O'Degans. I'll send you a report by one of our young men—*Harvard Law Review*, all that—on the situation. . . . Must be beautiful at Shad Point this time of the year."

"My sister, damn her—sweet woman—is priest-washed. Look, Ken, you ever want to play some golf, feel free to bring up your foursome. Liberty Hall."

"Keep that in mind. You couldn't change your sister's mind?"

"Pauline? Not even if I converted and kissed the ring."

Two weeks later Tyler Starkweather's bank stocks were sold to the Shore-Export interests at a good price. . . . He told Kelly Hayes, the caretaker, son of his father's old chauffeur, "Well, I'm a fully retired man, Kelly. Where's my old man's wheelchair?"

"You'll be frisking about a long time yet, sir."

Kelly's wife, Anne, cooked and kept house for Tyler. It was an easy task for the Hayes couple. Tyler never entertained at home, never brought a woman to the house; even if the Hayes pair knew from certain signs servants detect that there was some long-standing affair with a female in the city, where he spent usually two nights a week. (Anne said, "They'll find him dead in some whore's bed, mark my words.")

Tyler really didn't mind retiring. It had been hard work and too many crises after the death of H.H., the long decline and passing of his father, and always at his back Nicholas Brooks and some of the O'Degans putting warm but firm family pressure on him, expanding the bank more than he felt safe. Taking risks that H.H. and his father would have frowned on.

Nicholas had not aged well. He had become a shaggy old man of piquant irregularities. Still a hedonist, involved in a few scandals no one cared about anymore. His base was often a vast California ranch; the press reported orgies, wild doings for some time. The years had intensified Nick's search for pleasures. *Newsweek* once reported he was said to have remarked, "They don't have to be too ardent anymore, just used to waiting."

Johnny O'Degan spent part of the year with his wife, Pauline, and four daughters in Switzerland, where he was active in the Starkweather-Unity Bank's dealings on the international money exchange. In futures in cocoa beans, olive oil, sugar, and other commodities through the bank's various European branches or connections.

When Nicholas Brooks died in 1969, it was discovered he had been married in 1943 in Lima, Peru. The woman, Alicia Soriano-Fuertes, now dead, and there was a daughter, Chepita de Ortega, whom the courts accepted as Nick Brooks' heir. His estate was a disappointment; he had lived too high, spent much, and his holdings had been mostly invested in railroad stocks and oil companies. Airline travel had destroyed much of the passenger rail travel and bankruptcies sent many lines into receivership. Several Middle East countries seized or nationalized oil resources where Nick had huge holdings, and payment was promised, but little was made. The daughter sold the ranch and the Brooks' estate interest in the Starkweather-Unity banks to some people in Boston who had bought heavily into Shore-Export, and they began to press the O'Degans for control.

It was rather sardonic, Tyler mused wryly over his morning

toast, coffee, a baked apple, and several assorted vitamin pills that Anne Hayes set down in order before him, to see in the morning *Times* a half-page advertisement showing his grandfather's picture of *Sea Witch* reproduced under the headline S-U SAILING THE SEA TO SAFE BANKING SINCE 1863.

The rest of the text was a prose poem: how the bank was not merely your good neighbor, your silent partner, your guardian angel (federally insured), but that you were welcome to use the restrooms, travel services, and view its collection of rare coins and "the original ledgers of Howard Harrison Starkweather, kept in his own hand."

Tyler had put in a claim for the little black marble clock and the oil painting of *Sea Witch* as personal property of the Starkweathers, and was thinking it was too bad the Starkweather name was still attached to the banking business. He would have liked to talk it over with someone, just gossip a bit; but there was no one among the bankers, brokers, clubmen he was close to anymore. There were men he liked playing bridge with most every day at one of the three clubs he belonged to. Elderly men, self-preoccupied, redundant. Two or three generations away from their days on Ivy League football teams, the bed-dominated nights with *Follies* girls, memories of Hoover and that "son of a bitch FDR," whom Tyler had rather admired and had voted for several times (once too often, he felt).

Tyler had served in World War II in the Pacific theater, New Guinea, the Palaus under Mac, a show horse of a general. There were still two or three fellow ex-colonels surviving with whom he could cut up touches of their days of island-hopping and standing at attention on the deck of the *Big Mo*, while the little Japanese in top hats and officers in badly fitted uniforms, tight-faced samurai, stood grimly dour as some signed a document. But the colonels were retired either to Santa Barbara, or to Waco, Texas, one in a sanitarium expecting the Kremlin's doomsday atomic bombers over any day, just before cocktails.

Tyler enjoyed people, tried to eat lunch in company, played golf with friends from Scarsdale, East Orange. Sometimes in bad weather he took out his father's collection of Japanese *ukiyoe* prints. Some of the Harunubos, Utamaras were rather erotic; several of them he took away as gifts on his two nights in town.

He was reading a lot, going through H.H.'s set of Balzac with a tranquil delight in the *Comédie Humaine*. No wonder the old boy liked Balzac; all that drive for money and power, a desire to take a city, to seize hold of what seemed within reach.

On May 10, 1972, Kelly Hayes laid the morning *Times* beside Tyler's plate of kippers.

MEDFORD-STARKWEATHER BANK LOSES $78 MILLION

LONDON—Medford-Starkweather, one of Britain's best-regarded banks, affiliated with Starkweather-Unity of New York, said Monday it stands to lose up to $78.2 million through unauthorized currency transactions at its branch in Lugano, Switzerland.

A spokesman in London said the Lugano branch manager and his foreign-currency dealer have been suspended pending the outcome of an investigation.

The Federal Banking Commission in Geneva, Switzerland, said it had also opened an investigation to find out whether any criminal offenses were committed. A spoksman said all losses were covered by the London central office and that there was no need to close down the Lugano office. The bank said it made its statement "to remove any disquiet which rumor or uncertainty might engender."

The Lugano case was the latest in a series that has hurt European banks in the high-risk field of foreign-exchange dealings. In the worst, the West German Bankhaus Wetzluft had to close down with a loss of almost $200 million, affecting many depositors and sending shock waves through the international markets.

It was reported that the losses developed when the head of the Lugano branch's foreign-exchange department and his assistants began speculating in the money markets with huge sums of cash.

Foreign-exchange dealers said such activity has been common in European banking circles, where government supervision is much less stringent than that in the United States.

"Much of the time the international foreign exchanges operate like a vast gambling casino with none of the central bank authorities able to impose the proper control over what is going on," one trader said.

"Shall I have Anne heat up a fresh pair of kippers?"

"What? Oh. No, Kelly. These are still hot enough." He ate the

371

kippers with relish and a sense of amusement, and wondered why. He had nothing against his sister Pauline's husband. But it was clear Johnny O'Degan might be implicated, perhaps was the leading guilty figure; as for the manager, he most likely was only a front for Johnny's endeavors and speculations.

The scandal over the losses by Medford-Starkweather in currency dealings in the end forced the O'Degans from the Starkweather-Unity Bank. The Boston group made a pretense of mercy; they would not make trouble for Johnny O'Degan; he could stay in Switzerland with his brood of daughters. But all O'Degan interests in Starkweather-Unity Bank & Trust would have to be sold to the Boston group. They would place their own men in principal positions of control.

They were a strong, driving group, audacious and original when they took over. There was no proven truth in the Street rumors that they were a front for the Mafia or a raid of second- and third-generation Irish come to big business and seeking a clout on the money markets of the world. They were not, as far as Tyler knew, even Texans. He felt they lacked impeccable antecedents in banking and was certain they were unorthodox in their methods. As the 1970's unrolled, several of their coups were rather dangerously close to investigation. But the branch banks prospered and expanded into new territory. The eagle or hawk (there was some confusion just what bird H.H. had originally picked for his emblem) appeared in many new shopping centers, in real estate developments with names like Greentop Terrace, Oak Tree Acres, Peach Tree Estates.

The great stables and garages of Starkweather Manor contained a treasure house of classical old cars: Rolls, Mercers, Stutz Bearcats. Even three Star-Falcons, now as rare, as one envious guest said, "as a Cape of Good Hope triangular stamp."

Tyler and Kelly Hayes cherished the old cars, but who owned them? Starkweather Manor, the house and its surrounding hundred acres, had been given by H.H.'s heirs to the Starkweather Foundation, which kept the place as a kind of museum while contemplating just what to do with the huge old structure. Tyler had taken over a special E Series 1956 Mercedes car as his own, and Kelly Hayes had put it in splendid working order with a new clutch system.

Tyler was driving into the city on the night of April 19, 1975, the car radio tuned in on the news when, as he put it later, "the dulcet tones of the newsmonger came on."

"There is definite news tonight that Starkweather-Unity Bank, long rumored in deep trouble, is expected to be taken over soon by new administrators. A story in the *Wall Street Journal* states:

"'The mighty have come low. One or more banks should complete a deal to acquire financially troubled Starkweather-Unity Bank of New York in the next few weeks, Wall Street sources report.

"'Negotiations seem in work amid a continuing runoff of depositors' funds, a cutback in bank personnel, and a drastic ebb in employee morale.

"'Starkweather-Unity, the fifth-largest bank in the United States, with headquarters on Wall Street, disclosed in February it had again lost millions in the foreign-exchange market because of unauthorized transactions.

"'Bank losses for six months totaled $85 million, of which $55 million involved the foreign-exchange fiasco, a spokesman said. So Starkweather-Unity skipped dividend payments on its common and preferred stock, the first major American bank to do so since the Depression.

"'He added, since the beginning of the year, the bank's total assets have dropped from $6 billion to $4 billion as the institution sold off part of its portfolio holdings to meet financial responsibilities.

"'Said the spokesman, depositor withdrawals have slowed from $180 million a week at the height of the disclosure of financial trouble, but it was still running at $30 million a week, mostly in withdrawals of corporate cash.

"'The last full week before Starkweather-Unity announced suspension of its dividends, domestic deposits and foreign deposits totaled over $23 billion.

"'Both U.S. and foreign banks have expressed interest in acquiring Starkweather-Unity Bank & Trust Company.'

"In Washington the oil situation faces a new crisis. . . ."

Tyler turned off the radio and hunted in the pocket of his topcoat. He had not read the *Wall Street Journal* and had brought it along to read later in bed. He unfolded the paper and turned to the front page, picked up the story.

* * *

Former Treasury Secretary Elmo Whitkin, Starkweather-Unity's new chairman, recently visited Washington to gain support for legislation that would be needed if Starkweather-Unity were involved in a merger with a bank out of New York State. Under present banking laws, a commercial bank cannot cross a state line to buy into another bank.

Bank of America and Wells Fargo were among the California banks that have made inquiries to take over S-U. Two Chicago banks also expressed interest: Continental Illinois National Bank & Trust Company and First National Bank of Chicago.

Foreign banks with branches in various states would not be prevented under U.S. banking laws from acquiring Starkweather-Unity.

Also several major New York banks are looking over the project. Manufacturers Hanover Trust, which loaned Starkweather-Unity $36 million, is considered a serious prospect for the merger.

A Wall Street source said it would be "destructive" for the stockholders if the bank were split up among several banks. If it were split up, it would be a liquidation, not a merger. So an effort is being made to set up an acquisition by only one bank.

None of the surviving Starkweather family holds any position or connection with Starkweather-Unity.

Tyler had pulled up to the side of the highway to read the news item. A county patrol car pulled alongside. A wide-faced officer waved. "Having any trouble, Mr. Starkweather?"

"Oh, hello, Kaminsky. No. Just studying something."

"Yeah, well, don't get bumped in the prat. Real crazies driving these days."

Tyler read slowly in the range of the dashboard lights:

The Federal Reserve Board already has performed a $15 billion capital infusion into the Starkweather-Unity Bank and the bank plans a $90 million offering to its shareholders later this year.

But about 250 of the bank's top officers who work at its home office and its 105 New York City area branches are being terminated along with 406 other higher and lower employees. "Morale is not good," a bank personnel source said.

Withdrawal has occurred primarily in corporate certificates

of deposit and foreign accounts. Corporate officials are informing Starkweather-Unity they need assurances regarding its true financial condition.

' So far the Federal Reserve Board, the Comptroller of the Currency, and the Federal Deposit Insurance Corporation all are involved in the Starkweather-Unity negotiations.

Tyler tore out the story and folded it with care. Should he give up going into the city? No, actually (he laughed out loud as he put the car in motion) the news had made him raunchy. As he read, he had been aware he was getting a hard-on. Must be hereditary. Thank God for a randy grandfather.

Tyler parked the car in a garage on Bleecker Street and bought four bottles of Mumm Sec at the East Village Gourmet Mart. In a corner flower shop he added a ceramic pot hanging on woven ropes, the pot containing a plant with spear-shaped leaves, silver on one side, lavender-purple on the other. So burdened, he crossed to an old brownstone house and walked up three flights, past floors smelling of spicy cooking, dark doggy corners, a graffito: GOD IS A WOMAN. He knocked at a door painted Chinese red. The door had three locks. It was a neighborhood of muggers, rip-offs, of the last aging hippies dropping acid, smoking a lid of grass. The narcs had once asked Tyler to spread against a wall for a frisk for hash, meth, smack.

The stereos below were remembering Janis Joplin; someplace a vacuum cleaner announced its invisible presence.

Tyler knocked twice on the door and it opened. Margo stood there, a dark cigarillo hanging from a lower lip. She rather large in girth, hair a color too dark to be true, the dressing gown he had given her two years before open, revealing Dacron slacks. He was used to nature's cruelty to aging women.

He kissed her cheek. "Hello, sweets."

She smiled and fondled his back. They were old—she was older than he was—but there was the warmth of lovers who welcomed each meeting. If a bit slower and more casual than youth might act it, still these two had come around to these last years invulnerable to irony and with no exuberant hopes. This spared them, she said, much fraudulent rhetoric.

The studio had been made by knocking out connecting walls of

375

three small rooms. It was not neat, but there was some kind of order. The studio bed had a wild red-and-orange pattern of some Asian design; the walls held large paintings by Margo of already-outworn periods of twentieth-century art. A semicubist view of Lower New York, dated 1919; some Mexican peasants barefoot, a donkey backed by soldiers carrying rifles and live chickens; a surreal oil, beautifully painted, of the backside of a slim nude, her rounded, dimpled buttocks repeated in the curves and dents of the fruit on the table behind her, and out beyond the open window a large curtain in the sky drawing back to show the stardusted backdrop.

"Bubbly? *Mamma mia*, what the hell are you celebrating, *amore mio?*"

"Just existing—me, *thee*. Not any other special specific relevant damn thing."

"That witch on the *Today Show* on TV said the old family bank has gone down the drain. That give you your jollies, Ty?"

He slipped off his hat and topcoat and moved his hand under the robe, grasped the melons of his love. He looked into her eyes, those eyes bracketed in sweet wrinkles, eyes still bold and fierce for all that. And yes, he supposed, a bit cruel. But that was Margo, and his life was as complete as it would ever be; we are maybe without much significance but to each other.

He removed her cigarillo and kissed her mouth. "Happy day."

It was six years now since he had passed the ratty little Haute Volée Art Gallery on Eighth Street, showing a window full of some drippy abstractions made by colors dropped down in puddles on raw canvas: EXHIBITION—CRIVELLI.

The large dyke with the amber beads who ran the gallery had not wanted to give him Margo's address. But he bought a three-by-six abstraction of two broad red brush strokes looping around each other on a black canvas. He paid out one hundred and fifty dollars and was given an address on Sixth Avenue which turned out to be out of date. A postman he met on University Place broke all rules, for a folded bill, and gave Tyler the new address of Margo Crivelli.

She hadn't shown much surprise when he knocked on the red door with its three locks and she saw a slim old man in the well-cut suit and Italian narrow-brimmed hat. Neat, sun-tanned, white-haired, a Ronald Colman mustache surviving past middle age.

"The ghost walks," she said. "God damn it, mister, you've become old."

"Well, Margo, there is a lot more of you. Hello."

"All right, cut the compliments. Come in."

It went very well after that. They hugged, took in each other's odor like friendly dogs, grasped hands. He said the right things when she showed him her new style of painting: smears, drips, colors running across blank canvas, flat patternings hiding their meanings. He knew some of the art-gallery-world jargon. He nodded. "Valid, *very* valid."

They were as ardent as they had been in their youth a million light-years ago, only a bit slower, perhaps, Tyler admitted. They were certainly jollier now, for they admitted they had no family problems, no doubts, turmoils, or tensions. Ludicrous to others, perhaps, this old couple, but they saw their meetings as jocose dramas.

It didn't matter that Margo had been married twice, once to a Spanish smuggler of Mexican pre-Columbian art into the United States, most of the artifacts fakes. Again married to a hard-hat bastard who knocked her about, a steelworker who fell from the fiftieth floor of one of the city's Twin Towers one noon, he full of boilermakers. Life was a onetime experience, she said once when she and Tyler were drunk, "a surface like a patina, see? Raw in spots, overpolished down to the nerve ends in other places. See?"

She'd had several shows of her paintings, gone through various avant-garde periods, as her walls showed.

Now this night, as she lit a cigarillo and Tyler opened a bottle of Mumm, she said, "This abstract crappola kick I'm on, it's our times. I think it's the core of the *merde* of our era, the total stupefaction of art." (The cork popped.) "Hey, *don't* waste it! Pour."

Tyler didn't mind her talk of her painting. It meant very little to him, but it gave her satisfaction to gripe after a hard life, such disappointments, sorrows. It had not made her cynical, it had just polished that sardonic immediacy of outrage she had always had. She was a delight to him, in her raffish gaiety and battered talents.

With a Caesar salad, a chicken stewed in bay leaves and tomatoes, they finished off the bottle of champagne, taking another bottle to bed with them on the studio couch. After the two old bodies gallantly went to thumping about in a most satisfactory fashion in the

377

act of love, they lay back on the various cushions, their glasses refilled.

"So it's all gone, *amoroso*? H. H. Starkweather *et* Company, the Starkweather-Unity Bank and Trust Company. Well, your grandfather, he had too much machismo pride. The bastard, he was going to build a dynasty. Kicked me out on my ass when it looked like I was going to bring a little dago strain into his bourgeois hangups." She lifted her glass. "Up his—"

"I think I'm the only one, Margo, who understood H.H. He had to keep moving to stay upright. He had this duty, he felt, to make things grow, make money earn its keep. He had this old New England idea—he felt responsible to others; that Protestant ethic—save, serve, make a buck. He knew he was out of date. . . . Said to me in 1929, 'Historical inevitability, Ty, is the joker in the deck.' In the end he didn't give a damn."

"Ty, you need another drink. *Tenere l'anima coi denti*. The only thing to do with money is throw it into the Trevi Fountain in Rome and make a wish."

For one moment Tyler felt a twinge of guilt and a shiver under his skin that all that had gone before in the family, the bank, could still be a dubious menace hovering over our two old naked bags of bones. We must all cauterize our conscience.

Margo had once quoted *The Cloud of Unknowing*: "Look forward, and let the backwards be. . . ."

One of the presentation gold watches H.H. had given to each of his grandchildren in the early part of the century, at the groundbreaking of a new version of the bank, now ticked on Margo's night table, the table stained by white rings left by wet glasses. A tugboat hooted in the East River, sounding in the studio like a plaintive oboe. After a while they both slept, snoring slightly.